"Don't bait m..., ...," John said.
"You're p...

"So what are you going ... ... 's
where you screwed up, j... ... t
Neiman's are carpeted."

"So if we were at Neiman's, we'd be having sex?"

"If we were at Neiman's, sex would be the last thing on my mind."

"Then maybe I didn't screw up after all."

"In your *dreams*, repo man."

She tried to shove him aside, only to have him grab her wrist and pull her back.

"You made a big mistake when you forced me to come in here. I'm one of those men you can't trust to behave himself."

He pulled her close and smothered her mouth with a burning, reckless, unrelenting kiss . . . Anger bubbled inside her, but she didn't know if she was mad at him for being a presumptuous, kiss-stealing tyrant, or mad at herself for being so hot for him whether she liked it or not . . .

"A delightful, funny read with a unique twist as a former trophy wife discovers herself, and true love, in the most unexpected place. A total winner!"

—Susan Mallery, *USA Today* bestselling author of *The Marcelli Princess*

Please turn the page for more praise for Jane Graves, and turn to the back of this book for a preview of her upcoming novel, *Tall Tales and Wedding Veils*.

Hot Wheels
and High Heels

———

JANE GRAVES

FOREVER

NEW YORK   BOSTON

Copyright © 2007 by Jane Graves
Excerpt from *Tall Tales and Wedding Veils* copyright © 2007 by Jane Graves. All rights reserved. Except as permitted under the U.S. Copyright Act of 1976, no part of this publication may be reproduced, distributed, or transmitted in any form or by any means, or stored in a database or retrieval system, without the prior written permission of the publisher.

Forever is an imprint of Grand Central Publishing.
The Forever name and logo is a trademark of Hachette Book Group, Inc.

Cover design by Diane Luger
Cover illustration by Mike Storrings
Book design by Giorgetta Bell McRee

Forever
Hachette Book Group
237 Park Avenue
New York, NY 10017
Visit our Web site at www.HachetteBookGroup.com

Printed in the United States of America

First Printing: July 2007

10 9 8 7 6 5 4 3

ACKNOWLEDGMENTS

I'd like to thank Michele Bidelspach, for her enthusiasm about my writing and her editing expertise; Beth de Guzman, who thought readers might like a crazy story about a trophy wife who becomes a repo agent; the Foxes, for being a funny and talented group of women I love to hang out with; my husband, Brian, and my daughter, Charlotte, for their never-ending support; and my sweet kitty, Isabel, who so kindly keeps my lap warm while I write.

Hot Wheels
and High Heels

Chapter 1

On July twenty-fifth, Darcy McDaniel lost her house, her husband, and her self-respect. Then things really went downhill.

Looking back, she should have known something was up. After all, her husband, Warren, hoarded money like a survivalist hoards ammo, yet he made reservations at a five-star resort in Cancún, handed her two airline tickets, told her to grab her friend Carolyn, and live it up for a week. As he hustled her out the door, Darcy remembered thinking that even though he was fifty-seven, he was still a little young for senility. Unfortunately, she took his sudden generosity as a *good* thing, and that was about as far as her thought process on the matter went.

She and Carolyn spent a glorious week in Cancún. Scantily clad waiters brought them pitchers of margaritas while they lolled in beach chairs and dragged their toes in the sand. They ate the most superb gourmet food; had spa treatments involving hot rocks, cold compresses, and Alonzo's magical hands; and soaked up enough sun to give their skin a healthy glow without turning it into lizard hide.

After flying back to Dallas, they air-kissed and promised

to make a trip to Mexico an annual tradition. Darcy hopped into her Mercedes Roadster, put down the top, and sped out of long-term parking at DFW. She jacked up the radio and savored the last moments of her vacation before going home to Warren.

At four-thirty in the afternoon, the Texas sun beat down on her shoulders like a blowtorch, but she liked the feel of the wind tossing her hair and the appreciative smiles of the men she zipped past, some of them young enough to be her . . . younger brothers. She smiled back, knowing they figured she was thirty, tops. Actually, she was thirty-nine, with the big four-oh only a few weeks away. She surprised herself by not caring about that. Thanks to her personal trainer, her hair colorist, and the miracle that was Botox, it was a secret no one ever had to know.

She stopped at Doggie Domain to pick up Pepé, who was delighted to see her. The *tap, tap, tap* of his tiny toenails, along with his buggy little eyes staring up at her adoringly, made her heart melt. She scooped him up and rubbed her cheek over his silky hair, inhaling the aroma of vanilla-scented doggie shampoo. Long-haired Chihuahuas weren't any less neurotic than short-haired ones, but all that hair did help cushion the frantic beating of their little hearts. Still, Pepé's was thumping even faster than normal, because it always freaked him out a little to be away from home. But since Warren didn't communicate well with other species, letting Pepé stay with people who spoke dog—particularly dog with a Mexican accent—was better for all concerned.

By the time Darcy reached Plano, it was nearly five o'clock. She drove down Preston Road, which was flanked by immaculate strip malls, restaurants, and movie theaters. Everything in Plano was brand-new and squeaky clean, unless of course you crossed Central Expressway into old east Plano, which was what Plano used to be before it became home base for a substantial segment of corporate America. Over there you'd better have a damned good car alarm and hang on to your wallet with both hands. She'd grown up in east Plano, so she knew for a fact it was a good place to be *from*.

A few minutes later, Darcy was motoring down Briarwood Lane, heading for her house at the end of the block. On either side of the street, huge two-story brick houses stood as monuments to upward mobility, with massive front doors inset with etched glass, arched windows, pristine landscaping, and a swimming pool in every backyard. Coming home to a place she loved after a week of being pampered put her in such a fabulous mood that when Warren got home, she was going to hand him a glass of water and a little blue pill and show him her appreciation. She swung into the alley, then pulled into her driveway, hit the garage door opener, and got a shock.

Two unfamiliar cars sat in the garage.

Her first thought was that since Warren had a thing for cars, he'd done a little buying or trading while she was out of town. That theory might have held water, except one of the cars was a Buick sedan and the other a Ford Explorer, and Warren would never have bought any vehicles so painfully ordinary.

Houseguests? While she was away?

She grabbed Pepé and got out of the car. On her way

through the garage to the back door, she noticed a car seat in the back of the SUV.

Houseguests with *kids?*

She went inside and set Pepé down. He trotted off with a jingle of dog tags. When she rounded the corner into the kitchen, she got another surprise. Four strangers sat at her breakfast-room table.

And Warren was nowhere in sight.

Odd little chills snaked up her spine. She put her handbag on the kitchen counter. Several boxes sat along one wall, a few of them standing open. She had no idea what that was all about.

She feigned a friendly smile. "Uh . . . hello?"

A thirtysomething man in a rumpled polo shirt was holding up a forkful of pasta, as if he'd stopped mid-bite when he heard her come in. The nondescript woman beside him looked equally dumbstruck, an expression that exaggerated the frown lines around her mouth. The ponytailed preschool girl kicked her feet back and forth and blinked curiously. The baby sitting in a high chair smashed a graham cracker in his fist, then deposited the crumbs all over Darcy's marble tile floor.

The man stood up, his brows drawing together like dueling caterpillars. "Who are you?"

Darcy eased back, feeling a little defensive. Wasn't she the one who should be asking that question?

"You must be friends of Warren's," she said.

"Warren?" the man said. "Warren McDaniel?"

"Yes. I'm his wife, Darcy."

"His *wife?*"

At first Darcy took his surprise to mean that he thought a woman her age—you know, thirty—couldn't possibly be married to a man as old as Warren. Most people thought that. Even *she* thought that. But something else lurked behind this man's confusion.

"Yes," she said carefully. "His wife. Didn't he tell you he was married?"

After the man and his wife exchanged a few more of those stunned looks, he cleared his throat. "Actually, he . . ."

"He what?"

The man swallowed hard, his Adam's apple bobbing wildly. "He told us you were . . . uh . . ."

"Uh, *what?*"

"Dead."

Darcy went totally still. It took a full ten seconds for her to even comprehend the word, then another five or so to find her voice. "Warren told you I was *dead?*"

"Yes. He said there was a car accident in Cancún. Those Mexican cabdrivers, you know. It was very, uh . . . tragic."

Tragic? *Tragic?* The only *tragedy* here was just how delusional these people were. Or maybe it was Warren who was delusional.

Or . . .

Or maybe she really was dead.

For a moment Darcy actually considered that *The Sixth Sense* might be more than just escapist entertainment. Still, she was quite certain she hadn't gone to heaven in the backseat of a Mexican cab. Now, she had taken a spill off a jet ski and sucked in a little surf, but she'd made it back to the beach still breathing. And she'd driven home from the airport, hadn't she? Everyone knew if a dead person tried to drive, his hands passed right through the steering wheel. She'd seen *Ghost*. That mind-over-matter thing was way harder than it looked.

No, the problem here wasn't her death, or lack of it, but the fact that she didn't know who the hell these people were—and that her husband was missing in action.

"Where's Warren?" she asked.

When they shrugged, she felt her confusion melt into frustration, which oozed into annoyance. Finally she just let it loose.

"Excuse me, but . . . who *are* you people?"

She spoke a little louder than she'd intended, and they recoiled as if she'd physically shoved them. The baby stopped littering her breakfast-room floor, screwing up his face as if he was going to cry. Pepé's buggy little eyes grew even buggier. The woman fiddled with the silver bracelet she wore and deferred to her husband. When he shot her a helpless look, she turned back to Darcy, shrugging weakly.

"I guess with you being, you know, dead and all, your husband didn't tell you he . . ."

"He *what?*"

"Sold the house."

Wooziness overcame her. *Warren sold the house.* The words whacked the outside of her skull, trying desperately to get through. Entry was denied.

"We had to make a decision quickly," the man said, "but we had cash and were ready to buy, and it was such a steal, especially with all the contents thrown in. This big house at the price he was asking . . . well, you understand. We couldn't say no."

Darcy started to shake a little, sure she was going to be sick. But she managed to hold up her palms, laughing a little in that way people do when they know there has to be some mistake. "There has to be some mistake," she said, in case they missed the laugh.

"No," the man said. "No mistake. I can show you the closing papers."

The guy dug through a kitchen drawer and produced a stack of legal-sized paper and shoved it at her. She saw only one thing clearly before her vision went all blurry. Warren's signature.

Good God, he'd actually done it.

She was about to shout, *This is my house, too! How could he sell it without my signature?*

Then she remembered the papers *she'd* signed fourteen years ago before they got married, the ones that short-circuited Texas's community property laws. Warren had the right to do anything he wanted to with this house, and she couldn't do a thing about it.

Consciousness seemed to fade a little, leaving her dazed and confused. Then a horrendous thought jerked her back to reality.

"Where are my things?" she said, her voice rising with panic. "My clothes? My shoes? My jewelry?"

The woman and her husband exchanged those glances again.

"Tell me!"

"He took your jewelry with him," the woman said, "but he left everything else. So this morning we called Goodwill—"

Darcy actually screamed. Or, at least, she thought she did, but it was hard to tell when the world was moving in slow motion and her head felt as if it were underwater, where voices get muffled.

She raced to the front entry and scrambled up the stairs, images of street people filling her mind. She saw them huddled in doorways wearing her Emilio Pucci pants and smoking Camel nonfilters. Stretched out on park benches, using her Gucci jackets as pillows. Carrying drug paraphernalia in her Fendi bag. And whatever clothes of hers they weren't wearing were stuffed inside rusty shopping carts, suffocating beneath something flowered and polyester from the Kathie Lee Collection.

Darcy went into the master bedroom and threw open the closet door. It was like looking into an eclipse, because she was blinded by the most pedestrian clothing she'd ever seen. Cotton T-shirts. Sneakers and flip-flops. Enough denim that Levi Strauss had to be feeling the shortage. They were clothes only a mother could love—the mother downstairs with the husband and two kids and the title to Darcy's house.

She ran to the jewelry box on her dresser and yanked open the door. It was empty. Visions of pawnshops danced in her head, their grimy glass cases displaying her gold Lacroix bracelet, her diamond chandelier earrings, her Cartier watch. As she stood there sucking in sharp, horrified breaths and gaping at the black hole where her jewelry used to be, the truth finally sank in.

It was gone. Everything was gone. What the *hell* had Warren done to her?

Strangely, it hadn't occurred to her yet to question the why of the situation. She was still dealing with the what, when, where, and how. She ran back down the stairs and wheeled around to the living room, where she spied the French art deco vase she'd gotten at the Moonsong Gallery on McKinney Street. Whatever Warren's plans were, they clearly didn't include her, so when it hit home that she'd gone from having everything to having nothing, she was determined that she wasn't leaving this house without *something*.

She grabbed the vase and stuck it under her arm. She took the silver candlesticks from the mantle, plunked them inside the vase, and grabbed the Waterford clock from the end table. She spied the wine rack in the dining room and started toward it, intending to snatch the bottle of 1996 Penfolds Grange Shiraz that these people were going to drink over her dead body.

She had to hand it to the new homeowners. They knew temporary insanity when they saw it, and they were smart enough to back off and call 911. But that didn't slow Darcy down. She knew she was slipping off the deep end, but she was caught in one of those weird out-of-body experiences where she was watching herself doing something stupid but couldn't stop. She told them she didn't care what Warren had done. She didn't care if they had a ream of closing papers. She didn't care what kind of evil prenuptial agreement she'd signed. The things in this house were hers, and she wasn't letting them go without a fight.

Just when she was wishing for a third hand so she could grab the Tarkay serigraph off the wall, she heard a rapid-fire knock at the door.

Plano's finest had arrived.

Cop number one was an older guy who looked like a hound dog minus the floppy ears. Cop number two was a cute young guy who'd been there a couple of times when their security alarm had gone off by mistake. He'd been friendly beyond the call of duty, giving her a few suggestive smiles in spite of the fact that he wore a wedding ring. Now he was looking at her as if she were a crazed asylum escapee. But that was only fair, because she was feeling a little differently about him, too. Those other times, she'd noticed how cute his legs looked in his summer cop shorts and the way his green eyes sparkled by the light of her foyer chandelier. Now she saw the Gestapo coming to drag her kicking and screaming from her home.

After getting the gist of the situation, the cops managed to pry everything away from her but the bottle of wine, which she had a death grip on. The new homeowners just shoved her handbag at her and waved at the cops to take her away, figuring it was more important to get rid of the crazy woman than it was to have a nice red with dinner.

She scooped up Pepé on her way out the door. Young cop escorted her to her car while old cop spoke to the new homeowners. He came back a few minutes later to tell her that the people had no desire to press charges in spite of the way she'd behaved, as long as she swore she would never step foot in their house again. She countered that the prenup she'd signed didn't cover the things in the house she and Warren had bought since they were married, so he had no right to sell them. Old cop said fine, but that was something that had to be sorted out between her lawyer and her husband's, and for now it would be best if she just left the neighborhood.

Darcy's hands shook as she started her car and backed out of the driveway. She drove down the alley and swung back onto Briarwood Lane just in time to see the cops take a left onto Thornberry. As soon as they were out of sight, she did a one-eighty in the cul-de-sac and headed back down the street, stopping at the curb to have one last look at her house.

Her house? It wasn't her house.

It had never been her house.

At that moment, she wished Mercedes-Benz had taken luxury one step further and installed a corkscrew in the dashboard. Then again, it was probably a good thing they hadn't, or she'd be chugging that two-hundred-dollar bottle of wine like a can of Old Milwaukee.

Okay. She had to get a grip. Talk to Warren. Find out why he'd done this to her. She pulled out her cell phone and called Warren's office to talk to his secretary. If anyone would know where he was, Lucy would. She was an earthy little woman utterly lacking in fashion sense, which gave her that much more room in her brain for things like efficiency and professionalism and organizational skills. So Darcy was surprised when the woman greeting her sounded a little befuddled. She told Darcy she hadn't seen Warren for the past two days, and he had a client presentation this afternoon. Did she have any idea where he was?

Stunned, Darcy hung up the phone. This couldn't be happening. Warren had kissed his job good-bye, along with that big, beautiful paycheck?

That led her to another thought that made her even queasier than before. Warren could subsist a long time on the profit from the house, but not in the style to which he was accustomed. But if he piled a few more assets on top of it . . .

Darcy called information, who then connected her to

their bank. She asked about their checking accounts. The perky little clerk on the other end informed her that all three of them had been cleaned out and closed two days ago.

Darcy's stomach did a slow, sickening heave, and she had to swallow hard to get rid of the feeling that she was going to throw up. She yanked out her credit cards, flipping one of them over so she could dial the 800 number on the back. The customer-service rep informed her that recent large purchases plus a big cash advance had run the card right up to its limit.

No. Not her credit cards. Please, God, not her credit cards.

She knew it was pointless, but she called about the others, too. Same story. Now she knew the whole ugly, painful truth: Warren was a one-man demolition team hell-bent on destroying her life.

Darcy gripped the steering wheel so hard her fingers ached, and she took deep breaths to drive oxygen back to her brain so she wouldn't keel over onto the passenger seat. Not one dime of cash was left, not one dollar of open credit. Warren had all kinds of other investments, but she didn't have a clue what they were.

As if he'd left any of them for her.

Glancing back at the house, she saw a tear-clouded image of the new homeowners peeking out the plantation shutters, clearly wondering if she was on the verge of going nuts and taking hostages. That led her to yet another revelation. They would be sleeping in her bed tonight. She wouldn't.

Despair edged into panic. Where was she supposed to go now?

She thought about her friends, only to realize that most of them weren't really friends at all. They were women she went to lunch with, women she shopped with, women she went to Cancún with while her husband was yanking her life out from under her. But they weren't really friends if she was afraid to not show up to something for fear she'd be the one they talked about. Carolyn was the only one she'd even consider staying with, but Carolyn's husband didn't like her friends dropping by for coffee, much less moving in.

Finally she realized that, outside of a homeless shelter, there was only one place she could go that wouldn't cost her money or cause unnecessary gossip in the circles she and Warren ran in. And the thought of it made a shudder undulate down her spine.

You've got no choice. It's that or share a bathroom with forty other women.

She wiped her eyes so she could see enough to drive, then started her car. She left her neighborhood and drove down Preston Road. When she reached Park Boulevard, she gritted her teeth, turned left, and headed toward east Plano.

Ten minutes later, she drove into Wingate Manufactured Home Park, her eyes still so clouded with tears that the place almost looked habitable. She pulled to the side of the road in front of the double-wide on lot 38G, a vinyl-clad structure with plastic shutters and a limp metal awning. A pot of pink geraniums sat beside the front door, wilting in the heat, and Christmas lights drooped over the picture window in the living room. *"Clayton, take down the damned lights,"* her mother would say, and her father would say, *"Not if I'm gonna have to put them up again next year."*

Darcy sat in the car a long time, unable to bear going inside, overcome by the most terrible feeling that she had come full circle when all she'd ever wanted to do was stay put halfway around.

Chapter 2

When John Stark looked up from his desk to find himself staring down the barrel of a gun, he really wasn't all that surprised. From the moment the kid had walked into his office, his swaggering gait and *screw-you* expression said he had more bravado than brains, and that was always a reason for a heads-up.

As usual, John's instincts had been right on target.

"So, whatcha think now, repo man?" the kid said, holding the gun at a ninety-degree angle with his elbow locked, like in every B-grade gangbanger movie ever made. "Still think I need to make up those back payments? Huh? Or are you gonna give me back my damned car?"

John let out a silent sigh. If anyone else had been in the office, the kid might have thought twice about pulling this crap. But Tony was out on a repossession, Amy had left for class, and the floozy of a clerk John had hired a few days ago wouldn't have been much help even if he hadn't fired her this afternoon. Then again, maybe she could have asphyxiated the kid with a can of Aqua Net, or stabbed him with a nail file, or maybe just talked him into a coma. In her hands, any of those weapons could have been deadly.

John tried to remember if he'd seen the kid before in his former life, maybe busted him for drag racing or picked him up for shoplifting, but no bells rang. He was maybe nineteen or twenty, as tensely coiled as a starving pit bull, with an angel-of-death tattoo on his upper arm and the reshuffled nose of a street fighter. At six-three, two-twenty, John's size alone made most men think twice about messing with him, and if the only weapons between him and this kid had been their bare hands, he could easily have taken him down. Unfortunately, a firearm had a way of evening things out.

John stood up carefully and moved around his desk. "I'll give your car back. But like I said, you have to make up the back payments, pay the impound fee—"

"Bullshit! I don't have to make up no back payments!"

John cringed. Profanity he could tolerate. Any accent in the world was fine by him. But for God's sake, did the kid have to use a double negative?

"If I don't have the appropriate paperwork," John said, "I can't release the car. You'll have to take it up with your finance company."

"I'm taking it up with *you*."

The kid shook the gun, and a heightened sense of uneasiness slid along John's nerves, telling him he'd better tread softly. This kid was a little more agitated than the average person whose car had turned up missing, which told John that a little crack might be swimming around in his veins, which made this situation more unpredictable than he cared to mess with.

He weighed his options. One repossession was hardly worth getting blown away over. Then again, if he got in the habit of simply handing over the cars he'd taken the time and trouble to legally steal, he'd have armed dead-beats lined up around the block demanding their vehicles back.

"Hey, repo man! I'm *talking* to you!"

John held up his palms. "Take it easy." He carefully opened a file drawer and pulled out a key ring. "Here's the key to the impound lot. Just take your car and get out."

He lobbed the key to the kid. But—doggone it—his aim was off.

Way off.

The kid lunged for the key and missed. It clattered to the tile floor, and the second the kid's gaze turned south to follow it, John stepped forward, clamped his hand on the kid's wrist, and backed him against the wall. He smacked the gun from his hand, then pushed him facedown on the ground and planted a knee in his back. With one hand pressed to the kid's neck, he held his face to the floor, and with his other hand he reached for the cell phone in his pocket.

While he was having a word with the 911 operator, the door to the outer office swung open and Tony walked in. He glanced into John's office, stopping short and staring down at the kid. "Damn. I leave for an hour and miss all the fun?"

John flipped his phone shut and looked at Tony. "Grab the cuffs from my desk drawer."

Tony gave him the handcuffs, and in seconds John had the kid subdued. Then he came to his feet, wincing at the dull pain that throbbed in his knee.

"So, what's the deal?" Tony asked. "Did you feel like taking a trip down memory lane and arresting someone?"

"He wanted his car back. Pulled a gun."

"Bad move, kid," Tony said. "Guess you didn't know who you were messing with. Next time you might want to think twice before pulling a gun on the nice repo man."

That prompted the kid to let out a string of curse words directed at everything from Tony's parentage to his intellect to his religious affiliation. The kid might have been a little deficient where proper English was concerned, but John had to give him points for creativity.

A few minutes later, the cops showed up, two guys John had never seen before, both of them so young that he wondered if the Plano PD had taken to trolling high schools looking for recruits. He told them what had happened and that he would come to the station later to make a statement. They stuffed the kid into the back of a patrol car and took off.

John collapsed in his desk chair with a heavy sigh. *I should have listened to my family and gone with the Subway franchise*, he thought. Unfortunately, eight years as an auto theft detective with the Plano PD had taught him more about repossessing cars than making sandwiches. After all, who knew more about how to steal cars than a cop who went after car thieves?

Tony tossed some paperwork onto John's desk. "Got the Viper."

"Any trouble?"

"Nah. The guy about wet his pants when I said I was repossessing his car. All he was worried about was the neighbors seeing me."

Well, that was nothing new. Most of John's business involved repossessing the high-dollar assets of west Plano doctors, lawyers, and other assorted bigwigs whose fortunes were tied to stock market trends and overspending wives. Those guys rarely gave him the kind of trouble he got from lowlifes whose fortunes came from dealing drugs.

Tony looked around. "Hey, where's the girl? Uh . . . What was her name?"

"Rona? Fired her this afternoon."

Tony blinked. "Now why did you go and do that?"

"She had the brain of an amoeba."

"Brain? Who was looking at her brain?" Tony popped a Tic Tac into his mouth. "We finally get a decent-looking woman around here, and you get all hung up on competency. What's the matter with you?"

"I have a business to run."

"I was going to *marry* that woman. Till death do us part. I was in *love*."

"You were in love with her thirty-eight Ds."

"No. We had a cosmic connection. I could feel it."

"What was her name again?"

Tony blinked, then gave John a smug smile. "Rhonda. You thought I didn't remember, didn't you?"

"No, buddy. You're right on top of things."

"So why'd you fire her? I mean, specifically."

"She painted her nails at her desk. Stunk like hell, but I let it go. She talked on the phone for an hour. I looked the other way. Then she started to file."

"That's a good thing, isn't it?"

"Yeah. Until I heard her singing the alphabet."

Tony winced. "Well, if she could get most of the way to Z—"

"I swear to God I'll vote for a chimpanzee in the next

presidential election if he promises to do something about the damned educational system."

"Did she cry when you fired her?" Tony asked.

John winced at the memory. "Of course. And that made the experience even more enjoyable."

"So right now she's probably feeling pretty down, huh?"

"I expect so."

Tony raised his eyebrows. "You have her home number, right?"

John shook his head, wondering if he'd been like Tony at twenty-eight, looking around every corner for an opportunity to get laid. He guessed he must have been. But late-night liaisons with predawn departures just didn't do it for him anymore, and no woman had ever come along whom he cared to get permanent with.

Of course, being a loser in the marriage department had made him a real standout in his family full of . . . well, *families*. At their last reunion in Tyler, his female relatives from across the state of Texas had chattered about him in hushed whispers, speculating how such a handsome man could have reached age forty-two without making it to the altar at least once.

"Look how he's tossing back the Jack. I bet he has a drinking problem."

"Maybe the trouble's down south. Size may not matter, but functionality's another thing entirely."

"Suppose all that macho's for show? Uncle Raymond the bricklayer went queer, you know. I mean, who'd have ever thought that?"

After that weekend, John had left believing that "bless your heart" was actually his last name.

If he'd been living a few centuries ago, everyone would have just said "he's not the marrying kind" and let it go at that. Now they speculated on exactly which part of his anatomy or personality was defective and thanked God those mutant strands of DNA hadn't infiltrated their branches of the family tree.

The truth was that while he had no shortage of women in his life, marriage just didn't appeal to him. Never had. Maybe it was because he'd watched virtually everyone he knew walk into matrimony and right back out of it again. It took some guys two or three times to get the picture. It was as if they were hitting themselves in the head with hammers and trying to figure out where all the pain was coming from.

"Go ahead," he told Tony, flipping open a file and scribbling down the number. "Give *Rhonda* a call. I'm sure she'll be delighted to hear from you."

"Yep. As long as I tell her what a bastard you were to fire her."

The phone rang, and John picked it up. After a short conversation, he hung up with a smile of satisfaction.

"What's up?" Tony asked.

"Got a line on a car. It may not be there for long, though. Mind dropping me off so I can pick it up?"

"Sure."

John grabbed a key from his desk drawer, grateful he had one for this particular car. Hot-wiring could make a mess of a steering column, and there was always danger of damage whenever he grabbed one with the tow truck. Those were usually his only options, but every once in a while he dealt with a company that kept a key for every vehicle it financed in case somebody stopped making the payments. And that meant all he had to do was unlock the car and drive it away, which was the easiest five hundred bucks a man could make.

As he and Tony closed up shop and headed out, John felt a whole lot better than he had a few minutes ago. Yeah, it had been a hell of a day, but he had no doubt that getting behind the wheel of a sweet little Mercedes Roadster was going to perk him right up.

~

Darcy grabbed Pepé and trudged up the wooden steps that led to her parents' front door, wincing as they groaned painfully, shrunken as they were from years of shriveling in the blazing Texas sun. She knocked, and a few seconds later her mother came to the door wearing a pink bathrobe, her hair in a towel. When she saw her daughter's state of distress, her eyes got big and horrified. She shoved the screen door open and pulled Darcy inside.

"Darcy? What's wrong? You look like hell. Have you been crying? What's happened?"

It was the rapid-fire interrogation of a woman who lives with the absolute certainty that some dreadful event is always lurking just around the corner, waiting to snatch her up in its cold, clammy grasp. Of course, she was never right about that, and Darcy's father never let her forget it.

Today, though, Lyla Dumphries was going to be vindicated.

Darcy gave her the gist of the situation, and Lyla wheezed in a breath and grasped her throat as if she were stroking out.

"Did you hear that, Clayton? Warren left Darcy. Just like that. He left her high and dry without a dime to her name!"

"Uh-huh. I heard."

"See, I told you it couldn't last. Didn't I tell you it couldn't last?"

"It lasted . . . what? Fourteen years?" He returned to his Naugahyde throne in the living room and snapped open his newspaper. "Pretty good run, if you ask me."

"Other people are living in her house, for God's sake!"

"It's big enough. She won't even run into them."

Lyla huffed with disgust and turned to Darcy. "Forget your father. You know how useless he is in a crisis. Sit down."

She dragged Darcy to the kitchen table and slid into a chair beside her, grabbing her cigarettes and lighting one with the practiced *flick-puff-exhale* of a thirty-year smoker. She tossed the lighter onto the kitchen table, her brows drawn together and her mouth drooping in a taut, worried frown.

"So you're telling me there's no money left? None at all? He took every penny?"

Oh, God. It sounded way worse when somebody said it out loud. "Yes," Darcy said, her voice shuddering. "Every penny."

"I can't believe this is happening. Didn't you put anything away? Anything at all?"

Darcy felt like a fool. Sure, *now* she could see she should have developed an alternative plan somewhere along the line, like maybe siphoning money from their joint accounts and sticking it under the mattress. Hindsight sucked.

"I have a hundred and eighty-three dollars in my wallet," she said. "Plus a few pesos."

Lyla groaned, taking several short puffs on her cigarette, interspersed with a lot of eye shifting and fingernail tapping. She had long since given up the idea of rising to the top of society as a whole, but she could damn well be the cream of the crop at Wingate Manufactured Home Park. Unfortunately, most of that status came from the fact that her daughter was married to a *chief financial officer* at a *big corporation* in *west Plano* and lived in a *gated community* of homes worth over *half a million dollars*. Those buzz words piqued all kinds of interest among people who watched *Wheel of Fortune* and dreamed of winning a plasma TV.

"So, what did you do?" Lyla asked.

"I haven't done anything yet," Darcy said. "I just found out."

"No. I mean, what did you do to make him leave you?"

Darcy drew back. "I didn't *do* anything!"

"Of course you did. It's not hard to hang on to a man once you've hooked him. Even a rich one. You had to have done something."

"I'm telling you, I didn't do anything! Everything was fine when I left, and then when I came home—"

"Oh, God. It was the sex, wasn't it? You stopped giving him sex."

Darcy groaned. "Mom—"

"Haven't I told you how dangerous that is? If you

don't give a man sex, he's out the door. Haven't I *told* you that?"

"If it's so damned dangerous," Clayton muttered from the living room, "how come I don't get any?"

Lyla hurled a look of disgust over her shoulder. "Because I'm *hoping* you'll leave."

Darcy closed her eyes, wishing she'd had the foresight to put her fingers in her ears and *la-la-la* her way through that. Why did every visit to her parents' house have to be a trip through Dysfunction Junction?

She remembered the first time she'd shown her mother Warren's house. Lyla stood in the entry, gazing around as if she'd passed through the gates of heaven and was basking in paradise. Then she'd pulled Darcy aside and gave her a simple three-point plan on how to hang on to the rich man she'd managed to snag: *Stay thin, don't let even one strand of gray hair show, and never, ever have a headache at bedtime.*

"Maybe there's another reason he disappeared," Lyla said. "After all, maybe this wasn't his fault. Maybe he has a brain tumor. Did you stop to think about that? Brain tumors make people do crazy things."

Darcy gave her mother a deadpan look. "Do you actually think he has a brain tumor?"

"Hard to say. When we were over at your house last Christmas, he seemed a little distracted. Then again, if he'd had a brain tumor last Christmas, he'd probably be dead by now." She ground out her cigarette and reached for another one. "You know, I read in the *Star* about a man who was abducted by aliens. Disappeared just like that."

"Uh-huh," Clayton said. "Warren was abducted by

aliens. And the head alien said, 'Sure, take a few days to sell your house before we beam you up.'"

"Like you know what happens in outer space?" Lyla snapped, then turned back to Darcy. "Anyway, the guy's wife thought he'd run off with another woman. I guess in a way he had, since it turned out he was having sex with a little green woman with great big eyeballs."

Over the years, Darcy had trained herself not to picture Warren doing it with anyone else since she'd had the feeling a few times that he might have been. But not once had she imagined that the other woman was . . . well, an other*worldly* woman.

"He wasn't abducted by aliens," Darcy said, as if somebody had to.

"Then what's your explanation? Do you suppose it *is* another woman? Is that what's going on?"

"I don't know."

"Is she younger than you?"

Darcy looked at her mother dumbly. "If I don't even know if she exists, how do I know if she's younger?"

"Oh, she's younger. Believe me. They're *always* younger." She glanced at the sunflower clock on the kitchen wall. "Clayton! Go take a shower. We're due at the clubhouse in forty-five minutes."

"You're leaving?" Darcy asked.

"Have to," Lyla said. "Monthly potluck. I'd stay home, but I'm the committee chairman this year. If I'm not there, Roxanne will move in and take all the credit."

Roxanne LaCroix was Lyla's neighbor across the street who was supposedly her best friend, but both of them had elevated backstabbing to an Olympic event.

"You can come if you want to," Lyla said.

Darcy thought about the clubhouse, which consisted of a Coke machine, a scruffy pool table, a galley kitchen with yellowed linoleum, and plenty of folding tables for bingo night.

"Uh . . . no, thanks," Darcy said.

With a squeak of his La-Z-Boy, Clayton rose from his chair and came to the kitchen table, newspaper in hand. "You can stay in the spare bedroom," he told Darcy. "Your mother will feed you. Here's thirty bucks to fill up your gas tank."

"My gas tank?"

"After you look at these." He tossed the newspaper down on the table, then ambled down the hall.

Lyla glanced at the section of the paper he'd given Darcy, then whipped around and shouted, "You want her to get a *job?*"

But Clayton had already disappeared. If he was going to drop a bomb, he knew to stay clear of the fallout.

Lyla huffed with irritation. "Didn't I tell you he was useless in a crisis?"

For once, her mother was right. After all, Darcy had been an employee once—a receptionist at a big manufacturing company—and she hadn't liked it in the least. She had to be at her desk at some ungodly hour of the morning, she got only an hour for lunch, and as much as she liked talking on the phone, after a while the ringing drove her nuts. If Warren hadn't worked there as a senior accounting manager and eventually taken her away from all that, she'd have been forced to rethink employment as a means of making a living.

Marry rich, Darcy. It's your only hope.

She'd heard those words from the moment she realized

boys didn't have cooties to the day she said "I do." Her mother believed every woman needed a man to take care of her, and the richer he was, the better. And if you couldn't find a rich one, you made do with whatever you could get and then spent the rest of your life bitching about the monthly shortfall and trying to make him into something he wasn't.

Lyla stabbed out her cigarette and rose from the table. "I have to go do my hair. In the meantime, I suggest you make a few phone calls and see if you can find your husband. And when you do, tell him you're sorry for whatever you've done, and then pretend nothing ever happened."

"Sorry? What do I have to be *sorry* about?"

"Whatever you did to make him leave you."

"Haven't you heard a word I've said? I didn't *do* anything!"

Lyla shook her finger like a cranky schoolmarm. "Do you like pretty clothes? A big house to live in? Lunch at those fancy restaurants? You're not twenty-five anymore, you know. Do you think you've still got what it takes to snag another man who can give you a lifestyle like that?"

Darcy felt a slap of reality. Her impending birthday hadn't meant a thing to her two hours ago when she had the money to look thirty. But now she pictured her roots growing out. Her Botox wearing off. The lump of Play-Doh her body was going to become if she couldn't pay Vlad to push her to exercise.

As those horrific thoughts swept through her mind, she quivered with dread. All she wanted was for Warren to surface with some kind of plausible explanation—or even a not-so-plausible one that was at least semi-believable—so she could get her life back again and pretend all this had never happened.

Lyla went to her bedroom to make herself as presentable as nature would allow. Darcy found leftover chicken in the fridge for Pepé, and then she fixed herself a drink with the only ingredients she could find: diet Coke and Wild Turkey. After her parents left the house, she drained that glass and filled another one, then picked up the phone and made calls to Warren's friends, his golf buddies, and his CPA. Nobody had seen a single hair on his mostly bald head. Or, if they had, they weren't telling her.

She hung up and took stock of her situation. It didn't look good. She had a hundred and eighty-three dollars, a couple of suitcases full of clothes that would be perfect as long as she moved to a Mexican resort for the rest of her life, and a dog she loved dearly but who was about as useful in a crisis as dryer lint.

But she did still have her Mercedes. Thank God she still had that.

She glanced out the window and adored her car for a moment, taking a mental tour of the interior, with its walnut door panels and its heated seats and its Thermo-Tronic climate control, not to mention the intoxicating smell of the black leather seats. Maybe everything else in her life had gone to hell, but no one was taking her car away from her.

Except maybe those guys out there stealing it.

Chapter 3

As John unlocked the door of the Mercedes Roadster, he experienced the same thrill he always did whenever he was in the presence of a truly extraordinary vehicle. He couldn't wait to feel the walnut-inlaid steering wheel beneath his palms, smell the leather, hear the thunder of three hundred horses under the hood. It was a convertible, earning it extra points, and firemist red with black interior, which were exactly the colors he would pick if fate ever chose to drop fifty thousand discretionary dollars in his lap. It was getting near dusk, but he'd bet this baby would glow in the dark.

Parked behind the Roadster was a '91 Corolla, blue with rust accents, with a Jack-in-the-Box antenna ball and a purple rosary hanging from the rearview mirror. Since that vehicle was typical for those that resided at Wingate Manufactured Home Park, the Mercedes Roadster stuck out like a champion show dog in a pack of mangy mutts.

Tony gave a low whistle, running his hand over the fender of the car with utmost appreciation. "Man, one of these days I'm going to buy one of these instead of stealing other people's."

"Yep," John said. "Nice car. Now, keep an eye on that double-wide until I can get it out of here."

He unlocked the driver's door and opened it so he could check out the vehicle identification number, careful as always to see that the numbers matched. Nothing on earth caused a bigger mess than grabbing the wrong car.

"The VIN matches," John said.

"Okay, then," Tony said. "I'm out of here. There's a certain depressed woman who needs me tonight. I'll just give her a call. . . ." He paused. "Uh-oh. We've got trouble."

John heard a door slam. He looked over his shoulder to see a woman tearing down the front steps of the double-wide, teetering on ridiculously high heels as she ran across a lawn that was more weeds than grass. Christ, a woman could break an ankle in shoes like those.

"Hey, you!" she shouted. "Get away from my car!"

John stood up. She halted in front of him, coiling her perfectly manicured hands into fists and resting them on her hips. And he couldn't help noticing the tight white pants that followed the curve of those hips and the lime-green off-the-shoulder shirt she wore that was just short enough to reveal an inch of skin below it—smooth, tanned skin that said she was a poolside lounger who wore just the right SPF. And her hair—long, dark, and silky—looked as if she'd just stepped out of a shampoo commercial.

Although she was nice to look at, he'd discovered long ago that high-maintenance women only made his life hell, and she was clearly one of those. Anytime one of them popped up on his radar, he ran the other way.

She flicked a strand of dark, glossy hair over her

shoulder and skewered him with an angry glare. "What are you doing with my car?"

"Returning it to its owner."

"I *am* its owner."

"Nope. This car is owned by Atlas Financial Services."

"What are you talking about?"

"I'm repossessing it."

She drew back with a stunned expression. "*Repossessing* it?"

"That's what happens when you don't make the payments."

"Hold on. Wait a minute. Payments? What do you mean, 'payments'?"

Not only was she high maintenance, she was dumb as dirt. Dangerous combination. It meant she had the basic motor function to start shopping but not enough brain power to tell her when to stop.

"It was financed," he told her. Slowly, so she'd get the picture. "By your husband."

"No. There are no payments. My husband has plenty of money. He pays cash for everything."

"Maybe for everything else, but not for this."

"You're not listening to me," she said sharply. "You clearly have the wrong car."

"Nope. The VIN matches."

"VIN?"

"Vehicle identification number."

"Maybe somebody gave you the wrong number."

"And the wrong number matches? What are the odds?"

He turned to get into the car, but she grabbed his arm. "Hey! I'm telling you you've made a mistake!"

John let out a breath of irritation. He rarely bothered to explain himself, but since it might be the quickest way out of here, he pulled the repossession order from his pocket.

"Warren McDaniel," he read. "Is that your husband's name?"

"Yes. But you must have the wrong Warren McDaniel."

John rattled off the social security number. "Is that your husband's?"

"Yes, but—"

"Is this a Mercedes SLK350 Roadster?"

"Of course it is. But—"

"The vehicle identification number matches."

"Okay, but—"

"And the loan is sixty days delinquent."

"Well, you *say* it is, but—"

"So tell me where I'm out of line by taking this car."

She snatched the order out of his hand and tore it up, tossing the pieces into the air for the evening breeze to carry away, then planted her fists on her hips again.

Tony's eyes widened. "Oops," he told her. "Big mistake. John's real funny about his paperwork."

"Will you shut up?" John snapped. "I'll handle this."

Tony held up his hands in surrender and went over to lean against the fender of his 4x4, popping a Tic Tac and not even bothering to hide his smirk of amusement. John, on the other hand, was not amused in the least.

"That did you no good at all," John told her. "I don't have to have paperwork to take the car." He slid into the convertible and stuck the key into the ignition.

"Wait a minute. Where did you get a key?"

"Some loan companies keep a copy. Makes life easier when their cars have to be repossessed."

"They can't do that!"

"They can until the loan is paid off." He shut the door.

"No! You are *not* taking my car!"

The hell he wasn't.

He started the engine and revved it a little. As he was reaching for the gearshift, though, she circled around the front of the car, turned, and leaned against the hood.

"Hey!" he shouted. "Get out of the way!"

She didn't move, so he laid on the horn. She jumped a little but stayed put.

Shit. What now? He couldn't keep honking. If he did, pretty soon an audience would gather, and in his profession that could only lead to disaster.

He looked over his shoulder. Unfortunately, the crappy Corolla parked behind him hadn't decided to move of its own accord. It was hugging the Roadster's bumper so close he had no room to back up.

Enough was enough.

John ripped open the door and strode around to where she stood. "Get away from the car."

She held the fingers of one hand in front of her, apparently overcome with a sudden need to inspect her fifty-dollar manicure.

Okay. He could physically remove her. Hell, he could pick up three of her and never break a sweat. But as soon as he did, she'd start screaming, and the neighbors would come running, and assault charges would be filed, and he sure as hell didn't want to deal with any of that.

"I said get away from the car," he repeated, injecting

as much venom into his voice as he possibly could. Intimidation was his strong suit. This expression and this voice had brought felony suspects to their knees. But she merely glanced at him nonchalantly as if to say, *You are absolutely boring me to death,* then went back to checking out her perfectly polished nails.

"I'm warning you," he said. "I'm a very stubborn man."

"And I'm a stubborn woman."

"I'll stand here all night if I have to."

"How nice. We can watch the sun come up together."

"It's supposed to rain."

She glanced at the sky, where a brilliant Texas sun had just slipped below the horizon. "I believe we'd need some clouds for that."

He glanced at the hose coiled haphazardly near the front steps of the mobile home. "Not if I haul out a garden hose."

She whipped around. "You wouldn't *dare.*"

"Try me."

"You're a horrible, *horrible* man."

"Why? Because it's my job to pick up a car that hasn't been paid for?"

"No. Because you run a business that thrives on the misfortune of others."

"You mean those misfortunate people who refuse to honor their commitments and pay their bills?"

"Some people are down on their luck. Ever stop to think about that?"

"Yeah. A few are. But most of them squander their money. That's not misfortune. That's misallocation."

"I didn't *misallocate* anything! It was my husband who didn't make the payments, not me!"

"I don't care who missed the payments. The loan on this car is delinquent, so it's my job to take it back."

"You don't understand! My husband left me. He took everything. This car is the only thing I have left!"

John made a scoffing noise and started to tell her she might want to take that up with a divorce attorney, but all at once her challenging expression fell away, and her face crumpled. He froze, overcome by a horrible sense of foreboding.

Oh, God. She was going to cry. Sure enough, her eyes began to glisten. Her lips tightened.

"No," he said, holding up his hand. "For God's sake, don't cry."

"I can't help it."

John glanced at Tony, who had conveniently turned his attention to the yard next door, where a stray dog was peeing on a crape myrtle tree.

"Yeah, you can," John said. "Really. You can help it. Just . . . don't."

But then a tear ran down her cheek, and another, and John knew he was in for a deluge.

"You have no idea what I've been through," she sobbed. "None at all."

"No. You're right. I don't. And I really don't think you should tell—"

"I came home from a vacation today and found out that my husband had left me!"

John closed his eyes. Here it came. The whole damned story.

"He took everything. He sold our house. There was

another family living there. I actually walked through the door to find *another family living in my house.* Can you believe it? And he cleaned out our bank accounts. Ran up our credit cards. Now all I have is my dog and . . ." She ran her hand over the hood of the car, tears rolling down her face. "And my beautiful, *beautiful* car."

She buried her face in her hands, and pretty soon her shoulders were shaking with sobs, and John wished to God he were anywhere else. For a few seconds, though, he wondered what kind of man would sell a house right out from under his wife. But the truth, of course, was that no man would. It had to be a lie. People living in her house when she came home? *Please.* She was playing him, pure and simple, and it was time he put his foot down, tears or no tears.

Stand firm. Stand tough. You can do it.

"It doesn't matter what your story is," he told her. "I don't have any choice about this. All the legalities are in place. Once they send me the repossession order—"

"Warren gave me this car as an anniversary present last year," she went on, as if John hadn't even spoken. "It had one of those big red bows on it. You know. The kind you see on TV commercials."

John bowed his head. *Shoot me now.*

"It was so beautiful, and I was so excited, but now he's stopped making the payments and I'm going to lose it." She flicked her gaze to the mobile home, rolling her tear-filled eyes. "And now look where I've ended up. My beautiful house is gone, and I'm stuck living with my parents. And that's not an easy thing to do, let me tell you."

One glance at the mobile home told John that even if

she was lying about everything else, she probably wasn't lying about that.

She sniffed. "Do you think . . ."

"What?"

"Do you think you could give me a break? Let me keep my car long enough for me to make up the back payments?"

"No. I really can't—"

"Please. If you just let me keep it, I swear I'll get the money together. How much do I need?"

"You don't understand. I have to take the car."

"How *much?*"

He sighed. "Twenty-four hundred dollars."

Her jaw dropped. "Twenty-four hundred? For only two months of payments?"

"Plus the impound fee."

And then she was crying all over again.

Okay. That did it. Tomorrow morning, first thing, he was going to be on the phone with the Subway corporate office, begging for a franchise. From now on, it was going to be just him, cold cuts, and a squirt bottle full of mayo.

"Listen," he said, "if you promise you won't give me any more problems, I'll give you a break on the impound fee." He pulled out a business card and gave it to her. "The car will be at my place for thirty days. If you come up with the back payments, I'll waive the impound fee and you can have it back."

"The impound fee doesn't mean a thing if I don't have the money for the payments."

"That's the best I can do."

She dropped her head to her hands again, and John

felt like a total idiot standing there listening to her cry. He didn't give a damn if she was lying or not. He just wanted it to *stop*.

Then slowly she raised her head and wiped her eyes, as if maybe she was getting a grip.

"Okay," she said, sliding John's card into her pocket. "I understand. If you say Warren didn't make the payments, then I guess he didn't. And that means you have every right to take my car away from me."

Thank God. She was finally coming to her senses.

"Even if it is the only thing I have left in the whole world."

And making him feel like crap in the process.

"I'd look the other way if I could," he told her, trying to sound sympathetic even though he sucked at it. "But I can't. That's just the way it is."

She nodded again. "I know. You're only doing your job. And I'm sorry I'm falling apart. You shouldn't have to deal with that."

She moved away from the car. The tear that had started a line of mascara trickling down her face erased his image of her as that cold-as-ice, picture-perfect woman who'd raced up to the car a minute ago. Those big brown eyes filled with tears made her look more like Bambi after Mommy Deer got blown away, and he was the big bad hunter who'd done her in.

"Go ahead and take my car," she said. "It's all yours. I promise I won't give you any more trouble."

Against all odds, he was starting to believe she really was telling him the truth. Still, it didn't change a thing. He had a job to do, and it was time he got to it. He turned to get in the car.

"Wait a minute," she said.

Oh, God. What now?

She waved her hand. "Never mind. It's stupid."

"What?"

"I just . . ."

"What?"

She let out a shaky breath. "Would you mind if . . . if I sat in it one more time? Just to say good-bye?"

John grimaced. "Say good-bye?"

"Please."

Surely to God this wasn't really happening. He glanced over at Tony again, who rolled his eyes and held up his palms, sign language for *Sorry, buddy. You're on your own.*

With a sigh of resignation, John opened the door for her, and she slid into the driver's seat. She paused for a moment, her gaze wandering around the car. Then she took a deep, cleansing breath, lifted her hand, and touched the dashboard, moving her fingertips lightly across the leather surface. In spite of her phony fingernails, John couldn't help but notice that she had beautiful hands. Small, perfectly formed, looking as soft as the pricey leather she was touching.

And glittering with precious stones. *High maintenance, remember?*

He had no doubt that every fight with a woman like her would cost a man a fortune. Makeup jewelry didn't come cheap. Still, even though he wasn't too fond of what was on the inside, it didn't stop him from admiring what was on the outside in spite of her obvious cosmetic enhancements.

He watched as she moved her hand to the CD changer,

her fingertips tripping lightly over the buttons in a mesmerizing motion, as if she could make it play through
the sheer electricity of her touch. He had no doubt she
and the stereo made beautiful music together every time
she turned it on.

He shifted his gaze to the curve of her shoulder, let
it linger there a moment, then moved it down along her
arm, where her lightly tanned skin was so golden and
perfect that sun goddesses everywhere had to be crying
with envy.

Look the other way.

But that was damn near impossible when she turned
her attention to the passenger seat and stroked it in a
slow, sultry motion, causing her silver bracelets to clink
together. An image formed in John's mind of her hand
moving across a man's body, leaving a trail of scorched
nerve endings in its wake.

His body in particular.

No. Don't go there. Don't you even think *of going
there.*

Before he could rid his mind of the thought, though,
she moved her hand to the gearshift. Taking another deep
breath, she circled her hand over the knob and flexed
her fingers. Then slowly she dragged her hand down the
length of it in a long, languorous stroke, and his mouth
went dry as dust.

The whole thing made him feel as if he was peeping
through her bedroom blinds, but he couldn't look away.
And just when he thought his mind couldn't fall any further into the gutter, she took hold of the steering wheel
with her other hand and leaned in and kissed it.

Holy shit.

Even though the sun had gone down, a hot trickle of sweat ran down his chest and melted into his shirt. Cherry-red lips meeting polished walnut—good *God,* he'd never imagined what an erotic sight that could be. But then he also couldn't have imagined when he got out of bed that morning that he'd be jealous of a steering wheel. The only problem with her leaning in to kiss it was that he couldn't see what mesmerizing things she might be doing with her other hand now.

Deep breath. It'll all be over in a minute.

She held that position for a moment, her lips touching the smooth walnut inlay in a light caress. Finally she leaned away from the wheel and put her hands in her lap, which told John the show was over. Now if he could just get her out of there before she lit two cigarettes and handed one to the car, he might be able to get this vehicle to the impound lot and call it a day.

He opened the door and automatically reached down to help her out of the car. Now one of those hands that had just made sweet, sweet love to a Mercedes Roadster was nestled inside his, and it was every bit as warm and soft as he had imagined. His thumb brushed against her wedding ring—a multicarat monstrosity that dwarfed her small hand—and he found himself wondering if she really would be getting a divorce.

Then he wondered why he was wondering.

After she stood, he tried to pull his hand away, but she tightened her grip and stared soulfully into his eyes.

"Drive it carefully, okay?"

Damn it. So much for his plan to take this sporty little vehicle on a pedal-to-the-metal trip down a farm-to-market road just to see what it could do.

As she walked back toward the mobile home, he slid into the driver's seat. This had been a real red-letter day. First a kid with a gun, and then a crying woman with a car fetish.

Oh, hell. As if he was much better? She might have a car fetish, but he clearly had a fetish about watching her act out her car fetish.

Subway, here I come. And I'm not kidding about that.

Then he lifted his hand to start the car and got a shock.

The key was gone.

He stared dumbly at the ignition. *Where was the damned key?*

He whipped around. The woman looked back over her shoulder, and the moment their eyes met, she ran.

In no time, John was out of the car and flying across the yard, but she already had a big head start. She reached the porch steps, scrambled up them, and scurried inside the mobile home. At the same time John's foot hit the top step, she slammed the door and flicked the deadbolt.

He grabbed the doorknob. Rattled it.

Shit!

He smacked the door with his fist, letting out a string of curse words so potent they practically wilted the scraggly shrubs beside the porch steps. He couldn't believe it. He simply couldn't believe it. He'd bought it. The story, the tears, the fond farewell that would have been right at home in a cheap porn flick. All of it. What was he? Some kind of moron?

He heard a tapping noise. Turning to the window, he

saw the woman looking through the blinds. She held up the key and waggled it, a sly victory smile spreading across her face.

If John had been pissed before, he was livid now. And when she blew him a kiss, it was all he could do not to plow straight through the window and go for her pretty little throat.

He spun around, trotted down the steps, and strode back to Tony's car.

"So I guess she grabbed the key?" Tony said.

"You're very intuitive." John yanked open the passenger door. "Get in."

Tony climbed into the driver's seat. "That Roadster's nice and everything, but if I were you, I'd be going after the gorgeous woman."

John looked at Tony with disbelief. "Are you *kidding* me?"

"Hell, no. She was hot."

"She was a lunatic."

"Nice body."

"Addled brain."

"Now, see, there you go again. That brain thing. Which reminds me that I need to call Rhonda. I want to make sure it's my shoulder she leans on in her time of need."

"Rona," John snapped.

"What?"

"Her name is *Rona.*"

Tony blinked. "Then why did you tell me it was Rhonda?"

"Just drive the car, will you?"

Hot or not, John wanted nothing to do with any woman

who was conniving. Phony. Manipulative. Shameless. Particularly when she was telling lies, manufacturing tears, kissing steering wheels, and palming keys.

This wasn't over yet. One way or another, he was grabbing that Mercedes Roadster. And when he did, he'd make sure she never set foot in it again.

~

Darcy peered out the blinds, watching the 4x4 disappear down the street and breathing a huge sigh of relief. But her heart was still thumping like crazy. Outwitting a man had never been a major undertaking for her, but then she'd never tried to get the better of one who was the size of a redwood tree. She was lucky he hadn't caught her, or he'd have snapped her in half like a piece of kindling.

When he'd risen up beside her car to his full six feet, umpteen inches, she'd nearly choked. He had a chest like granite and shoulders so broad they blocked out the setting sun. His thick, dark hair was meticulously clipped, and his tense, watchful eyes were equally under control, fixing on their targets with military precision. His intimidating scowl told her that smiling wasn't in his repertoire of facial expressions, even in the wake of her heartfelt sob story. Some women would have said he was handsome, but only those who liked men who could chew a sack of nails into a wad of bubble gum.

She pulled out the card he'd given her. John Stark. Lone Star Repossessions. White card stock. Black letters. No fancy logo. More evidence to support the theory that he was a no-frills kind of guy who came, saw, and conquered. Only now she'd outsmarted him, which meant she'd undoubtedly moved to the top of his hit list.

Fortunately, it was after hours, and he wouldn't be able to come up with another key from the loan company tonight. But by tomorrow morning she needed to move her car to a place where he couldn't find it.

Oh, God. How depressing was that? She was only a few hours into being broke, and already she was thinking like a deadbeat.

She went back to the kitchen table, stuck his business card in her purse, and picked up what was left of her drink, which she downed in a single gulp. She couldn't believe Warren had financed a car. She'd always imagined he just wrote a check and that was that. Light was dawning so brightly on her situation that it practically blinded her.

She went to the living room and sat in her father's recliner. Picking up the remote, she ran the channels. An infomercial. A country music video. A *Friends* rerun. When she came to the *Jerry Springer* show, she laid down the clicker and sat back to watch. It wasn't her usual choice of programming, but it was the only opportunity she had right now to revel in somebody else's misfortune for a while and forget about her own.

By the time Jerry signed off, Darcy's eyes were getting heavy. Pepé had jumped into her lap and was sleeping soundly. She was about to doze off herself, anesthetized by the drone of the TV, the bourbon she'd ingested, and the mind-numbing predicament that had become her life, when she heard a loud noise.

She opened her eyes and listened. An engine?

Yes. A very *big* engine. Oversized trucks were a dime

a dozen in the average Texas trailer park, but this one seemed higher than usual on the noise-pollution scale. She shooed Pepé off her lap and went to the window. When she flicked down the blinds, she was shocked at what she saw.

The repo man was already back.

Chapter 4

Parked at the curb was a large flatbed truck, and Darcy's car was up on it, secured in place. She had no idea how he'd managed to make that happen. Now he was sliding behind the wheel of the truck, preparing to drive away.

Darcy let go of the blinds with a clatter and yanked open the door. She hurried down the porch steps and across the yard, muttering a curse every time her heels hit clumps of crabgrass and twisted her ankles.

"Hey, you! *Stop!*" She reached the street, circled around to the driver's door, where the window was down. She had to crane her neck to look up at him sitting in the cab. She pounded on the door. "What do you think you're *doing?*"

He looked down at her. "Do we really have to go over this again?"

"How did you get my car up on this truck?"

"Repo magic."

She banged her fist on the door again. "I can't *believe* you're doing this!"

"Of course you can believe it. What you can't believe is that I did it so quickly."

Boy, he had *that* right. She made it a policy never to

underestimate her adversaries, but she'd underestimated this one big time.

Darcy heard a barrage of barking. She turned to see Pepé galloping through the grass, dodging dandelions as tall as he was. He came to a halt beside her, looking up at the large man in the mammoth truck and barking wildly.

"Well, now," he said. "You should have told me you had a dangerous watchdog. I wouldn't have dared step foot back here again."

Darcy scooped Pepé up and held him close to her chest, finally wrapping her fingers around his muzzle to stem the tide of barking. "Dogs always know what kind of people they're dealing with, and he doesn't like you. What does that tell you?"

"That I'm on a minimongrel's hit list?"

Darcy all but snarled herself. "You are *so* pitiful."

"*I'm* pitiful?"

"Yes. I mean, look at this truck. *Really.*"

"Okay. I'll bite. What's wrong with my truck?"

"Don't you know what they say about men who drive big trucks?"

"That they can haul a lot of cars to impound lots?"

"No," she said. "That they're compensating for something."

"Oh, yeah?" He raised an eyebrow. "If I were you, I don't believe I'd take *their* word for that."

The low, throaty tone of his voice caught Darcy off guard. Large, stubborn men had never held much appeal for her—they were far too hard to control—but then her gaze drifted to his hands gripping the steering wheel, big, strong hands that looked as if they could grab a charging bull by the horns and flip him over like a pancake. Large truck notwithstanding, according to *them,* big hands meant a big—

"You have my card," he said, putting the truck in gear. "You know the drill. Twenty-four hundred bucks, plus the impound fee, and the car's all yours again."

"Wait a minute! You told me you wouldn't charge me the impound fee!"

"I believe that was before you ran off with the key and slammed the door in my face."

And she didn't regret that one bit. What she regretted was that she hadn't had the foresight to park her car two blocks away before he showed up again.

He started to pull away from the curb, then braked to a halt again. "Oh," he said, "one more thing. I need to return something you gave me earlier."

"What's that?"

He touched his fingertips to his lips and blew her a kiss.

When Darcy's mouth fell open with surprise, he hit the gas and took off. She snapped her mouth shut again, all kinds of homicidal feelings welling up inside her.

Soon, though, her anger gave way to utter hopelessness. She stood under the harsh streetlamp, listening to the chirp of crickets and the faint but irate voices of the neighbors having a high-volume discussion, and watching the truck's taillights until they became nothing more than twinkly dots in the distance.

So that was it. Now she really had lost everything.

An hour later, her mother and father returned home. Ten minutes after that, her mother still refused to believe she was no longer going to have the occasional privilege of joining her daughter on a trip around town in a fifty-thousand-dollar sports car.

"I told you, Mom," Darcy said for the third time. "It was *repossessed.*"

Lyla lit a cigarette and took a heavy drag. "But does that make any sense? Any at all? What was Warren doing financing a car?"

Her questions came quickly, even though about half her words were slurred. Somebody had clearly spiked the potluck punch, and her mother had been very thirsty.

"I don't know," Darcy said. "Maybe he was having money problems I didn't know about."

"They can't just take your car right out from under you," Lyla said. "There has to be a law against that."

"Nope," Clayton said from the living room. "But there are laws against not paying your bills."

"For God's sake!" Lyla snapped. "There are extenuating circumstances!"

"The loan company won't care much about those."

"You have to do something! Get Darcy's car back!"

"That would require making up the back payments."

"Will you stop being such a tightwad? She's your daughter!" She turned to Darcy. "How much are the back payments?"

"Twenty-four hundred dollars."

Lyla froze. "Oh," she said, and reached for the bottle of Wild Turkey in the lower cabinet.

Great. The one time Darcy needed her mother's outrage, it had fizzled like a lit match in a mud puddle. *Thanks a lot, Mom. Drink up.*

Lyla poured a hefty amount of bourbon into a glass. In

the living room, Clayton settled into his recliner, ran the TV dial, and landed on a monster truck rally.

"We could loan you money," Lyla said, "but we just got back from Vegas. Damned slots. Swear to God they're tighter every time we go."

Which was about four times a year. Darcy knew that whatever her mother hadn't lost at the blackjack table last week had undoubtedly been invested in the Texas state lottery this week. No eighty-three-million-dollar jackpot was getting past her.

Unfortunately, Warren had shared her mother's love of gambling. He also shared her inability to know when to stop, always gambling away every penny he came with and then some. *"It's just entertainment,"* he'd always told her, but sometimes she had the feeling he was going to entertain himself right into the poorhouse.

"Did you make some calls?" Lyla asked. "Try to find Warren?"

"Yes. Nobody knows where he is."

"Try again tomorrow. When a man is having an affair, he can never keep his mouth shut about it. Somebody will know what he's up to."

Darcy could barely concentrate on the horrible things she was sure Warren had done, much less on those she hadn't proven yet. She just couldn't make sense of it. If he'd wanted to leave her, all he had to do was hire a divorce lawyer, and considering the prenup she'd signed, it didn't even have to be a very good one. He still would have ended up with the lion's share of all they owned. Yet he'd cashed out everything and disappeared. *Why?*

She thought about reporting him as a missing person, but she'd seen enough cop shows to know that if it looked as if he'd left of his own accord, the police wouldn't do anything. Selling the house and cleaning out the bank accounts certainly seemed to point to a voluntary absence.

"Talk to an attorney," Lyla said. "Eventually you should be able to get something out of this mess."

"Assuming Warren shows up again," Clayton said. "And even if he does, how long will it take to get him into court?"

Forever, of course. Everyone knew the American judicial system moved with the speed of an asthmatic snail.

Lyla tossed down the shot, stuck the glass in the sink, and announced she was going to bed. As she stumbled toward the hall, Darcy was struck by the most surreal feeling that her life with Warren had been a dream and now she'd woken up to a horrible reality.

"Mom?"

Lyla stopped at the doorway. "What?"

Darcy's voice came out in a choked whisper. "I have nothing left. What am I going to do?"

She teared up a little, and she thought she saw a flicker of sympathy in her mother's eyes. After all, Darcy was undergoing the biggest crisis of her life. Of course her mother would sympathize. In spite of her accusations that this was all her daughter's fault, in the end, blood was thicker than—

"You might as well stop crying," Lyla snapped. "You'll only make your mascara run. No woman ever won a man back when her makeup was a mess."

With that, she turned and headed down the hall, swaying like a willow in a light breeze. There was nothing like a few warm fuzzies from her mother to make Darcy feel as if everything was going to be just fine.

"I have a car I can loan you," her father said, his eyes never leaving the television.

"What kind of car?" Darcy asked, wiping her eyes.

"One with four tires that runs. Come with me to the shop in the morning to get it. Be ready to leave at seven-thirty."

Clayton picked up the remote and turned up the volume on the TV, shutting out any potential complaints Darcy might have about the crack-of-dawn departure. But seven-thirty? Who in his right mind got up at that ungodly hour of the morning?

Pepé brushed against Darcy's ankle. She scooped him up and held him against her shoulder, his nose snuffing against her ear, and his whole body trembling. He let out a little doggy sigh that matched Darcy's mood exactly.

"I know, sweetie," she murmured, stroking his furry ears. "But look at the bright side. If I can't pay to get my car back, it means we never have to see that awful repo man again."

And the thought of that actually made her feel better— until she remembered that the luggage she'd brought home from Mexico was still in the trunk of her car, which was currently sitting in the impound lot of Lone Star Repossessions.

Darcy had always had difficulty relating to her father. Growing up, she'd known him primarily as the balding head sticking up over the black vinyl recliner and the empty chair at the breakfast table during deer season. He was a man with perpetual grease beneath his fingernails and a permanent frown on his face, a man whose life had been scripted for him since the fateful day in '67 when he hit a home run with Lyla Scarsdale in the backseat of his GTO. Shortly after their shotgun wedding and the birth of their daughter seven months after that, her father discovered his mechanic's salary was never going to afford his wife the lifestyle to which she desperately wanted to become accustomed.

And now, as he presented Darcy with the keys to her new loaner car parked on the grease-stained floor of his mechanic shop, she could see he'd been absolutely correct. The car had four tires and ran. It also had sun-bleached paint, hail damage, and a headliner that drooped like the hem of a twenty-year-old skirt. It hadn't been the most beautiful car when it was fresh off the lot fifteen years ago, and age hadn't improved it in the least.

"You can use it as long as you need to," her father said.

"Why? Because nobody else on earth would get near it?"

"It'll get you where you need to go. That's all that counts."

Darcy cringed when she thought about what her first stop today was going to be. John Stark thought he'd had the last laugh last night, but if he saw her driving this car today, the hilarity would begin all over again.

"The tires were shot, so I put on new ones last week," her father said. "So at least that part of the car is safe."

"Are there parts that *aren't* safe?"

"The transmission's a little slow. Just be careful pulling out into busy intersections."

Good Lord. "The tires are probably worth more than the car itself."

When her father offered no argument against that, Darcy sighed. Just what she wanted to be driving. Four tires whose value was diminished by the car attached to them.

She looked out the door to her father's pickup truck. She'd never had any desire to be seen behind the wheel of one of those, but anything beat this heap.

"Dad?"

"Yeah?"

"Just for today, could you let me drive your truck?"

"Nope."

"I'll bring it back in two hours."

"Nope."

"One hour."

"Nope."

"But—"

"*Nobody* drives my truck."

Darcy put her fists on her hips. "So you're telling me if Dale Earnhardt came back to life and wanted to drive your truck, you'd tell him to forget it?"

"Darcy, if God himself offered me heaven on a silver platter for the keys, I'd tell *him* to forget it."

Darcy didn't think the exclusive use of a Ford F-150 was worth eternal damnation, but that was her father. And since her mother quit driving after the train-crossing incident three years ago, they were a one-vehicle family, so grabbing her mother's keys and taking off wasn't an option.

"Besides," her father said, "you don't know how to drive a car that has a manual transmission."

Okay, so she'd forgotten about that.

As long as she stayed in east Plano, she wouldn't run into anyone she knew. And she had to drive the old car only as long as it took her to find Warren, put her hands around his throat, and squeeze some of the money he'd taken right back out of him.

Warren. Where in the world was he?

No. She couldn't think about him now. She had to concentrate on the problem at hand—getting back what few possessions she had so she could begin to feel normal again.

"Watch your pressure gauges," her father said. "It leaks oil."

Darcy sighed. "Anything else?"

"Yeah. The latch is broken on the driver's door. You'll have to crawl in from the passenger side."

This could *not* be happening.

Her father opened the door for her, and she climbed inside none too gracefully, putting one knee on the passenger seat, then turning around to plop behind the wheel. She started the car. It gasped and sputtered, reminding her of her great-aunt Gertie, who had continued to smoke even as emphysema was driving her into the grave.

Darcy closed her eyes. Every time she thought she'd hit rock bottom, she sank a little lower.

⁓

"The stock market's on a downturn. Unemployment is up. Interest rates are on the rise." John tossed the business section of the *Dallas Morning News* onto his desk. "If this keeps up, I might actually make a decent profit one of these days."

Tony leaned against the door frame, morning coffee in hand. "In other words, what's bad for America is good for John Stark?"

"It's hard to stay in this business when people don't default on their loans."

"Hey, we already have plenty of work. You got that Mercedes, didn't you?"

"Finally."

"Did she give you any trouble when you went back with the tow truck?"

Now *that* put a smile on John's face. "Not a bit."

"Ah. A smile. Does that mean you finally got your priorities straight?"

"What?"

"You're focusing on the woman as much as the car?"

John frowned. "I told you. She's a nutcase."

"So you're not going to see her again?"

"I repossessed her car. Just how amenable do you think she'd be if I said, 'Hey, baby, wanna go out?' " As if he'd even consider it.

"Well," Tony said, "I agree it doesn't usually set the stage very well, but I've dated women whose cars I've taken."

"You'd find a way to date a woman if you shot her mother."

"Hmm. There's a pickup scenario I hadn't considered, but—"

Just then the door to the outer office opened. Both men craned their necks around to see who it was.

"Well I'll be damned," Tony said. "Speak of the devil. What's she doing here?"

Actually, after taking inventory of her car last night, John had been expecting her. "She had luggage in the trunk of her car. I assume she's here to pick it up."

"Well, then. Here's your chance to get the Mercedes *and* the girl."

John just shook his head. Tony's preoccupation with the opposite sex was an amazing thing to behold. When he wasn't thinking about women, he was drinking with them, eating with them, showering with them, or sleeping with them. Being surrounded by all that estrogen was bound to get him into trouble someday.

The men went to the outer office. John's gaze automatically drifted to the woman's snug little pants, which ended just below her knees, then upward to a stretchy blue top. Following her curves up and down and all around reminded him that it had been a while since he'd gotten up close and personal with a woman, but he had no intention of ending that streak with a marginally insane one.

She stood there with her purse draped over one shoulder, jingling her keys, as if she expected this visit to be a short one. Good. He couldn't think of anything he wanted more.

Tony gave her a brilliant smile and stuck out his hand. "Hi, there. We didn't get a chance to meet last night. I'm Tony McCaffrey."

She shook Tony's hand, giving him a smile of her own. "Darcy McDaniel."

"What brings you here today?"

"Knock it off, Tony," John said. "This isn't social hour.

You know why she's here. She's getting her luggage, and then she's leaving."

Darcy turned to John, her smile evaporating. "Well, aren't you Mr. Hospitality."

"Don't mind John," Tony said. "He's all business." Leaning closer to Darcy, he whispered, "He doesn't know a thing about pleasure."

She raised an eyebrow at John. "Is that so?"

John shot Tony a look of irritation. "Come help me with her stuff."

A few moments later, they brought her luggage out of the back room—all five pieces of it.

"How long were you on vacation?" John asked.

"A week."

He stopped short. "You went on a weeklong vacation and took all this luggage with you?"

"Why not?"

"It's an awful lot to lug around."

"I don't *lug*. That's what porters and limousine drivers are for."

Of course. What was he thinking?

He handed her the form to sign that said she'd picked up her possessions and that they were in good condition. She stopped halfway through her signature and looked around the office.

"Wait a minute. Where's my wine?"

"Wine?" John said.

"It was on the floor of the front seat. A bottle of Shiraz."

"Never saw it."

"It probably rolled under the seat. I want it back."

John sighed. "How about I just give you ten bucks and we call it even?"

"Ten dollars?" Darcy said. "Are you kidding me? It's a two-hundred-dollar bottle of wine!"

"Two hundred dollars? Who in his right mind pays two hundred dollars for one bottle of wine?"

"A person with discriminating taste."

"Who loves to throw away money."

"You clearly know nothing about the finer things in life."

"I know the value of a buck. Doesn't get any finer than that."

"Don't worry," Tony said. "I'll get the wine for you."

"Why, thank you," she said, giving him a pleasant smile. "I do believe you're one of the sweetest men I've ever met."

Tony grinned at John. "You hear that, John? I'm sweet."

"Just get the damned wine, will you?"

Tony gave Darcy a wink, grabbed a set of keys, and headed out the door. She turned and gave John a look that could have curdled milk. "Is there a single ounce of gentlemanly behavior inside you at all?"

"Sure there is. And it all comes pouring out the moment I encounter a lady."

"You're still mad because I outsmarted you and grabbed that key. Maybe it's time you got over that."

"Actually, I got over that about the time I drove off with your car and left you standing in the middle of the street."

"How does it feel to take a car away from a woman who has nothing left in the world?"

"So you're sticking to that story, are you?"

"It's the truth."

"Your husband actually sold your house while you were on a vacation?"

"Yes."

"You came home to other people living there. That's hard to believe."

"Not when he practically gave it away."

"Your address was in west Plano. High-rent district. And now you're living with your parents in a trailer park?"

"With no money, what else am I supposed to do?"

"Then you don't have a job?"

She lifted her nose a notch. "Since I've been married, I haven't *had* to work."

"That doesn't surprise me." He grabbed a garment bag, slung it over the handle of the biggest suitcase, then took the handle of the next smallest one and headed for the door. Darcy just stood there.

"What are you waiting for?" he said. "Porters and limo drivers don't generally happen by this way, and I'm only making one trip."

She gave him a dirty look and grabbed the carry-on bag and another bag with wheels, and they went to the parking lot. The only car there that wasn't his or Tony's looked as if it was on its last leg.

"Nice ride," John said.

She unlocked the trunk. "It's your fault I have to drive it."

"Steal it from a junkyard?"

"No, stealing would be *your* thing. If you must know, I borrowed it from my father."

"So what did you do to your father to warrant a punishment like this?"

"Just put my luggage in the trunk, will you?"

He'd just finished loading up the car when Tony came around the corner of the building and handed her the bottle of wine. "Here you go, sweetheart." He looked at the car, wincing painfully. "Yours?"

"I'm afraid so."

"For the love of God, John. Nobody should have to drive a heap like that. Give her back her car, will you?"

"So you'd like to make up her back payments?"

"Uh . . . no." He turned to Darcy. "Sorry."

She smiled at him. "You're still a very sweet man." Then she shot John a look that said, *And you're not.*

"I'm real sorry about what your husband did to you," Tony said. "What are your plans now?"

"I'm not completely sure," Darcy said. "But I'll manage."

"That's going to be a tough thing to do with no job," John said.

"Some people work hard," she said smugly. "Other people work smart."

"I'm surprised you're interested in working at all."

"If you are," Tony said, "we have a job opening here."

John whipped around. "No, we don't."

"Yeah, we do," Tony told Darcy. "John fired our clerk yesterday."

"Well, thank you so much for thinking of me," Darcy said, showering Tony with that glowing smile again. Then she turned to John, and the glow vanished. "But I'm afraid the management here is a little overbearing for my taste."

"I'm quite sure it is," John said. "And you couldn't handle the job, anyway."

"Handle what? Picking up a phone and saying hello? Pulling open a file cabinet and stuffing folders into it?" She made a scoffing noise. "I can't imagine the person who *couldn't* handle it."

"Well, in that case," he said with a deadpan expression, "the job's all yours."

"And I'll take you up on that," she said, "the day hell freezes over."

With that, she circled around, got in the passenger door of that god-awful car, and shimmied over to the driver's seat. It was a hard thing to pull off gracefully, and John had to admit she did a pretty good job of it.

Tony grinned. "She's one of a kind, isn't she?"

That was the understatement of the century.

John watched as she stuck her nose in the air and motored out of his parking lot, that crappy old car gasping for every inch of ground it covered. As much as she drove him nuts, he couldn't help being curious about how she was going to pull herself out of the hole her husband had dug for her. It would be an interesting thing to watch. From a distance, anyway. Wearing body armor. With a weapon in each hand. And his brain on full alert.

No matter how beautiful she might be, behind that pretty face was a woman who could turn any man's life upside down before he even knew what hit him.

~

That man was infuriating.

Darcy fumed most of the way home, wondering how

she'd had the misfortune not only to have her husband leave her penniless, but then to have a man like John Stark pop up to make life hell for her. Thank God she finally had her luggage back, which meant that from now on, Lone Star Repossessions would be nothing more than a very bad memory.

It was time to concentrate on other things, such as where Warren was and how she could get back some of the money he'd taken away. She still couldn't fathom why he'd disappeared the way he had. While their relationship had never been overly warm, they'd never been hostile to each other, and taking everything they had and leaving was just about as hostile as it got.

She'd met Warren when she went to work for the big manufacturing company where he used to be an accountant. He had just made the leap to upper management about the time he divorced his wife of twenty years.

But it wasn't until he and Darcy had been married for several months that she realized the extent of his midlife crisis. Sometimes she'd see him looking in the mirror when he thought he was alone, checking out the hairline and the wrinkles and the love handles, and an aura of quiet desperation would fill the air around him. Warren always seemed to have the sense that time wasn't just marching on but was running wildly around him in ever-tightening circles, closing in on him until escape was impossible.

Ironically, right now Darcy was feeling the same way. Was that why he had left? Because she wasn't the fresh young woman he'd married? Because she was no longer enough compensation for the way he felt about himself?

And if that was true, would any other man be interested in her?

As that sickening feeling took hold, Darcy let herself entertain the fantasy that one of her mother's theories was actually true. Maybe Warren really did have that brain tumor. It had made him go a little crazy, but in a few days he would find his way home, they'd get him a little chemo, and everything would be right with the world again. When she arrived at her parents' house five minutes later, though, a sense of impending doom overcame her.

A police car was parked at the curb.

She pulled Gertie up behind it and killed the engine, then went into the house. Her mother was talking to a detective from the Plano Police Department.

"Mom? What's wrong?"

Lyla grabbed Darcy's arm, her face ghost-white. "Brace yourself, Darcy. Something terrible's happened. It's . . . it's Warren."

It's true. The brain tumor finally caught up to him, and they've found his body.

But the detective quickly relieved her of that crazy scenario by offering her an even crazier one. As it turned out, not only had Warren cashed in everything he and Darcy had, an IRS audit at Sybersense Systems revealed that a few days before Darcy had returned from Mexico, he'd embezzled three hundred thousand dollars.

And now he'd skipped the country.

Chapter 5

Darcy already knew her husband was a no-good, deserting, asset-grabbing jerk. But the last thing she'd expected was that he'd turn out to be a criminal.

The detective questioned her at length, trying to find out if she might have any idea where Warren was, but his questions only muddled her mind and made the situation seem even more surreal. They'd discovered that Warren had substantial gambling debts, which gave him all kinds of motive to embezzle. Worst of all, as a chief financial officer of a major corporation, he had the knowledge to successfully hide any money that hadn't gone to loan sharks, which meant that Darcy would probably never see a dime of it again.

At least she had her answer now. Put quite simply, Warren was a lousy gambler who amassed a huge amount of debt and was reluctant to have his knees broken. But she had news for him. If she ever saw him again, his knees would be the least of what she'd break.

Darcy spent the rest of the day with her head in a murky cloud of disbelief. As evening approached, she was ready to dive headfirst into a glass of alcohol. She thought about opening the bottle of Shiraz Tony had rescued from her car, but now the wine she might have once had with Chinese takeout seemed more valuable than gold.

Instead she chugged some Wild Turkey with her mother, then sat like a zombie in front of a NASCAR race with her father while her mother did the *TV Guide* crossword puzzle. At ten o'clock, Darcy stumbled to bed in a haze of lower-class mediocrity.

The next morning she was shaken from sleep by late-morning sunlight bursting through the window, the kind that turns pupils into pinpoints and aggravates the hell out of a tears-and-bourbon headache. Pepé was standing on her stomach, staring down at her like a child whose alcoholic mother has been tipping the bottle again. She pulled him down to the bed, turned on her side, and cuddled him against her.

She wished she could lapse into a coma so she wouldn't have to face the day. But sooner or later she had to get out of this bed and do *something,* though she didn't have a clue what. The urge to draw a warm bath and haul out the razor blades had passed, but in its place was a scary little ball of nerves that felt permanently stuck in her stomach.

She had no money and no means of getting any. No man on the horizon willing to step into Warren's shoes. What was she going to do?

Finally she pushed the covers away and sat up, the blood vessels in her temples on the verge of exploding. She shuffled to the kitchen and fed Pepé some of the unrecognizable animal parts in a can that her father had found, left over from a few months ago when Duke the Wonder Dog had gone to the great duck hunt in the sky. Pepé wolfed down one plateful of it and looked up for more. Darcy sighed. Her dog was so nondiscriminating sometimes that she wondered if he really was hers or whether puppies had been switched at birth.

Darcy pulled out a chair and plopped down at the table, feeling like Raggedy Ann in the midst of a major depressive episode. And that depression took an even bigger nosedive when her mother showed her the business section of the *Dallas Morning News*.

SYBERSENSE EXEC EMBEZZLES $300,000.

"Now the whole world is going to know about it," Lyla said, puffing away on her Virginia Slims as if the Surgeon General had never weighed in on the issue. "You married a criminal, Darcy. How could you have married a criminal?"

Darcy wanted to beat her head against the table. "He wasn't a criminal when I married him."

"Maybe he was. Maybe he just hid it really well all these years."

"Mom—"

"Forget it. It doesn't matter now. What matters is that the detective said you'll never see any of that money again, so it's time to start thinking about what to do now."

"She might consider getting that job we talked about," her father said.

"Clayton, will you shut up about that? Now that Warren is gone for sure, she needs more than a paycheck. She needs another husband."

"She doesn't need a man to take care of her."

"You're right. She doesn't. As long as she doesn't mind eating out of a Dumpster."

Thanks, Mom. I need a horrible image like that to haunt me twenty-four hours a day.

"First things first, Darcy. Put yourself together. You'll

feel better. No woman feels good when she looks like hell."

Darcy wasn't sure she'd feel good if she *didn't* look like hell, but it was worth a shot. Forty-five minutes later, she came back out to the kitchen, her hair dried and her makeup on, and wearing a print skirt, a knit top, and her Claudia Ciuti sandals. Her mother gave her a once-over.

"That skirt's really not your color."

"It's a print skirt, Mom. Which color isn't me?"

"All of them. Are you hungry?"

Darcy poured a cup of coffee. "No, thanks."

"No. You should eat something." Lyla opened the pantry door. "Let's see . . . I have some bagels—no, wait. They're a little green." She moved some stuff around. "Oh. Here are some Pop Tarts. And some instant oatmeal. And one of those muffin mixes with the dehydrated strawberries." She searched through the shelves a while longer. "And some Froot Loops."

Dumpster-diving was looking better all the time. "Pop Tarts, I guess." Flavored rubber between two pieces of cardboard. She couldn't wait.

Lyla shoved two Pop Tarts into the toaster, then went to the kitchen sink to put some dishes into the dishwasher.

"Oh, my *God!*"

Darcy just about spilled her coffee. "What?"

"Will you look at that! A limousine!"

Darcy rose and looked out the window over the sink. Sure enough, a sleek black limo sat at the curb.

"What do you suppose it's doing here?" Lyla said.

"I don't know, but somebody's getting out."

"It's a woman," Lyla said. "At least I think it's a woman. She's coming this way!"

There were three sharp raps at the door. Darcy opened it and came face-to-face with a short, compact woman wearing a black shirt, black jeans, black boots. Her dark hair was cut in a short, utilitarian style, and she wore not a speck of makeup or a single piece of jewelry. She held her hands behind her in military-ready fashion, looking at Darcy with a grim, almost lethal expression.

"Yes?" Darcy said.

"I'm looking for Darcy McDaniel."

"I'm Darcy McDaniel."

"Mr. Bridges would like to speak with you."

"Excuse me?"

"Jeremy Bridges."

Darcy blinked with surprise. She knew that name. He owned Sybersense Systems, the software company Warren worked for, along with about a dozen other companies. He was one of those computer wonder boys who had turned a tiny software company into a huge conglomerate, going from ordinary citizen to multimillionaire in a very short period of time. She'd asked Warren once what he was like and had gotten two words in response: *young* and *eccentric*. That hadn't been much to go on, so Darcy wasn't quite sure what she was in for now. But with her mother all but shoving her out the door, it looked as if she was going to find out.

Darcy followed the woman down the stairs and across the yard. The woman opened the rear door of the limousine. With the tinted windows, at first all Darcy saw inside was black. She climbed inside and sat down, and when she turned to face the man on the seat beside her, she got the shock of her life.

This was Jeremy Bridges?

He lounged against the opposite door, his arm along the back of the seat, wearing a pair of khaki shorts, a faded Hawaiian shirt, and flip-flops, holding a bottle of Corona against his knee. A lock of sandy brown hair fell carelessly across his forehead, and a day's growth of beard darkened his cheeks and chin. Interventions by a hairstylist, a wardrobe consultant, and a sommelier were definitely in order.

But wait a minute. This couldn't be him. She knew Bridges was in his late thirties, and this guy looked like a college kid who'd rented a limo with his buddies to go for a joy ride.

"Hi, Darcy," he said. "I'm Jeremy Bridges."

Darcy blinked. Blinked again. *Impossible.* "Uh . . . hello, Mr. Bridges."

"Jeremy. You don't mind chatting with me for a minute, do you?"

Soft Texas drawl. Pleasant smile. Disarming manner. Those things should have put her at ease, but they didn't. Anytime reality didn't meet expectation, she always went on guard.

"No," she said. "Not at all."

Then Darcy realized the woman who'd summoned her had climbed into the limo behind her and was sitting on the seat across from them. Jeremy nodded in her direction.

"Darcy, this is Bernadette Hogan."

Darcy swallowed hard. "Hello."

A curt nod was her only acknowledgment. Who in the world was she? Business associate? Relative? Prison parolee?

"Bernie is my bodyguard," Jeremy said.

Darcy blinked. "Bodyguard?"

"We've had a few incidents. Too many nutcases out there think kidnapping a rich guy is a great moneymaking opportunity."

"Well," Darcy said, trying to sound cordial, "I don't believe I've ever heard of a woman acting as a bodyguard before."

Bernie raised her chin ever so slightly, her dark eyes narrowing.

"But I'm sure you're very good at it," Darcy added.

"Bernie is ex-military," Jeremy said. "And a martial arts expert. She runs five miles a day unless it's raining. Then she runs ten." He leaned in and whispered, "She's rumored to have once killed a man with a Popsicle stick."

Darcy glanced back at Bernie and swallowed hard. Forget the Popsicle stick. She could probably kill a man with a cotton ball.

"Bernie," Jeremy said, "why don't you wait outside for just a minute while I talk to Darcy? I think you're making her nervous."

Without a word, Bernie got out of the car. She closed the door and stood beside it with her arms folded, waiting vigilantly for one of the residents of Wingate Manufactured Home Park to get the urge to kidnap a multimillionaire.

"Lovely woman," Darcy said, even though the "lovely" didn't fit, and the jury was still out on "woman."

"Uh-huh." Jeremy took a swig of his beer, then rested it on his knee again. "You're staring."

Darcy blinked. "Oh. I'm sorry. It's just that . . ."

"Yeah, I know. I don't look like a millionaire. That's what you're thinking, isn't it?"

"Uh . . ."

"You know, I can't imagine anyone with money going for that rich-guy look. If a man has enough money that he doesn't have to answer to anyone, why would he put on a suit coat and wear a noose around his neck?"

Actually, that made a lot of sense to Darcy. In her mind, though, millionaire still equaled Armani. "But you do have a limousine."

"Dallas traffic sucks. It's more comfortable to have somebody else drive while I watch TV and have a beer. Wait a minute—where are my manners? Would you like a beer?"

"Uh . . . no, thanks."

"If you'd rather have a shot of caffeine, I think I have a couple of Mountain Dews in the fridge."

Beer? Mountain Dew? What was this, a tailgate party at the Super Bowl? "No, thanks. I'm fine."

"So," he said, "where do you suppose Warren is, and what has he done with my three hundred thousand dollars?"

Darcy cringed, feeling guilty by association, even though she was as much in the dark as Jeremy. "I'm afraid I don't know."

"Yeah, that's what you told the police. I was hoping you'd have a different story for me."

"A different story? I don't understand."

"Are you covering for Warren?"

Darcy nearly choked. "Covering for him? Why would I be doing that? He ran off with everything I own!"

"So the police told me."

"I came back from a vacation and he'd disappeared.

He'd sold our house. Cashed in our assets. Ran up our credit cards. He took *everything*."

"Yeah, you'd think something like that would really piss a woman off. But they're funny sometimes. Guys crap all over them, but still they cover for them."

"No. I assure you, I don't have the first clue where my husband is. And he should be glad of that. If I ever see him again, I just might . . ."

Her voice trailed off, and Jeremy smiled. "What? Put your knee where it would inflict the most damage?"

"Well, I wouldn't have put it that way, but—"

"But the thought has crossed your mind."

She opened her mouth to speak, then closed it again.

"Good. That means we're on the same page. So you had no warning that he was getting ready to take off?"

"None at all."

"No weird behavior? Odd phone calls?"

"Not that I remember."

"Is there anywhere in particular he likes to travel outside the United States?"

"He tends to gravitate toward anyplace there's a casino, but I'm afraid that doesn't narrow it down much."

Jeremy took out a business card. "This number will get me directly. If you happen to remember something, let me know, will you?"

"Of course," she said, taking the card. "But I have to tell you, I'm surprised you're bothering to chase down such a tiny sum of money." She gave him a flattering smile. "You probably make three hundred thousand dollars every day before lunch."

"Uh-huh. But I didn't get where I am by allowing people to steal from me. Anytime one of my employees sticks his hand in the cookie jar"—he leaned in and emphasized every word—"I take it *very* personally."

His no-nonsense expression sounded a warning bell, telling Darcy this was a man she should never underestimate. He might look like an overgrown kid, but he sounded like Tony Soprano.

He nodded toward her parents' mobile home. "You're probably taking it a little personally yourself."

He didn't know the half of it. "How did you know where I was living now?"

"It's one of the perks of being filthy rich. I can find out anything I want to." He smiled. "So how are you getting along now that your husband cleaned you out?"

Darcy sighed. "I'm managing."

"Hope you stuck a few bucks under your mattress for a rainy day."

Darcy was getting a little tired of hearing that. First from her mother and now from this man. Was it really so unbelievable that she hadn't foreseen a day when her husband would walk off with every dime she had?

"Let's just say that maintaining a decent lifestyle is going to be difficult," she said.

"Do you have a job?"

Now he'd morphed into her father, and she didn't want to hear that, either. But the truth was that without a job, maintaining *any* lifestyle was going to be a challenge.

"No, I don't."

"How old are you?" he asked.

Did he have to hit every sore spot she had? She smiled indulgently, trying not to act as offended as she was. "Now, Jeremy, don't you know that's a question you should never ask a lady?"

"Let's put it this way. You're considerably younger than Warren."

"Yes."

"How long have you been married?"

"Fourteen years."

"You know, I've always wondered something. Maybe you can help me out." He rubbed his chin thoughtfully. "Why do you suppose beautiful young women marry men old enough to be their fathers?"

Darcy was stunned. Over the years, she knew friends and acquaintances had wondered the same thing about her, but no one had ever come right out and asked. And certainly not a total stranger.

"Love is unpredictable," she said. "Who knows when it will strike?"

"Ah. Now I understand. It's all about *love*. I assumed you married Warren for his money."

Her mouth fell open. "I did *not* marry Warren for his money!"

"You're pretty uptight about losing the material stuff. What about losing the man you love?"

Darcy glared at him. "When a woman finds out her husband is a criminal, it's amazing how quickly love fades."

"When a beautiful young woman marries an older man, I'm thinking love doesn't have much to do with it."

"You don't know *anything* about my relationship with Warren!"

"Hey, take it easy, will you? You're assuming I think that's a bad thing." He shrugged offhandedly. "Personally, I've never had much luck with love, either. It requires at least a little bit of selflessness, and just between

you and me, I've never lived a selfless day in my life."
He smiled. "I have a feeling we're a lot alike. Two people
with their eyes always on the bottom line."

"If my eyes are on the bottom line," she said, her voice
escalating, "it's because Warren left me with nothing. Do
you know what it feels like to live with your parents in a
mobile home? To drive a car so old it leaves a trail of oil
on the street behind you? To pass right by Starbucks because you can't even afford to stop for a cup of *coffee?*"

Jeremy drew back. "No Starbucks? My God. Please
tell me it isn't so."

"This conversation is over."

Darcy turned to get out of the car, wanting to put as
much distance as possible between her and Richie Rich.
There was nothing she hated more than a microscopic
examination of her motives, especially from a man, and
especially when that man was right.

"Wait a minute," Jeremy said.

Slowly she turned back, glaring at him. "What?"

"Does this mean you won't be looking for another man
to take Warren's place?"

As he spoke, he slid his hand along the top of the seat
behind her head. Darcy froze, watching its advance out
of the corner of her eye. He hooked his finger around a
strand of her hair, then pulled back slowly until it fell
away and fluttered to her shoulder again.

"Darcy, don't you know there are men out there who
can offer you far more than Warren ever did?"

He continued to stare at her, his eyes full of promise.
Somehow the tide had turned, making Darcy's stomach
quiver with excitement. She pictured lounging around
his palatial home. Dining at the Mansion on Turtle Creek

as often as other people ate Big Macs. Tooling around town in this very limousine, cursing the tinted windows because they kept the world from seeing her inside it.

Wearing a wedding ring that would make her current four-carat stone look like something she'd pulled out of a box of Cracker Jack.

Jeremy Bridges could buy and sell Warren a hundred times over, making all her problems go away with a single swipe of his pen. Was it possible her luck had turned? That maybe, just *maybe,* she was on the verge of finding a gold-plated way out of this mess?

She lazily looked him up and down, letting a soft, sensual expression ease across her face. She dropped her voice to a seductive murmur.

"Are you applying for the job?"

His eyebrows rose with interest, and when his gaze went to her lips and hovered there, Darcy knew for a fact what was on his mind. Just the thought of it made her mouth go dry.

Then, inexplicably, he leaned away, settling back against the seat with a knowing smile. "No, but it's interesting to know you're hiring. How about I put a notice on the job board at the next Millionaire's Club meeting?"

Humiliation shot through Darcy, and it was all she could do to keep her chin up and her gaze steady. He'd dangled the bait, and she'd snapped at it like a starving carp.

Well, the cat was out of the bag now. Further denial would only make her look like a bigger fool.

"You might want to reconsider," she told him. "You wouldn't *believe* the benefits that come with the job."

"I don't doubt that for a moment." His gaze drifted to

her breasts, then slowly rose again. "If you'd consider hiring on a short-term contract, maybe we could talk."

"Sorry, Bridges. I *marry* rich. I don't give it away on a one-shot basis."

With one last go-to-hell look, she opened the limo door and got out, resisting the urge to slam it behind her. She never thought she'd be glad that Warren had bilked his boss out of three hundred thousand dollars, but she sure as hell was now.

She only wished it had been three million.

As the driver started the car, Bernie slid back into the seat across from Jeremy and shut the door behind her.

"Does she know where her husband is?" she asked.

"Nope."

"You sure about that?"

"He was her meal ticket, and dinner's over. If she sees him again, I have no doubt she'll bust his balls."

Jeremy tapped on the Plexiglas between him and his driver, and he pulled away from the curb. "So, what did you think of her?" he asked Bernie. "On a scale of one to ten."

"What criteria?"

"Looks."

"Seven. Too much phony stuff going on."

"I don't mind the phony stuff, as long as it's well done. I'd give her a nine."

"What would have bumped her to a ten? A D-cup instead of a C?"

Jeremy grinned. "Of course not. That would make me a very shallow man."

"She's a gold digger."

"They're all gold diggers."

"She's a gold digger at rock bottom. Dangerous combination."

"I was at rock bottom once."

"Then you've found your soul mate. Shall I make reservations in Vegas?"

"Now, Bernie. You know marriage isn't my thing. By the time my lawyers got the prenup drafted, we'd both be dead and gone."

"You'll be dead and gone eventually, anyway. You have more money than God. Why not spread it around a little?"

"I've never been very good at sharing."

"In other words, you're selfish."

Jeremy smiled. "You don't like me very much, do you, Bernie?"

"What's to like? I don't give a rat's ass about your money."

"My scintillating personality, maybe?"

"You have the personal habits of a frat boy. You think *Jackass* is quality TV programming. You go through women like a chain smoker goes through a pack of Camels. The next time somebody moves in to grab you, I'm just going to stand back and let it happen. That'll teach 'em."

"Nah. You'd never pass up an opportunity for a little hand-to-hand combat."

"Don't bank on that."

"This is gross insubordination. You're fired."

"Right. Good luck finding somebody else who'll put up with you."

She folded her arms and turned to look out the window, scouring the landscape for evildoers. Jeremy couldn't help but smile. So few people in his life did anything but kiss his ass; a bodyguard with a bad attitude was actually a breath of fresh air.

Darcy McDaniel had a bit of an attitude herself.

Sorry, Bridges. I marry rich. I don't give it away on a one-shot basis.

That had been a blatant, in-your-face, I-am-what-I-am remark that he hadn't seen coming. Once he had people nailed, they generally backed away, groveling and making excuses. Not this woman. Even when she didn't have a dime to her name, she stuck her nose in the air and looked at him as if he were a slug slithering down the sidewalk.

He took the last swig of his beer and tossed the bottle into the trash, trying to decide what was next on his agenda for the day. Over the years, he'd discovered that he didn't much like the day-to-day operations of running a conglomerate of companies, so he hired smart people in suits who popped Maalox like candy and let them do what they did best. He took meetings here and there to keep his finger on the pulse, spent a few hours every day monitoring things, and that was about it. Playing the young, eccentric millionaire in the business world had always given him an edge with his competition because they never took him nearly as seriously as they should, but even that was getting to be a bore.

His hands-off approach worried people sometimes, but even if the worst happened and it all fell apart tomorrow, he had so much put away that he'd still be set for life. It was as if he had a fistful of Monopoly money and landed on Boardwalk every time around, so why knock himself out to make more?

Darcy, on the other hand, had just lost every dime she had, and that was fertile ground for all kinds of interesting behavior. Warren had dealt his wife a really crappy hand, and Jeremy couldn't think of anything more entertaining than keeping tabs on her to see how she played it.

Chapter 6

The moment Darcy stepped back in the trailer, her mother dragged her to the kitchen table, sat her down, and started in with a barrage of questions, all of them centered around why a wealthy and important man like Jeremy Bridges had taken time out of his day to come see her.

"He thought I might know where Warren is," Darcy said.

Lyla's expression became panicked. "But you don't. You have no idea. He doesn't think you had anything to do with Warren embezzling from him, does he?"

"To tell you the truth, Mom, I don't give much of a damn what Jeremy Bridges thinks about anything."

"Oh, God. You didn't *tell* him that, did you?"

"In so many words."

Her mother gasped. "But he's a very wealthy man!"

"Like a man can't be wealthy *and* be a jerk?"

"I can't believe you're blowing this opportunity. I can't *believe* it!"

What her mother didn't realize was that it was only an opportunity if her target was at least a little open to the possibility of being hooked. This man . . . no way. So why hang around and be humiliated?

"You're broke," Lyla said. "Your husband is clearly not coming back. A man like Jeremy Bridges comes to see you, and you refuse to turn on at least a *little* charm?"

Fortunately, Darcy's cell phone rang in the middle of the inquisition. She looked at the caller ID. Carolyn. She pressed the TALK button and got hit with yet another round of questions. Carolyn had seen the article that morning about Warren, which begged the question: Since when did Carolyn read the business section?

"Oh, you poor thing!" Carolyn said. "Why didn't you let me know what was happening? You have to tell me everything!"

Darcy sighed at the thought of going through it all over again. But given a choice between that and hanging around listening to her mother's incessant harping, she decided it was the lesser of two evils.

"Meet me at our Starbucks," she told Carolyn, "and I'll tell you all about it."

A few minutes later, Darcy was driving west on Park Boulevard toward Central Expressway, the boundary between east and west Plano. The moment she crossed over it, she felt like Dorothy opening the farmhouse door and seeing Oz. Everything seemed to go from black and white to Technicolor.

She may have been raised on the east side, but *this* was her place. *These* were her people. Shopping malls and shiny new office buildings and gas-guzzling SUVs and huge houses with lush landscaping and decorator window treatments and high-definition TVs.

And Starbucks. *Ahh*. That little slice of heaven where you pay for your coffee by the adjective and inhale pastries fit for royalty. With almost no money in her pocket,

Darcy knew the last thing she should be doing was spending a good percentage of it on a cup of coffee, but right now she needed her table by the window with sunlight streaming in and the aroma of coffee and brownies and macadamia-nut cookies to make her feel normal again, at least for a little while.

When she arrived, Carolyn was already there, sipping her usual Mocha Frappuccino. She was a woman prone to excessive gossip, wearing out her credit cards, and doing the kind of charity work that involved lots of teas and galas and silent auctions. But since almost all the women Darcy knew had those same characteristics, she figured she might as well hang out with the one with the most fashion sense.

Darcy went to the counter and ordered a Caramel Macchiato. She took a sip and let her eyes close, the sweetened caffeine hitting her system like an anvil dropped from a fourth-story window. Ah, *God,* it was good. For a moment, it almost made her forget just how destitute she was.

"Okay," Carolyn said when Darcy sat down. "You have *got* to tell me what's been going on."

Darcy filled her in on the whole story, and when she got to the part about the family living in her house, she thought Carolyn was going to stroke out.

"And now I'm living with my parents," Darcy said.

"Oh, God. In their trailer?"

Darcy sighed. "Yeah."

"You know I'd let you stay with me, but Ralph is so unreasonable."

She had that right. The Lord of the Manor didn't like

Carolyn's friends dropping by socially, much less taking up residence.

"So what are you going to do now?" Carolyn asked.

"I don't know."

"I'd loan you some money, but . . ." She sighed. "Ralph is so unreasonable."

She had that right, too. Once when he thought Carolyn was spending too much money, he took away her credit cards for a whole month. Carolyn would have fared better trying to kick a heroin addiction. If she loaned money to a friend, he'd probably cut her off for life.

"Do you have anything left that's worth anything?" Carolyn asked. "Something you can sell?"

Darcy thought about the jewelry she'd taken with her to Mexico. Unfortunately, they'd stayed at a beach resort, so she'd brought along mostly costume stuff. She wouldn't be able to sell that for much.

Then she looked down at her wedding ring. Its emerald-cut center stone had the four Cs in spades, surrounded by stones that were smaller but no less spectacular, all of them set in platinum.

"Just my wedding ring," she said.

Carolyn gasped. "You can't sell that!"

"Don't worry," Darcy said. "I wouldn't think of it."

And not because of any lingering nostalgia about her marriage gone awry. Husband or no husband, this ring was her symbol to every store clerk, spa attendant, and waiter in town that she was a woman of means, and therefore she was to receive the utmost in customer service. Now that she was destitute, she needed that symbol more than ever. No way would she consider taking it off, unless she found another man who could replace it with an even bigger one.

But ring or no ring, just sitting in her Starbucks now, she felt like an imposter, as if everybody here could see through her and right to her blue-collar roots.

"I wonder who else read that article?" Darcy said.

"Well, let's see," Carolyn said. "There was Gail Howard, Barbara Barrett, Colette Ward—"

"What?"

"They're just the ones who called me this morning."

"Called you? Why did they call you?"

"Because I'm your best friend, and they wanted to know what was going on."

"Oh, they did? Well, tell them it's none of their business."

"I don't think they're being catty," Carolyn said. "I think they're just concerned."

"Wrong," Darcy said. "If they were concerned, they'd have called me themselves. Calling you meant they were on a gossip-gathering mission."

"Well, last year when Gail divorced Larry because she found out he had a thing for cheap prostitutes, we called Barbara to see what was going on, didn't we? And last month when Barbara's son was arrested for cocaine possession, we called Colette. And when—"

"No. Those things were different."

"How were they different?"

Darcy thought about that for a moment. Truthfully, they weren't different at all. It was just the way things were in her world. Or what used to be her world. Just because you smiled to somebody's face didn't mean you weren't taking secret pleasure in the fact that their misfortune wasn't yours.

Now that it *was* hers, Darcy was rethinking that policy.

"Okay, so it isn't different," she admitted. She took another sip of her coffee, savoring every drop as if it were her last. And the way things were going, it just might be. "My father thinks I should get a job."

Carolyn shuddered. "Doing what?"

"I don't know."

"Didn't you used to be a receptionist?"

"Yes. A long time ago. That's how I met Warren."

"Hmm."

"What?"

"Do you want to get married again?"

"To the right man." *One who's breathing. With money.*

"I read in *Cosmopolitan* that forty percent of all people find their spouses at work. You met Warren there. Why not do it again?"

Darcy went still for a moment, turning the idea over in her mind, examining it from all angles. The longer she considered it, the more it gained momentum. Was Carolyn actually making sense?

Warren wasn't the only man on the planet with deep pockets who might be looking for a beautiful woman to shower with the finer things in life. Hooking a man like Jeremy Bridges might be out of the question, but finding another highly paid upper-management type certainly wasn't. Darcy hadn't been blessed with an overabundance of talents, but she'd never had any trouble attracting the opposite sex. She'd just have to be very careful to choose a workplace filled with professional men with large bank accounts. And while she was hunting for her next husband, a regular paycheck would allow her to put a few bucks in a bank account of her own.

Men had all kinds of foibles and insecurities. All she had to do was find one who was divorced and having a nice little midlife crisis that a hot car or hair-replacement surgery hadn't been able to relieve, and snagging him would be a breeze. She'd just be playing to her strengths. Wasn't that always a smart thing to do?

For the first time since her life fell apart, she actually felt hopeful.

"That's not such a bad idea," Darcy said. "A job may be just the thing I need."

"There you go. Now you have a plan." Carolyn checked her watch. "I'd better go. I'd stick around longer, but I have to go home and fix lunch. Ralph's working from home today, and—"

"I know, I know. He's so unreasonable."

Carolyn sighed.

"Carolyn? Why don't you just divorce him?"

She shrugged weakly. "Because I love him?"

Oh, God. Because she *loved* him? What was *with* some women? "Then at least take the 'kick me' sign off your back, will you?"

Carolyn shrugged again. Was there such a thing as a human invertebrate?

"I have to go, too," Darcy said. "It's time to start job hunting."

"Don't you mean manhunting?"

Darcy smiled. "One and the same."

At nine o'clock the next morning, Darcy sat in the lobby of the A-1 Employment Agency, filling out a job application and a questionnaire about her skills. Unfortunately, it appeared that in the fourteen years she'd been married to Warren, a technological revolution had passed her by. Good thing she'd made an appointment with a man. She needed an edge, and that was about the only thing she had in her favor.

A few minutes later, Darcy was summoned into the employment counselor's office. She put on her best air of confidence and entitlement, fully prepared to unleash every charm she had on him if that was what it took to land a really plum assignment. But one look at the guy, and she banished those thoughts immediately.

He was young. No, not just young. Any bartender on earth would card him in a heartbeat. When his face broke into a boyish grin, she was actually relieved not to see a set of braces.

"Ms. McDaniel," he said, standing as she came through the door. "Come on in here and we'll have a chat."

She sat in the chair in front of his desk, eyeing his name plate. Scott Connolly. They'd probably called him *Little Scotty Connolly*. Last week. In the third grade.

"Okie dokie," he said, plopping down into his pseudo-leather executive chair like a kid in front of a video game. "Let's see what we have here." He slouched back in his chair, swiveling back and forth as he looked at her application.

His expression turned grim. "Your most recent experience was fifteen years ago?"

"Yes."

He frowned. "Hmm. I'm not seeing much computer

experience. Do you know anything besides Word? Power-Point? Excel? Maybe a little accounting software?"

It sounded like *blah, blah, blah* to Darcy's ears. "I don't know much about those." As in, *nothing.* "But I'm a fast learner."

"Most companies want you to hit the ground running. What about office machines? Typing speed?"

She opened her mouth to speak, then closed it again.

"You're a little short on qualifications."

"But all I'm looking for is a receptionist job. Answering phones. Making coffee. Greeting people." *Male people with lots of money.*

"You really have been out of the workforce for a while, haven't you? These days they expect receptionists to do more than just say howdy. Even copiers these days are so complicated you practically need an engineering degree to run them. They want receptionists who can back up other employees. Handle overflow work. Companies are all tightening their belts, so they want lots of bang for their buck."

"Just send me on an interview. I'll get the job."

"Sorry. No can do."

"Excuse me?"

"Can't send out unqualified candidates. You might think about taking some junior college classes. A lot of older women are going back to school."

Darcy's eyes sprang open wide with horror. "Older women? Just how old do you think I am?"

"I don't know. Forty?"

Forty? Oh, God. Were her roots showing? "I'm *not* forty." *And I won't be for another couple of weeks.*

Little Scotty just shrugged.

"Don't you have anything I might be qualified for?" she asked.

"Maybe you should consider something in the food service industry."

She shuddered.

"Or how about a department store? They're always hiring."

Well, wouldn't that be wonderful? Selling clothes and cosmetics to women she used to buy them with? That would be the ultimate humiliation. And just how was she supposed to meet men like that?

"No, thank you." Darcy stood up. It was clear that Junior here wasn't going to be able to help her. It was time to go straight to the source—the companies themselves—and show this little twit just how employable she was.

⁓

Darcy had no idea just how unemployable she was.

By the end of the day, she'd visited the Human Resources departments at six major corporations in west Plano. The applications she'd filled out had netted her only two interviews, because most of them stopped the process at that stage with the words she didn't want to hear: *You have no experience. Thanks, but no thanks.*

After her last stop, she got into Gertie and sat there, wondering what to do next. Little Scotty had been right. They all wanted her to be "computer literate." Not only that, but the phone systems she saw today looked like the instrument panels of 747s and came complete with voice mail systems so convoluted it took a flow chart to follow them. They expected a receptionist to do all sorts of mousing around on a computer in addition to looking good, saying hello, and making coffee. Sometime in the past fifteen years, a race of three-handed receptionists had to have surfaced who could actually perform all those functions at once.

As the day progressed, she'd moved from the certainty that she was going to walk right into a cushy job and find the man of her financial dreams to the uncertainty of whether she'd be able to find a job at all. The very idea that all she was qualified to do was put on a paper hat and flip burgers scared her to death. It was even possible that if she went head-to-head with a McTeenager for that job, she'd come out on the losing end.

She rested her forehead on Gertie's steering wheel, trying to keep from falling apart, trying to think of a way out of this horrible mess.

Well, she thought as she slowly raised her head, *there might be one place she could get a job . . . .*

No. That was nuts. Even though she was facing the possibility of lifelong poverty, she still had a little bit of pride. The last thing she wanted to do was go back and beg for a job from the crabbiest man alive.

Then she thought about the alternative, which was taking up permanent residence in Dysfunction Junction with no ticket out. At least she could get a little money ahead and some recent job experience so she could get back on her feet again.

Oh, God. Was she actually considering this?

Yes. She was. At least it was a job she knew she could handle. With only a few people in the office, their phone system couldn't possibly have more than a few lines coming in, and the copier looked as if it had been ripped right out of the 1980s. The big boss clearly needed a personality transplant, but maybe he'd be out of the office most of the time stealing cars from poor, unfortunate people like her and she wouldn't have to see him very often.

It wasn't just *a* solution to her problem. Right now, it looked like her *only* solution. Bright and early in the morning, she was going to pay John Stark a visit, and she wasn't leaving until he gave her that job.

Chapter 7

At eight o'clock the next morning, John was in the storage room at the office, digging around for a file he swore had simply disintegrated into thin air. He'd been through practically every box in the place, but still he couldn't find it. He'd had so many clerks through here—both temporary ones and permanent ones who didn't work out—that the filing system was in shambles. He closed that box and shoved it aside, too, with a sigh of disgust. Every moment he had to spend doing crap like this was a moment he wasn't making money bringing in cars.

He picked up his coffee cup and came out of the storage room, surprised to see a woman sitting at the clerk's desk chatting with Tony. And the moment he realized who the woman was, he could already feel his day going downhill.

An article in the paper a few days ago told him that the man who'd left Darcy McDaniel with nothing had also embezzled from his employer and skipped the country. John found it interesting that she was married to a man who'd turned criminal, which was almost as interesting as the fact that he was fifty-seven years old. Knowing she'd married a man old enough to be her father, along with the fact that she hadn't held a job in fourteen years, told him all kinds of things about her, and none of them were good.

"What are you doing here?" he asked.

Darcy slowly turned her gaze to meet his. "I changed my mind."

"What?"

"I'm accepting your job offer."

He looked at her dumbly. "I didn't make you a job offer."

Tony turned to John. "Uh, yeah, I think you did."

"No, I didn't."

"Yeah, you did. When she said she could handle the job, you said, 'Well, then. In that case, the job's all yours.'"

"You think I *meant* that? I didn't mean that!"

"I think there's some kind of law that says you can't Indian give where jobs are concerned."

"That's crap."

Tony held up his palms as if to say, *Hey, man, if you want to go to jail, it's up to you.*

John turned to Darcy. "You're not working here."

"Why not?"

"I don't have to answer that."

"So you're going to hire that woman who came in here this morning?" Tony asked. "The one who had to have time off every week to see her parole officer? Or how about the one who you were going to hire until you checked her references?" He turned to Darcy. "She once brought a gun to work and shot a copy machine."

"I don't have bad references," Darcy said.

"I'm betting you don't have *any* references," John said.

She smiled sweetly. "Which means they can't be bad."

"You told me you didn't have to work when you were married. Have you ever even held a job?"

"Of course I have. It's just been a few years."

"How many is a few?"

"Come on, John!" Tony said. "Does it really matter? Look at that stack of filing. We can't find crap around here. And I'm sick of answering the phone."

"No, you're sick of having to deal with whatever woman woke up in your bed that morning because there's nobody here to screen your calls."

"Uh, yeah. That, too."

"Don't worry. I'm on it." Darcy grabbed a pen and a sticky note, talking as she wrote. "Tell any woman . . . who calls for Tony . . . that he moved to Guam . . . and won't be coming . . . *back*." She pulled the note off and stuck it to the telephone, then folded her hands on the desk and smiled up at Tony.

He flashed her a smile in return. "Now that's what I call a steep learning curve."

"My office," John snapped.

With a roll of his eyes, Tony followed John into his office. They closed the door, and through the glass Darcy could see John's face turning tense and crabby. She was an eavesdropping expert, but still she made out only about half of what they said. She heard "loose cannon" and "combative" and "nutcase," and something that sounded like "refrain" but was probably "insane." Then more stuff from Tony about how somebody needed to be doing the job, so why not her?

From John she heard "outa your mind, blah, blah, blah," and then "Fine. Send her in here."

Tony came out of John's office. "He wants to see you." He leaned in and whispered, "Try not to piss him off."

Darcy went into John's office to find him sitting behind his desk, scowling like a bulldog without a bone.

"Sit," he said.

She did.

"I saw an article in the paper yesterday," John said. "It appears that your husband not only skipped out on you, but he also embezzled three hundred thousand dollars from the company where he worked. Do you happen to know anything about that?"

Good heavens. Had everyone in the Dallas metroplex seen that article?

"It came as just as much of a shock to me as it did to his employer," Darcy said. "I didn't know anything about what my husband was up to."

"So you never acquired any of your husband's bad habits? I'm not fond of employees stealing from me."

"He embezzled to cover gambling debts. Gambling makes me nervous. I've never even bought a lottery ticket."

"Good. The lottery is a waste of money. Do you smoke?"

"No."

"Do drugs?"

"Of course not."

"Amy does most of the skip tracing around here, along with the database and accounting management. All I need is somebody to back her up. To type a little. Copy. File. Answer the phone. Keep my clients informed."

"I didn't see another woman working here."

"She's part-time. She works around her college schedule. Does that job description sound like something you could handle?"

"Of course."

"You'll be required to deal with all kinds of people, from the filthy rich to the scum of the earth. Think you can handle that?"

Filthy rich? Maybe there were going to be some man-hunting possibilities around here after all. No, wait. He probably meant to say *ex*-filthy rich, or they wouldn't have defaulted on their car loans. That left the scum of the earth.

Oh, joy.

"Of course," she told John. "I'm very good with people."

"A guy came in here the other day waving a gun around and demanding I give him his car back. What would you do if that happened?"

"What did you do?"

"Knocked the gun out of his hand, shoved him down face-first on the ground, and called the cops."

"Well, I suppose I'd just have to sweet-talk that gun right out of his hand."

"Good luck with that."

She gave him a knowing smile. "Never underestimate the power of a woman."

"Uh-huh. Recite the alphabet."

"What?"

"And no singing."

This man was nuts. She recited *A* to *Z*, enunciating *L, M, N,* and *O* so it didn't sound like "elemeno." John seemed pleased by that. Go figure.

"You have no skills," he said. "You have no references. All you've ever done is irritate me. There's no reason on earth for me to hire you. Tell me why you think I should."

"Tony thinks you should."

"Tony would hire a woman with a lobotomy if he thought she was hot."

She gave him a sly smile. "But that's never a consideration for you?"

"I have a business to run."

"Then Tony was right?" She folded her arms on the edge of his desk and gave John a smoldering look. "You're all business and no pleasure?"

"The number-one pleasure in my life right now is keeping this business running with as little hassle as possible."

"What a pity," she said, smiling seductively. "You don't know what you're missing."

"Then I won't miss it, will I?"

"I have other qualifications, you know. The kind that don't show up on a résumé."

He sat back in his chair, eyeing her carefully. "Oh, really?"

Okay. She had him on the hook. She was very good at engaging in verbal foreplay without ever getting physical, and this man was going to be no exception.

"I know things have been a little shaky between us up to now," she told him, "but I think you and I could eventually get along *very* well."

"Oh, you do?"

"Of course. Don't you?"

When his gaze fell to her breasts, her hope soared that her lack of qualifications wasn't going to be an issue. Then he met her eyes again. "I take it you're offering to show me what I'm missing?"

Her heart skipped a little. He wasn't following the script. They were supposed to be talking in circles with lots of innuendo but never getting anywhere.

She held her gaze steady. "Well. One never knows what the future might hold, does one?"

"You seem to be saying you'd be willing to have sex with me someday if I give you this job now. Is that correct?"

Darcy almost swallowed her tongue. That was what she wanted him to think, of course, but she hadn't expected him to actually *say* it. And she certainly never expected to have to actually *do* it.

"Uh . . . as I said, all kinds of things might happen in the future."

"Sorry. I don't extend credit. If you owe me, you pay up now."

Darcy felt a shot of apprehension. "Are you saying this job depends on me having sex with you?"

"What if it does?"

"Then I'd say there's a lawsuit in there somewhere."

"He said/she said testimony never gets a person convicted."

"That would depend on who's testifying."

"Sorry, Darcy. You wouldn't stand a chance across the aisle from me in a courtroom."

"Oh, yeah? What makes you say that?"

"The eighteen years of experience I have testifying in court cases."

"What?"

"I used to be a cop."

Darcy swallowed hard. A cop?

Slowly and deliberately he rose from his chair, his size as intimidating as ever, even more so now that she knew he'd spent eighteen years armed and dangerous. He went to the window between his office and the outer office and closed the blinds. He walked to the outside window and did the same. Then he turned around.

"Stand up."

Nervousness crept through her. "I'm quite comfortable, thank you."

"Part of working for me is remembering who's the boss."

She lifted her chin, determined not to let him get to her. There was no way he was serious about this, and she was going to get a tremendous amount of joy out of watching him back down.

She uncrossed her legs and stood up, resisting the urge to fold her arms over her breasts. She forced a casual smile. "Won't Tony wonder what's going on?"

"No wondering involved. He'll know."

"So is this one of your regular hiring practices?"

"Nope. But since he's probably got his ear to the door right now, I expect he'll figure it out."

He started toward her. She faced him, trying to hold her ground, but a second later he was looming over her, all wide chest and broad shoulders and hotter-than-hell expression. She automatically took a step backward. With his desk behind her, though, she was trapped. He stood so close to her that she could actually feel the heat radiating from his body, and all at once she had a flash of the kind of hot, sweaty, down-and-dirty sex she'd always fantasized about but never experienced. Instinctively she knew John Stark was the man who could deliver it.

But not here. Not now. As a matter of fact, not *ever*. In fantasies, men did as they were told. Reality was another thing entirely.

"Most men start with flowers and candlelight," she said.

"Most women aren't putting out to get a job."

"Maybe we could do this another time."

"Nope. It's now or never."

Don't worry. He's bluffing. Just hold your ground.

He touched a fingertip to her throat, then dragged it down until it reached the first button on her shirt. She closed her eyes, her breath coming faster. Such a tiny part of him was touching such a tiny part of her. So why did it feel as if her whole body was on fire?

"What's the matter?" he asked.

She opened her eyes. "Nothing. Nothing at all."

"You've already made it clear that you're willing to give to get. If so, it's time to start giving."

"But surely you don't want to do it here."

"Surely I do."

He circled his fingertip around the button, making his intent known, dragging the moment out so long that Darcy had a hard time maintaining what little composure she had left. Most men had insecurities a woman could capitalize on in order to control a situation, but she sensed this man hadn't had an insecure moment since the day he was born. She felt like a gazelle cornered by a lion—a very large, very domineering lion who could take down that gazelle anytime he wanted to.

With a practiced flick of his fingertips, he opened the button.

Darcy smacked her palm against his chest and pushed him away. "You can't be serious about this! What kind of man demands sex in return for a job?"

"I don't remember demanding sex. But I do remember you offering it."

"Well, I'm *not* offering! I don't want to have anything to do with you! You can take your job and *shove it!*"

"Is that so?"

"Yes, that's so!"

"Then you're hired."

Darcy froze. *What* did he say?

"Just for the record," John said, "I've never done a horizontal interview, and I never will. And don't you *ever* work for a man who would, or you'll be up to your neck in the kind of trouble you don't want to deal with. You're getting a little old to be relying on sexual manipulation to get the things you want, anyway. Better dust off that brain and start using it instead."

Darcy was flabbergasted. "Just how old do you think I am?"

"Forty."

"I am *not* forty!"

"You're at least within shouting distance of it."

It must be true. She really did look forty. Was her Botox wearing off already?

Darcy felt sick. It wasn't just Little Scotty. If John thought she actually looked her age, too . . . oh, *God.* Her body hadn't come with a maintenance contract, and repairs weren't going to come cheap.

And that meant she really *did* need a job.

"I'll give you a one-week trial," he said. "If you do the job, then the job is yours. If you screw it up, you're out of here." Then he mentioned a monthly salary figure that sounded like the Christmas tip Darcy had given her hairstylist. "Be here at eight on Monday morning."

Still reeling from this turn of events, Darcy tried to get a grip. Dictatorial men had never sat well with her, and this one was as demanding as they came. She wanted to object to something. Anything. Just to let him know she wasn't a woman who took whatever a man dished out.

She lifted her chin. "I didn't say I was accepting your offer. Maybe I don't like those terms."

"Are you telling me you don't want the job?"

Darcy gritted her teeth. She hated this. *Hated* it. "No, I want the job, but—"

"Then I'll see you on Monday."

John sat down behind his desk again, opened a file, and began to read, as if she weren't even in the room, as if sex with her really had been the last thing on his mind. In the end, that bothered Darcy most of all. Just because she didn't want a man didn't mean she didn't want him to want her.

At least, she was pretty sure she didn't want him.

No. She had to get that out of her mind. His collar was too blue and his bankbook too lightweight for her purposes. If she was ever going to get back on top again, the last thing she needed to do was lower her standards to sexy working-class Neanderthal.

She grabbed her purse and left his office. Tony was

still hanging around, clearly waiting to see the outcome of their closed-door session. Right now her insides felt like mush, and she hoped her face wasn't as flushed as it felt.

"Well?" he asked.

She mustered up her best victory smile. "I'll see you at eight on Monday morning."

Tony grinned. "I knew John didn't stand a chance."

She winked at him and left the building, wishing she felt as confident about the situation as she'd just made herself out to be.

Men were usually so easy. All she had to do was get them interested. To get them to see the possibilities for the future, even if there weren't any, and pretty soon they were tripping all over themselves to give her what she wanted. So what was wrong with John? He'd hired her when she *refused* to have sex with him? What was the *matter* with him?

It could only mean that he had some kind of ulterior motive she hadn't discovered yet, which meant she had to stay on her toes. She'd never met a man she couldn't manipulate, but it was clear now that she was going to have to work overtime to stay ahead of this one.

Chapter 8

When Darcy arrived at Lone Star Repossessions on Monday morning, John came out of his office looking as big and authoritative as he always did, and she couldn't help but remember the way he'd backed her up against his desk. Just the memory of it made her blood heat up. If he ever reached out and touched one of her buttons again, she'd probably melt right onto the cheap tile floor.

But why? Her taste had never run to men like him, who regarded anyone in their vicinity as their minions to command, and she didn't imagine him treating the women he dated any differently. She wanted to ask him if he ever smiled, or whether those muscles had atrophied so much that it was no longer possible. Then she decided that insulting the boss probably wasn't the best way to start off on the right foot.

"You actually showed up," he said.

"Did you think I wouldn't?"

"Yes. I thought you wouldn't."

"Why, thank you so much for that vote of confidence. I assume this is my desk?"

She set her purse down and turned to see another woman approaching. She was maybe in her early thirties, five-two if she was standing up really straight, with a natural, freckles-over-the-nose beauty that made her seem warm and friendly. She gave Darcy a big smile and held out her hand.

"Hi. I'm Amy."

Darcy shook her hand. "I'm Darcy."

"Amy's going to get you started," John said. "Whatever she says goes." He turned to Amy. "I'm going after the Tahoe, but I should be back within the hour."

With that, he grabbed a set of keys and left the office, closing the door behind him with a solid *thunk.*

Amy smiled. "I'd tell you John isn't always that abrupt, but most of the time he is."

Wonderful.

For the next hour, Amy gave Darcy a rundown of how the repo business worked. She told her about the vehicle records and the condition and inventory reports they did on all the cars they repossessed, and she gave her an overview of the client database and collections information.

"I handle a lot of that stuff now, but as time goes on, you can take over a lot of it. Mostly what I do is skip tracing. Finding the cars so John and Tony can go after them. Most of the time it's pretty straightforward, but if people know the repo man is after them, sometimes they go to all kinds of lengths to hide their cars."

Darcy didn't doubt that. She'd certainly been prepared to hide a certain Mercedes Roadster if John hadn't shown up so quickly to grab it again.

Then Amy told her a few funny stories about things that had happened to John and Tony when they were repossessing cars, from naked people running out into the street trying to stop them to repossessing a car only to have its transmission die in the middle of Central Expressway to taking inventory on a car and finding a stash of gay porn in the trunk.

"Of course," Amy said, "the best story of all was the one about the Mercedes John was trying to repossess. A woman faked him out and ran off with the key. Can you imagine that?"

The smile that crossed Amy's lips told Darcy she knew exactly which woman had accomplished that particular feat. She closed her eyes with embarrassment. "I can't believe John told you that."

"He didn't. Tony did. John wouldn't have admitted a woman got the better of him in a million years."

"I was desperate, Amy. Really. I didn't have anything left but that car, and—"

"Don't worry," Amy said, her smile growing broader. "That was the best laugh I've had in a long time."

Darcy was finding more and more to like about this woman all the time.

"Why don't you just take some time today to go through the files and the database system and get familiar with them?" Amy said. "I have class this afternoon, but tomorrow morning I can answer any questions you have."

For the rest of the morning, Darcy poked around on the computer and flipped through files, and she was surprised to learn that they were practically a who's who of rich folks who had fallen on hard times. Hers wasn't the only high-dollar vehicle to have been repossessed. She'd always assumed rich people were, well, *rich,* and therefore they could pay their bills. She'd never really thought about how they might look good on the surface yet be up to their eyeballs in debt.

Like Warren, for instance.

Wait a minute. What was this?

She pulled one out of the stack. Larry Howard? Gail's ex-husband? Surely not. There had to be a lot of Larry Howards in a city the size of Plano. But when she scanned the page, sure enough the car in question was a red 1968 Corvette.

Darcy wondered if Gail knew her ex-husband had defaulted on his car loan. After he'd embarrassed her by engaging in all that clandestine sex with cheap hookers, she'd probably love hearing that he appeared to be as financially deficient as he was morally deficient. Darcy wondered how many more of her other friends and acquaintances had been victims of the repo man and she'd never known it.

Later, as she was filing billing records, she made another interesting discovery. John's fee for bringing in her car had been five hundred dollars. A few weeks ago, that wouldn't have sounded like much money, but now it seemed like a fortune, particularly in light of what John was paying her. She made a mental note to approach him about a salary increase just as soon as she thought he might not bite her head off for asking.

The morning went quickly, and around noontime Amy came back to her desk.

"It's lunchtime," she said. "You want to go out?"

Unfortunately, lunching out had moved beyond Darcy's means. Brown bagging was *so* low class, but at least it meant she could eat on her parents' dime instead of her own.

"Uh . . . no. I brought something from home."

"I have a two-for-one coupon for Taco Hut," Amy said.

"We can share it and get Neato Burritos for half price. Put your lunch in the fridge and you can eat it tomorrow."

Okay. So Taco Hut wasn't exactly lunching out. Eating in a place like that consisted of filling your stomach with a pseudo-food product to sustain life. But she had to admit that anything that was half price these days got her attention.

Ten minutes later, they walked in the door of Taco Hut. The décor was every bit as horrific as Darcy had imagined, with a color scheme of purple, aqua, and orange that would keep a narcoleptic awake. They ordered Neato Burritos from a high school kid who tossed the food on the tray with all the delicacy of a butcher slapping meat onto a conveyor belt. When Darcy unwrapped hers, it was squashed flat and looked so unappetizing that she almost wrapped it back up again. But hunger drove her to finally dig in.

She couldn't believe it. It was love at first bite.

She'd been to five-star restaurants serving the finest Southwestern cuisine whose entrees hadn't tasted this good. How could that be? How could she have found heaven for a dollar fifty? It wasn't the most stunning presentation she'd ever seen, but getting so much bang for her buck these days really put a smile on her face.

"Can't help noticing," Amy said. "That's a gorgeous ring you're wearing."

"Thank you."

"So you're married?"

"Not really. I'm getting a divorce."

Which reminded her that sooner or later she was going to have to hire an attorney and deal with the fact that her husband had skipped the country. How did you go about divorcing a man who you couldn't find? And even if she could find him, how was she going to pay for a divorce?

"I'm so sorry," Amy said, continuing to stare at her ring with a look of confusion.

"John must not have told you," Darcy said.

"Told me what?"

"Why I'm wearing a four-carat diamond but working as a clerk at a repo company making next to nothing and eating lunch at Taco Hut."

"No. He didn't."

Darcy didn't know why she confided in Amy exactly, except that girls share, and she seemed to be more genuine than most. Darcy gave Amy the *Readers' Digest* version of her marital horror story. When she described her homecoming from Mexico and subsequently finding out her husband was a criminal, Amy's mouth fell open.

"You poor thing!" Amy said. "How could he *do* that to you?"

"I've been asking myself that same question."

"Well, I'm glad John hired you. It's good for you, and it'll be good for him."

Darcy shook her head. "I'm not so sure he feels that way."

"Well, he should. For once we'll have a clerk who clearly has a brain. The last few he hired were a little lacking in that department."

"So why did he hire them?"

"It's just hard to find good employees. He's hired two repo guys in the last couple of months, but they didn't work out. One of them was just lazy. Wouldn't get out and hustle. The other one got his first paycheck, then blew all of it before he showed up to earn another one.

As you can well imagine, that didn't set well with John. Business is picking up, so he's ready to get another tow truck or two just as soon as he can find the repo guys to use them."

Darcy laid down her burrito. "Amy? Can I ask you a question? Confidentially?"

"Sure."

She leaned closer and spoke quietly. "How in the world do you deal with a man like John?"

"What do you mean?"

"Isn't he hard to work for? I mean, he's crabby all the time. He never cracks a smile. He orders people around like some kind of third-world dictator. Does he *ever* lighten up?"

Amy smiled. "Actually, not very often. And he's been that way for a *very* long time."

"Well, I don't have many options myself, but if I were you, I'd find a new place to work."

Amy's smile grew brighter still. "I guess John didn't tell you."

"Tell me what?"

"My full name."

"What?"

"It's Amy Stark."

Darcy froze.

"I'm John's sister."

Darcy sat back, stunned. John's *sister?* This cute little woman who gave the word *perky* an entirely new meaning? She actually shared the same gene pool with Tall, Dark, and Exasperating?

Then Darcy remembered what she'd just said about

him. She closed her eyes, wishing she'd had the sense to keep her big mouth shut.

"Amy, I'm *so* sorry. Really. I shouldn't have said that about John. I don't know why I—"

"Don't apologize," she said. "You're only speaking the truth."

"So why do you work for him?"

Amy smiled. "Don't let what's on the surface fool you. There's a lot more going on inside John's head than you realize. You'll discover that soon enough. Just always remember that his bark is *way* worse than his bite."

Darcy was having a hard time imagining that.

That afternoon, Amy headed off to class about the time John came back. He mumbled something that sounded like hello, then strode past her, went into his office, and closed the door. She told herself that was a good thing. If he didn't talk to her, they couldn't fight.

A few minutes later, a FedEx man came into the office. He greeted Darcy and asked her to sign for the envelope he was carrying. She did, assuming it was for John. It wasn't.

It was for her.

Then she saw the return address. Jeremy Bridges?

The delivery man left the office, and Darcy ripped open the envelope, wondering what in the world could be inside. She pulled out a small envelope and was even more confused.

A Starbucks gift card?

A handwritten note accompanied it. *Enjoyed our chat. Have a cup of coffee on me. Jeremy.*

At first she was confused. Then she remembered telling him that since Warren had cleaned her out, she couldn't even afford to stop for a cup of coffee anymore. So Bridges was giving her one.

She frowned. Probably *exactly* one. This was probably a five-dollar card for *one* cup of coffee. And of course he'd enjoyed their chat. He was a man who clearly enjoyed humiliating people.

Jerk.

Darcy tossed the card aside. But after a few minutes, she glanced back at it. After a few more minutes, curiosity finally overtook her.

She flipped the card over and found an 800 number on the back. She dialed it, and a customer service rep came on the line. She gave him the number on the card and asked what its value was.

She heard the click of fingers on a keyboard. Then . . . silence.

"Hello?" she said.

"Just a minute," he said. "That can't be right." More clicking. More silence. Finally he spoke again.

"A thousand dollars."

Darcy nearly dropped the phone. "Did you say a thousand dollars?"

"Yes."

"As in a one with three zeroes?"

"Yes, ma'am."

"Uh . . . thank you," she said, and hung up the phone. Was Jeremy Bridges completely out of his *mind?*

Yes, she wanted Starbucks coffee. Every day, if she could get it. But now that she had absolutely nothing in the world, she would gladly have traded that daily dose of caffeine for clothes on her back and gas in her car.

She called the service rep back.

"Yes, ma'am?"

"I'm the one you just talked to with the thousand-dollar card. Is it possible for me to get a refund for that?"

"Oh, yes, ma'am."

Darcy's heart soared. *Jackpot!*

"Just turn in the card along with the receipt, and any of our stores will be happy to give you whatever amount is remaining on it."

Her elation fizzled. "I have to have the receipt?"

"I'm afraid so."

"But it's a gift card. If somebody's giving a gift, who gives the receipt along with it?"

"Sorry. Those are the rules."

Damn.

She thanked the guy and hung up. How could Bridges do this to her? Didn't he *know* how destitute she was?

Maybe not. Maybe she hadn't made it completely clear. Maybe he didn't know she literally had nothing left in the world. Surely if he knew how much she needed more practical things, he'd sympathize with her and hand over the receipt.

Assuming he'd kept it.

No. Think positive.

She fished through her purse and found the business card he'd given her. She dialed the number on it. He'd said it was his cell phone, but still she didn't expect—

"Jeremy Bridges."

Darcy came to attention. This really was his cell phone. And he really had answered it himself.

"Uh . . . hello, Jeremy. This is Darcy McDaniel."

"Darcy! So good to hear from you."

He sounded pretty jovial, considering how they'd

parted. Then again, he *had* sent her a thousand-dollar gift card, so surely there were no hard feelings on his part after their disagreement the other day. Maybe this would be easier than she thought.

"I'm just calling . . . well, I'm calling to tell you that I got the gift card, and while it's a very thoughtful thing to do—"

"No, you can't have the receipt."

Darcy's mouth fell open. "What?"

"I said you can't have the receipt."

"Uh . . . I don't want the receipt."

"Of course you do. You want to cash out the card."

"No. Really. I don't."

"Then what do you want?"

She opened her mouth to say something, and several seconds later it was still hanging open. She was so utterly shocked at just how dead-on his accusation was that she couldn't think of a thing to say.

Then she got mad.

"You are *such* a jerk," she said. "You spend a thousand dollars, and all I get out of it is *coffee?*"

"You get far more than coffee. They have cookies, too. And pastries. And I think some of them have started carrying sandwiches and—"

"You know what I mean!"

"Hey, I think it's kinda stupid, too. But you did say you couldn't afford Starbucks anymore."

"I also said I was driving a crappy car and living in my parents' mobile home. A thousand dollars would go a long way toward fixing *those* problems."

"Now, Darcy. What would happen if I just gave you a car? Or apartment rent?"

"Uh . . . I'd have something respectable to drive and a decent place to live?"

"But how would you ever expect to grow as a person?"

Was this man completely out of his mind? "I've got news for you, Bridges. Growing as a person is just about last on my to-do list."

"I'm quite sure it is. And number one on that list is getting back all the luxuries you've lost. Enjoy the coffee, Darcy."

Click.

Darcy held out the phone, staring at it dumbly, then hung it up with a sigh of frustration. He was toying with her, plain and simple. That was the only explanation. He wasn't actually going to help her. Instead, he liked watching her flounder around, trying to keep her head above water while he dangled the luxuries of life in front of her, reminding her of what she couldn't have. But what good would it do her to have a four-dollar cup of coffee if she couldn't put gas in old Gertie?

The door to John's office opened, and he stuck his head out. "I was on the phone. What did the FedEx guy leave?"

"The FedEx wasn't for you," she said. "It was for me."

He came out of his office and stood over her desk. "You? Who sent you a FedEx here?"

Before Darcy could move the envelope out of his way, John grabbed it and read the return address.

"Jeremy Bridges?"

"Give me that!"

"Isn't he the guy your husband embezzled all that money from?"

Darcy paused. "Yes."

John glanced around her desk. "What did he send you?"

"That's none of your business."

"New rule. If you're on the clock, it's my business."

She rolled her eyes. "If you must know, he sent me a Starbucks gift card."

"Huh?"

"You heard me."

John held up his hand. "Wait a minute. Do you know this guy?"

"Not really."

"Your husband embezzles from him, and he sends you a gift?"

"He's just a very sympathetic person," she said, hoping her nose wasn't growing as she spoke. "He came to see me the other day. He just wants me to have one of the luxuries Warren took away from me."

"You're broke. Couldn't he have sprung for something a little more useful?"

"The rich are different, John. A man like Jeremy doesn't even think about necessities. It's all about luxury."

She almost choked on that. A man who swilled beer and dressed like a Jimmy Buffett groupie had a little way to go as far as a luxury mentality was concerned.

"Luxury?" John said. "Starbucks? What kind of idiot pays four bucks for a cup of coffee?"

"That's exactly the reaction I'd expect from a man who drinks Maxwell House."

"Damn fine coffee. And a real bargain, too."

"Oh, yeah? Well, who needs bargain coffee when I have"—she nonchalantly *tap, tap, tapped* the gift card against her desk, then held it up with a smug smile—"a thousand dollars?"

John's eyebrows flew up. "A thousand dollars' worth of *coffee?*"

Finally. It was about time she impressed him with something. But instead of giving her the look of awe she expected, he shook his head with disapproval.

"What's wrong?" she said.

"That's a lot of money."

"He's a very generous man."

"Generous?" John placed his palms on Darcy's desk, meeting her eye-to-eye. "Let me tell you something. Any man who gives a woman a thousand dollars' worth of anything expects something in return. And I guarantee you that 'something' is more than a peck on the cheek. Is that really what you're looking for?"

"He hasn't asked me for anything."

"Not yet, he hasn't."

"Why don't you let me worry about Jeremy Bridges's motives?"

"Just remember where you heard it first."

With that, John turned and went back into his office, and Darcy had to resist the urge to hurl her stapler at his door. She'd never met a man so infuriatingly sure of himself in her entire life.

What she hated most, though, was that he was right. Jeremy was neither sympathetic nor generous. He had "ulterior motive" stamped all over him. And no matter how abruptly he'd hung up on her today, she had a feeling she hadn't heard the last of him yet.

Chapter 9

Darcy's first week on the job passed without too many problems. Gradually she learned more about word processing, and Amy started teaching her how to run some of the reports. By Thursday she'd done away with the "to be filed" pile. She was relieved when the weekend came and John hadn't found a reason to fire her yet, but when she rose on Saturday morning, she wished she was back at the office. Her father was at his shop, as he always was on Saturday, which left her at home to be her mother's target du jour.

"I still can't believe you're working in a place like that," Lyla said, digging the last cigarette out of a pack and lighting it. "What were you thinking when you took that job?"

Darcy shoved her half-eaten bowl of Froot Loops away, visions of brunch at the Palm dancing inside her head. "I told you, Mom. I wasn't exactly overwhelmed with job offers."

"Doesn't some nice CEO need a girl Friday?"

"This isn't the 1950s. Even receptionists have to know a lot of things. A lot of things I don't."

"You can stay here as long as you need to, but even

without paying rent, you have expenses. Your hair and nails alone will cost half your paycheck. And what about clothes? Are you going to dress out of your luggage from now on? Isn't it a little scary to think about doing that forever? It would scare me, that's for sure."

Darcy had learned long ago that there wasn't much her mother wasn't scared of. Her life had always been governed by fear: fear of aging, fear of heights, fear of ghosts, fear of nuclear war, fear of the number thirteen, fear of trains. And spiders. She didn't like spiders. Anytime a spider sat down beside her, all hell broke loose.

But right now, Darcy had to admit she was starting to feel a little of that fear herself. It *was* a crappy, low-paying, dead-end job. Using it as a springboard to something better was going to take a very long time.

"I'd suggest you find yourself another man, and fast," Lyla said. "And don't sign a prenup this time. That way if it doesn't work out, at least you can get a big divorce settlement. Then you can do it all over again."

"Actually, Mom, when I get married again, I'd like it to last for a little while."

"Right. Statistics show that half of all marriages these days end in divorce."

"You and Dad are still married."

"Stop being naïve, Darcy. Your father would have left me ages ago if some other woman would have him."

Darcy sighed. Just what a kid wanted to hear. That if her father were only a better man, he'd have left her mother. She wasn't good enough for him to want to stay, but he wasn't good enough to find a replacement, which meant they were living in a state of mutually assured misery.

All at once, Lyla leaped out of her chair and made shooing movements with her hands. "Pepé! Off the sofa!"

As Pepé scrambled away, Lyla turned to Darcy. "That dog's behavior is atrocious. He needs a good trainer."

"Trainers cost money."

"You used to have plenty of that, and still you did nothing."

"*Mom—*"

"It's a good thing you never had children. They'd have turned into juvenile delinquents." She gasped. "Darcy! He's peeing in the corner again!"

Darcy put her hand to her forehead. "It's because you're shouting at him, Mom!" she whispered loudly. "You can't shout at him!"

"Of course I can shout at him! It's my house, isn't it?"

"I'm not arguing with your *right* to shout. I'm just telling you—" She let out a heavy sigh. "Oh, never mind. I'll clean it up."

"I'm going across the street to Roxanne's. Her dog doesn't pee on the rug."

"That's because she keeps him tied up in the backyard."

"Which means he can't pee on the rug."

Lyla glared at Pepé, and he stared up at her as if she were Medusa with a headful of writhing snakes. Then Lyla grabbed another pack of cigarettes and her keys and left the house, shutting the door behind her with a huff of disgust.

Darcy went to the kitchen for the P-B-Gone she'd bought yesterday, knowing she couldn't stay there much longer. Dog shrinks cost a fortune. Then again, so did people shrinks. Eventually she was going to go nuts, commit matricide, and end up in an institution for the criminally insane.

Okay, so maybe that wouldn't be so bad. At least she'd have free room and board, along with the precious solitude only a rubber room could provide.

After she cleaned up the mess, Pepé trotted over, and she scooped him up to calm his delicate nerves. She had to get out of there before she turned into one of those sad little people who had no means of support, who lived in their parents' basements and watched infomercials. She needed an apartment of her own. But how long would it be before she could get the money together for that?

She looked down at her wedding ring.

No. She couldn't do it. Even though it was the only thing she had left with any value at all, it was also the only thing she had left of her former life, and she just couldn't let it go.

She sighed. If only she made the kind of money John and Tony did for bringing in cars, she could have an apartment deposit in no time.

Wait a minute.

Darcy froze as an idea entered her mind. She turned it over, examined it from all angles, and after a few moments, she came to a stunning conclusion.

Forget being a clerk. She could become a repossession agent.

All John had done to go after her Mercedes the first time was get the key from the finance company. If she hadn't interfered, he'd have just driven it away. All that had been required was a key and a driver's license. Like she couldn't handle that? Amy did say John had been trying to hire another repossession agent. He just didn't realize that someone was right under his nose.

A sense of excitement built inside her, making her feel like a prospector who'd happened onto a vein of gold. She pictured checks for hundreds of dollars rolling in with dazzling regularity, in contrast to her piddly biweekly salary. This was the solution to her problem. Only one thing stood in her way.

She had to talk John into letting her do it.

~

"No way," John said. "You get that out of your head right now. I am *not* teaching you to repossess cars."

Darcy leaned forward and rested her forearms on his desk. "Just give me one good reason why you won't."

If John needed any more evidence that Darcy was a lunatic, this was it. What a hell of a thing to get hit with first thing Monday morning.

"I don't have to give you a reason. I'm the boss."

She sat back in her chair, eyeing him with irritation. "It's because I'm a woman, isn't it?"

"That doesn't help your case any."

"Are you really that sexist?"

"It's not sexism. It's just a fact that in this business, the bigger and badder you are, the less likely people are to give you any crap."

"Tony's not as big as you are, yet he manages to do the job."

"Tony doesn't need size with that mouth of his. He could talk anyone into anything."

"I'm good with people, too."

"I'm not talking about polite chatter at tea. I'm talking about the ability to talk your way into and out of difficult situations. People in this business can be a pain in the ass to deal with. They don't want you to take their cars. Some of them go to great lengths to keep you from doing it. Say, like, combative women who cry, throw fits, and steal keys."

He could tell she wanted to come back at that, but for once she was smart enough to hold her tongue.

"I'll tell you what," she said. "I'll do both jobs. You let me do a repo every now and then, and I'll still take care of the administrative stuff."

"It's not as easy as it looks."

"Oh, yeah? What's so tough about putting a key into the ignition of a car and driving it back here?"

"Some of the dealers keep keys on hand. Others give us the key code, and we have to go to a locksmith to get the keys cut. But for most of the cars, we have to use other means to take them. Sometimes we use the tow truck. Sometimes we pick the locks to break in, and if they're older cars, we hot-wire them. Do you know how to do any of those things?"

"Well, no. But you can let me do the ones that have keys, and you guys can do the rest."

"Wrong. I'm not handing you the easy ones."

"Then teach me how to do the other stuff."

"Nope."

"Come on, John! You got five hundred dollars for bringing in my car!"

"I deserved twice that for having to deal with you."

Darcy sat back and glared at him. "Did anyone ever tell you how unreasonable you are?"

"I don't have to be reasonable. I'm the boss. And if you want to keep drawing a paycheck, you'll go back out there and do what I hired you to do."

He stacked up some papers on his desk, stuck them in a file folder, and stood up. "I'm going to be out of the office for a few hours. While I'm gone, I want you to get the direct mail ads together so they can be sent out today. And while you're at it, wash every thought you've had about repossessing cars out of your mind, because I don't want to hear another word about it."

With that, he circled his desk to leave the building, feeling her go-to-hell look boring into his back all the way out the door.

As John was leaving the building, Darcy shot him a really scathing go-to-hell look, then returned to her desk to resume her low-paying, dead-end job. But she wasn't going to have to do it for long. John might have said no this time, but she wasn't deterred. What he didn't know was that she had another quality she hadn't even unleashed yet. She never took no for an answer.

She just hadn't yet figured out a way to make him say yes.

The trouble was, if he wouldn't let her go after the jobs they had keys for, he'd have to teach her how to hot-wire a car or grab one with the tow truck. And getting him to do that clearly wasn't going to happen.

With a heavy sigh, she started in on the task John had commanded her to, muttering under her breath the whole time. *Because I'm the boss.* If she heard that man say that one more time, she was going to scream.

By the time she finished running off copies of the letters, stuffing the envelopes and attaching the address labels, it was lunchtime. Once again, Taco Hut was calling to her. It was becoming an addiction more powerful than heroin, and if she didn't kick the habit, her hips were going to be as wide as a city bus.

Just one more day. Then you can start that twelve-step program at Burrito Eaters Anonymous.

She grabbed her purse and left the building, locking the door behind her. As she was opening Gertie's passenger door, she heard the rumble of a truck engine. Turning around, she saw Tony coming through the gate with a late-model Lexus on the back of the tow truck. He waved to her, then circled the building to put it in the impound lot.

Darcy looked after him longingly. It seemed like such an easy thing to do for such a large amount of money. But if John wouldn't show her—

And that was when it struck her.

If she could grab a car and bring it in all by herself, he'd have to pay her for it, and he'd also have to admit she could do the job. But that would require her to have skills he refused to teach her.

Fortunately, John wasn't the only repo man around here.

She walked around the building and down to the impound lot. Tony already had the car down off the truck, and she still didn't know how it was done.

"Hey, Darcy."

"Hi, Tony. Nice-looking car you picked up. Did you have any trouble?"

"Nope. The guy works in an office building near Park and the Tollway. He'd driven it to work. I don't think he ever even knew I took it."

"You know, I was pretty confused myself when John came back for my car that night. By the time I got out there, he already had it up on the truck, just like you had this one. And I thought to myself, Now how in the world did he do that?"

"So you didn't see him do it?"

"He said it was repo magic."

Tony made a scoffing noise. "Magic, my ass. Watch."

He hit a lever, and slowly the bed of the truck began to tilt down until it met the pavement.

Oh . . . so *that* was how it worked.

She watched exactly where Tony hooked a tow chain underneath the carriage of the car.

"Now, if we have to use the tow truck," he said, "sometimes it means we haven't got a key, which means we can't get inside to release the steering column, which means we can't tow it behind the truck. But that also means it won't roll up the ramp when we pull it."

"So what do you do?"

"Just give it short little jerks like this."

He hit another lever, then quickly released it several times, inching the car up the ramp.

"If the tires aren't rolling, doesn't that mess them up?"

"Nah. Not if you're moving the car over a short distance like this."

In less than a minute, he had the car up there. Then

he hit the lever and tilted the bed of the truck horizontal again.

"That's all there is to it?"

"Yep."

"No wonder John grabbed my car so quickly. So you don't have to be strong to do this?"

"Nope. The truck does all the work. And John went first class with this one. Automatic transmission, cruise control, air conditioning, power everything."

Darcy couldn't believe it. This was what John told her she wasn't qualified to do?

"You make all that money just doing that?" she asked.

"Well, there is a downside every once in a while. Sometimes people shoot at you."

Darcy gulped. "What?"

"Oh, that hardly ever happens," he said, pulling out a Tic Tac and popping it into his mouth. "If you don't push people, they generally don't push back. I can usually leave them smiling."

Particularly if they're women, Darcy thought.

"Thank you for the explanation," she said to Tony, giving him a smile of gratitude. "I like knowing how you gentlemen do your jobs."

"Anytime, sweetheart."

Okay. She had the knowledge. Now all she needed was a target.

She went to Taco Hut, grabbed lunch, and by the time she came back to the office, she was already hatching a plan. It involved the tow truck, Larry Howard's Corvette, and a nice big check John was going to be forced to write when she brought the car in. All that remained for her to do now was keep her eyes open for a time when nobody else was at the office so she could grab the truck and put it to good use.

Over the next several days, Darcy watched for her opportunity, but it was Friday before it materialized. John announced on Thursday that he was taking Friday off. Amy was going to be in class all afternoon. And Tony was spending the day going to the banks and finance companies who had responded to their direct mail advertising to drum up some new business.

Which meant she'd be in the office by herself.

A week ago she'd have never considered doing what she was thinking about doing now. But now that she saw how simple it was going to be . . .

Look out, Larry.

At three o'clock on Friday afternoon, Darcy pulled the tow truck into the alley behind Larry's house. He lived three doors down from the house Darcy had occupied for fourteen years, which was why his ex-wife, Gail, and Darcy had been friends. The Howards' divorce had been a contentious one. In the end, Larry had gotten the house, and Gail had gotten everything else, which was only fair considering what a cheating bastard Larry had turned out to be.

With a bit of maneuvering, Darcy backed the truck into the driveway and brought it to a halt near the garage door. She got out, her heart beating like crazy. She couldn't have imagined a scenario under which she'd be stealing a car, but then again, she couldn't have imagined a scenario under which she'd be desperate for the five hundred bucks she was going to get for stealing a car, either.

Because Larry's house was on a corner lot, it was a simple matter to leave the truck in the driveway, then circle around the house and walk to the flower bed near the front porch. Once there, she searched through the river rock surrounding the base of the shrubs. When she didn't see what she was looking for, she was afraid her plan was going to be foiled before it even got under way.

Wait. There it is.

She picked up a rock that was a little bigger and a different color than the others. It really wasn't a rock at all. Holding her breath, she turned it over and slid open the compartment.

Bingo.

Darcy knew Gail Howard had hidden this key against the possibility that someday she'd lock herself out of her house, because Darcy had been with her when that day came to pass. Now the key opened the door for Darcy just as easily as it had for Gail.

Once inside, Darcy moved quickly to the kitchen, through the utility room, and opened the door to the garage.

There it was. Larry's Corvette.

By night he was Midlife Crisis Man, tooling around town in—as Gail always put it—his shiny red substitute penis. By day, though, he was a real estate agent, which meant he opted for a big old Cadillac to haul prospective buyers around to look at homes, which meant that right now the Cadillac was out and the Corvette was in.

Darcy hit the button to the garage door opener. She hooked up the car, and in no time she had it loaded on the truck. She couldn't believe it. It really was as easy as Tony had said. She closed the garage door, locked the rear door, and hid the key back inside the rock.

She hopped back into the cab of the tow truck, and as she carefully pulled out of the alley back onto the street again, she could barely drive for all the back-patting she was treating herself to. She couldn't wait to see the look on John's face when she pulled into the impound lot with this car. He'd have to admit she could do the job, and she'd push to do it again. Her bank account would grow, and soon she'd be able to buy some new clothes. She'd be able to keep her hair appointments so she wouldn't go gray. Drive a respectable car. Eventually she could buy a modest condo in west Plano, where she'd use what she'd learned all these years watching HGTV to create chic décor on a dime. And when she was finally back to her old self again, she'd be the kind of woman who could turn the head of a wealthy, important man, and the world would be right again.

Ah. Life was going to be *good*.

When she arrived back at the office, she was thrilled to see John in the parking lot, getting out of his car. She didn't know why he was here on his day off, but she was glad he was. Maybe he'd cut her a check on the spot. If he did, she was heading to the mall as fast as Gertie could get her there.

She pulled into the lot, brought the truck to a halt, and killed the engine. As John approached, she opened the door and hopped out.

"Darcy?" he said, looking stunned. "What have you done?"

"What does it look like?" she said with a grin. "I repossessed a car."

"But . . . I don't get it. How did you . . . ?"

"I saw this repossession order come across my desk a few days ago," she said, excitement bubbling up inside her. "Turned out I knew the guy. Larry Howard. He's the ex-husband of a friend of mine. He and Warren used to hang out at the country club together. I know his ex-wife, so I knew she used to keep a house key in one of those fake rocks in their flower bed. So I went to Larry's house, got the key, opened his front door—"

"You *what?*"

"Don't worry. He wasn't there. I called ahead to make sure he was at work. He's a real estate agent, so he drives his Cadillac to work, which meant his Corvette would be in his garage at home. Sure enough, it was. I just hit the button for the garage door, hooked the car up, pulled it up the ramp, and"—she waved her arm at the car—"voilà."

John's eyes widened, a look of subdued panic edging across his face. "Are you telling me you took a car from a locked garage?"

"Yep. I told you I could do the job. You didn't believe me." She folded her arms with a smile of supreme satisfaction. "I believe you owe me a repossession fee?"

But for some reason, John didn't seem to be in any hurry to grab his checkbook and a pen. And she noticed he wasn't exactly smiling. In fact, he looked downright pissed.

"John," she said carefully, "what's the matter? Is there something—"

"You can't take a car from a locked garage! *It's against the law!*"

Darcy recoiled. "Against the law?"

"Yes!"

"But why? He wasn't making his payments!"

"That doesn't mean you can break into his garage to take the car! And you sure as hell can't take a tour of his house when he's not there! That's breaking and entering!"

"Now, hold on. I may have done a little entering, but there was no breaking. I told you I had a key."

"It doesn't matter if you had a key or not! If it isn't your property, you have no authorization to enter it!" He paced away a few steps, running his hand through his hair. "I don't believe this. I just don't *believe*—"

"Wait a minute!" Darcy said. "Larry won't know I didn't have authority to take it. Won't he just figure the repo man finally caught up to him?"

John whipped around. "No. You don't know deadbeats. They always know their rights. And they can't wait to use them against you."

"So . . . what are we going to do?"

He strode back to her, his eyes narrowed angrily. "Listen to me, Darcy. The only reason there's a 'we' here is because my name is on the truck. If I knew of a way to save my ass without saving yours, I'd do it in a heartbeat."

Darcy hoped he didn't actually mean that. Then again, judging from the way steam was blowing out his ears, maybe he did.

"Did anyone see you take the car?" he asked.

"I don't think so. The garage has an alley entrance."

John looked at his watch. "It's almost four o'clock. Do you think Larry will be home yet?"

"I doubt it."

"Is the repossession order in the truck?"

"Yes."

He climbed behind the wheel, then looked down at Darcy. "Get in."

The last thing Darcy wanted was to be in a small, closed-in space with a large, angry man. Especially when that man was John. "Uh . . . whatever you're doing, do you really need me?"

"You're not weaseling out of this. If something goes wrong and I end up going down for this, you're going down, too."

"So what are we going to do?"

"The only thing we can. Put the damned thing back."

Darcy sat quietly in the cab of the tow truck as John drove to Larry's house in miserable, abject, screaming silence, gripping the steering wheel so hard his knuckles whitened. Okay, so he wasn't happy about this. She could see his point. But all they had to do was put the car back, and everything would be fine.

John pulled the tow truck to a halt a few doors down from Larry's house. "Go get the key and open the garage door," he told Darcy. "I'm driving around to the alley to wait for you. Now move it."

Darcy scrambled out of the truck's cab, circled around the house, and walked to the flower bed beside the front porch, where she grabbed the key from the rock. She let herself into the house, and a minute later she opened the door leading from the utility room to the garage and hit the button for the garage door opener.

The moment the door was up, John unloaded the Corvette back into the garage, shooting Darcy several scathing looks that told her that even when the car was back in place, this issue wasn't over. Not by a long shot.

"I'm going to pull back into the alley," he told her as he opened the driver's door to get back into the truck. "You go put the key back. And for God's sake, make sure nobody sees you."

Darcy nodded. As soon as John pulled away, she lowered the garage door again and made her way back through the house. When she reached the front door, she stopped to peer out the peephole to ensure nobody was standing on the front porch.

All clear.

She slipped out the door and went to the flower bed, where she bent over to retrieve the phony rock. She had just returned the key and slid the compartment closed when she heard a voice behind her.

"What do you think you're doing?"

Darcy whipped around to see a woman standing on the sidewalk. At first it didn't dawn on Darcy who she was, but the baby stroller she was pushing, the mom clothes, the suspicious look on her face, and the fact that Darcy was three doors down from where she used to live finally jogged her memory. The last time Darcy had seen this woman, she was calling 911 and having her escorted out of her house.

"I asked you what you're doing," the woman snapped.

"Uh . . . nothing."

"Nothing? Why are you digging around in Mr. Howard's flower bed?"

Darcy couldn't think of a single thing to say. All she

could do was stand there with her mouth hanging open, which undoubtedly made her look every bit as guilty as she was.

"You're not supposed to come back to this neighborhood. The police told you that." The woman dove into a diaper bag and pulled out a cell phone.

"What are you doing?" Darcy asked.

"Calling the cops."

"No!"

As Darcy hurried down the sidewalk to stop her, the woman reached her other hand into the diaper bag, pulled out a canister, and held it up. "Stay away!"

Darcy screeched to a halt. Pepper spray? Was she *kidding?*

Okay, so Darcy had acted a little insane the day she lost everything. But she hadn't actually *attacked* anyone, had she?

Using her thumb, the woman poked the cell phone in her other hand. Three buttons: nine, one, and one.

"Wait!" Darcy said. "Don't do that! I wasn't doing anything wrong! I swear I wasn't!"

"You went crazy in my house. Then you were told to stay away. Now you're back, acting suspiciously. That's reason enough for me to call the cops."

Darcy sensed she wasn't going to convince this woman that this wasn't a job for the Plano PD, which meant it was time to get out of there.

She spun around and took off, circling the side of the house and sprinting into the alley. She ran up to the tow truck, yanked open the passenger door, and climbed in.

"Darcy?" John said. "What's the matter?"

She slammed the door. "We need to get out of here."

"What's going on? Did somebody see you?"

"John, let's go."

"Darcy? What happened?"

"John—"

"I swear to God, if you screwed this up—"

"Hey! Do you want to deal with the cops?"

John's eyebrows flew up. "Cops? Hell, no!"

"Then *drive!*"

John had no idea what was up, but the last thing he wanted was to come face-to-face with the police. He hit the gas and drove to the end of the alley, then made a right onto Thornberry. He'd driven about a block before they met a police car coming the opposite direction. He gave the cop a casual wave of his fingertips and kept on driving.

"Darcy," he said, talking through clenched teeth, "what happened back there?"

"Nothing, really," she said nonchalantly. "Everything's fine."

"The cops showed up! Everything is *not* fine!"

Darcy rolled her eyes and started in on the story, and the more she talked, the closer John came to blowing his stack.

He'd always prided himself on his remarkably even temper. When he was a cop, nothing bothered him, because he never took anything personally. He could take down suspects, listen to their sob stories or their foul mouths, shrug his shoulders, and call it a good day's work. It had taken the woman sitting beside him to make him lose his cool, and he wasn't sure if he'd ever find it again.

"But we got out of there before the cops showed up," Darcy said brightly. "So no harm done, right?"

He glared at her. "No harm done? Are you *kidding* me?"

"Well, nobody's in jail, are they?"

"That's what you call 'no harm'? That we weren't both arrested?"

"Hey, I didn't know that woman was going to happen by. And as far as taking the car in the first place, it was just a beginner's mistake. If you'd shown me how to do it right, I wouldn't have done it wrong."

"You weren't supposed to do it at all!"

"I was just showing some initiative. I thought employers liked that."

"What I like," he said sharply, "is an employee who keeps her hands off my tow truck."

Darcy rolled her eyes. "You sound just like my father. What is it with men and their trucks, anyway?"

"You *stole* mine!"

"Stole it? I can't steal it. I work for you."

"You were *not* authorized to drive it. And you sure as hell weren't authorized to repossess a car with it. How did you even know how to use the tow truck?"

"Tony showed me how."

"He *what?*"

"Don't be mad at him. He didn't know I wanted to learn how to do it myself. I just . . . you know. Acted curious."

And Tony couldn't resist those fluttering eyelashes. He was definitely a dead man.

John braked at a stoplight. "I ought to fire you for this."

"No," Darcy said, looking a little panicked. "Now, there's no reason to do that. My being a clerk has nothing to do with this. I'm doing a good job with that, aren't I?"

"Yes, you are. But—"

"If you fire me, you'll be without a clerk all over again. And you know how hard it is to find decent employees."

John thought about Rona and the alphabet. God, he couldn't take *that* again.

"If you fire me, you'll have one less person to order around. And you know how much you like to do that."

He gave her an admonishing look, then followed it up with an angry glare, because he had no intention of giving in.

"I need this job, John." She paused, looking pitiful. "Do I still have it?"

Get tough. Take no crap. She's a nutcase. Fire her now, before she drives your business right into the ground.

But now she was looking at him with a plaintive expression, silently pleading with those gorgeous green eyes, and he felt himself waver. What was it about this woman? Hadn't she messed with his mind, his business, his *life* enough already? Why would he even consider letting her stay?

Because he was a sucker. A sap. A spineless jellyfish of a man whose good sense went right out the window when he looked at a beautiful woman. What other explanation could there possibly be?

"John . . . ?"

"Yes! Okay! You still have a job!"

"Thank you."

"A *clerk* job. But it comes with a warning." He pointed a finger inches from her nose. "If you even *look* in the direction of my tow truck again, you're a dead woman. And it won't be one of those pretty murders, like closed head trauma or a quick strangulation. There will be blood, and there will be violence. By the time I'm finished with you, the guys in Homicide will have to do DNA testing to ID your body. Do you hear me?"

Darcy made a face. "Good Lord. Leave it to a former cop to come up with a threat like that."

"Do you *hear* me?"

"Yes, John. I hear you."

The light changed, and he hit the gas. "How in the hell did you get it in your head to do this, anyway?"

"I told you before. I need to make more money."

"You wouldn't need more money if you learned to live within your means."

"My means right now allow me to live with my parents, drive a beat-up car, and eat Taco Hut burritos."

"There are people worse off than that."

"I have nothing but the clothes I took with me to Mexico. That's it. Unless you want me showing up at work in a swimsuit in the next few days, I have to buy some more clothes."

"Borrow some from your mother."

"Right. She's three sizes bigger than I am." As if size were the only consideration. "I need an advance on my salary."

He looked at her skeptically. "How much?"

"At least five hundred dollars. A thousand would be better."

"For *clothes?*"

"Yes. And even that won't buy much."

John opened his mouth to say something else, only to

shut it again. A thousand bucks for a clothes-shopping trip? That was ridiculous. There was only one way this woman was ever going to learn the value of a dollar. And once she did, maybe she'd get the idea of quick money out of her mind and keep her hands off his tow truck.

When they arrived back at the office, he opened the driver's door and got out of the truck. "Come with me."

She scrambled out the passenger door, hurrying to keep up. "Where are we going?"

"I'm taking you clothes shopping."

She grabbed his arm. "Wait a minute. *You're* taking me shopping?"

"That's right. I wouldn't put it past you showing up to work in a swimsuit just to make a point. You do that, and I never will get Tony to leave the office."

"You're giving me an advance against my salary?"

He thought about it for a moment, then said, "Nope. I'm buying."

"*You're* buying? As in, spending *your* money to buy *me* clothes? What do you want in return?"

He paused. "Nothing."

She eyed him warily. "I don't have to pay you back?"

"That's right."

"I don't believe you."

"Take it or leave it. It's up to you."

By the way her eyes shifted back and forth suspiciously, he knew she smelled a rat, but in order to go shopping right now, she'd probably *eat* a rat.

"I'll take it," she said.

Chapter 10

As John drove his SUV down Central Expressway in the direction of Collin Creek Mall, Darcy couldn't shake the feeling that he was up to something. Not that she minded men buying her things, but John was the last man she'd expected to do that, particularly after what had just happened.

Don't look a gift horse in the mouth.

Still, men like him wouldn't be caught dead in a women's clothing store. If by some wild stretch of the imagination they ended up with a woman at a mall, they hung out in Radio Shack or supersized something at the food court. It was a fact that men who got dragged to malls owned more small electronic devices and had more clogged arteries than anyone else on the planet.

"Hope your credit card is warmed up," Darcy said.

"All I'm spending is a hundred bucks."

Darcy slumped with dismay. So that was why he appeared to be so generous—because he was actually being a tightwad?

"Then what's the point of shopping at all? I need more than a pair of cheap shoes."

"Oh, you'll get more than that. Much more."

He slowed the car, then veered off the freeway onto the service road.

"You got off too soon," Darcy told him. "The mall is two exits away."

"Nope. This is the right exit."

"Now, John. You might be able to find every sports bar and hardware store in the city of Plano, but when it comes to shopping malls, I'm the one who—"

That was when she saw it. Looming like a giant gray monster on the horizon, surrounded by a sea of compact cars, soccer moms, battered shopping carts, and screaming kids. John turned into the parking lot, and Darcy's mouth dropped open.

"You're taking me shopping at *Wal-Mart?*"

"That's right. Damn fine store. If it doesn't have it, you don't need it."

"You don't understand. I need clothes. Not waffle irons and garden tools."

"That reminds me. I need some line for my weed eater."

"Are you trying to be funny?"

"No. I really do need some line for my weed eater."

Darcy looked back at the building, her mouth dry with dread. The closest she wanted to get to this place was to daydream about marrying a cultured descendant of Sam Walton's—one who'd had a prominent place in his last will and testament.

John pulled into a parking space and killed the engine.

"I'm not going in there," Darcy said.

"You know, if you'd bought normal clothes all these

years and saved the rest, you wouldn't be in this mess right now."

"Define 'normal.' "

"Jeans. T-shirts. Stuff like that."

"I have jeans and T-shirts." *Had,* she reminded herself. *Had.* Her whole life was past tense.

"Uh-huh. Jeans that look like Levi's, but because of some initials sewn onto the hip pocket, they cost a hundred bucks."

"A hundred bucks? You're insulting me."

"I think it's time you learned the value of a dollar."

"So you're taking it upon yourself to show me?"

"That's right. A buck goes a whole lot further here than it does at the Galleria."

"How about a compromise? Collin Creek Mall is right down the street."

"Yeah? And how far would a hundred bucks go there?"

Further than at the Galleria, but not by much. *Damn.*

John got out of the car, circled around, and opened her door. Putting his forearm on the roof, he leaned in.

"Time to get real, sweetheart. You're broke, you have no clothes, and I was serious about the swimsuit thing."

"I am *not* shopping in that place."

"Fine. Maybe Neiman Marcus is having a shoe sale. You can buy one for your left foot."

"What if somebody I know sees me in there?"

"Then they're as broke as you are. Now, come on."

She rolled her eyes and got out of the car. John took her by the arm and led her into the store, as if he expected her to bolt at any moment.

"Why is there a cop at the front door?" she asked.

"Because they're expecting you to shoplift."

Once they were inside, Darcy's nose was hit with a bizarre combination of aromas: Popcorn. Garden chemicals. Big Macs. Something was very wrong when all three of those could be inhaled in the same breath. And children were everywhere—running down the aisles, sitting in strollers and screaming, or playing games of whiney emotional blackmail to score supersized boxes of Milk Duds.

John led her past the costume jewelry and the vinyl handbags to the women's clothing department. It was even more horrifying than she'd anticipated. She'd never seen so much cheap polyester in her life. And flowers. The bigger the clothes, the bolder the print. What was *that* all about?

She picked delicately through a rack of cotton shirts. At $4.99 apiece, she could take ten of them and blow only half her budget. Unfortunately, *one* was one too many.

"Nope," John said. "If I'm buying, I get to pick."

"So that's why you offered to foot the bill? So you can tell me what to buy?"

"So I can show you how to get the most for your money. It's a lesson you need to learn."

Okay. Darcy had two choices here. She could throw herself on the mercy of a man to pick out her clothes, a man who wouldn't know haute couture if Versace himself waved it around in front of him.

Or she could have nothing.

"What size do you wear?" John asked.

Darcy sighed with resignation. "Six."

"Hmm," he said as he flipped through the rack. "I'm not seeing many of those."

"No kidding."

He pulled a shirt off the rack and held it up. "Here you go."

"That's hideous."

"It's a perfectly good shirt."

"For my great-grandmother."

"What? You don't like my taste?"

She let her gaze slither down his body and back up again, turning her nose up as if she'd gotten a whiff of dog poop. "Well, you're not exactly GQ material."

"Well, there's that lifelong dream shot to hell." He worked his way through a rack of Capri pants. "Well, now. Aren't these nice?"

He grabbed a pair and held them up. They were pink. No, *pink* didn't begin to describe the color of those pants.

"I can't buy those," Darcy said. "Somebody spilled Pepto-Bismol on them."

"They'll fade in the wash."

"The stitching is crooked."

"I'm not paying enough for it to be straight."

"I hate pink. How about the white ones instead?"

"How about you try on what I give you?"

He shoved the Capris at her. He grabbed two more shirts and a pair of pants, then something off another rack that made Darcy cringe. Had broomstick skirts *ever* been in style?

"Would it be possible," she said, "for you to place that lovely garment back on the rack? I don't want to show up at the soup kitchen wearing the same clothes as another street person, now, do I?"

"Do I need to remind you who's footing the bill?"

With a roll of her eyes, she took the clothes and headed for the dressing room.

"I want to see everything you try on," he called out.

Oh, *God.* Not only did she have to put these awful clothes on, but she had to model them, too?

The counter in the dressing room was serviced by a woman approximately the size and shape of a troll doll, with fiercely frizzed red hair straight from a bottle of Nice 'n Easy. She wore a blue smock and a name badge that read "Twyla."

"How many you got, honey?" she said.

This was beyond humiliating. Darcy was used to a saleswoman escorting her to a private fitting room, where she brought in the latest fashions for her scrutiny, along with a glass of Chardonnay and a deliciously subservient attitude. But here was this woman sorting through the clothes, counting every item to ensure Darcy didn't shoplift.

Shoplift. Good God. If she were inclined to steal, wouldn't she do it from a better place than this?

"You'll like the Capri pants," the old lady said. "Bought some of them myself."

Darcy shuddered. *This is just a bad dream,* she told herself. *You'll wake up in a moment and it'll all be over.*

She put on the pink Capris and the blouse. They fit. Sort of. A puckered seam here, a crooked collar there. She walked out of the dressing room to find John leaning against a wall, his arms folded. He pushed away from the wall and took a step or two toward her, eyeing her critically, then held up his index finger and spun it around. She rolled her eyes and turned in a circle. He put his hand on his chin, narrowing his eyes.

"Not bad."

"Yes, bad."

"Those pants are definitely your color."

"This isn't anybody's color. If you put a chameleon on them, the poor thing would commit suicide."

"They should hold up pretty well in the wash."

"I don't wash. I dry clean."

"Not on your salary, you don't. We'll take it. Go try on some more."

She glared at him. "Doesn't it embarrass you to hang around in a women's clothing department?"

"I grew up with Amy in the house. Nothing embarrasses me where women are concerned."

"I find that hard to believe."

"Shall I go buy some tampons to prove it?"

Darcy had never met a more infuriatingly uncontrollable man in her life.

She headed back to the dressing room and put on another shirt and a pair of pants, which were wrong in every way possible, and trudged back out to where John stood.

"Looks good," he said.

"As long as I'm heading to prison."

"It's perfect for work. Very utilitarian."

With yet another roll of her eyes, she turned back to the dressing room. She went in and out several more times, adding whatever clothes to the pile John directed her to until she had approached the hundred-dollar mark.

"Hold on," John said. "One more thing."

He reached to a nearby rack in an adjoining department and held up one of the most hideous garments Darcy had ever seen: a hot-pink nightgown with feathers around the hem. It looked like a bad Valentine's Day joke.

She stared at him dumbly. "You expect me to try that on?"

"It's pink. Your favorite color. And it's on sale. Seven ninety-nine. Hell of a bargain."

"What happened to utilitarian?"

He gave her a provocative smile. "Some clothes are just for fun."

She yanked it out of his hand and headed for the dressing room again.

"Now you be sure to let me know how it fits," John said. "And details are appreciated."

His smirk of amusement said he was getting a bang out of knocking her exquisite taste in clothing down a peg or two. And he was so smug about shopping in the women's department that she couldn't even embarrass him about that.

Darcy went into the dressing room, tossed the nightgown aside, and started to put her own clothes back on, only to stop short and stare at it again.

Maybe there was a way to knock that smug expression off his face after all.

She put on the nightgown. The hem came to the middle of her thighs, its feathers tickling her legs. It was cut low, but not criminally so, and she showed less skin wearing this than she did wearing a swimsuit. The only law enforcement entity that could legitimately arrest her for wearing this in public was the fashion police.

She opened the door to the dressing room and came slinking out. Fortunately Twyla had left her station to return clothes to racks, so there was nobody around to suggest to her that modeling this particular garment might be a bad idea. She caught sight of John in the electronics department across the aisle. He clearly thought their shopping expedition was over.

Not yet it wasn't.

With a sway of her hips, she moved toward him. Along the way she caught the attention of a thirtysomething man carrying a garden hose and another one pushing a shopping cart containing two giant-sized bags of dog food. They stopped and stared openmouthed. As she drew closer to the electronics counter, the clerk behind it, a gangly young man with braces, looked up. When his eyes widened, John saw his expression and turned around. His jaw dropped.

"Darcy! What are you doing?"

"I'm sorry," she said sheepishly to the other men. "I don't mean to be such an exhibitionist." She nodded toward John. "It's my boyfriend. He told me if I didn't model the clothes I wanted to buy for him, I couldn't have them." She pouted pitifully. "And I really, *really* want this pretty nightie."

"*What?*" John said.

"I believe those were the instructions you gave me."

"Regular clothes! Not lingerie!"

Darcy turned to the men and whispered, "Imagine what it's like when I'm shopping for bras."

"I can imagine that," the clerk said.

"Me, too," said another man.

"Planning on buying any today?" the third one said.

"That's it!" John grabbed Darcy's wrist and dragged her back to the dressing room. He shoved her into the first compartment he came to, followed her inside, and closed the door behind them.

"What the hell do you think you're doing?"

She blinked innocently. "You told me you wanted to see everything I tried on."

"I assumed you had common sense. Clearly that's not the case."

"So you don't like it?" She ran her hands down the sides of the nightgown, then fluffed the feathers with her fingertips. "Personally, I think it's one of your better selections."

"You made me sound like some kind of domineering pervert out there!"

"Just as I suspected. Some things *do* embarrass you." She gave him a sly smile. "Maybe I should put you to the tampon challenge after all."

"Maybe you should stop acting like a fool. When you're dressed like this, do you think you can trust men to behave themselves?"

Darcy narrowed her eyes. "You know, I thought you were being generous. Helping me out a little. Then you bring me to this god-awful place and dress me up like Frump Barbie just so you can laugh your head off."

"And then you come waltzing out in Prostitute Barbie's nightgown."

"You picked it out."

"I picked it out because it was ugly as hell. I wouldn't want to see that thing in private, much less in public."

She gave him a sarcastic smile. "So do you want me to take it off?"

John narrowed his eyes. "You really like to flaunt it, don't you?"

"And you really like to watch me when I do."

She expected an objection to that. It never came.

Instead, he dropped his gaze to her breasts and let it

hover there for several long, tantalizing moments. When he looked up again, something new was stirring in his expression. Just the force of his unspoken message caused her to take an unintentional step back until she felt the coldness of the mirror on her bare shoulders.

"Don't bait me, Darcy," John said, his voice low and charged with intensity. "You're playing with fire."

"So what are you going to do? We're not in your office, which of course is the ideal place for illicit sex. We're at Wal-Mart. That's where you screwed up, John. At least the dressing rooms at Neiman's are carpeted."

"So if we were at Neiman's, we'd be having sex right now?"

"If we were at Neiman's, sex would be the *last* thing on my mind."

"Then maybe I didn't screw up after all."

"In your *dreams,* repo man."

She swiped her hand against his arm to shove him aside, only to have him grab her wrist and pull her back.

"You made a big mistake when you forced me to drag you in here," John said.

"Oh, yeah? Why is that?"

"Because I'm one of those men you can't trust to behave himself."

With that, he slid his other hand around her waist, pulled her up next to him, and smothered her mouth with his. It shocked her so much that her first reaction was to pull away, but she had nowhere to go. John leaned into her, crowding her against the mirror, at the same time he thrust his hand into her hair, crushing it in his fist to hold her in place as his mouth moved over hers. It was a burning, reckless, unrelenting kiss she never would have expected from a man so utterly in control of everything.

But wasn't that what he was doing right now? Taking complete control of *her?*

Anger bubbled up inside her, but she didn't know if she was mad at him for being a presumptuous, clothes-picking, kiss-stealing tyrant, or mad at herself for being so hot for him whether she liked it or not.

So damned hot.

She couldn't deny it. She'd had this in the back of her mind almost from the first moment they met. And now that it was happening, she didn't give a damn about the circumstances.

No. Wrong. Don't you dare give in to this. Somehow, some way, you're going to regret it.

But she was too far gone, and there was no stopping now. She skimmed her hands along his chest to his shoulders, then looped her arms around his neck. He felt so good beneath her hands—so hard and solid and powerful—and just touching him made a tiny moan of satisfaction rise in her throat. She'd lied before. He *was* GQ material, as long as they did a spread of ruggedly sexy men wearing designer birthday suits.

He grasped her thigh just beneath the feathered hem of her gown, and shivers zoomed all the way to her toes. That was no cliché. Her toes felt as if she'd stuck them in an electrical socket. He moved his palm slowly up her thigh, replacing the shivers with heat that seemed to melt right into her bones.

He pulled away until his lips just brushed hers. "You don't know what you do to me," he murmured, his voice a harsh whisper. "God, Darcy, I . . ."

But he didn't finish the thought. He tilted his head and dove in again at a new angle designed to take even more of her mouth with his. *Ahh,* this was what it was like to be kissed by a man who really knew how, how to hold her, how to touch her, how to drown her with feeling. From day one, every interaction between them had been a power struggle of some kind, but now, as she thought about the fourteen long years she'd spent on the receiving end of ordinary, bland, boring kisses, she decided if John wanted to whack her over the head and drag her back to his cave, she'd hand him a club.

Then a thought sparked to life, deep in the back of her mind.

Power struggle?

You don't know what you do to me . . .

Slowly Darcy fought her way back to consciousness, just enough to realize what was happening. That age-old feeling surged through her, an underlying power from all her beauty-queen years that was so strong it superseded everything else.

As soon as she had a man sexually, she had him every other way there was.

She melted away from John and opened her eyes, watching as he opened his and looked down at her with a heavy-lidded expression of pure desire.

"Let's get out of here," he said, the husky tone of his voice telling her exactly where he'd like to go, which was anywhere with a bed. She caressed the back of his neck with her fingertips, leaning in to press her breasts against his chest and turn her lips close to his ear.

"How about some real clothes, John?" she murmured.

"Take me someplace nice. Then we'll go wherever you want to."

John's expression faltered. He blinked, as if trying to get his bearings, then backed away a little, his face suddenly clouded with suspicion.

"So that's the game we're playing?"

Darcy leaned away. "What?"

"Do you intend to spend the rest of your life begging men to throw you a bone?"

"Throw me a . . ." She yanked herself away from him. "Hey, I didn't *ask* you to bring me here! And I didn't ask you to kiss me!"

"But you didn't ask me to stop, did you?"

"Were you looking for a way to recoup that hundred dollars you offered to spend? For all that stunning generosity, you thought I ought to sleep with you?"

"You know better than that," John said hotly. "I offered you a hundred bucks with no strings attached, and I meant it. And that was pretty damned generous, if you ask me. What pisses me off is that you're trying to con me into more."

"Of course I want more! I feel as if I've lost my whole life! And just being in this place makes me feel as if there's no hope of ever getting it back. I've already been humiliated enough for one lifetime, but you're determined to heap on more!"

"I'm trying to *help* you! You're the one who humiliated yourself by walking out of here wearing that thing!"

"I swear to God I'll wear a gunny sack before I take *anything* from you!"

"Right. This coming from a woman who married a wealthy man old enough to be her father. Was that a love match, Darcy? Or did you just like all those expensive things he gave you in return for sex?"

His accusation hit so close to home that Darcy's cheeks flushed with humiliation. "Get out."

"Darcy—"

"I said get *out!*"

He glared at her a moment more, then ripped open the door and stalked out of the dressing room. Shaking with anger, Darcy changed back into the clothes she'd worn into the store. He didn't understand what it was like to have everything, then lose everything. He just didn't. She hated these clothes. She hated this store. She hated what her life had become.

But most of all, she hated John.

She dumped the pile of clothes onto the counter outside the dressing room. Twyla had returned, and her wide-eyed expression said she'd heard every word of their argument, but the fact that she hadn't sent for security told Darcy that she took her entertainment wherever she could get it. John stood outside the dressing room waiting for her, but she didn't even glance in his direction. She just headed for the front of the store.

Without a word, he followed her out to his car. As he stuck the key in the ignition, she ventured a sidelong glance. He wore that stone-faced expression she'd seen dozens of times before, the one that said, *I'm right, you're wrong, and that's that*, which made it clear to Darcy that she was getting no apology from him.

All the way to back to the office, she looked out the passenger window, refusing to speak to him until he pulled into the parking lot and came to a halt next to Gertie.

"I'll see you at work on Monday morning," she told him. "Assuming, of course, that I decide to come back."

She yanked open the car door and got out. She pulled her keys from her purse and opened Gertie's passenger door. John didn't drive away. He just sat there watching her less-than-graceful crawl over the seat to get behind the wheel, and she felt humiliated all over again. But it wasn't until she was out of the parking lot heading for her parents' house that the full extent of the day's disgrace hit her hard.

Yes, she was mad at him. Furious, to be exact. But she was also mad at herself. She'd made a very big mistake. John had given her a hundred bucks. Why had she asked for more? Shouldn't she have known that somehow he'd throw that right back in her face?

She'd told him she didn't know if she was coming back on Monday morning, but in light of this, she didn't know how she could even consider it.

If she were smart, from now on she'd stay as far away from John Stark as possible.

John sat in the parking lot, watching that god-awful car of Darcy's sputter down the street. There was nothing about that woman that didn't infuriate him. Absolutely nothing. But he had to admit that the longer he thought about it, the more his anger faltered.

Yes, she'd asked for more than he'd offered her. Practically threw herself at him to get it. But desperate situations made for desperate people, and Darcy was more desperate than most. And would she even have done that if he hadn't kissed her in the first place?

He couldn't believe it. He'd kissed her. Then essentially propositioned her. Had he actually intended to go through with that? He'd never been dumb about women, so what was the matter with him now?

Grow up. You're forty-two, not seventeen.

The truth was that he'd always felt superior to other men who had no self-control in the presence of a beautiful woman. He was probably the only man on earth who could go into a strip club and come out with dollar bills still in his pocket. Tony—never. He'd convert half his paycheck into thong stuffers.

But Darcy . . . what made her so different?

She was full of sharp edges—the least of which were her sarcastic mouth and her devious mind—but the moment he'd felt her give in and dissolve in his arms, so soft and warm and willing, he'd quite simply lost his mind. He'd felt like a kid who was dying to get laid and didn't much care what he had to do to make it happen.

But that didn't mean she was blameless in this situation. After all, he wouldn't have kissed her if she hadn't provoked him by wearing that slutty little nightgown. What kind of woman walks around in public wearing practically nothing?

Then again, she wouldn't have worn the slutty little nightgown if he hadn't pulled it off the rack in the first place. And he wouldn't have pulled it off the rack in the first place if he'd just let her pick out whatever she wanted.

Unfortunately, as he played the blame game backward, it all ended up squarely back in his lap.

He'd wanted to teach her a lesson. Knock her attitude down a peg or two. But subjecting her to his scrutiny with every piece of clothing she put on had been taking things a little too far. He could have just given her the hundred bucks and let her buy whatever she wanted to. But no. He had to be a bastard about it to make his point. Amy harped on that constantly. Said it was his tragic flaw. He had to inform everyone else of what was wrong with their lives and tell them exactly how to go about improving them. Because, of course, he was such a genius with his own life.

Well, *crap*.

It would probably be best for both of them if he fired her or if she quit and that was the last they ever saw of each other, but still he couldn't shake the feeling that he needed to do something to make this right again. But he didn't have a clue what that might be.

Chapter 11

Maybe you need to try Internet dating," Lyla said. "They say you can search for exactly the kind of man you want. You just tell them you want one with a good job and who makes a lot of money."

Darcy sighed and muted the TV. "I don't think Internet dating is as easy as that, Mom. If it were, every woman on earth would be ordering a rich man."

"Roxanne's daughter found a boyfriend on the Internet."

"You mean the one who stole five thousand dollars from her and went back to his ex-wife?"

"She's a homely girl who dresses funny. That was the best she could do. You have more going for you, as long as you don't let yourself go."

Darcy hit the mute button again and brought the sound back up. God forbid she miss one more moment of *Celebrity Makeovers.* And then when this was over at four o'clock, it was time for a *Wheel of Fortune* marathon on the Game Show Network.

She sighed. Saturday in the Dumphries household was a *very* long day.

But what did it matter? She felt so rotten after what

happened yesterday with John that she didn't feel like doing anything else, anyway. She still hadn't decided if she wanted to go back to work on Monday morning or not. Then again, she wasn't completely sure that, even if she decided to go back, there would still be a job open.

And then she thought about that kiss.

Her eyes drifted closed as she imagined it all over again. That was just her luck these days, wasn't it? To find a man who could kiss like that but who was also the most maddening one she'd ever known.

"My God. Darcy!"

Darcy's eyes snapped open to find her mother leaning close and peering at her hair. Darcy drew back. "What?"

"You have gray showing!"

Darcy sat up straight. "No, I don't."

Lyla grabbed Darcy's chin and turned her head. "Oh, yes, you do. Right there at your temples."

Darcy put her hand to her head. Surely not. She'd missed her regular appointment to have her hair cut and colored last week—these days she was finding it more difficult than usual to spare a hundred and twenty dollars—but she thought she had a little time before the problem became critical.

"You're letting yourself go," Lyla said, panic rising in her voice. "You can't do that. Men don't look twice at women with gray hair."

Darcy ran to the bathroom and peered in the mirror. Her mother was right. She had roots.

She sat down on the toilet lid, her heart thudding, trying not to panic, but it was a hard-won battle. Maybe hats were coming back in style. But even if that were true, she'd have to buy hats. She might as well pay to have her hair colored.

Lyla came to the bathroom door. "I was right, wasn't I?"

"Yes, you were right," Darcy muttered. "What am I going to do? I can't afford to have my hair done."

"Color it yourself. I color mine."

And look how that had turned out.

Her mother had opted for blond at an early age and had never given it up, so getting beneath all the chemicals to discover her real hair color would be like excavating King Tut's tomb. She had the eyebrows of a brunette, the skin tone of a blond, and the personality of a brassy redhead. But the hair itself?

Maybe the world would never know.

"I am *not* coloring it myself," Darcy said.

"Well, fine, Miss Snooty Britches. Go gray. See if I care."

Okay. She had to get a grip here. Since she didn't have highlights, her hair was all one color. Why couldn't she color it herself? As long as she picked out something that was close to her natural hair color, how badly could she screw it up?

She ran to the drugstore, bought hair color in a dark ash brown that promised a hundred percent gray coverage or her money back, then came home and locked herself in the bathroom. It wasn't hard to apply, and thirty minutes later, as she was rinsing it out, she was congratulating herself on this money-saving option. Was it really worth paying a colorist a hundred bucks just to do this? No. Of course it wasn't.

She towel-dried her hair, went to the mirror, and stifled a scream.

This wasn't dark ash brown. This was black. Coal black. Midnight black. Goth black. Black-hole black.

She grabbed the blow dryer, hoping her hair would look lighter once it was dry. It did. By about half a shade. But since it was about three shades darker than her natural color, she still looked undead.

She stared at herself in the mirror, tears coming to her eyes, trying to tell herself it wasn't as bad as she thought. At least not a single strand of gray showed. But that was only because this horrible color had scared away all the surface gray, then seeped into her skull to ferret out any hair that was even *thinking* of looking old.

This was it. Her life was over. She might as well haul out those razor blades. What was the point of going on now? She'd rather be dead than be walking man repellent.

She heard her mother shout from the other room. "Darcy! Come quick!"

"No! I'm never coming out of this bathroom again as long as I live!"

Okay, so she sounded like a thirteen-year-old drama queen, but with hair like this, she was entitled to.

"No!" her mother shouted. "You have to see this!"

Darcy grabbed a towel, wound it around the dye job from hell, and went to the living room, expecting to see the aliens her mother had always believed in making crop circles in the front yard. Instead Lyla held a big, beautiful gold box wrapped with a blue ribbon. Darcy recognized that kind of box. It came from Amaryllis.

"It was just delivered with your name on it," Lyla said. "What do you suppose is in it?"

Her mother set the box down. Darcy opened it, and she couldn't believe what she saw.

Clothes. Gorgeous clothes. Shirts and pants and skirts. Everything she pulled out elicited a gasp from her mother, and Darcy gasped a few times herself. Who in the world could have sent her—

Jeremy. He'd done it again. Only this time he'd graduated from coffee to couture, finally stepping up to the plate with something that was not only useful, but *fashionable*. Beautiful, glorious clothes from her favorite store, in just the colors she loved. How had he known?

"There's no card," Lyla said. "Who do you suppose all this is from?"

"The only man I know right now who can afford to shop at Amaryllis."

Her mother's face went blank for a moment, and then her eyebrows shot up. "Of course! Jeremy Bridges! Oh, my God! This is even better than that coffee he gave you! Do you suppose he's actually getting serious?"

Darcy wanted to believe that. She wanted to believe Jeremy was putting aside his game playing to pursue an actual relationship. She still remembered the sarcastic lilt in his voice when he refused to give her the receipt for the Starbucks card, but maybe this was his way of making up for that.

And maybe not.

"I don't trust him," Darcy said.

"Trust him? Of course you trust him. What's not to trust about any man who gives you beautiful things like this?" She picked up the sleeve of one of the shirts. "The tags have been removed. I wonder how much he spent?"

Darcy wondered, too. Just how far had he gone this time to rattle her cage? If he'd spent a thousand dollars on coffee . . .

"I'll get the catalog. We can add it up." She started to rise, then sat back down again. "Never mind. I left it at the office."

"Then call the store. You know all the staff there. I *have* to know."

Darcy found the number and called the store. Betty came on the line, an older woman who'd worked there since Darcy could remember.

"Hi, Betty. It's Darcy McDaniel."

"Ms. McDaniel! So nice to hear from you. It's been far too long since you've been in."

Darcy loved that fawning attitude. Betty knew how to kiss ass with the best of them.

"I was hoping you could tell me something. A gentleman was in there recently to buy me a gift, and I was wondering—"

Wait a minute. This would get her nowhere. Jeremy wouldn't have come in himself. He would have sent a personal shopper, which would have been a woman, and since dozens of women came in there every day, would Betty even have known . . .

"Oh, yes," Betty said. "A gentleman certainly was in here last night. I assume you got the delivery today?"

So Jeremy had actually come in there himself? The very thought of that put a smile on Darcy's face.

"Yes," Darcy said. "I just received it. Uh . . . Betty? Just between you and me . . ."

"Yes?"

"How much did he spend?"

"Hmm . . . I don't remember exactly. Let me look."

A minute later she came back on the phone, her voice

low and confidential. "Three hundred and eighty-four dollars."

Darcy felt a shot of disappointment. He'd spent only three hundred and eighty-four dollars on clothes when he'd gone a full thousand on coffee?

"That's all?" she said.

"Storewide clearance sale," Betty added.

Thank God. That explained the pitiful price tag. "Did he say anything about me when he was in there?"

"No, not really. Actually, he didn't talk much at all. He brought one of our catalogs in, opened it, and pointed to what he wanted."

Darcy blinked. "What?"

"And he kept saying, 'No pink. She doesn't like pink.' He wouldn't even consider mauve or rose."

Darcy froze. It couldn't be.

For a moment she just stood there, gripping the phone, as her mind circled back to her Wal-Mart shopping excursion. Only two men on earth knew she hated pink. One of them had skipped the country.

The other one was John.

On Monday morning, John arrived at work just after eight o'clock, relieved to see Darcy's car there. At least she'd shown up today, which meant it was possible she wasn't going to hate him for the rest of her life.

He went inside the building. She wasn't at her desk, but he saw a light on in the storeroom and figured she was in there getting supplies or fishing through old records. He went to the coffeepot for a shot of caffeine, then headed to his office. He still didn't know how she was going to react to everything, and he wasn't sure he wanted to know.

Don't say a word if she doesn't. Just go about your business as usual.

That was hard to do, though, when he was still reeling from his traumatic experience on Friday night. The Galleria was every woman's dream and every man's nightmare, one of those malls where everybody dresses up to go shopping and they charge you to breathe the air. Fortunately, there had been a big sale at that ridiculous store Darcy loved, so he'd been able to buy more with less. He'd grabbed that catalog from her desk that he'd seen her browsing through at lunch. Even though at this point in her life it was nothing but a wish book, still she'd circled several items she liked, so those were the ones he'd bought. The whole time his mind had been screaming that it was a waste of money, but he just hadn't been able to stop himself.

He discovered a woman's clothing store was like a grocery store, because pink really wasn't pink. It was *shrimp.* Purple was *eggplant.* Green was *kiwi.* And yellow could either be *banana* or *lemon,* depending on how loud a yellow it was. The saleswoman kept offering him all these choices, and in the end he'd simply told her if it was circled in the catalog, it was a size six, and it wasn't *shrimp,* to stick it in a shopping bag.

Then he handed the salesclerk his credit card and pretended he really wasn't spending such an outrageous amount of money. He was a man who was careful about the disposition of every dime he made, but he'd had to cough up nearly four hundred dollars before his conscience had even begun to leave him alone. By the time he left the store, he'd actually broken a sweat. He never spent that much money all in one place unless it was a gun shop, an electronics counter, or a car dealership.

He only hoped she'd see the clothes as the peace offering they were and not flip out and tell him again that she refused to take anything he gave her. He had no idea what he'd do if she did *that* again.

He turned on the light in his office, and the first thing he saw was an envelope in the middle of his desk. Curious, he set down his mug and opened it. It contained cash. A lot of cash. He counted it and got a shock.

Three hundred and eighty-four dollars?

Just then, the door to the storeroom opened and Darcy came out. She was carrying a few office supplies, which she deposited on her desk. Her hair seemed different today. Darker, maybe? Maybe not. Finally he just decided it looked different because she had it in a ponytail instead of down around her shoulders. And her clothes . . .

Wait a minute. This wasn't what he'd bought for her. Instead, she wore a pair of white pants that fit a little awkwardly and a knit shirt exactly like ones he'd seen recently that were priced two for ten dollars.

Slowly the truth came to him. She wasn't wearing Donna Whozits or Calvin Whatever.

She was wearing Sam Walton.

She went to the coffeepot to pour herself a cup. He left his office and grabbed a stack of repossession orders from the top of a file cabinet. He mumbled a "good morning," and she mumbled one back. He pretended to thumb through the stack while she wiped stray drops of water off the table where the coffeepot sat, but soon he couldn't stand the silence any longer.

"You returned the clothes," he said.

She paused. "Yes."

"You didn't have the receipt."

"They know me there."

John nodded. "The shirt you're wearing now is nice."

"Thank you. I do love wearing popular styles. As it turns out, one of my mother's friends has one just like it."

"And the pants. I see you bypassed the pink ones."

"When it's my dime, I can buy whatever I want to."

Which made him wonder where she'd gotten the money, since she'd returned to him all the money he'd spent. Then he looked down at her left hand.

Her wedding ring was gone.

When he met her eyes again, it was clear she'd seen him staring. She turned away, straightening the coffee and filters and stir sticks for the third time. "It didn't go with my wardrobe anymore. Nothing's worse than wearing overstated jewelry with . . ." She stopped and looked down at herself. "Understated clothes."

What she didn't mention was that she'd pawned that overstated jewelry to get the money to buy the understated clothes it didn't go with.

"I thought you hated Wal-Mart," he said.

"I do. I thought you hated high-priced clothing stores."

"I do."

"So why did you go there?" Darcy asked.

"Temporary insanity. Why did you cash it all in for a return trip to Wal-Mart?"

She gave him a chastising look. "John. How else am I supposed to teach you the value of a dollar?"

She turned and walked back to her desk, and John felt

something shift inside him, and suddenly he was filled with a new kind of awareness he hadn't expected. *She's more than you thought she was. A whole lot more.*

"Oh," she said. "I almost forgot."

She pulled something from a small sack on her desk and tossed it to him. He caught it on the fly.

A package of weed eater line?

Darcy met his gaze for a moment, cracked a tiny smile, then sat down at her desk to get to work.

John knew the moment she found another rich man, she'd be back to her old habits again, dressing in outrageously priced clothes. But just for now . . .

She would have looked like a million bucks in those clothes from Amaryllis, but somehow, in the clothes from Wal-Mart, she looked like a million and one.

～

When Darcy had worn expensive clothes and her hair had been just the right color, all John had ever done was grump at her. Now that she was wearing cheap clothes and had hair only Morticia Adams could love, he seemed pleased. She wasn't sure she understood that completely, but she could tell that her second trip to Wal-Mart had changed the way John looked at her, and she was surprised at how good that made her feel.

Tony showed up about eight-thirty, coasting by with his usual grin and cheery "Good morning." He went to his desk, took out his phone, and had a hush-hush conversation with a person who was clearly of the opposite sex. Tony was one of those men a woman couldn't help liking, and Darcy could only imagine how many broken hearts he'd left in his wake.

Amy arrived next and complimented Darcy on her new clothes, because that was what nice women did whether they liked what you were wearing or not. Then her gaze drifted up to Darcy's hair, and a look of distress came over her face.

"Oh, sweetie," she whispered. "What happened?"

Darcy closed her eyes. "Is it that obvious? I thought since John and Tony didn't say anything, maybe it didn't look so bad."

"Men are oblivious. Did the color kick in a little too much?"

"A little? I look like Elvira, Mistress of the Dark."

"Did you try to do something about it?"

"I can't afford to have somebody fix it."

Amy smiled. "Don't worry. I know how to fix it."

Darcy brightened. "You do? How?"

"Last year I dyed my hair auburn. Or, at least, I thought it was going to be auburn. I ended up looking like Raggedy Ann. So I got on the Internet and found some stuff that'll lift out permanent color. I still have some left."

"So it really works?"

"Like a charm."

"Can you bring it in tomorrow?"

"Sweetie, this is a crisis. Come home with me at lunch. We'll fix it today."

When noontime came, Darcy and Amy dropped by Taco Hut to pick up some burritos, then went to Amy's apartment. It was a small one-bedroom, but it was in a nice complex near the mall with a fountain out front, a clubhouse, and a nice swimming pool. A few months ago, Darcy would have thought it was painfully modest. Given where she was living now, it felt like heaven on earth.

True to Amy's word, the stuff to fix Darcy's hair worked. After only five minutes, it lifted out most of the color she'd put on, but the gray was still mostly masked. It was still darker than her natural color, but at least she no longer looked like a creature of the night.

"Your hair must pick up color really easily," Amy told her. "Next time get a lighter shade and don't leave it on so long."

Darcy nodded. Lesson learned. Now that she knew of something that would fix any goofs she happened to make, she wasn't so afraid of doing her hair herself.

With the hair-color crisis averted, they reheated the burritos and sat down to eat. Darcy wouldn't ever have thought it, but she really enjoyed being with Amy. She was smart and cute and down-to-earth, one of those sun-shiny women for whom the glass was always half full. When Darcy thought about how few people in her life fit that description, she realized how much she'd been missing. Carolyn was meek and neurotic, and the rest of the women she knew were either sarcastic or conceited, sometimes both at the same time.

"Work has been interesting today," Amy said.

"Really? Why?"

"Something's different between you and John."

At that out-of-the-blue statement, Darcy's heart skipped. "What makes you say that?"

"You weren't sniping at each other this morning."

"We weren't? Oh. Well, I'll have to make a concerted effort to be more sarcastic this afternoon. It is part of my job description."

"It's part of John's, too, but he sure is falling down on the job. When you gave him the morning report, he actually smiled at you."

"Did he? I must have blinked and missed it."

"He watches you all the time, you know."

Darcy rolled her eyes. "I know. Tony's the same way. A woman walks by, and their eyes follow. It's a man thing."

"Nope. There's more to it than that."

"Amy? What are you trying to say?"

"Nothing, really. I've just never seen my brother act this way around a woman. John's very methodical. His eyes don't generally go wandering around of their own accord. But lately they've had a life all their own." She paused. "So have yours."

"Amy!"

"Okay, okay. So don't tell me what's going on. I'll get the scoop from John."

"John won't tell you a thing."

"So there's something to tell?"

"No!" Darcy huffed with irritation. "Tell me the truth. Have you ever seen two people more wrong for each other than John and me?"

"It sure does look that way, doesn't it? But sometimes two wrongs *do* make a right."

No. They were oil and water. Fire and ice. Night and day. Immovable object and irresistible force. Two vastly different people who would only end up making each other miserable.

Wouldn't they?

Yes. Of course they would. And there was nothing more to be said about it.

As they finished lunch, Darcy found herself looking around Amy's place with an advanced case of apartment envy. She thought about the perpetual cloud of cigarette smoke in her parents' house that was sending her mother down the road to lung cancer. She thought about the blaring NASCAR races her father watched. She thought about Pepé peeing on the rug and her mother shouting. But most of all, she thought about how living with her parents was a horrible reminder of what she was going to become if she didn't get out of there, and fast.

"Do you like living here?" Darcy asked.

"Yeah," Amy said. "It's nice."

"How much is a one-bedroom apartment?"

"Seven hundred a month."

Darcy's hope sank. "That much? How can you afford that?"

"I saved up money before I quit my full-time job to go back to school. Are you looking for an apartment?"

"Not at that price."

"Don't worry. This place has a lot of frills. That's why it's kinda expensive. You can find an apartment cheaper than this."

"How much cheaper?"

"Depends on where the apartment is."

Darcy had a terrible feeling that meant east Plano.

She had a paycheck coming on Friday. With luck, that along with the money she had left after pawning her wedding ring would probably pay her first month's rent and a deposit on a modest apartment. Probably an extremely modest apartment. But it didn't matter. Anything that wasn't her parents' house would seem like a dream come true.

Come Saturday, she was going to find herself a new place to live.

Chapter 12

Darcy had no idea how difficult finding an apartment was going to be. She had to immediately strike at least a dozen complexes from consideration because they were just too expensive. Those that were left weren't exactly beautiful, and even they had standards she was having a hard time living up to. She'd worn some of the clothes from her old life that she'd taken with her to Mexico, trying to look like a woman of means, but to her surprise, her designer clothes and accessories hadn't impressed a single one of the apartment managers.

Loreli Apartments pointed out her stunning lack of credit, since not one credit card in fourteen years had been in her name. Woodlawn Village said her lack of employment history was a problem, but after she'd been on the job for six months, they might be able to rent to her. One particularly creepy assistant manager at Forest Villa suggested that if they became very close friends very quickly, maybe he could persuade the manager to overlook the deficits in her application. She informed him that she'd rather sleep in her car than sleep with him, a remark that became even more deliciously scathing when he looked out the window and saw what lovely condition that particular car was in.

Creekwood Apartments was just about her last hope.

She drove into the parking lot, wondering where that name had come from. There was no creek, and there were no woods. Creepwood might have made better sense, judging from the people she saw loitering around. Or just plain Crapwood.

She pulled into a parking space between a red Chevy that had a couple of dented fenders and an ancient Lincoln Continental with fuzzy dice hanging from the rearview mirror. Where, exactly, did one go to buy a pair of those?

Darcy went into the manager's office, a dreary place with dollar-store art, fake potted plants, and glaring fluorescent lighting. A large, unpleasant-looking woman sat slumped behind the desk wearing a pair of navy-blue stretch pants and a smock top. Her chair was turned around so she could see the portable television on top of a nearby file cabinet, which was tuned to a *Brady Bunch* rerun.

She turned around as Darcy approached.

"Hello," Darcy said. "I'm looking for a—"

Darcy stopped short, stunned into silence. She knew that face. At least, she had twenty years ago.

Charmin Brubaker?

No. It couldn't be. The Charmin she remembered from high school may have been a screaming bitch, but she'd also been bone-thin and knew how to dress. This woman had hair like a Brillo pad, wrinkles like a bloodhound, and a 3X body stuffed inside 2X pants. No *way* could this be Charmin.

But it was.

In the blink of an eye, Darcy was transported back twenty-two years to high school, an era that hadn't exactly been known for its sweetness and light. Charmin had never liked anyone prettier or more popular than she was, which meant she had really hated Darcy. The bickering and backstabbing escalated over the years to culminate in the ultimate showdown: the race for prom queen their senior year. Darcy had taken great delight in winning that battle then. She only hoped Charmin wasn't going to take great delight in denying her an apartment now.

"Why, Charmin!" Darcy said with a bright smile. "It's been such a long time! Imagine running into you!"

As soon as recognition registered in Charmin's eyes, her lip curled into a subtle sneer. "Yeah. Imagine that."

Darcy had hoped Charmin's looks were gone because she had traded them in for a pleasant personality, one that had allowed her to let go of any lingering grudges she happened to be holding on to.

No such luck.

Charmin eyed her up and down. "What are you doing here?"

Darcy wanted to say she'd lost her way in a bad neighborhood and had stopped to ask directions, but the truth was all she had.

"I'm looking for an apartment."

Charmin drew back suspiciously. She knew something was up. And the last thing Darcy wanted was to delve into what that something was.

"You want to live here?" Charmin said. "Why?"

"Well . . . why not?"

There were about a hundred reasons why not, but since

Charmin probably lived there herself, she couldn't voice any of them without admitting she lived in a dump. She sat back in her squeaky chair, steepling her sausagelike fingers together, her eyes flicking to Darcy's left hand.

"Heard you married some rich old guy. What happened with that?"

"We're no longer together."

"Hmm. Too bad. What did you do? Blow the whole settlement?"

Darcy lifted her chin a notch. "Do you have an apartment available or not?"

Charmin narrowed her lying eyes. "No."

"The sign out front says you do."

"I might have one unit left. But it's only one bedroom."

"That's fine."

"It's by the pool."

"Good. I love to sunbathe."

"That's where all the loud parties are."

"Not a problem. I like a festive atmosphere."

"There's a registered sex offender in the same building."

"I have pepper spray."

"Rumor has it the tenants next door are running a meth lab."

Darcy drew back. "And you haven't reported them?"

Charmin shrugged. "No grounds for a search warrant yet. And they pay their rent on time."

Darcy waited for Charmin to add that somebody had been murdered there in a satanic ritual or that the tenant upstairs was a suicidal pyromaniac. Finally, though, she pushed her considerable bulk out of her squeaky chair and grabbed a key from a board on the wall behind her. Darcy followed her out of the office.

They walked through the complex, Darcy sidestepping cracks in the sidewalk so large they could swallow a small child. And through it all, she could feel the loathing rolling off Charmin like sweat off a prizefighter. But at the heart of it was nothing more than a bad case of envy. She quite simply hated the fact that she had a face full of wrinkles and a butt the size of Wisconsin and her old nemesis didn't.

Suddenly a door across the parking lot opened, and a large woman appeared wearing a bright purple peignoir. She had Texas big hair, teased and bleached to within an inch of its life.

"Charmin!" she shouted. "You gonna get my garbage disposal fixed, or what?"

"I told you the repairman will be out tomorrow!"

"That's what you told me two days ago!"

"He'll be there when he gets there!"

The woman rolled her eyes and slammed her door.

"Well," Darcy said, a little horrified, "she seems like an interesting woman. Lovely peignoir."

"Evidently she's working today."

"Working?"

"She's a massage therapist. How much money she makes depends on what a man wants massaged."

"She's very . . . large."

"That's because Georgette used to be George."

A transsexual hooker. Now Darcy had heard it all.

Charmin turned into the breezeway of one of the buildings, where a pair of broken flower pots sat beside a rusty bicycle.

Ignore that. They're outside your apartment, not inside.

Across the breezeway, Darcy heard a door creak open. Turning, she saw a tall, gangly man wearing a pair of tattered gym shorts and no shirt. He had several days' growth of beard and probably hadn't showered in recent memory. A cigarette hung from his lower lip, burned almost down to the filter. He peered through the crack, shifting his eyes back and forth between her and Charmin as if he were following a Ping-Pong match.

"Nothing to look at here, Bob," Charmin said curtly. "Go back inside."

His eyes moved madly for a few more seconds, then locked onto Darcy's. She'd seen eyes like those before. On *America's Most Wanted*. Finally he shut the door again and locked it.

"Who was that?" Darcy said.

"Crazy Bob."

"Why do you call him Crazy Bob?"

"Because he thinks government satellites are reading his mind."

"Is he the sex offender?"

"Nah. He's a school teacher."

School teacher? Well, at least that explained why Johnny couldn't read. Courtesy of Crazy Bob, though, Johnny could probably spin a hell of a conspiracy theory.

"I assume he's harmless?" Darcy asked.

"Nothing yet," Charmin said. "But you might want to hang on to that pepper spray until he gets his meds straightened out again."

Charmin pushed open the door to apartment 827, and Darcy followed her inside, hoping for the best but ready to accept the worst.

And there it was. The worst.

The disinfectant smell in the air said that someone had at least attempted to clean the unit, but lack of a spit-polished sparkle was the least of its problems. The kitchen, just off the short entry hall, had marble-patterned laminate countertops dotted with cigarette burns, and the stainless-steel sink had lost its luster years ago. The appliances looked like the ones they gave away on *The Newly-wed Game* in the 1960s. They were that color they called *avocado*. They should have called it *bile*. And she guessed she had a linoleum allergy, because the moment she felt that ugly crap beneath her feet, her eyes teared up.

"All the appliances come with the unit," Charmin said. "Even the washer and dryer. You don't get those every day."

And most particularly not ones like these. Dented, dinged, and decrepit.

They went into the living room to find banged-up woodwork and miniblinds hanging askew. The green carpet was so ratty it looked as if a cat had clawed up a miniature golf course.

Charmin led her down the hall to another room.

"Well," Darcy said, "this is a nice closet."

"It's the bedroom," Charmin snapped.

Charmin was sarcasm impaired. Always had been. Darcy had spent four years in high school messing with her mind, during those few times when she could find her mind to mess with it. It had been wonderful recreation back then, but somehow over the years the fun quotient had slipped a little.

And then there was the bathroom. More ugly linoleum, cigarette burns, and beat-up blinds. *Dear God, I can't live in this place!*

"How much?" she asked.

"Five hundred a month," Charmin said, and Darcy swore it sounded like five gazillion. Still, it was the cheapest thing she'd found. Unfortunately, there was a reason for that.

"Pets?"

"Small dogs only. Cats claw the drapes. Three-hundred dollar deposit."

So there it was. Five gazillion for the monthly rent, three gazillion to keep Pepé. She decided right then that what Charmin didn't know wouldn't hurt her. She might not know Darcy had a dog as long as she kept the blinds closed and was careful when and where she walked him. If she got caught, *then* she'd deal with the deposit issue.

"Never mind," Darcy said. "My ex will take the dog."

Yeah, right. Like Warren would be resurfacing for custody of an animal he'd never liked in the first place.

Back at the manager's office, Darcy filled out an application and handed it to Charmin.

"You're working for a repossession service?" Charmin asked.

No way to gloss over that. "Yes."

"You say you're the office manager."

Her job title was technically *Peon,* but Charmin didn't need to know that. "That's right."

"How about references?"

The same questions she'd gotten everywhere else. "I've never rented an apartment before."

"Is there anyone who can attest to your financial responsibility?"

Darcy opened her mouth to speak, realized she didn't have anything to say, and closed it again.

Charmin gave her a sigh of phony regret. "You're not giving me much to go on here. We only rent to responsible people."

"Come on, Charmin. I saw what's wandering around this complex. You're telling me they're all upstanding citizens?"

"I'll need first and last month's rent, plus a security deposit."

"I have that." Barely. It had amazed Darcy just how little she could get for a ring that was worth so much.

"Your application says you've been on your job only a few weeks. And it's your only one in fourteen years."

"Come on, Charmin. I'm in a bad spot here. Can you give me a break?"

Charmin's expression turned smug. "Maybe." She looked down at Darcy's feet. "Hmm. Nice shoes."

Darcy was used to women looking at her with shoe envy. But Charmin's eyebrows moved with a weird kind of cattiness Darcy couldn't quite read.

"So you're what?" Charmin said. "A size seven?"

"Six."

"Hmm." Bitchy smile. "So am I."

Light dawned slowly on that, but when it did, Darcy went on red alert. "What are you saying?"

"I'll give you what you want. As long as I get something I want."

"You think you're getting my *shoes?*" Darcy made a truly inelegant noise. "You're not getting my shoes."

"Oh, yeah? Then you're not getting the apartment."

"You've got to be joking."

"Do I look like I'm joking?"

Darcy looked at that face. Nope. No levity there. What

kind of person held a dumb high school grudge for twenty-two years?

One whose mother had named her after toilet paper.

In a fit of disgust, Darcy yanked off her shoes and kicked them over to Charmin, who collected them and put them behind her desk.

"Okay," Charmin said, turning back to the application. "Now, about the matter of credit references . . ." Charmin's gaze drifted to Darcy's lap. "Nice bag."

No. Charmin was *not* getting her Biasia bag. Darcy eased it protectively out of sight. "It's a knockoff."

"No, it's not. If it was a knockoff, you wouldn't be trying to hide it."

Thinking just her shoes would appease Charmin was like tossing a single dog biscuit to the Hound of Hell and expecting entry into the Netherworld.

"Does the owner of this place know you're an extortionist?" Darcy asked.

"I can commit murder as long as I keep the occupancy rate up and the delinquency rate down."

Darcy stood up, turned her purse upside down, spilled its contents onto Charmin's desk, and slammed the purse down beside them.

"There. It's all yours."

Charmin gave her a catty smile of satisfaction. "Oh, my. You need something to put your things in, don't you?" She fished through a lower desk drawer and offered Darcy a choice of solutions. She nodded to her right hand. "Paper?" Then her left. "Or plastic?"

Darcy ripped the plastic bag out of Charmin's hand and stuffed the contents of her purse into it, taking comfort in the fact that the woman didn't stand a chance of looking stylish no matter what she wore. Draping a Biasia bag over her shoulder and putting Claudia Ciutis on her feet was like putting a silver-trimmed saddle on a big fat mule.

Darcy slid the money across the desk, then reached for the lease copy and the key, but Charmin slid it out of her grasp. Then she leaned in and lowered her voice. "Spill it, Darcy. How'd you go from living high on the hog to living in a place like this? There's gotta be a story there."

"It's none of your business."

"Did you sign one of those pesky prenups? End up with nothing?"

"Actually, I didn't know what nothing was until I pulled into the parking lot of this place."

"And yet here you are." Charmin leaned back with a smug expression. "The bigger they are, the harder they fall, huh?"

Darcy grabbed the plastic grocery bag, her copy of the lease and the key, and left the office to the sound of Charmin snickering behind her. Every time she thought she'd been humiliated as much as was humanly possible, it happened all over again.

She got into Gertie and sat there for a moment, tears filling her eyes. How had this happened to her? How?

All she wanted was to go back home again. She wanted to sit on the chintz sofa in her family room and watch *Oprah* by the light streaming through her palladium windows. She wanted to have her friends over and gossip about whoever wasn't there. She wanted to do lunch at outrageously expensive restaurants with elegant menu items like truffled risotto and crème fraîche, then flip out her platinum AmEx and tip generously.

But mostly she wanted to invite Warren into a dark alley and act out her castration fantasies.

Fueled by that thought, she decided she wasn't going to give in. Someday, some way, she was going to get back on top again. And the most beautiful fantasy of all was that Jeremy Bridges would reappear, stop playing games, fall madly in love with her, and put a ring on her finger. When that happened, she was going to go back into that apartment office, wave the ring under Charmin's nose, blind her with the refraction of the light as it bounced off that hefty stone, and watch her entire body go green with envy.

Then she thought about John.

The memory of that kiss still made her face hot. Ever since she'd realized he was the one who'd bought her those clothes, he looked different to her, like a man who might actually have a heart beneath that gruff exterior. But hearts didn't pay the bills, and if she judged men on whether or not they could kiss, she'd be broke for the rest of her life.

⁓

"I still don't know what to do about that Corvette," Amy said, sticking her head into John's office. "If he doesn't drive it to work or anywhere else regularly and keeps it in that garage when he isn't driving it, there's not much you can do but stake him out."

John tossed his pen on the desk. "I don't want to take the time right now. It hasn't been delinquent that long."

And truth be told, John still had a bad taste in his mouth

about that one. After all, how many times in three years had he actually put a car *back?*

"What about the Infiniti?" Amy said, taking a seat in the chair in front of his desk. "I thought you had that one."

"It was blocked at the curb with a car on either end. The owner wouldn't come to the door. I'll have to go to the guy's office tomorrow morning."

"He works in Arlington. That's nearly fifty miles from here."

"I've driven farther to pick up a car."

Amy gave him a sly smile. "I just didn't think you'd want to be out of the office that long."

"Why not?"

"If you're not here, you can't engage in your new favorite recreation."

"What's that?"

"Staring at Darcy."

John looked away. "You know she's not my type."

"Come on, John. Men practically break their necks doing double takes at her. I can't imagine a man whose type she *wouldn't* be."

"Looks aren't everything. You know how I hate high-maintenance women."

"Maybe. But I've seen the way you look at her."

"Are you sure you're not thinking of Tony?"

"Nope. He backed away from her right off the bat."

"Wrong. Tony doesn't think *any* woman is off limits."

"Now, John. Even he's smart enough to know that you don't mess with the boss's girl."

"Amy, don't you have somebody else you can irritate?"

"Hey, you harass me all the time about the men I date."

"And you harass me about the women I don't date," John said.

"You'd be a lot happier if you had a woman in your life."

"I have plenty of women in my life."

"Yeah, for one night each. You pick a woman to death. Nobody's ever good enough for you."

"That's not true."

"Sure it is. How about Jennifer? Remember her?"

Yeah, he remembered her. Big eyes, big boobs, and a big space between her ears. She tended bar at McMillan's. While Tony had been hitting on one of the waitresses, Jennifer had hit on John. They'd dated exactly three weeks before he couldn't take it anymore.

"You dumped her because she didn't know the name of the first man to walk on the moon," Amy said.

"The woman had never watched a documentary in her life. She watched Saturday morning cartoons and *America's Funniest Home Videos*."

The truth was that most women eventually bored him. They all smiled the same, talked the same, looked the same. If he hung around long enough, they eventually became clingy. And every last one of them had marriage on their minds.

But Darcy . . .

She might have marriage on her mind, but not to a man like him. And he couldn't imagine her ever being clingy. Bossy and belligerent, maybe, but not clingy. But different wasn't necessarily good, was it?

Then again, maybe it was. Every day was a new day

with her. He never knew what to expect. Yeah, she was marginally insane, but at least crazy beat boring.

Just then the outer door opened, and Darcy came into the office. She wore a flowered skirt from Wal-Mart, one he'd originally picked off the rack, and a knit top that clung to her breasts and highlighted every curve. When she looked that good wearing cheap clothes, he couldn't imagine why she'd want to waste money on the upscale stuff.

"See what I mean?" Amy said.

John slowly dragged his eyes away. "Huh?"

"You're staring at her again."

"I wasn't staring."

Amy rolled her eyes.

Darcy reached for a pen, scribbled something on a notepad, then came into John's office.

"I rented an apartment this weekend," she said. "This is my new address. I'm sure you'll want to update your personnel records."

He looked at the address and felt a shot of trepidation. "That's Creekwood Apartments."

"Yes. I'm moving in on Saturday."

"It's a hellhole."

"Yeah, but at least it's *my* hellhole."

"I worked that neighborhood as a patrol cop. It's full of scum. You can't live there."

"Sorry, John. It's a done deal."

"Why don't you just keep on staying with your parents?"

"You haven't met my parents, or you wouldn't ask that."

"Darcy, I'm telling you—"

"Hey! Are you offering to raise my salary three hundred dollars a month so I can live someplace decent?"

"Uh . . . no."

"Then I don't want to hear any more about it."

With that, she raised her chin in that irritating way she had of telling him the case was closed, then left his office and went back to her desk.

"See what I mean?" John said. "She's nuts."

Amy shook her head. "Sometimes you're so blind it scares me."

"What are you talking about?"

"First you bash her because she's helpless and high maintenance. And now, when she's finally trying to do something for herself, you bash her all over again."

"But that place is dangerous."

"True. But give her a few points for trying, will you?"

It just drove him nuts when people did dumb things, and he generally felt obligated to tell them about it. But this was one woman who wouldn't listen if he told her to pull her head out of a lion's mouth.

He didn't know who'd be crazy enough to take the job, but sooner or later somebody needed to save that woman from herself.

Chapter 13

The next Saturday morning, Darcy put on a pair of shorts and a T-shirt, stuck her hair in a ponytail, and got down to the business of making her new apartment livable. She had decided to rent a minimal amount of furniture for the first few months until she could collect enough hand-me-downs and garage sale items to furnish the place. Once that was delivered, she ran to Wal-Mart to get glasses, silverware, bed linens, cleaning supplies, dog food, and a couple of sacks of groceries. Her mother gave her an old set of stoneware and a few pots and pans. A microwave was going to have to come after her next paycheck.

By that evening, she had actually created something resembling a place a person could live. As the sun began to go down, the natural light in the apartment dimmed, and if she squinted, she could almost make herself believe her living room looked homey. Pepé wasn't too sure about the new place, though, spending most of his time under the bed. He'd get used to it eventually. At least she hoped he would. Anything that made Pepé nervous generally resulted in excessive urination in all the wrong places.

Darcy had just started thinking about hitting a Taco Hut drive-through for dinner when there was a knock at her door. She looked out the peephole to find her parents standing in the breezeway. Evidently her father had gotten home from the shop, and her mother had insisted on coming by. Great. She'd moved out to get away from them, and here they were again.

She swung open the door. As they came inside, Lyla looked back over her shoulder. "My God. Who is that awful man in the apartment across from you?"

"Crazy Bob," Darcy said.

Lyla's hand slipped to her throat. "Why do they call him Crazy Bob?"

"Because he thinks government satellites are reading his mind."

"Oh! You know, I read something about that in the *National Enquirer.* They beam all sorts of things into a person's head." She gave Darcy a knowing look. "He might not be as crazy as you think."

"Nope," Clayton said. "He's definitely as crazy as you think."

"Oh, yeah?" Lyla said. "You wait until the government fills *your* brain with microwaves. We'll see who's the smart one then."

"So what do you think, Dad?" Darcy said. "Is this a gorgeous apartment, or what?"

Clayton gave the apartment a cursory once-over, the part he could see from the front door, anyway. "It's a roof over your head. Rangers are on the radio. I'll be in the car."

Well, at least her father thought it was okay. Then again, Gertie was his idea of an acceptable mode of transportation, too, so what did that say about his opinion?

Lyla walked into the living room, and her face crinkled with disgust. "This furniture is awful."

"Rental furniture doesn't tend to be attractive."

"The blinds are bent."

"I'm lucky there are any at all."

"And look at this dreadful carpet."

"It has plenty of old stains, so any new ones won't show."

"Darcy, why did you insist on moving? You could have stayed with us as long as you needed to."

Not and keep my sanity. "I just needed my own place."

"What is a man going to think when he comes here to pick you up for a date?"

Darcy closed her eyes with frustration. Well, at least there was one good thing about her mother coming for a visit. It gave Darcy the absolute assurance that getting a place of her own had been the right thing to do.

Then she heard another knock at the door. She went back to the entry hall and looked out the peephole. She blinked with surprise. Blinked again. Was that who she thought it was?

"It's Jeremy Bridges," she told her mother.

Lyla's jaw dropped. "Jeremy Bridges is here? *Now?*"

"Yes."

"You can't let him in," her mother said. "The moment he sees this apartment, he'll turn right around and leave again. He'll be gone, Darcy. Don't you dare open that door!" Then she grabbed Darcy's arm. "No. Wait. On second thought, you have to. If he made it through the front gate and wasn't scared off . . ." Then she groaned. "My God! Look at you! You're a mess!"

She pulled the elastic out of Darcy's hair.

"Mom! What are you—"

"Be still." She fluffed Darcy's hair around her shoulders. "There's nothing you can do about what you're wearing. Just be sure to stand up straight." She shook her finger at Darcy. "And don't screw this up!"

With a roll of her eyes, Darcy opened the door. Through the peephole she hadn't gotten a good look at Jeremy, but now that she did, she couldn't believe the transformation.

Gone was the Hawaiian grunge look. Instead he wore a pair of khaki pants, a Lacoste shirt, and loafers. Casual yet stylish. It looked as if he'd gotten a haircut. A shave. In one hand he carried a basket wrapped in blue-tinted cellophane and topped with a satin bow. She had no idea what *that* was all about.

Now that they were both standing, she had to look up to meet his eyes—sharp, intelligent, nothing-gets-past-me eyes she'd been wary of from the first time she'd climbed into his limousine.

And then there was that smile.

"Hello, Darcy."

"Hello, Jeremy." She eyed him up and down. "Was a trip to Margaritaville not on the agenda today?"

"This is millionaire casual. I thought you'd enjoy the look."

Actually, she did. What woman wouldn't? But even though he had the money of a millionaire, he was someone else at heart.

In the distance, Darcy saw the tail end of his limousine inching away, the driver probably looking for a place to park. Her advice: west Plano.

She glanced around warily. "So where's your guard dog?"

"I persuaded Bernie to stay in the car. But don't worry. I cracked the windows."

"Darcy!" her mother said. "Don't just stand there! Invite Mr. Bridges in!"

Darcy sighed and opened the door wider. He came across the threshold and strode past the kitchen doorway and into the living room.

"Jeremy, this is my mother, Lyla Dumphries."

Her mother lifted her hand, limp-wristed, her head cocked. "Mr. Bridges. What a *pleasure* to meet you."

"Why, I had no idea I'd be meeting your mother, Darcy," Jeremy said. "It's easy to see where you get your beauty."

Then he kissed her mother's hand. He actually *kissed her hand.* Darcy thought she was going to barf. And her mother *giggled.* Toss one millionaire her way, and she turned into Blanche DuBois.

"So . . . ," Lyla said. "I understand you and Darcy have been getting to know each other?"

"Why, yes, we have," Jeremy said.

"No, we haven't," Darcy said. "I'm simply a means by which Mr. Bridges entertains himself."

"Well," he said, "good entertainment *is* hard to come by."

"I find that hard to believe from a man who could buy Disney World."

"Darcy!" Lyla whispered angrily. "Show some respect!"

Respect? Just because the guy was made of money?

Well, okay. That *was* a good reason. If only he'd get

real about being interested in her, with the kind of interest that might eventually lead to the altar, she might take him seriously. But until he convinced her he wasn't just yanking her around, she had no intention of putting up with it.

"To what do we owe the honor of this visit?" Lyla said.

"I just dropped by to see your daughter's new place."

"How did you even know I moved?" Darcy asked.

"Come on, Darcy. I'm disgustingly rich, and money talks. Is there anything I can't find out?" He gazed around the room. "Love what you've done with the place. It's stunning."

"Yeah," Darcy said, "it stunned me, too, the first time I saw it."

"It's temporary, of course," Lyla said. "My daughter has met with difficult times of late caused by that scheming husband of hers. But of course you know that. He also caused you some problems."

"That embezzling thing? Haven't given it another thought. If it got Warren out of the picture"—he turned and gave Darcy a suggestive smile—"it was worth it."

Darcy rolled her eyes. "You are *so* full of crap."

"Darcy Elaine Dumphries! *What* did you say?"

"Trust me, Mom. He's probably got a battalion of private investigators looking for Warren and that three hundred grand." She turned to Jeremy. "Why are you here? Really?"

"I brought you a housewarming gift."

He set the basket down on the bar between the kitchen and the living room.

"Did you hear that, Darcy? A gift! How nice!"

"Yeah," Darcy said. "Nice."

"Well, aren't you going to open it?" her mother said.

Letting out a sigh, Darcy pulled the bow loose until the cellophane fell away. That was all it took for her mother to dive right in. She pulled out a small tin.

"Beluga caviar! That's the expensive kind, isn't it?"

"Outrageously so," Jeremy said.

Okay. Now Darcy knew why he was here. He was at it again. A thousand dollars' worth of Starbucks coffee and now Beluga caviar. She'd had it only once before, and it had been exquisite. At a hundred and fifty dollars an ounce, it better have been.

Lyla extracted a silver box from the basket. "Oh, my *God.* Waterford wineglasses?"

Waterford? This from the man with Mountain Dew in his limo fridge?

"Tell the truth," Darcy said to Jeremy. "There's no Waterford around your house, is there? I'm thinking . . . Tupperware?"

"God, no," Jeremy said.

"*God,* no!" Lyla echoed.

"I just bring home those big plastic cups every time I go to a Cowboy's game."

Lyla stared at him blankly for a moment before she figured out that he was joking. Or maybe he wasn't. With this guy, it was hard to say. Finally she giggled nervously before turning a scolding glare to Darcy. "You're lucky Mr. Bridges has a sense of humor. I wouldn't blame him if he took back his generous gifts."

She fished through the basket some more. "Ohmygod! Darcy! Godiva chocolate!"

"It's only four pounds," Jeremy said. "I'm afraid that's the biggest box they make."

Darcy thought about how she always went for the dark chocolate ganache first and how the flavor made her taste buds quiver with joy. But she wasn't going to give Jeremy the satisfaction of going gaga over it. She'd wait until he was long gone before eating the majority of it in one sitting.

"Oooh! Perfume!" her mother said.

Darcy looked at the box. It couldn't be. Clive Christian No. 1?

The last time she was in Nordstrom, she'd looked longingly at the lead crystal bottle trimmed with gold-plated sterling, knowing full well Warren would have heart failure if she bought two-thousand-dollar-an-ounce perfume. And for the cost of one ounce of that perfume, she could pay her rent for months. Why was Bridges doing this to her?

Lyla pulled out another box. "Dog biscuits?"

"They're from the Pampered Pet," Jeremy said. "Treats for the discerning dog."

"How did you know I had a—" Darcy sighed. "Oh, never mind."

Jeremy opened the box, pulled out a mini dog biscuit, and called Pepé over. He wolfed it down, then looked up at Jeremy with total adoration.

"Look at that," Jeremy said. "Your dog has good taste."

"Uh-huh. Pepé's a real connoisseur. He also eats rubber bands and carpet fuzz."

"And one last thing," Jeremy said, reaching into the

basket and pulling out an envelope. He handed it to Darcy.

"What's this?"

"A gift certificate for a consultation with Hiro Kasamotsu, feng shui master to the stars."

"Huh?"

"Just say the word, and I'll have him on a plane from Los Angeles to Dallas. First class, of course. No butt-to-butt coach seat or Motel 6 for Master Kasamotsu."

Darcy looked at him dumbly. "You're kidding, right?"

Jeremy grinned. "I knew you'd be surprised."

"A *what* master?" Lyla asked.

"Feng shui is an ancient art," Jeremy explained. "Supposedly if you get all your furniture and mirrors and plants in the proper place in your house, it brings good fortune." He leaned toward Lyla and spoke confidentially. "From what I'm told, all the big celebrities have their houses feng shuied."

"Ohh!" Lyla said, even though she didn't have a clue what Jeremy was talking about. The only master her mother was familiar with was Thigh Master. She wouldn't know a thing about feng shui until they started selling how-to videos on the Home Shopping Network.

"Feng shui?" Darcy said. "In this place? Are you out of your mind?"

"What?" Jeremy said. "You don't want your new home filled with harmony and prosperity?"

"Forget the harmony. Let's talk prosperity. How about some cold, hard cash? That I could use."

Jeremy smiled. "Who was it who said, 'Take care

of the luxuries, and the necessities will take care of themselves'?"

"A woman who wasn't dead flat broke. *That's* who."

"Darcy!" Lyla snapped, then turned back to Jeremy. "I hope you'll overlook my daughter's surly attitude. She's been under a lot of pressure lately." She gave him a simpering smile. "The gifts are just lovely."

"Thank you, Lyla."

"Well," Lyla said, looking back and forth between them. "I suppose I should be going." She held her hand out to Jeremy again. "It was so nice to meet you."

"Nice to meet you, too, Lyla. I hope we see each other again sometime soon."

Her mother smiled coquettishly, then turned her back to Jeremy and gave Darcy an evil eye that could have withered a redwood tree, mouthing the words *Behave yourself.*

Darcy could already hear her mother at the next potluck. She would be telling everyone that her daughter was seeing *the owner of several big corporations* who lived in a *five-million-dollar mansion* and owned *an island off the coast of Belize* and had a *bodyguard* because he was such an *important man.*

Yeah, that sounded pretty good. But when all Darcy got out of the deal was the opportunity to smell good while her hips expanded from eating fish eggs and chocolate in a harmonious environment, what difference did it make?

After her mother left the apartment, Darcy went back to the basket and stuffed all the items back inside it.

"Call me paranoid," Jeremy said, "but I'm getting the impression you don't like my gifts."

"Yeah? What was your first clue?"

"I sure did impress your mother."

"That's because my mother is easily impressed."

"I give you all these *lovely* housewarming gifts, and this is the thanks I get? I do believe you've hurt my feelings."

"Come on, Bridges. You don't have any feelings to hurt. All this is just ridiculous, and you know it."

"Ridiculous, huh? Tell me, Darcy. Would it have been so ridiculous a few weeks ago coming from your husband?" He inched closer. "Tell me that if you hadn't lost everything, somewhere along the line you wouldn't have had some weird Asian guy flitting through your house, moving furniture around and creating a water garden in the middle of your living room."

Darcy opened her mouth to object, only to close it again. Yes, she probably would have. But now that her life had turned upside down, spending money for things like that seemed kind of . . . silly.

"I just thought a woman who's used to the finer things in life would jump at the chance to have a few of them again," Jeremy said.

"What I'd be happy to have right now is food on the table, gas in my car, and rent in my landlord's pocket."

"You're talking about maintenance."

"You bet I am."

"Gifts are free." He inched closer. "Maintenance has . . . strings."

As he said the words, his eyes seemed to darken with sexual suggestiveness, and suddenly the overgrown kid looked very much like the man he was.

Darcy looked away. "I don't have a clue what you're talking about."

"Come on, Darcy. You're a lot of things, but clueless isn't one of them."

She faced him. "What do you really want from me?"

"Why, sex, of course."

"You give me useless gifts like these and then expect me to sleep with you?"

"So you're saying you have a price, but I just haven't found it yet?"

"I'm not interested."

"Sure you are." He opened the Waterford box and extracted one of the wineglasses. He held it up, the light playing through the cut crystal. He traced his finger slowly around the rim. "Did you know if you wet your finger, then run it around the rim of a crystal glass, it sings?"

Yes, she did. When she and Warren first got married and he'd shown her that, she remembered thinking, *When you're rich, the glasses sing. Imagine that.*

"How did you know that?" she asked him. "You drink out of the good plastic."

"I went to millionaire finishing school. The instructors were really strict." He set the glass down on the bar and picked up the tin of caviar. "Did you know they recently limited the export of caviar to the United States because the sturgeon that produces it is an endangered species?" He turned the tin over in his hand, looking down at it reverently. "Imagine what a single ounce must cost now."

One hell of a lot. And she wouldn't mind trying it again sometime.

"What about the Godiva chocolate?" she asked. "Do you have any interesting facts about that?"

"Nope. Premium chocolate pretty much speaks for itself." He picked up the perfume bottle. "I don't know a thing about perfumes, but I've been assured they don't come any more expensive than this one."

He opened the bottle as he spoke, then dabbed some on his fingertip. In a slow, deliberate motion, he touched the pulse point beneath Darcy's ear. As he dragged it downward, the subtle notes of jasmine and sandalwood wafted up to her nose.

With her mother here oohing and aahing, it had been easy to downplay her reaction to these things. But now, with Jeremy's deep baritone voice narrating an even better life than the one she'd lost, she couldn't help imagining what it would be like to have this kind of opulence every day of her life.

Leaning to within inches of her neck, Jeremy inhaled softly, then made a sound of approval. "Do you remember what it was like?" he murmured. "To live like a princess?"

Of course she remembered. She tried to put it out of her mind most of the time, and most of the time she was successful. But with these things right in front of her, memories came racing back. Part of her wanted desperately to dive headfirst into that basket and overdose on chocolate and caviar. To bathe in expensive perfume. To drink the best wine out of Waterford crystal. To have a weird little Asian man bringing harmony and prosperity to her new home, a home also occupied by a wealthy man ready to lay the best life had to offer right at her feet.

But she didn't trust this man. Not by a long shot.

"You can have any woman on the planet," she said. "Why me?"

"I've been asking myself that same question."

"Come to any conclusions?"

He came closer still. "Lust is unpredictable. Who knows when it will strike?"

Lust. Exactly. This was all a game to him to see just how much it took to get her into bed. That the moment she gave him what he wanted, he'd laugh his way right out her front door. Or . . .

Or there was always the possibility that once she gave him what he wanted in a way he couldn't forget, he'd find his way back for more. One thing would lead to another, and she'd have him wanting her. *Needing* her. And then she'd have him right where she wanted him.

He closed his hand around her wrist, stroking the tender skin with his thumb. "Come to my house tonight, and I'll show you what real luxury is."

Which was clearly going to involve seven-hundred-thread-count Egyptian sheets.

He took another step forward and closed the gap between them, staring at her lips the whole time. She knew what he intended, and something in the back of her mind was screaming at her to stop him. But the closer his lips came to hers, the more that little voice faded into the distance.

Just kiss him. Kiss him like you've never kissed a man before, and sooner or later, you'll have everything you ever—

Knock! Knock! Knock!

At the loud raps on the door, they both jerked back.

"Damn," Jeremy said. "It's probably Bernie, checking to see if the bad guys swooped in through the back door."

Damn was right. Darcy was ready to kill whoever

was on the other side of that door for their *impeccable* timing.

She backed away slowly, then turned and went to the door. She opened it, expecting to find Bernie, and got a shock.

"John?" she said incredulously. "What are you doing here?"

"Well, I didn't just happen to be in the neighborhood, that's for sure." He brushed past her, taking an immediate right into her kitchen, where he set the stuff he held down on the counter—a toolbox, a Home Depot sack, and a box from Pizza Hut.

"I can't believe you're living in this dump," he said.

"John—go away."

He upended the sack on her kitchen counter, and some kind of hardware tumbled out.

"What's that?" she asked.

"A deadbolt."

"I have a lock."

"In the door handle. That's useless."

"How did you know my door didn't already have a deadbolt?"

"I told you I know this complex. The owner's a tightwad."

"But there's a chain lock, too."

"One good kick and that's history. How safe do you think that makes you?"

"John—*stop!*"

He ignored her, grabbing the deadbolt along with a drill out of his toolbox. He turned to head back to the front door, and that was when he looked across the counter between the kitchen and living room and saw Jeremy.

"John," Darcy said, "this is Jeremy Bridges. Jeremy, my boss, John Stark."

John eyed Jeremy for a moment, then set down the drill and the deadbolt and came into the living room. He moved slowly, clearly taking the time to analyze the situation he'd just walked into. The men shook hands the way men do unless they have a real good reason not to, all the while sizing each other up. Money versus might. Both formidable powers.

"So you're the man who repossessed Darcy's Mercedes," Jeremy said.

"So you're the man Darcy's husband embezzled three hundred thousand dollars from," John responded.

There was a long silence as both men stared each other down. Finally John spoke to Darcy, but his eyes never left Jeremy.

"Darcy? Have I interrupted something here?"

She wanted to say, *Yes! I have a millionaire on the hook, and you're messing things up. Go away!*

But then John turned and met her eyes, and her brain replayed the words he'd spoken a moment ago. *"One good kick and that's history. How safe do you think that makes you?"*

The strangest feeling came over her. She'd fought with John from the second they'd met. He was irritating and exasperating and thought he knew what was best for her every moment of every day, and he was doing it again tonight. But right now she couldn't get around one undeniable fact that gave her a whole new awareness of him. Jeremy had brought her expensive but frivolous gifts.

John had brought her food and safety.

Maybe he had an ulterior motive, too, but Darcy sensed

none of that. Suddenly the man who drove her crazy had filled her with the most amazing sense of warmth and comfort, overshadowing every need or desire she'd felt before he knocked on her door. Within a few minutes, she'd probably be fighting with him all over again, but still . . . right now . . .

She wanted one of these men to leave. And it wasn't John.

"Uh . . . no," she told him. "You didn't interrupt anything. I think you're right. I really do need that deadbolt."

"That's not a problem," Jeremy said. "I'll send someone over to take care of it tomorrow."

"No," John said. "She shouldn't spend a single night in this place without decent locks."

Jeremy's expression tightened with irritation. "Then I'll send someone over tonight."

"No," Darcy said. "There's really no point in doing that. Not when John's already here. He can take care of it."

"I'm sure he has something better to do than play handyman."

"Nope," John said. "Can't think of a single thing."

He spoke in an even tone of voice, but the warning was there just the same. *Back off, buddy. I have this situation under control.*

Jeremy turned to Darcy. "My car's waiting."

A beautiful, luxurious limousine, complete with a millionaire making his move. She was insane to give that up, and she couldn't imagine that tomorrow she wouldn't be filled with a whole lot of regret over that. But just for tonight, insanity seemed like a wonderful state to be in.

"Maybe another time," she said.

Jeremy raised his chin a millimeter or two, a muscle in his jaw twitching. In one swoop, he'd been dismissed by a woman and one-upped by another man. He clearly didn't like that in the least, but he was smart enough to know when he'd lost the battle. Whether he still wanted to fight the war remained to be seen.

He headed for the door. Darcy followed. When they reached it, he turned back, lowering his voice so only she could hear.

"A woman like you isn't cut out to struggle, Darcy." He glanced at John, his gaze tight. "Remember that."

He left her apartment, and she closed the door behind him.

Chapter 14

J eremy got into the limo, barely closing the door behind him before reaching into the fridge for a beer.

"Back so soon?" Bernie said.

He popped the cap of the beer and took a swig, then looked out the window, amazed that in spite of the squalor that was Creekwood Apartments, he hadn't been able to entice Darcy to spend an evening in paradise. This whole situation with her was becoming an irritation he wanted to settle in his favor, but for the first time he wasn't quite sure how to go about doing that.

"She's staying in tonight," he said.

"So she didn't like your extravagant but heartfelt gifts?"

"She liked them just fine."

"Is that why you were in there for only twenty minutes?"

Jeremy clenched his teeth with frustration. "Seems I have a little competition."

"You mean she found a guy richer than you? Works fast, doesn't she?"

"Actually, it's the man she works for."

"At the repo company?"

"Go figure."

"Did he happen to be the guy who showed up at her door a minute ago carrying the toolbox?"

"That's the one."

"Hmm."

"What's that supposed to mean?"

"What it means is that you'd better ramp it up. You're fighting six foot three inches of pure testosterone."

Yeah, some women had a real thing for the blue-collar type. But in the end, women like Darcy always knew who signed the checks.

"What's the matter?" Bernie asked. "Aren't you up to the challenge?"

"Of course I am."

"Just take her to Paris or something. That'll wow her."

"I won't have to. John Stark is just a distraction. I know which buttons of Darcy's to push, and they have nothing to do with hormones."

"Oh, I have no doubt you'll win in the end. The question is, what's it going to cost you?"

Jeremy took a swig of his beer, frustrated as hell because he was beginning to wonder about that himself. Not that he didn't have it to spend. But he hadn't gotten this far in life by paying more than market price for anything.

"She's just playing hard to get," he said.

"Never thought I'd see the day. I think you might actually like this woman."

"Now, Bernie. You know me better than that. Liking someone would require me to have a heart."

"True. My mistake." She eyed him up and down. "Then again, what's with the preppy look? You look like you're heading to a country club. And I know how you hate those."

"They're just normal clothes."

"Nope. Normal for you is a Cowboys T-shirt, crappy jeans, and tennis shoes. Yet now you're going for the rich-guy look. Trying to impress someone?"

"Bernie, you want to shut up?"

"Sure, boss," she said, smiling a little as she turned away. "Whatever you say."

God, she was *such* a know-it-all. One of these days he was going to fire her for real.

At first this had only been a game. But now, when it looked as if there was a possibility he could lose . . .

It was time he got down to business.

John plugged in the drill and ripped through the dead-bolt packaging to install the lock in Darcy's door, moving with the authority of a man used to firing up power tools and repairing things. Warren had never fixed anything around the house. Replacing lightbulbs and putting new batteries in the TV remote were about the only things he'd been able to handle.

While John worked, Darcy busied herself by arranging a few things in her pantry closet, but several times her gaze wandered in his direction. She noticed his taut expression as he pressed the drill to the door, the fluid, agile way he switched from one tool to another, his forearm muscles flexing as he twisted the screwdriver. And those hands again. Big, strong, *talented* hands. Now that she knew what it felt like to have them roaming over her body, just looking at them now made her mouth go dry.

She turned away. This was ridiculous. Getting hot over a man with tools? Was there any bigger cliché than that?

John had the door open as he worked on the lock, and suddenly he looked up, focusing on something outside. He slowly rose to his full height, his voice booming across the breezeway. "Hey! What are you looking at?"

Darcy looked around the doorway to see Crazy Bob peeking out his door. He wore his usual gym shorts without a shirt, that cigarette dangling from his lower lip and his eyes shifting back and forth crazily.

"Beat it!" John said.

He ducked back inside his apartment in a flurry of door slamming and lock turning.

"Weirdo," John muttered, kneeling beside the door again. "You watch out for guys like him."

"He's probably harmless."

"That's what somebody has said at one time or another about every serial killer in history."

"He's a school teacher."

"That figures." John shook his head with disgust. "Damned educational system."

A few minutes later, he had the lock installed. He came to his feet a little stiffly, then twisted the key in the lock to test it. He handed her the key. "There. It's in. I'm hungry. Let's eat."

"How do you know I haven't already had dinner?"

"Have you?"

"No."

"Then let's eat."

They went to the kitchen, where Darcy pulled down

two of the stoneware plates she'd put away earlier. John grabbed the pizza box and set it on the kitchen table, and they both sat down.

"So," he said, eyeing the gift basket on the bar. "I take it Rich Boy is hitting on you?"

"It's just a housewarming present."

"I don't like him."

"You met him for two minutes."

"Doesn't matter. I don't like him."

"That's because you're not a woman."

"Why would you want a guy like him?"

"Gee, John, I don't know. Maybe because he's worth *millions?*"

"That money thing again. You really do need to get over your fascination with the color green." He glanced at the basket again. "So, what's in there, anyway?"

Darcy shrugged. "Just a few luxuries. Chocolate. Caviar. That kind of thing."

"It's like I told you before. Expensive gifts mean that someday he's going to expect something in return."

"You bought me half the clothes at Amaryllis. What's the difference?"

"I didn't give you those clothes because I wanted to sleep with you. I gave you those clothes because I acted like an ass."

Darcy sat back with surprise. "Did you actually say that out loud?"

"What?"

"That you acted like an ass."

"I don't know what you're talking about."

"But you just said—"

"I think you're hearing things. Better have that checked

out." He grabbed three pieces of pizza and put them on his plate. Darcy just stared at him.

"So are you going to eat or what?" John asked.

Darcy took a piece of pizza, smiling to herself. She had a feeling that witnessing an admission of asslike behavior from John was like seeing a falling star. It happened only once a blue moon, and if she blinked, she'd miss it. But that didn't mean she couldn't tuck the memory away to savor for some time to come.

As John dug in to his pizza, Darcy picked the pepperoni slices off hers and pushed them aside.

"What are you doing?" John asked.

"What does it look like I'm doing?"

"Now you have cheese pizza."

"You didn't bother to ask me what I liked. You just showed up with a pizza."

"Who on earth doesn't like pepperoni pizza?"

"See, there you go. You naturally assume everyone shares your point of view about everything. Probably just about *nobody* does, but you're so bullheaded that you won't listen to see if they do or not. So you just go on thinking you're right about everything."

"Just because other people don't share my point of view doesn't mean it's not the right one."

"How would you know if they share it or not if you never listen to what anyone else has to say?"

"You're exaggerating."

"Not according to Amy."

"Oh, yeah? What evil things has my sister been saying about me?"

"Actually, I was the one saying evil things. You might

have told me she was your sister before I told her how crabby and dictatorial I thought you were."

John had the nerve to smile at that.

"But it ended up being okay," Darcy said. "She agreed with me."

"That figures."

John chomped into a slice of pizza, consuming half of it in one bite. At that rate, she figured he'd have eaten half the pizza before she'd even nibbled on one piece.

"Do you have any brothers or sisters?" he asked.

"No. I'm an only child."

"Why did your parents stop with one kid?"

Darcy laughed. "Are you kidding? My parents didn't even want *me*."

"What?"

"I was born seven months after they got married. My mother always told me that if she hadn't gotten pregnant and had me, she would have been a movie star or a socialite or something equally important. So instead she tried to drive me down that path. Did you know I was once a runner-up for Miss Texas?"

"Oh, yeah? Almost went to the big one, huh?"

"My mother had me in pageants from the time I was four. Dressed me up in silly costumes. I could do a baton routine before I was six years old. By the time I was eight, the batons were on fire. That impressed the hell out of the judges. I never made Miss America, but I did do my mother proud and marry a rich man." She sighed. "And look what happened with that."

"We don't always get what we want. Sometimes we just have to play the hands we're dealt."

"So what did you want that you didn't get?" she asked,

not really expecting an answer. John seemed like the kind of man who went out and took whatever he wanted and didn't let anything get in his way.

"I got what I wanted," he said. "And then I lost it."

"What?"

"All I ever wanted to be was a cop."

"So why did you quit?"

Darkness settled over his face. "Blew out my knee."

"On the job? What happened?"

"I'd love to say I was chasing down a murder suspect and was shot as I was taking him out. At least then I'd have a good story to tell. But no. I was playing softball three years ago. I slid into home, caught my cleat in the dirt, twisted my knee, and that was that."

"The limp is barely noticeable."

"Doesn't matter. It slows me down. When you can't pass the physical, you can't be a cop."

"So you miss it a lot."

"Every day of my life."

"And stealing cars is the next best thing?"

"There is no next best thing."

Darcy heard a note of wistfulness in his voice. How hard must it have been for him to watch the only profession he'd ever wanted go by the wayside in a freak accident?

"My family thought I ought to open a Subway franchise," he said.

Darcy laughed. "You? Making sandwiches?"

"Supposedly it can be pretty profitable."

"Well, then. By all means consider it."

"Some days I actually do. The repo business can get a little ugly sometimes. Then I think about being trapped behind that counter for the rest of my life . . ." He sighed. "Just can't see it."

Darcy couldn't see it, either.

"Your mother wanted you to be Miss America," he said. "What did you want?"

She shrugged. "I didn't have any big dreams."

"Oh, come on. Everybody does."

Darcy thought about it for a minute. "I did have something when I was a kid. But it sounds silly now."

"What?"

"I watched the Olympics when I was nine years old. I never missed one second of the ice-skating competition. I wanted to be Dorothy Hamill."

"Oh, yeah? Did you take skating lessons?"

"God, no. My mother wouldn't let me within ten feet of a pair of ice skates. What if I fell and bruised my knee? Broke my arm? Cut myself? How would I ever cover that up in my baton twirling outfit?"

"Ah."

"I wanted Dorothy's haircut, too, but of course I couldn't have that, either. 'The judges like long hair,' she kept telling me, and that was that. She always thought that would be my meal ticket. Making it to Miss America. I'm afraid if my fortunes don't turn around pretty soon, she's going to have me dusting off my twirling routines and running for *Mrs.* America."

"Except you're not a Mrs. anymore."

"I am until I can get a divorce. My mother's going to have to work fast."

Darcy heard the jingle of dog tags and turned to see Pepé peering around the doorway.

"Well, look at that," John said. "It's Micro Mutt."

At the sound of John's voice, Pepé crouched down, making himself even smaller than he already was. John grabbed a pepperoni from Darcy's plate and leaned over, holding it out.

"Hey, you want a pepperoni? Looks like we're going to have plenty."

Pepé considered it, only to have fear overcome his usual food curiosity. He scurried back into the entry hall, looking up at John like Fay Wray staring up at King Kong.

"So he won't eat pepperoni either?" John said. "What's wrong with you two?"

"You just scared him earlier."

"I did?"

"With the drill. He's not crazy about loud noises. Warren used to yell at him."

"Why?"

"Because he got underfoot. Because he shed. Because he peed on the rug. But he only peed on the rug because Warren yelled at him. Once that cycle got going, it was tough to break."

"Your husband sounds like a real jerk."

Darcy almost disagreed with John out of sheer habit, but how could she argue with that?

A few minutes later, they finished the pizza. As Darcy rose from the table and grabbed their plates, John crushed the empty pizza box, twisting and smashing it until it wasn't much bigger than a softball, then tossed it into the trash can. She had no doubt he could tear a telephone book in half and never break a sweat.

"It's getting late," John said. "I should go. But I want you to be careful around this place. Night and day. Watch going to your car. And don't leave anything lying around outside your apartment, or it'll be gone."

"Aren't you being a little paranoid?"

"I was a cop, remember? I know what I'm talking about. When I was in patrol, we once broke up a meth lab in one of these apartments."

Darcy decided this probably wasn't the time to tell him a new generation of that particular brand of entrepreneur just might be living next door.

"Don't worry," she said. "I have a watchdog."

"Uh-huh. One who runs from power drills and pepperoni. Have you considered getting a real dog? A big one with teeth and a bad attitude?"

"Hey! Pepé's got attitude! He once bit the mailman's ankle."

"Did he draw blood?"

"No, but he did snag the guy's sock."

"You're not taking this seriously."

"I'll be fine," she told him as she stuck the dishes in the dishwasher. "At least Pepé barks. That's a good thing. And I always carry pepper spray."

"Forget pepper spray. Tomorrow I'll bring you a gun."

"Will you *stop?*"

He held up his hand. "Fine. I'm out of here. Just remember what I've told you."

He went to the counter to pick up his toolbox. As Darcy was leaning over to close the door of the dishwasher so she could follow him out of the kitchen, she saw movement out of the corner of her eye. She spun around. Something was crawling along the counter.

The biggest, ugliest roach she'd ever seen.

She screamed and backed away, banging her leg on the open dishwasher and almost falling into it. John turned, saw the roach, grabbed a newspaper Darcy had left on the kitchen counter, and smacked the bug. Then he ripped off a paper towel, scooped up the carcass, and deposited it, along with the newspaper, in the trash.

As John was wiping the counter, then washing his hands, Darcy just stood there with her hand at her throat, frozen with revulsion. She'd seen genetically enhanced creatures in horror movies that weren't that hideous.

"Are you"—she swallowed hard—"are you sure it's dead?"

"Yep," John said. "Flat as a pancake."

Slowly her eyes drifted closed. "I can't do this."

"Do what?"

"I can't live here. I know I talk big, like it's nothing, but I can't."

He turned around, drying his hands with a paper towel. "It was just a bug, Darcy."

"No. It's everything. This place is horrible. It smells funny. The neighbors are insane. And those who aren't insane are probably criminals." Tears came to her eyes. She tried to fight it, but she couldn't. "There are holes in the wall. The plumbing hasn't backed up yet, but you can bet it's going to. Gross things crawl out of the woodwork. *I can't do this*."

"Sure you can."

"No, I can't. Even though I've got a barking dog and pepper spray and you were so sweet to come over here and install that deadbolt . . ." She let out a shaky sigh. "Maybe I should go back and live with my parents."

He took her by the shoulders. "No. You're staying right here."

"But you said it yourself. This is a hellhole."

"And you said something, too. It's *your* hellhole. And that means a lot."

Something was wrong here. John was supposed to be saying things like, "*If you see another bug, just whack the damned thing. You're bigger than it is*," and "*Hey, you were the one who wanted move into a place like this, so don't bitch*."

Instead, he eased closer and rubbed his hands along her upper arms. "I know you didn't ask for this. But you can do it. I know you can."

She wasn't convinced of that, but whenever John declared anything, it always sounded like something you could take to the bank. His grip softened until it was more like a caress, those big, strong hands surprisingly gentle. But the gentler he became, the more awkward she felt. Being with John when he was tough and authoritative was one thing. Being with him when he was like this was something else entirely.

"You're a complicated woman, Darcy," he murmured. "Sometimes I have a hard time keeping up."

She had no idea what he meant by that. She couldn't imagine John having a hard time keeping up with anything, and she'd never thought of herself as complicated. On the outside, maybe. It took a lot of intricate rituals to keep herself looking good. But she'd never stopped to think much about what was on the inside.

"Complicated?" she said.

"Bridges expected you to go with him tonight, didn't he?"

"Yes."

"Why didn't you?"

Actually, the answer to that wasn't complicated at all, and thinking about it made her feel warm all over again. Jeremy had brought her what she wanted.

John had brought her what she needed.

"Because I love pizza, of course," she said. "But just for the record, if I'd known it was pepperoni, I'd have opted for the limo."

To her surprise, his mouth softened into a warm smile. "Then it's a good thing I didn't open the box before he left, isn't it?"

It was the first time she'd seen a smile on his face that wasn't accompanying a sarcastic remark. As sexy as his rugged, tough-as-nails demeanor could be, that smile catapulted his already-handsome face into an entirely new realm.

"You don't do that very often," she said.

"What?"

"Smile."

"I have to do it sparingly," he said. "I have a reputation to protect, you know."

A long silence stretched between them, but their eyes were locked together in some kind of mutual expectation that gave Darcy goose bumps.

"Did I hear you correctly earlier?" he murmured.

"What?"

"You said I was sweet."

"Yeah. I guess I did, didn't I?"

That smile again. "Wait until Tony hears that."

Their voices were quieter now, and still they stared at each other.

"You're complicated, too, you know," Darcy said.

"I am?"

"Yes. Why did you come by with the deadbolt?"

"This place isn't safe, and since you're a better clerk than I thought you'd be, it'd be a real pain to lose you now."

"So Tony was right? You're all about business?"

His smile faded, replaced by a hot, penetrating gaze. "Tony doesn't know me as well as he thinks he does."

At the low, erotic tone of his voice, Darcy just about melted into the cheap linoleum. He set his palm on the counter beside her, and just his proximity made her breath come faster and her pulse kick up a notch. She swallowed hard, trying to maintain some kind of composure, but then he caught a strand of her hair with his fingertip and swept it slowly back over her shoulder, a tiny gesture that made a million of her nerve endings come to life. When he moved closer still, she put her hand against his chest in a pale attempt to stop him. But the minute it met bone and muscle, it became a useless appendage that just lay there in ecstasy.

For the past fourteen years, walking a flight of stairs had made her heart beat faster than it did when she was with her husband, but being with John made her feel as if she'd run a marathon. She knew what it felt like when he kissed her, and she wanted him to do it again.

No. Stop it. This is wrong, wrong, wrong.

They were oil and water. Fire and ice. Night and day. And if she didn't back off right now, the immovable object was going to meet the irresistible force, and God only knew what would happen then.

"Maybe this isn't a good idea," she said.

"Why not?"

"The last time we did this, all hell broke loose."

"Is it Bridges you want?"

An hour ago, she'd have said yes. No amount of physical pleasure could compensate for this pitiful lifestyle. But now, with John only inches away from taking her to heaven all over again, she wasn't so sure.

"I don't know," she whispered.

"Then I'll help you make up your mind," he said, and lowered his lips to hers.

Chapter 15

Darcy saw it coming, but still it was a shock when John's mouth fell against hers. Up until an hour ago, her brain was stuck in Wal-Mart, where she'd thought, *No way in hell will I ever let him do this again*, only to think now that she'd die if he didn't.

With one hand threaded through her hair and the other locked on her waist, he gave her one kiss after another, the deliciously steamy, insistent kisses of a man who knew what he wanted and took it. He pushed her right up next to the sink, the open dishwasher on her right and his thigh trapping her on the left. He was so big and demanding and overbearing that she should have told him to back off and let her have some say-so in this situation. Should have.

Didn't want to.

He reached over and flicked off the overhead light, leaving only the dim glow from the living room lamp to light the kitchen, and the sudden darkness in this unfamiliar place made what they were doing seem deliciously illicit, as if he'd pulled her into an office broom closet during a coffee break. As she wound her arms around his neck, he slid his hands from her hips to her thighs, then curled them around her bottom and dragged her up to her tiptoes, crushing her breasts against his chest. With the length of her body pressed against his, she felt his erection against her abdomen. Suddenly she knew what he wanted, and it was more than a little making out in the dark.

She dragged her mouth away from his and spoke breathlessly. "Wait a minute. What are we doing?"

He kissed her neck, then whispered in her ear, "Darcy, we've been dancing around this since the moment we met. And *God,* I hate to dance."

He was right. They'd been on a collision course since the Battle of Mercedes-Benz. All the banter, the sarcastic remarks, the sidelong glances, the inadvisable kisses in inadvisable places—now she realized all of it had been nothing more than a whole lot of vertical foreplay, and they were moving to the main event.

"I'm taking you to bed," he murmured. "And for the next couple of hours, we're not even coming up for air."

His words were a sexual one-two punch that almost knocked Darcy to her knees. This was what she wanted. To get swept away by electrifying sex with a man who knew how to deliver it. For a moment she imagined John simply hurling her down on the kitchen table and having his way with her. But then he took her by the hand, led her out of the kitchen and down the hall, moving so fast she had to trot to keep up, only to stop halfway there, push her against the wall, and kiss her all over again. After fourteen years of Warren's brand of sex—lights out, under the covers, over with before it even got started—this man scared her a little. Okay, maybe a lot.

But that only made it that much more exciting.

He unfastened one of her shirt buttons, then another.

He fought with the third one, his big fingers dueling wildly with the small button. With a groan of frustration, he grabbed the sides of the shirt and ripped it open all the way to her waist. Darcy gasped.

"Four ninety-nine," he said. "That's the beauty of cheap clothes. I'll buy you ten more."

Darcy was stunned. She couldn't have imagined a man wanting her so much he'd rip her clothes right off her body.

John peeled the shirt away from her shoulders. It fell to her elbows, gathering there and trapping her arms so she couldn't touch him. She wiggled and squirmed, but he just backed her up against the wall again and seduced her with that incredible mouth of his. This was going to be good, so good, the kind of fantasy sex she'd always imagined on those nights when she'd been in bed with Warren, staring at the ceiling and counting the minutes until it was over.

Finally John pulled the shirt off her arms and let it fall to the floor. She caught the fever, fumbling with his shirt buttons like a woman possessed. She unfastened only three of them before becoming impatient and slipping her hands inside to touch him skin-to-skin. He undid the rest, then yanked the shirt off completely. But when he reached for the clasp of her bra, all at once she was struck by the most horrific thought.

In about thirty seconds, she was going to be standing naked in the hall of her ugly new apartment. She was almost forty, with gravity working more of its evil on her with every moment that passed. John had already pegged her age just by looking at her Botoxed, microderm-abraded, cosmetically enhanced face. What was he going to think when he saw those places where the ravages of age couldn't be concealed?

She grabbed his hands. He stopped suddenly, breathing hard. "What?"

"I don't know about this."

"Don't know about what?"

"You were right about my age," she confessed.

"Okay."

"I'm . . ." She took a deep breath. "I'm almost forty."

"Okay."

"Things aren't necessarily where they used to be. They may be . . . you know . . . a few inches lower."

"Darcy, I don't care if you have one foot in the grave. You feel damned good to me."

"I think—"

"No. Don't think. That's your problem. You're thinking too much."

Before she knew what was happening, he'd swept her into his arms, carried her to her bedroom, and lay her on the bed. The only light in the room was the faint lamplight filtering in from the living room and the streetlamp outside, and she thanked God for that. Maybe he wouldn't see every imperfection she had.

He sat beside her and unhooked her bra, sweeping the cups aside, the lacy fabric tripping over her nipples. She held her breath as he looked down at her, staring at her for so long that she almost folded her arms across her chest. Then he put his palms against her ribs, slowly sliding them upward to take her breasts in his hands. He leaned in, kissing the swell of one, then the other.

"You're so beautiful," he murmured. "From the first moment I saw you, I thought you were so damned beautiful."

"The first moment you saw me, I was yelling at you."

"Make that *screamingly* beautiful."

He unzipped her shorts, hooked his fingers in the waist-band, and pulled them off along with her panties, leaving her naked. Self-consciousness seeped in again, but when he stood up and took off the rest of his clothes, she couldn't think about her own body. She was too enraptured looking at his. He had the chest and biceps and thighs of a mythological warrior, radiating power from every pore. As her gaze traveled south, she had a fleeting thought about how she'd told him that men with big trucks were compensating for something. She'd never been so glad to be wrong about something in her life.

Stretching out beside her, he slipped his hand between her legs, stroking her there. She was already unbearably hot and swollen, and when he dipped his head to take her nipple between his lips, she thought she'd die from the pleasure. Teasing, licking, sucking, stroking . . . so many incredible feelings all at once. Her hands curled into fists, her fingernails digging into her palms. And then his lips hovered over her ear again.

"Don't leave me in the dark," he whispered. "Tell me what you want."

John had always struck her as a man who took whatever he wanted and didn't much care who he trampled in the process. But against all odds, here he was being sweet all over again, saying words her husband hadn't uttered in fourteen years of marriage.

The truth was that she didn't know what to tell John, because she didn't know exactly what she wanted. This was good, but she doubted he'd want to keep it up forever. And even if she had known what to tell him, it would have embarrassed her to say it. So she reached down to his erection pressing against her thigh. She wrapped her hand around it, stroked the length of it, and said what she thought *he* wanted to hear.

"You. Inside me. Now."

With a muffled groan, he rose immediately and grabbed his jeans from the bedroom floor. She wondered what he was doing, and when he pulled out a condom, she felt a jolt of relief. She hadn't even thought about that. When a woman marries a man who's already had a vasectomy, she didn't *have* to think about those things. Thank God John had it covered.

He returned to the bed, parted her thighs, and hovered over her. For a moment he just stared down at her, his eyes shimmering in the near-darkness, killing her with anticipation.

Then he slid inside her.

She gasped at the sudden sensation of being filled completely, mindlessly curling her legs around him as he began to move inside her. She closed her eyes, stroking his back, loving the way his muscles flexed beneath his sweat-sheened skin. This was good. So good.

But as much as it excited her, if history was any indication, in a few minutes John was going to be the only one feeling *more* than good. It had always struck her as patently unfair that men could have something so easily that came so hard to—

Wait. She felt something.

No.

Hold on. Maybe. A stirring deep inside her, something trying to catch fire. She couldn't believe it. Oh, God . . . was it possible?

She arched against him, shifting her hips a little, trying to find just the right position. He picked up the pace, driving inside her, but the little flicker she'd felt began to slip away.

No, no, no! Concentrate. Think about sexy things.

Oh, hell. Like that made sense? She was having sex with the sexiest man she'd ever known. How much more sex could her brain fill up with?

She sensed him holding back. Gritting his teeth. Waiting to hear from her before going full speed ahead.

No. Don't concentrate. Stop thinking about it. That's your problem. John said it. You're thinking too hard. But you have to do something. He's waiting on you. Come on, come on, come on!

She squeezed her eyes closed, trying desperately to find that flicker again, but it wasn't going to happen.

Just as it hadn't happened for the past fourteen years.

Disappointment flooded through her. She'd eventually quit trying with Warren, finding it easier just to let him get there and think he took her there, too. And then she'd lain awake afterward, dreaming of sex with a man like John, assuming that if she ever had that opportunity, total sexual fulfillment would be a given.

It's okay. Just get it over with now. It'll be better next time.

Darcy took a deep breath. Everything she knew about faking an orgasm she'd learned from Meg Ryan, and the curtain was going up.

She started slowly, as always, just breathing a little harder. As he moved faster with more powerful strokes, she got a little vocal. And after a while, when she could tell he was close, she started in with some of Meg's *Yes!*

Yes! Yes! stuff, because that had always seemed really appropriate if a woman was truly on the edge. She congratulated herself, as she usually did, on just how exceptional her performance was. Or at least she thought it was, right up to the moment John stopped short and looked down at her as if she'd grown a second head.

"What are you doing?" he asked, breathing hard.

She froze. "What do you mean?"

"What's with all the hollering?"

What did he *think* was with it? "I'm...uh... excited?"

"Sweetheart, you're about as excited as a nun in church."

Oh, God. He knew. How did he know? *Drop back. Regroup. Get control again.* She gave him a sexy smile. "Baby, you have no *idea* how excited I am."

"Knock it off. Why are you faking it?"

Her smile vanished. "I'm *not* faking it!"

"Come on, Darcy. I know the phony stuff when I hear it."

"No. This is good. It really is. Will you just get *on* with it?"

Instead, he fell to one side and sat up. Judging from his still-raging erection, stopping clearly hadn't been an easy thing for him to do. And yet he had. What was *wrong* with this man?

"What are you doing?" Darcy said. "Men don't just *stop* in the middle of things!"

"This one does," John said, "when he's being lied to. Have you always faked it?"

Darcy opened her mouth to deny it one more time, but then he was staring down at her with that look on his face she was growing so accustomed to—the one that said he wasn't buying even a tiny white lie or a remote stretching of the truth.

She sat up and faced him, pulling the covers up to her chest and swiping her hair away from her face. "All right, John. You want the truth? Here's the truth. Sometimes it's just easier to give a man what he wants and get it over with."

"Really? Exactly what do you think a man wants?"

"To get off as fast as he can, as often as he can, with a minimum of hassle."

"Where most men are concerned, you're probably right."

"And a man also wants to believe that just the presence of his mighty rod in the vicinity of the bedroom is enough to bring a woman to orgasmic ecstasy."

"Did Warren subscribe to that particular fantasy?"

"Warren was the poster boy for that particular fantasy."

"So you decided to keep on faking it as long as he was signing the checks?"

Darcy wanted to get angry at that, but his words held so much truth that she just couldn't bring herself to.

"And if you're all wrapped up in the moment yourself," John said, "it's hard to keep your hands on the reins, isn't it?"

"What are you talking about?"

"Newsflash, Darcy. You're a little controlling."

She drew back. "Well, if *that* isn't the pot calling the kettle black, I don't know what is."

"That's a fair observation. Here's another one. I think

under different circumstances than the ones you've lived with in the past, you might actually like sex."

"It's not that I don't like it," she said. "It's just that . . ."

"What?"

"There are only certain ways that I . . . you know. And it's not all that common, so . . ."

John turned on the lamp and opened her nightstand drawer. Shoving some things aside, he pulled out a certain electronic device. "Is this one of those ways?"

"Put that back!"

"Hmm. Not exactly warm and fuzzy, is it?"

Darcy grabbed it from his hand, wondering how in the hell he knew the things he did. Men weren't supposed to understand women, which really gave women an edge. With John, she had no edge at all.

"To tell you the truth," she said, "up to now I haven't met a man who could top your average battery-powered device."

"Oh, yeah? Well, maybe if you stopped faking it and told a man the truth, you'd be tossing that thing in the trash."

He swung his legs over the side of the bed and stood up.

"Where are you going?" she asked.

Saying nothing, he grabbed his jeans and put them on, then his socks, and picked up his shoes.

"John?"

He turned and pointed at her. "When you're ready to lay off the phony stuff and get real, let me know."

He went into the hall, yanked on his shirt, and a few minutes later, she heard her front door open and close. Then . . . silence.

Darcy sat back against the headboard, shocked almost to tears. What the hell had just happened here?

She didn't understand it. The better she faked it, the happier Warren had seemed to be. She had no doubt he told all his golf buddies about just how good he was at satisfying his wife—his young, beautiful wife who was hot for him even after years of marriage.

What a joke.

It had always been a performance. A means to an end. No matter how she felt, the show always went on. But sometimes she'd lie awake afterward and think, *Is this all there is?* Then she'd wake up the next morning to her beautiful home and her cute little sports car and her platinum AmEx, and she'd forget.

Until the next time.

She'd bet half the men out there didn't care if they satisfied a woman, and the other half would be happy never knowing whether they had or not. But not John. He was in category number three, whatever the hell that was. When was he going to start behaving like other men and stop driving her crazy?

Then she remembered the front door. She got up to lock the deadbolt, turning it until she heard a reassuring little click. When she turned back around, she saw the gift basket on the bar between the kitchen and living room.

Chocolate. I need chocolate.

She tore open the Godiva box, grabbed a chocolate ganache, and took a bite. She sat down on the sofa, her eyes closed, chewing slowly, savoring every morsel. One bite, and she remembered. A little piece of heaven Warren had taken away from her.

A little piece of heaven Jeremy Bridges had replaced.

You're not cut out to struggle.

As she looked around this barren apartment, it scared her to think this was her life until she could find a way to make more money, win the lottery, or the heavens opened up and dropped thousands of dollars right into her lap. What scared her more was the way she was starting to feel about John, a man who wasn't much higher on the economic scale than she was, which meant that with him, security would never be a given. A deadbolt couldn't conquer everything that was wrong with her life right now.

But the way it had made her feel, along with so many other things tonight . . .

As she played every moment of this evening over in her mind, she realized she'd never been herself in front of a man before. She wasn't even sure she knew who the person was underneath all the subterfuge. Whoever she really was, though, John seemed to like her the most—the woman with the forty-year-old body who wore cheap clothes, drove a rattletrap, lived in a slum, and was terrified of bugs. At this rate, she might never figure him out.

Don't leave me in the dark. Tell me what you want.

But instead of telling him what he wanted to know, she'd told him what she thought he wanted to hear. Then she'd given him an earful of Meg Ryan. How dumb had that made her look?

At the time, it had irritated her beyond measure to have him call her on it. But now as she thought about it, she couldn't help but wonder what might happen if she brought John out of the dark and into the light. What kind of experience would he have in store for her then?

⌒

"It's perfect!" Amy said as she circled the chipped, dusty end table sitting in the middle of John's living room. "It's just the right size. Once it's refinished, it'll look great with my décor."

Décor? Amy didn't have décor. She had a houseful of orphaned furniture nobody else on the planet would touch. As John looked down at the ugly piece of furniture he'd almost hauled to the dump this morning, he couldn't imagine any amount of refinishing that would make it presentable.

"Did you find anything else when you were cleaning out the attic?" Amy asked.

"Yeah. A dead squirrel."

"No, thanks. Dead animals are *so* last year."

John picked up the end table and carried it out to Amy's SUV, stuck it in the back, and closed the door. Amy pulled out her keys.

"Oh," she said. "Meant to ask you. What was Darcy's new apartment like?"

John froze. "How would I know?"

"She moved in yesterday, right? I thought maybe you went by to see her."

"Why would I do that?"

"I don't know. You were harping about her living in a hellhole. I thought maybe you'd go by to check it out."

"Where Darcy lives is no business of mine."

"Come on, John. You think everybody's business is your business."

"Not hers."

Amy looked at him carefully. "Hmm. I thought things were okay between you two. I mean, there was the tow truck incident, but you seemed to have forgiven her for that." She grinned. "That took guts, didn't it?"

"She broke the law."

"Still took guts."

"If it's not one thing with her, it's another."

"Did something else happen?"

"None of your business."

"So my business is your business, but not the other way around?"

"Darcy is exactly what I thought she was. Phony through and through."

"You want to be more specific?"

"Nope."

"John, at the risk of beating a dead horse—"

"I don't want to hear anything that starts out like that."

"You'd be a lot happier with a woman in your life."

"Amy, go home."

She sighed. "Fine. Die alone. See if I care."

"Actually, I've been thinking about getting a dog. Dogs are always glad to see you. They don't have smart mouths. They don't try to manipulate you. And best of all, they don't let you pet them and then act as if they liked it when they really didn't."

Amy screwed up her face. "What in the hell are you talking about?"

"Never mind."

"Well," Amy said, looking over his shoulder, "speak of the devil."

John turned around to see a car coming down the street,

and by the clatter of the engine, there was no mistaking whose car it was. What was Darcy doing here?

She pulled to the curb and killed the engine, then scooted to the passenger door and got out. Pushing her sunglasses to the top of her head, she walked up to them, giving Amy a smile but avoiding looking at him. She wore that long, funny-looking skirt from Wal-Mart with all the permanent wrinkles in it that shouldn't have looked good on anyone, but on her somehow it did. Or maybe he was just remembering what was underneath the skirt.

Stop thinking about that. It'll only get you in trouble.

"Darcy?" John said. "What are you doing here?"

"Oh. Well . . . I just thought I'd return your toolbox. You left it at my apartment last night."

John winced. Amy turned to him with a sly smile. "So you went to Darcy's apartment last night, huh?"

"Amy, don't you need to be going?"

"Yeah. Sure. I'm going. And John?"

"What?"

"That dog you're thinking about getting? Not such a good idea. You know who man's best friend really is." She turned to Darcy. "See you at work tomorrow."

"Good-bye," Darcy said, then turned to John. "You're getting a dog?"

"No, I'm not getting a dog," he snapped. "Open your trunk."

As Amy drove away, Darcy unlocked the trunk and John got the toolbox out. He headed for his house. Darcy slammed the trunk closed and hurried after him. He climbed the steps to his porch, then turned around and glared at her. "What are you doing?"

"I thought we could talk for a minute."

"Do we really have anything to say to each other?"

"John, if I want to talk to you, you know I'll find a way. And who knows what that might involve?"

Now that was a threat he took seriously.

With a sigh of resignation, he finally just turned and walked inside, and she followed. He took the toolbox to his utility room, then went back to the kitchen to wash his dusty hands.

"Nice house," Darcy said.

"Darcy, on your scale of nice, this house is a negative number."

"Not these days, it isn't."

Good point. He rinsed his hands and reached for a dishtowel. "What do you want?"

"I told you. I just wanted to . . . you know. Talk."

"I have things to do."

"Like what?"

"I have to clean out my gutters."

"Gee, that sounds like fun."

"It's gotta be done."

"Actually, I was hoping we could do something . . . together."

There was no mistaking her meaning, and his mind went immediately to the ninety-five percent of last night that had gone perfectly rather than the five percent that hadn't.

No. Don't you ever forget that five percent.

He gave her a stern look. "There's no reason to go any further with this, Darcy. It was wrong from the beginning. You know I hate high-maintenance women."

She raised her chin. "Well, I don't think much of blue-collar men."

"All that mirror gazing and clothes shopping."

"All that beer drinking and sports watching."

"Nobody gets between me and the Cowboys on Sunday afternoons."

"And nobody gets between me and Neiman's on sale days." She sighed. "Okay, so now it's more like Wal-Mart and their Everyday Low Prices, but it won't be that way forever."

"Why is that so important to you?"

"What? To have nice things? To live in a place where I can turn on a light and not hear the patter of little roach feet?"

"You could have stayed with your parents."

"Once you meet them, you'll change that tune."

"I doubt I'll ever be meeting them. Like I said, we have no business being together. Now, it's time for me to get to those gutters." He brushed past her and walked out of the kitchen.

"John. Wait."

He turned back. "What?"

She let out a breath. "You told me to let you know."

He paused. "Know what?"

"When I was ready."

"Ready for what?"

Her eyes flitted around nervously before they finally settled on his again, and she spoke so quietly he could barely hear her. "To get real."

"Get real?" he said warily. "Don't you mean you're ready to see if you can fake it a little better?"

"Damn it, John, will you cut me some slack? This is hard enough for me to talk about."

Hard for her to talk about, and even harder for him to

take. It didn't do much for a man's ego when a woman faked it. He knew why she'd done it, why she'd always done it, but still it irritated him. Hell, there wasn't much about this woman that didn't irritate him. But he didn't like how last night had ended, and he decided he wasn't going to leave it at that.

"Okay, Darcy. We can give it another shot."

She nodded.

"But before things go any further between us, there are a few issues we need to address."

"Uh . . . like what?"

"Come with me."

Chapter 16

As John turned and headed down the hall, Darcy just stood there for several seconds, her heart racing, wondering what he was up to.

There was only one way to find out.

She followed him down the hall, her heart skipping a little when he went straight to his bedroom. His furniture was old, cheap, and out of style, and the room was pretty much devoid of anything decorative. An ugly blue chenille bedspread was draped crookedly over a king-sized bed. John sat down on the bed, leaned against the headboard, folded his arms, and stared at her hungrily.

"Take off your clothes."

Darcy recoiled. "What did you say?"

"Do as I tell you."

Suddenly her heart was beating ninety to nothing. John's ever-present displays of authority always irritated her, and she wondered if she shouldn't just call a halt to this before it got started. When it came right down to it, he still scared her a little. How was she ever supposed to feel comfortable around him when he seemed to be able to read her mind, but she was having such a hard time reading his?

But even though she didn't know what he was up to, just the memory of being with him last night was stronger than any resentment she felt. Whatever his game was, she had to play it if she expected to get anywhere. But all this daylight just wasn't going to cut it. She walked over to the drapes and started to close them.

"No," John said. "Leave them open."

She whipped around. "Why?"

"Because this time I want to get a good look at that body you think is so age-ravaged."

Darcy felt a little shiver of apprehension. It had been bad enough in the dark. Now he was going to see her in broad daylight? "Someone will see in."

"The window looks out on the backyard. I have a six-foot wood fence. We might shock a few squirrels, but that's it. Now, off with it."

"I will if you will."

"Nope. You will and I won't."

Okay. It wasn't as if he hadn't already seen her naked. And if she got that way, surely he wouldn't be far behind.

She kicked off her shoes, then pulled her knit shirt over her head and tossed it on the bed. The skirt came next. When it hit the floor, she kicked it aside. Down to her bra and panties, she circled the bed to go to him.

"All the way," John said.

She closed her eyes, gritting her teeth.

"I'm waiting."

With a sigh of disgust, she took off her bra and stepped out of her panties, refusing to act embarrassed, but so much light was streaming through that window that every bump, bulge, mole, scar, and wrinkle had to be showing up like the topography of the moon through a high-powered telescope. He stared at her with a gaze so hot that there was no mistaking what was on his mind. So why wasn't he *doing* something?

She put her fists on her hips. "Okay. I'm naked. Have we taken care of your stripper fetish yet?"

He jerked his head toward the bed beside him. "Lie down."

With as much dignity as she could muster, she circled around to the other side of the bed and sat down.

"Okay," she said. "It's your turn. Take off your clothes."

"In good time."

"But—"

"I told you to lie down."

"You're not playing fair."

"Did I ever say I would?"

"Damn it, John, you're doing it again! Do you always have to be in control of everything? When do *I* get to be in control?"

"When I say you can be in control."

She drew back with disbelief. "Did you just *hear* yourself? I'm not putting up with this!"

"Fine. Get up, get dressed, and leave."

His words jolted the indignation right out of her, because leaving was the last thing she wanted to do. She just wanted to have some kind of say-so in this situation. Just a little. Was that so much to ask?

Evidently so.

With a breath of disgust, she scooted forward and lay down on her back. He stretched out beside her, propped on one elbow. With him fully clothed and her stark naked, she felt completely at his mercy. Then again, she could be wearing a full-length parka and still feel as if she was at his mercy.

His gaze played slowly over her body—her face, her breasts, her hips, all the way down her legs to her feet—stopping here and there for long, concentrated stares.

"John? What are you doing?"

"Looking for the part that's not perfect. You're forty, you know. There has to be something." He sighed. "But I'm afraid I'm not having much luck."

"Then why don't you get naked and I'll see how lucky I can get?"

"Oh, no. Since my visual inspection came up empty, it's time for hands-on."

Darcy swallowed hard. Just the words *hands-on* made her skin quiver with anticipation.

John looked up and down her body, as if trying to decide where to start. Finally he put his hand on her shoulder, then ran his palm down her arm all the way to her fingertips, leaving a trail of goose bumps in its wake. Reversing the process, he grazed his hand back up her arm. He did the same to her other arm, then picked up a strand of her hair and twirled it around his finger. Tiny tingles raced across her scalp.

She knew what he was doing. This was thinly disguised foreplay. Long, drawn out, agonizing foreplay with a featherlight touch. And it was making her crazy.

He rested his palm against her chest, then dragged it downward, circling it around one breast, then the other, brushing his thumb lightly over her nipples. She closed her eyes, her breath coming faster.

"Hmm. No problem areas yet."

He stroked her abdomen, then ran his hand all the way down her leg past her knee. As he brought it back up, he shifted it inward, teasing his fingers along her inner thigh. Almost involuntarily, she opened her thighs a little more. *Higher*, she thought. *I think that's where the problem is.*

Instead, his hand glided around to her hip, and he leaned in to press a kiss to the side of her neck.

"What was that?" she whispered.

"Taste test."

Her heart jolted hard. He could do all the searching he wanted to with that truly gifted mouth. As she imagined it moving over every inch of her body, so much heat pooled between her legs that she thought the bed was going to catch fire.

John froze suddenly, raising his head and glancing down at her hip. "Wait. What's this?"

Her eyes sprang open. "What?"

"I think I feel something."

He ran his hand over Darcy's hip again, and when she realized what he must be talking about, her heart seized up. She sat up suddenly and pulled his hand away, looking at what was beneath it. She was barely able to croak out the word, it was so horrific. "Cellulite?"

"Yeah," he said with a grin. "Imagine that."

"You weren't supposed to actually *find* something!"

He pushed her down on her back again. "Thank God I did. I was beginning to think you really were perfect."

"I *am* perfect!"

"Stop with the body-image issues, Darcy. You're almost forty. You've got to expect a little imperfection. And perfect women are boring, anyway."

"Okay. Fine. You want imperfection? Well, I'm starting

to get a muffin top, too. You missed that. Does that make me even *more* interesting?"

"What's a muffin top?"

"The part of your waist that squishes over the top of your pants."

"Darcy, you're a lot of things, but squishy isn't one of them."

"I was thinking about getting liposuction this fall. Now I'd be lucky to afford a girdle." She sighed. "And what about my flabby arms? And then there are my saggy knees—"

"Okay, sweetheart. You're interesting enough. Let's get on with this."

He rose from the bed and moved to the foot of it, where he peeled off his T-shirt, revealing a body that was even more impressive in daylight than it had been in the dark. Contrary to her body, she didn't see anything even remotely *interesting* about his.

He threw the shirt aside and took off the rest of his clothes, and what lay beneath his jeans told her she hadn't been the only one getting turned on by his bodily inspection. He looked exactly like the dark, mysterious lover who had lived in the shadows of her mind for years. How was she to know he would actually come to life?

After putting on a condom, he pressed her legs apart, then put one knee between hers. Bracing a hand on either side of her shoulders, he loomed over her, fixing his gaze on hers.

"I want you to be still," he told her. "And when I say still, I mean no purposeful movement whatsoever. Do you understand?"

"But—"

He clamped his hand over her mouth. "And just a reminder. If I didn't induce it, I don't want to hear it. Got that?"

She nodded.

Slowly he removed his hand. "Last night I asked you to tell me what you wanted. I think you lied to me."

Darcy swallowed hard. "I . . . I just didn't know what to say."

"Clearly you didn't. So this time I'm not asking."

Which meant he intended to take her any way he wanted to, and her whole body flushed with anticipation. She waited for him to enter her again, but instead he angled his head and kissed the side of her neck. Then her collarbone. His lips would have felt heavenly, if only her nerves weren't tied up in knots from wondering what he was up to.

Rocking back on his knees, he circled his hands around her breasts, kissing the hollow between them, then trailed featherlight kisses down to her navel. He smoothed his hands along her sides, kissing her abdomen at the same time. But it wasn't until he grasped her hips and moved his mouth even lower that it finally dawned on her what he intended to do, and every nerve in her body tightened like a bowstring ready to snap.

"John—"

"Shhh . . . ," he said, his warm breath fanning her inner thigh. He parted her gently with his fingers.

"No, really. I can't. I just—" She gasped. His tongue. Oh, *God*. She'd never felt anything so incredible in her life.

"Please . . . ," she said, her breath coming faster. "Please don't . . ." But her plea must have sounded weak and unconvincing, because he showed no signs of stopping. Not that he would have stopped no matter what she said. That was John. He was a great big bully who insisted on having his way no matter what. So it would be silly of her to try to fight it, wouldn't it?

Oh, yes. It would.

As he stroked her with his tongue, Darcy's fingers flexed, drawing up handfuls of that ugly chenille bedspread. She'd always wondered about this. Listened to other women talk about it. But she'd never actually . . . *oh, my God.*

Her head felt as if it were in a hazy cloud of pure pleasure, her body rigid, her breath coming in sharp, shallow gasps. He'd told her not to move, but she couldn't help it when her hands strayed to his shoulders, clutching, her fingertips digging in. Soon a faint vibration took hold of her nerves, setting off a tremor of arousal that grew hotter every second. He licked and teased and flicked in just the right place, and she squirmed against him because it was so good she almost couldn't stand it, but he held her tightly and tormented her relentlessly until she was clawing his shoulders, arching up to meet him, begging for more, breathing harder as he pushed her higher. A deep, raspy moan rose in her throat that sounded as if it came from somebody else, a carnal, wanton woman so filled with lust she was ready to explode with it. She was close . . . so close . . . so *close* . . .

And then he backed away.

She reached for him. "John! No! Don't stop! Oh, God. *Please*—"

He rose above her, parted her thighs, and plunged

inside her, and that was all it took to send her over the edge.

A burst of energy shot through her, becoming a hard pulsing rhythm that took hold of her nerves and wouldn't let go. Tiny lights flashed on the insides of her eyelids, and she couldn't breathe. But she didn't care. Maybe he was killing her, but it didn't matter. He thrust inside her like a man possessed, reaching for release at the same time he forced every bit of pleasure from her body that it had to give.

"God . . . oh, God, *Darcy* . . ."

His muscles tensed and tightened, and then he fell forward and clung to her, a fierce groan rising in his throat as he came. She lifted her hips to take him as deeply as possible, relishing the feeling of her body joined so perfectly with his.

Finally he slowed, then stopped, turning to kiss her neck before falling to one side, his breath still coming in sharp gasps. She thought she must be dreaming because it just didn't happen like this. She felt as if he'd wiped her out completely, like a tidal wave crashing through a sea wall and leaving it a crumbled wreck. She couldn't think. She couldn't breathe. Tears leaked from the corners of her eyes and streaked down her temples.

"Darcy?"

She wiped away the tears. Oh, God. Where had those come from?

"What's wrong?"

"I don't know . . . I just . . ."

A sob choked her, and she clamped her mouth shut, knowing if she tried to talk again she'd only babble like a baby. She was the one who was supposed to turn men into blithering idiots, not the other way around. But John wasn't like other men. He stripped away every pretense she had. Yanked her out of every comfort zone. He was just so *big* and so *there* and so capable of rendering her into a sobbing frenzy of runaway emotions that she didn't know which way to turn to get away from the overwhelming feelings.

She only knew she had to. Right *now*.

She flung her legs over the side of the bed. He reached for her, but she wiggled out of his grasp and hurried into the bathroom, shutting the door behind her and locking it.

A few moments later, the doorknob rattled. "Darcy!"

"Go away!"

"Go *away?* What the hell is the matter?"

"Please just *go!*"

Darcy grabbed a bath towel, wrapped it around herself, and sat down on the edge of the tub, feeling weak as a wet tissue. Why was she acting so weird? Why couldn't she have held it together long enough to smile sweetly and say something like, *Real nice, baby. What do you do for an encore?*

Instead she'd locked herself in the bathroom like some kind of emotional wedding night virgin. He already thought she was half crazy. This confirmed that there was no "half" about it.

He knocked on the door again. "Darcy! Tell me what's wrong!"

"Nothing's wrong."

"When a woman locks herself in the bathroom and cries, there's something wrong!"

"No! I told you nothing's wrong!"

"It was good for you. I know it was. You can't tell me it wasn't!"

And that was the problem. It was good. So unbelievably and unexpectedly and overwhelmingly good that she'd lost her mind. Completely lost it.

"John! Just please go away. *Please!*"

"Where exactly do you expect me to go? It's my house!"

What a dope she was. Stuck in a man's bathroom, telling him *he* needed to leave?

"I don't get you, Darcy. Since when is great sex a problem? I never had a woman complain before. But what are you doing? Crying and locking yourself in the bathroom!"

"John, please . . ."

"I don't know why you're doing this, but you can be damned sure I'm getting to the bottom of it!"

She could hear it in his voice. He was going to claw through the door with his bare hands and then torture the truth right out of her. The average man wouldn't tear up his own house, but she wasn't so sure about John, and she waited for the door to come crashing down.

But now she heard nothing. She listened closely for a minute. Still nothing.

She dropped her head to her hands. He was probably just sitting out there, waiting for her to come out, and she'd have to eventually. But what then?

No man had ever made her feel like this before, as if she'd clawed her way through a barbed-wire fence to be with him again. Was she turning into one of those women who lost their heads over men? Look at Carolyn. Was she not telling the whole story? Did she put up with Ralph because once they slipped between the covers, he made her feel like *this?* Was that why he could control every other aspect of her life? Why she loved him when there was no obvious reason she should? If so, it had turned her into a mind-numbed idiot. And Darcy had the horrible feeling that she wasn't far behind. One cataclysmic orgasm, and she was on the verge of becoming a female fool.

The doorknob rattled again. Darcy jerked her head up in time to see the door swing open and John come into the bathroom.

She gasped. "John! How did you—"

"Bathroom doorknobs might as well not even have locks." He tossed a screwdriver onto the bathroom counter, wearing his usual hard-ass expression that said he was getting to the bottom of things no matter what.

Darcy sniffed a little and staggered to her feet. "I know I'm being dumb," she said through her tears. "Please don't kill me."

John opened his mouth to say something, only to clamp it shut again. As he stared at her tear-streaked face, his warrior stance slipped a little. Finally his whole body slumped with resignation.

"I just want to know why you're crying," he said helplessly. "That's all."

"I . . . I don't know."

"You make me crazy. You know that?"

"Uh-huh."

"I haven't had a clear thought since the moment I met you."

"I know."

"I'm not used to that."

"I know."

"Do you suppose all this crazy stuff is going to get better anytime soon?"

She shrugged weakly. "I don't know. But if I were you, I wouldn't hold my breath."

He shook his head slowly, then looked heavenward as if searching for a little divine guidance. When that didn't seem to be forthcoming, he let out a long, weary sigh and held out his arms.

"Come here."

She wobbled forward and fell against him, curling her arms around his waist and sobbing against his shoulder. He held her close, and she clung to him, overcome with the relief of being in his arms when she thought he might never want to hold her again. He stroked up and down her back, making little *shushing* sounds, and pretty soon her crying wound down.

"I just don't understand you," he said.

"I know. I don't understand me, either."

"Then how am I ever supposed to?"

"I think you understand more than you know."

"How's that?"

"You told me last night that I didn't like sex. You were right. Up to now, there hasn't been much about it to like."

"I'm trying to change that."

"I know. What happened just now . . ."

"Yes?"

She took a deep, shuddering breath. "It's never been like that for me. Never. It was just so . . . so . . ."

"Good?"

"God, yes."

"Then why are you crying?"

"I don't know. It just . . . happened."

He enveloped her in his arms again, kissing the top of her head. "Just don't lock me out," he said. "Okay? Never again."

She nodded. After all, what would be the point? No matter how much she tried to hide herself, he always found a way in.

⁓

On Monday morning, John got to the office early to look over some quarterly tax reports before heading out on a few repossessions, but his brain just wasn't in the game. Yesterday had been so good that he hadn't stopped thinking about it for two minutes. He hadn't wanted Darcy to leave his house last night, but she had to let her dog out, and quite frankly, she'd just about worn him out. Once she'd gotten over the hysterical crying fit he still didn't totally understand, she'd become like a kid in a candy store, going after him like a woman possessed. And that had been just fine with him.

Not that he didn't know the limitations of a relationship with a woman like her. He knew what kind of man she was looking for in the long run, and it wasn't one like him. And he wasn't looking for anything permanent at all. But that didn't mean he couldn't enjoy things in the short run. There was nothing wrong with a relationship that was based on sex. It came with no strings attached. Baggage didn't matter, because it was temporary. And then when it was time to walk away, nobody got hurt.

He looked back down at the pages on his desk, only

to see he'd pulled out the report for the wrong quarter. It had taken him ten minutes to realize it, since all he'd done from the time he sat down at his desk was sip coffee and stare off into space. This wasn't like him. Tax reports, by God, were serious business. But right now all he could think was, *To hell with Uncle Sam.*

No. Get it together. You have a business to run.

Then he had a horrible thought.

What if Darcy let on to Tony and Amy that the two of them were seeing each other? He'd protested so much about wanting nothing to do with her that if Tony found out, he'd rib John about it endlessly. And Amy. If she found out, she'd want to know just how serious it was, and no matter what he answered, she'd start planning the wedding. As flamboyant as Darcy could be, he was afraid she'd walk right into his office, throw her arms around his neck, and kiss him.

Please, God, don't let her do that.

A few minutes later, Amy got to work, followed shortly by Tony. Darcy arrived her usual ten minutes late. His nerves jangled a little when he saw her, and all kinds of erotic thoughts flooded his mind.

No. Concentrate. Watch for any indication that this thing's going to blow up in your face.

Darcy put her purse on her desk, then went to the coffeepot, poured herself a cup, and returned to her desk. She turned on her computer, then sat down and sipped her coffee as the screen came to life.

John breathed a sigh of relief. At least she hadn't walked into his office right off the bat and hit him with a great big public display of affection. It was even good that she hadn't immediately come into his office to say good morning. She didn't usually do that, so if she did it now, it might look suspicious.

A few minutes later, he headed to the coffeepot for a refill.

"Good morning, Darcy," he said as he poured, smiling a little, but not too much. Amy had a direct line of sight right to his face.

"Hi, John," Darcy said as she typed. "I'll have the morning report for you in just a few minutes."

He stood there a moment more, waiting for her to say something else. But she didn't even look up, so he just went back to his office, feeling a little disappointed. That was it?

No. This was a good thing, too. It appeared she wasn't going to be one of those needy, insecure women who would eventually ask him stuff like *What are you thinking?* and *Where is our relationship going?* and all that other nonsense.

For the next hour, he glanced at her repeatedly through his office window. He watched her file, particularly when she reached into a lower cabinet and her skirt pulled tight across that pretty little ass. He watched her talk on the telephone, twirling her hair around her finger. He watched her type not nearly as fast as a clerk ought to. He watched her cuss out the copier as she cleared a paper jam.

He watched her *breathe.*

Finally he got up to leave on a repossession. He told her he'd be back in a few hours. She acknowledged that with a nod, then got up to go to the storeroom.

Had it been a dream? Had he not had wild, screaming sex with her just yesterday? She was supposed to be gazing at him all day, giving him those suggestive little looks that said, *Can't wait until tonight*. What was *wrong* with her?

He picked up one car that morning, then hit two after lunch. When he got back to the office after the last repossession for the afternoon and passed by her desk, she barely looked up. He went into his office and stared at her through the window, but he finally got so frustrated that he closed the blinds so he wouldn't be tempted to count the number of times she blinked.

Finally, at about three-thirty, she came into his office. He looked up at her expectantly. She put a new set of repossession orders in his in-box, then turned around to leave. No sexy smile. No suggestive little wink. Nothing.

Enough was enough.

"Darcy," he snapped.

She turned around. "What?"

"Get back in here."

He came around his desk, closed the door, and glared down at her.

"What are you doing?"

She blinked. "What do you mean, what am I doing?"

"Have you forgotten we spent the whole day yesterday in bed together?"

"Of course not. How could I forget that?"

"Then why am I getting the cold shoulder today?"

"Cold shoulder?"

"You haven't spoken ten words to me all day."

"There have been a lot of days when I didn't speak ten words to you."

"Not after we spent an entire day in bed together."

"That's supposed to make me more chatty at work?"

"Where do we stand, Darcy? Are you just going to pretend nothing's happening between us?"

"*Is* something happening between us?"

"Of course it is!" he snapped. "We spent an entire day in bed together!"

"Yes, John. I remember. But that was just sex."

Her words startled him. Of course that was what it was. He'd already told himself that. He just hadn't expected *her* to say it.

"Just sex?" he said. "Was that all it was to you?"

"Was it something else to you?"

He froze, his mind suddenly failing him. He hadn't expected that, either. "Uh . . . maybe."

"Maybe?"

"I mean, we are seeing each other," John said. "Aren't we?"

"I don't know. Are we?"

"Will you *stop* talking in circles?" He let out a breath of frustration. "Would it have killed you to at least come in and say hello first thing this morning?"

"I just thought I should play it cool. Do we really want Amy and Tony knowing what we've been up to?"

"Saying hello tells them we've been sleeping together?"

"Better safe than sorry, right?"

Wrong. Saying hello wasn't a problem. Not unless she did something else along with it, like kiss him right out in front of everyone. But it was hard to know where to draw the line.

"Yeah," he said finally, a little confused. "I guess that's right. You know. Better safe than sorry."

"So we need to keep things hush-hush."

"Yeah," he said. "Hush-hush."

She started to leave, then turned back, leaning in and speaking softly. "John, in case you didn't know, any relationship that's *hush-hush* is always *just sex.*"

No. No way. He wasn't letting it go at that. He wasn't about to let her tell him yesterday meant nothing to her, because he knew better. He *knew* better.

He grabbed her by the arm and pulled her back.

"John? What are you—"

He dragged her up against him, took her face in his hands, and smothered her words with a kiss. Hard and deliberate at first, just to make the point, and then he eased up, stroking her cheeks with his thumbs, twining his tongue gently with hers. When he finally melted away from her, she dipped in to touch his lips one last time with hers, as if she couldn't bear for them to part. She opened her eyes, a dreamy expression filling her face.

"Does that feel like *just sex* to you?" he asked.

She sighed. "Uh . . . no."

"Damned right it doesn't."

He yanked open the door and walked out of his office, and Darcy followed.

"Tony! Amy!" John said.

They came to attention.

"Darcy and I are going to be seeing each other. As in dating, and everything that goes along with it." He pointed his finger at Tony. "I don't want you to tell me I'm doing something I swore I never would, because a man's entitled to change his mind. And you," he said, swinging that finger around to Amy. "This doesn't mean it's time to drag Darcy to pick out china patterns and start planning wedding showers." Then his finger came around to

Darcy. "I'll be at your apartment at seven o'clock tonight. I hope you like Chinese, because that's what I'm bringing for dinner." He fanned all of them with one last look that said they'd better toe that line, or else. "Everybody got that?"

There were murmurs of assent.

"Now get back to work."

He strode back to his office and closed the door behind him.

Darcy just stood there, staring at his closed door, amazed at this turn of events. Finally she walked over to Amy's desk, so stunned she could barely speak.

"I can't believe it," she whispered. "Did you hear what he just said?"

Amy grinned. "When you showed up at his house yesterday, I wondered what was going on between you two. Evidently quite a lot."

The most delicious little thrill raced through Darcy. She'd been so careful all day not to be one of those clingy women who thought she had a relationship with a man just because they had sex, even though it had just about killed her to keep her feelings to herself. Instinctively she knew if she assumed anything, a man like John would run for the hills. She had to wait for him to make the first move. But never in her wildest dreams had she imagined he'd make a move like this.

"I can't believe the bullheaded way he charged out here," Amy said with a grin. "That was unprecedented, even for him. He must really be a goner."

A goner? Darcy wondered what Amy meant by that. Their relationship might be more than sex, but it was a far cry from anything else. Someday Darcy intended to get married again, and it wouldn't be to a man like John.

At least, she didn't think it would.

Would it?

"What are you two chatting about over there?" Tony asked.

"None of your business," Amy said.

"John was quite the lunatic there, wasn't he?"

"Yep."

"Shall I tell him you're talking about him behind his back?"

"You do," Amy said, "and I'll tell all the women you're seeing about all the other women you're seeing. Pretty soon you'll be out in the cold, buster."

Tony grinned. "Well, then. By all means, talk away."

Chapter 17

Amy told Darcy that dealing with John was like feeding pigeons in the park. Even though the bread crumbs were good for them, if you threw them at them and demanded they eat, they'd run like crazy. But if you pretended you didn't care if they ate or not, pretty soon they'd come begging. John, she said, was the big, cranky bird in the middle of the flock who was starving and didn't even know it.

After Amy's insight into her brother's psyche, Darcy had planned on playing hard to get for at least a little while longer. Trouble was, playing hard to get was harder than it sounded. Every day Darcy told herself that this would be the evening when she'd say, *No, sorry, can't get together. I have other plans,* but every time the words were on the tip of her tongue, she'd think about his hands and his mouth and his big, strong body and the way he always knew what made her crazy with desire.

But it wasn't just the sex. It was the way he insinuated himself into her life as if he'd always been there. She knew it was merely his ever-present need to command any environment he found himself in, but Amy said it had to be a miracle straight from God that her brother had spent two whole weeks with a woman and he wasn't making up excuses not to see her.

This evening John sat on her sofa with his shoes kicked off and his gigantic feet on her coffee table, looking at the movie ads. Pepé was sprawled out beside him on the sofa. It had taken the dog no time at all to warm up to him, once he realized John wasn't going to yell at him and would pet him as long as he wanted the attention.

"Okay," John said. "Here's a movie we can see."

He rattled off the name of a new action-adventure flick. Darcy turned up her nose. "You're kidding, right?"

"What do you want to see?"

"That one with Julia Roberts."

"It's a chick flick."

"So?"

"So I hate chick flicks. We'll flip a coin."

Darcy knew better than to gamble. After all, look what had happened to Warren. And her gene pool didn't exactly produce the luckiest of people—her mother had never come home from Vegas with a dime to her name. So when Darcy called tails and it was heads, could she really be surprised?

"Oh, boy," she said with a sigh. "Two hours of gratuitous violence. I can't wait."

"Hey, I have to deal with weepy women the next time we go. You think I'm just dying to be subjected to that?"

"Why do I put up with you? You're the most insensitive man I've ever met."

He grabbed her arm and pulled her to the sofa beside him. Pepé scurried away, and in the next second, John had Darcy flat on her back, kissing that one spot at the junction of her neck and shoulder that drove her absolutely wild.

"No sensitivity?" he said, his lips tickling her ear. "I think you know better than that." He slid his hand beneath her shirt and closed it around her waist, kissing her at the same time.

Yes. She did know better.

"Thought you wanted to see a movie," she murmured.

"I do. As long as we can make out in the back row."

"You might miss an explosion or two."

"Oh. Good point." He stood up from the sofa and pulled her to her feet. "Then never mind on the making out. A man has to have his priorities."

Darcy took that as a challenge, and half an hour later, when they were sitting in the deserted back row of theater number six at Tinseltown, she managed to hold his attention significantly better than the movie did, even though it was filled with more guns and explosives per capita than any movie she'd seen in the past ten years. She decided when it was her turn to choose the next movie, she was going to pick the girliest, most estrogen-enhanced tear-jerker possible just so she could watch John squirm.

"Good movie," John said as they left the theater.

"You're kidding, right? A man's head actually exploded."

John grinned. "Yeah, that was great, wasn't it? You don't see something like that every day."

Thank God.

Just then the door to another theater opened, and half a dozen preschool boys swarmed out, followed by a mom-like woman with a chocolate smear on the arm of her blouse and a harried look on her face. One of the boys wore a paper crown and a big button on his shirt that said, "It's My Birthday!"

The mom murmured an apology and took the birthday boy by the hand, but before she could get a good hold on him, he jerked away from her and took off down the hall with the other five boys in screaming pursuit. She blew out a breath that puffed her bangs away from her forehead and took off after them.

Darcy shook her head. "That poor, poor woman."

"Why did you never have kids?" John said as they walked toward the lobby.

"Are you kidding? You just saw why not."

"All kids are like that."

"Exactly."

"So you never even thought about having any of your own?"

Darcy tossed her soda cup in a nearby trash can. "Oh, sure. I guess every woman thinks about it. But Warren thought he was too old. And now I am, too."

"I don't know. A lot of forty-year-old women are having babies."

Darcy grabbed his arm and pulled him to a halt. She looked left and right, then whispered, "I'm *not* forty!"

"But you're almost there, right?"

"*God,* you're infuriating."

She stalked off and John followed. She glanced over her shoulder and saw him smiling, which irritated her even more. They left the building and went into the parking lot, where the evening air felt like a blast furnace compared to the cool air inside the theater.

John strode alongside her. "So when's your birthday?"

"Can we talk about something else?"

"You and that age thing. Will you cut it out? People are living to ninety these days, so you're not even middle-aged. And age is just a number, anyway."

"*Age* is just a *number?*" She rolled her eyes. "You've been reading *Redbook,* haven't you?"

"Seriously. I don't see what the big deal is."

"Well, let's see. For one thing, if I don't color my hair on a regular basis, you'll see just how gray it really is."

"So what? Look here." He pointed to his temple, where a few gray hairs were showing through.

"Gray makes men look distinguished. It makes women look old."

"That's crap."

"No, it isn't. And if I don't get back in for more Botox, my forehead is going to look like a cotton shirt that got balled up in the dryer."

"Botox?" John said as they approached his SUV. "I don't know anyone who's actually done that."

"I don't know anyone who hasn't."

"Doesn't that wear off in six months or so?"

"Yes."

"Let it."

They reached the car, and Darcy faced him, laughing humorlessly. "You wouldn't like the result."

"What? A normal face? What's wrong with that?"

"You don't understand. In a matter of months, I'm going to look like a Shar-Pei."

He shrugged. "So what? I like dogs."

She smacked him on the arm. He grabbed her wrist, pulled her up next to him, and kissed her. "Wrinkles are no big deal. They give a person character."

"Wrinkles give *men* character. They give women hives."

"Some women worry too much about things like that. You're one of them."

"That's easy for men to say. Men only seem to get better. Women fall apart."

"Maybe if they didn't use all that crap to build themselves up so much, there wouldn't be so far to fall."

Darcy had to admit that was probably true. But since she was used to looking fabulous, taking it down several notches was a blow to her senses. And when she turned forty this Saturday, it was going to be the biggest blow of all.

A few minutes later they were driving back to her apartment. John had taken a route through west Plano that Darcy wished he hadn't, because it took them only blocks away from her old house. As they drove past the places she used to frequent—the Shops at Legacy, the Victorian Tea Room, her favorite Starbucks—she couldn't help imagining what her upcoming birthday would be like if her life hadn't taken such a drastic turn. Warren would undoubtedly "surprise" her with whatever lavish item she'd been hinting about for the past month, then take her out to the obligatory dinner at some overpriced restaurant, where she would have basked in all the opulence and reveled in the fact that even though she was a year older, she had enough money that she didn't have to look like it.

John pulled up to a stoplight at the corner of Legacy and Forest Glen, and suddenly insult was heaped on top of injury when Darcy found herself looking up a long, tree-shaded lane that led to one of the most familiar places of all to her: the clubhouse at Forest Glen Golf and Country Club.

With a silent sigh, she stared at the white-pillared, neo-Colonial brick mansion. The fountain out front was lit by floodlights and circled by pristine landscaping, accented by a collage of flowers lining the front walk that led to a pair of massive oak doors. In the distance, the rolling hills of the golf course were bathed in the bright orange hues of the setting sun.

At least twice a week for the past fourteen years, Darcy had crossed the threshold into that clubhouse, and as she looked at it now, it was almost inconceivable that it wasn't part of her life anymore.

"Warren and I had a membership there," Darcy murmured, nodding toward the clubhouse.

John glanced at it, then stared straight ahead, tapping his fingertips on the steering wheel as he waited for the light to change. "Pretty pretentious, if you ask me."

"Yes," she agreed. "It is."

"You miss it, don't you?"

"Hard not to. It was an easy life."

"Sometimes easy isn't best."

Still, she couldn't help the longing that overtook her, the sensation of being on the outside looking in. She hadn't been back to the club since her life turned upside down. She didn't even know if their membership was still paid up or whether Warren had jerked that out from under her, too. Not that she wanted to go there with the girls for Saturday lunch and martinis these days. A single meal would cost almost a whole day's salary, and did she really need all those catty eyes staring at her, thanking God her misfortune wasn't theirs?

Darcy felt the oddest kind of longing. It wasn't as if she wanted the life back that she'd lived with Warren. She didn't need that lavish lifestyle. She just wanted to know she had a comfortable little cushion between her and destitution. But there was no way that was ever going to happen on the salary she made right now.

She thought about asking John one more time if he would *please* make her a repossession agent in training, but she knew what the answer was going to be. If only she could come up with another way to grab Larry's car, she might get that ball rolling in the right direction. It was still her best bet for her first repossession. She was pretty sure Larry wouldn't pull out a gun and blow her head off, but she couldn't say that about a stranger whose car she was going after. Later, once she got John on board, he could teach her the subtleties of dealing with irate deadbeats.

But other than waiting for Larry to leave his house and then hoping she could follow him, she didn't know how to catch him with that Corvette outside his garage.

Then she had a thought.

She froze, her hand tightening on the console, and glanced back at the clubhouse. She knew where Larry went every Monday evening. The same place Warren used to go—to the club for their male bonding ritual of Scotch and cigars, a tradition that the men would miss only if the world came to an end. A plan started forming in Darcy's mind of a way to grab his keys, then his car. In no time that Corvette would be in the impound of Lone Star Repossessions where it belonged.

"Darcy?" John said. "What's the matter?"

Darcy whipped around. "What?"

"You have a funny look on your face."

"I do?"

John glanced over, narrowing his eyes. "Yeah. Like you're plotting something, and I'm not sure I'm going to like it."

She let a lazy smile come to her lips as she inched her hand over to rest against his thigh. "Oh, you'll like it. Trust me."

The light turned green, and John hit the gas. In seconds, he was driving just a little bit faster than the law allowed.

Darcy decided that first thing in the morning, she was going to research repossession law on the Internet so she'd know what she could and couldn't do so she wouldn't slip up again. As long as she was sure she'd be breaking no laws, and as long as she could talk Carolyn into helping her, and as long as Larry wasn't so down on his luck that he'd lost his country club membership, Monday evening she was going to put her plan into action.

"No, Darcy. No. I changed my mind. I can't do it. I can't help you steal a car."

Carolyn braked and turned into the parking lot of a strip mall on Parker Road and brought her car to a halt.

"Come on, Carolyn!" Darcy said. "You can't back out on me now!"

"Do I look like Ethel Mertz to you?"

"You barely have to do anything," Darcy said. "While Raoul is parking your car, I'll grab the key to Larry's car."

"What if there are two attendants on duty?"

"On a Monday night?"

"So what do I do while he's parking my car?"

"Just walk into the club like you always do."

She shook her head. "No. There's no way I'm doing this."

"Will you stop being so neurotic? I'll be the one doing the key stealing."

Carolyn sat there like a stubborn mule, refusing to budge. Good Lord. It must be hell to be that spineless.

Darcy sat back in her seat, her eyes narrowing. "Carolyn? Do you remember a certain New Year's party a few years ago?"

Carolyn's eyes widened.

"Madeline's husband . . ."

"Darcy—"

"And you . . ."

Carolyn gritted her teeth.

"In their pool house . . ."

"I'd had four martinis! And we didn't *do* anything!"

"Yeah? Well, Charlie sure had a hard time explaining that lipstick on his face to Madeline."

"You wouldn't dare say anything about that to anyone!"

"You're right. I wouldn't. Because friends stick together."

Carolyn fumed for a moment more, her lips pursed angrily. Finally she threw up her hands. "All right! I'll do it!" She put the car in gear. "God, you play dirty."

Darcy smiled. "Thanks, Carolyn. You're a true friend."

"Yeah. Friends forever. We can share a cell in Huntsville. Are you *sure* you have the authority to do this?"

"I showed you the repossession order, didn't I?"

"Wait a minute. How are you going to know which key to grab?"

"The car was manufactured in 1968. Keys looked different back then. No embedded computer chips."

"But how do you know there won't be other classic cars in the parking lot?"

"We'll scope it out once we get there just to make sure."

A minute later they were driving up the lane that led to the clubhouse. Darcy scanned the parking lot. "There's Larry's car."

"Do you see any other older cars?"

"No. Pull up to the valet stand."

Carolyn drove up, and Raoul stepped off the curb to open her door. Darcy got out the passenger side.

"Good evening, Mrs. Grant. Mrs. McDaniel. So nice to see both of you this evening."

Darcy and Carolyn greeted Raoul, then stepped up on the curb as if they were going into the club. Raoul slid behind the wheel of Carolyn's car and drove it toward the parking lot. Carolyn just stood there dumbly, as if she didn't know what to do.

"Go into the club," Darcy whispered. "And watch for anyone coming out."

"You didn't tell me I had to be a lookout!"

"Just *go*, will you?"

Carolyn scurried inside, and Darcy hurried over to the valet stand, ducking down to fish through the key hooks beneath it. At first they all looked alike, and for a moment she was afraid she wasn't going to find the right one.

Then she saw it. A key that was different. She pulled

it off the hook and saw that it was even on a Corvette key ring. *Thanks for the big red flag, Larry.*

"What are you doing?"

She stood up and spun around. Oh, God. *Larry?*

Over his shoulder, she saw Carolyn standing at the door with a panicked *I'm sorry but I couldn't stop him!* look on her face, probably wetting her pants at the same time.

"Gosh, Larry," Darcy stammered. "It's early. You're calling it a night already?"

"I have a date." He nodded at her hand. "That's my key."

Okay. She had one of two choices. She could make up some dumb story about why she picked up his key, hand it to him, and walk away, in which case she would have screwed up twice trying to repossess this car. Or she could flash the repo order, march right over to the parking lot, get in his car, and drive it away.

She took a deep breath, deciding she hadn't come this far to back down now. Gail always said Larry had no balls, so he probably wouldn't even try to stop her.

She pulled the repo order from her purse and held it up. "Sorry, Larry. You're busted."

He grabbed it from her, a look of disbelief passing over his face. "My car is being repossessed?"

She took the order back and stuffed it into her purse. "That's what happens when you don't pay your bills."

She skirted the valet stand and started toward the parking lot. For a moment she thought Larry was too dumbfounded to follow, but then he took off after her.

"You?" he said, striding alongside her. "You're the one repossessing my car?"

"That's right."

"I heard you fell on hard times with Warren being an embezzler and all, but . . . you're a *repo man?*"

"Do I look like a man to you, Larry?"

"You're not taking my car."

"Watch me."

"Darcy, give me the key."

She kept walking.

"Gimme the key!"

He reached for it, but she was quicker, stopping short and stuffing it down the front of her shirt into her bra. She doubted John would do something like that, but she had a few assets he didn't, so she might as well put them to good use.

Larry's eyes narrowed. "Don't think I won't go after that."

"No, you won't. It's common knowledge that you get excited reaching into a woman's bra only if you're paying for the privilege."

"That's not true! Gail made all that up!"

"Right." She kept on walking.

"Come on, Darcy!" Larry said, striding along beside her. "I'm just having a few financial problems right now. I'll clear things up with the bank in a few days."

"Fine. Once you're square with the bank, then you can have your car back."

She reached the Corvette, opened the door, and slid behind the wheel. She pulled out the key and stuck it in the ignition, then looked up at him with a sarcastic smile and a little wave of her fingertips.

"Bye-bye, Larry."

Feeling a surge of accomplishment, she started to turn

the key, only to see something out of the corner of her eye that made a shiver of apprehension run right up her spine.

A stick shift?

It took a moment or two for the sight to soak in. No. This could *not* be happening. *Damn it, damn it, damn it!* Why hadn't it occurred to her that a sports car might have a manual transmission?

Wait. There was no reason to panic. She'd seen Warren drive a car with a stick shift a million times. How hard could it be?

No. That was insane. It was like saying she'd watched a guy pedal a unicycle a million times, so of course she could do it, too. There was no way she could make it back to the office without wrecking this car, and if she did that, she knew John's horrific cop threat wouldn't be just a threat any longer.

"What's the matter?" Larry said.

She yanked the door open and got out of the car. Larry looked confused. Then he zeroed in on the gearshift, and a big, mocking grin came over his face. "You don't know how to drive a stick shift, do you?"

Darcy glared at him.

"Ha! You thought you had me, didn't you?" He held out his hand. "My key, please?"

She slapped the key into his hand. "You'd better watch out, Larry. I'll get this car sooner or later."

Larry opened the door. "Yeah? Well, you'll have to find it first."

"I found it this time, didn't I?"

"Yeah. Thanks for the tip-off." That mocking grin again. "Forewarned is forearmed."

He got into the car, started the engine, and hit the gas. As he squealed out of the parking lot, Darcy's hands curled into fists. She didn't know what it was going to take, but sooner or later, she was bringing in that car.

Chapter 18

A few days later, Darcy sat at her kitchen table going over her finances, wondering how she was going to pay her apartment rent when it came due on September first. When August arrived in Dallas, it brought with it the usual hundred-degree temperatures, along with humidity that would challenge even the most industrial-strength hair-care products. Before her life fell apart, the heat had been nothing more than an irritating nuisance. But now she had to air-condition a noninsulated apartment with west-facing windows, and the astronomical electric bill that produced was going to eat a good portion of her monthly income.

Basically, she couldn't afford to live in a decent apartment with good insulation, so she was going to have to pay a ridiculous amount for electricity, which meant she'd probably never be able to save enough money to move to a decent apartment with good insulation. Up to now, she'd never realized the world of catch-22 that poor people were stuck living in.

Okay. Maybe if she cut her own hair, drove only when she had to, and quit eating, she could afford to pay the rent, assuming nothing else went wrong.

Unfortunately, something did.

Gertie's air conditioner had been blowing progressively warmer, and when Darcy got in her car to go to work the next morning, the air actually felt hot instead of cold. She drove to her father's mechanic shop on her lunch hour, sweat sticking her hair to the back of her neck and trickling down her temples, hoping he could twist a screw or something and make it blow cold air again.

"Looks like a Freon problem," her father said. "Needs a recharge."

"What's that going to cost me?"

"Just the cost of the Freon, but on a car this old, it's in short supply. If it needs two cans, maybe a hundred bucks."

Darcy sighed. Another hundred dollars? "I'll have to come back in next week. I'm really short on money until payday."

"I'll take care of it. It's too damned hot for anybody to be driving around without air."

"Thanks, Dad. I'll pay you back."

"No need. You've got plenty of other things to worry about."

"No. I want to. It may be a little while, though, unless . . ."

"Unless what?"

"Unless I get the car I'm trying to repossess."

When she saw the look of astonishment on her father's face, she wished she'd kept her mouth shut.

"You're repossessing a car? I thought you were a clerk."

"I'm trying to get a promotion. I've gone after this one car twice already. The first time, it turned out I was kinda breaking the law, but nobody found out. The second time I could have driven it away without any problem, but the car had a manual transmission."

She couldn't remember the last time she'd seen her father smile, much less laugh. But slowly the corner of his mouth turned up, and he actually chuckled a little.

She frowned. "You're laughing at me."

"No, I'm not. I just never thought . . ." He shook his head in disbelief. "You want to be a repossession agent?"

"Why not? It pays pretty well. But my boss doesn't want me to get within ten feet of a car with a delinquent loan. He says it's a crummy job. People yell at you. And sometimes it's dangerous. But I know I can handle it. And if I can bring in just one car on my own, he'll have to admit it."

Her father's smile grew even bigger.

"Dad? Will you stop smiling? You're starting to freak me out."

He nodded toward his truck. "Get in."

"What?"

"Behind the wheel."

Darcy drew back. "Behind the wheel? Of *your* truck? The one you wouldn't let God himself drive?"

"Yep."

"Why?"

"If my little girl's gonna be a repo agent, I need to teach her how to drive a car with a manual transmission."

Darcy couldn't believe it. "You're going to help me?"

"Yes. But for God's sake, don't tell your mother."

"I guess she would flip out, wouldn't she? She didn't exactly raise me to steal cars."

"Uh-huh," her father said. "You might break a nail, and that'd be tragic."

Darcy slid behind the wheel of the truck, and her father got into the passenger seat. For maybe the first time in her adult life, her father looked different to her. Maybe he really wasn't the rock around her mother's neck Lyla always said he was. Maybe it was the other way around. Her father stayed up late watching TV every night of his life, claiming he had a hard time sleeping. But Darcy knew that during those late-night hours it was just him and the idiot box and no Lyla to contend with. A man grabbed his peace and quiet wherever he could.

She stuck her hand out for the keys, but her father held on to them, looking at her directly in a way he rarely did.

"This hasn't been easy for you, has it?" he said. "Since Warren left?"

She sighed. "No. It hasn't."

"Still, I'm glad he's gone. You can do better than him."

"Why? Because he's a criminal?"

"No. Because he was the wrong man for you."

"I don't know. Life was pretty easy. He gave me everything."

"You don't need a man to give you things. You're very capable."

Darcy sighed. "Come on, Dad. I'm not capable of much of anything, and you know it."

"Nah. You've always had a handle on things. You've been running your own show since kindergarten. Just because you haven't been taking care of yourself doesn't mean you can't."

Actually, in the past few weeks, Darcy had gotten these

strange little vibes that maybe it was a blessing that Warren was gone. Of course, it would have been even more of a blessing if he'd left behind a couple hundred thousand dollars for her, but a blessing just the same.

"Your mother needs taking care of," her father said. "Always has. But you're not your mother."

"You two have been married a long time."

"Yep."

"You had to get married."

"Didn't have to."

"Because of me."

"It was just what people did back then. The responsible ones still do."

"So what about now? I'm not a kid anymore, and these days people don't hang around if they don't want to."

"Old habits are hard to break."

"You still fight a lot."

"Like I said. Old habits." He shrugged. "I know it doesn't seem like it, but a lot of times it really isn't all that bad. Your mom throws a fit, and I do whatever I want to do, anyway. It's just what we do. If it didn't work for us, we'd have split up a long time ago."

"She's been on a rampage since Warren left me."

"She's just afraid for you, that's all. Believe it or not, she always just wants the best for you. She has a hell of a way of showing that sometimes, but it's the truth."

In her heart, Darcy had always known that. She just wished her mother would pick more calm and productive ways of demonstrating it.

An hour later, her father was probably regretting putting the transmission of his precious pickup through the trauma of Darcy's driving ineptitude, but finally she learned how to make the truck stop and go with a minimum of gear grinding and engine dying.

She couldn't wait to see the expression on John's face when she brought in a car all by herself without breaking the law to do it. She knew he'd launch into a tirade about it, but in the end she knew another truth: he'd respect her for the fact that she'd been able to pull it off. And for maybe the first time in her life, respect from a man was something she wanted to have.

"Speaking of stealing cars," her father said. "Would it help to know how to hot-wire one?"

Darcy smiled. This day just got better and better.

⁓

On Saturday morning, Darcy woke up, but it was a minute before she realized what day it was. When she did, she pulled the covers back over her head, wishing she could shut out the world. Today was G-Day. "G" as in geriatric.

Her fortieth birthday.

She'd already told her parents she didn't want them to make a fuss. No presents, no dinner out, no card, no nothing. She'd told Carolyn the same thing, threatening her with death if she showed up with a present or tried to drag her to La Maison for lunch. John would have no idea it was her birthday, so he wouldn't feel obligated to do anything. She wasn't even seeing him until later, anyway. He was working today, going after a few cars he hadn't been able to grab during the week. He told her to come to his house around seven o'clock. With luck, he'd take her straight to bed, and by the time she woke up, her birthday would be over. Then she'd just have to resign herself to living out the remainder of her years as an old woman.

She pulled the covers back over her head and slept till noon, hoping to make the day go by a little faster. Then, just as she was getting up to take a shower, she heard a knock at her door. She threw on a robe and looked out the peephole, surprised to see Amy.

She opened the door. "Amy! What are you doing here?"

Amy grinned. "Just dropped by to wish you a happy birthday."

With a painful groan, Darcy turned around and walked to her living room. Amy came inside and closed the door behind her. "What's the matter?"

"How did you know it was my birthday?"

"I'm nosy. I looked through your personnel records a few weeks ago, just in case it was coming up soon." She handed Darcy an envelope. "This is for you."

Darcy opened it. A Wal-Mart gift card?

A few months ago, she'd have turned her nose up at this. But now it felt as if Amy had given her pure gold. Just thinking of how much she could buy there for so little sent a little thrill right up her spine.

"This is great!" she said. "I need new dishtowels and a toaster and some other stuff for my kitchen." She gave Amy a hug. "Thank you."

"Why don't you get dressed and I'll go shopping with you? Unless you have something else planned today."

"No. Nothing. Not until tonight, anyway. I'm going to see John, and—" She stopped short, a terrible thought crossing her mind. "Amy. Please tell me you didn't say anything to him about my birthday."

"Didn't have to. He already knew. Apparently he was poking through personnel records, too."

Great. "I hope he's not planning anything."

"Truthfully, I don't know what he has in mind."

Darcy sat down on her sofa with a heavy sigh. "I just wanted this birthday to go by without anybody even mentioning it."

"But why? Birthdays are fun."

"Not when you're turning forty."

Amy waved her hand. "Forty's no big deal."

"Yeah, that's what John keeps saying. That forty's no big deal. Just because he passed right by it with no repercussions, he expects me to as well."

"Don't bet on that."

"What?"

"The 'no repercussions' thing."

"What do you mean?"

Amy sat down on the sofa beside Darcy. "He turned forty right after he had to quit the police force. That wasn't easy on him. It reminded him he was having to start over, only this time he wasn't a kid anymore. See, he wanted to come up through the ranks and eventually run the show. Given the fact that he thrives on being the boss, I think eventually he would have made police chief."

Darcy smiled. "It's not hard to imagine that, is it?"

"Nope. John has to be in charge of something, or he goes nuts. That's why he started his own business."

"He told me your family thought he ought to buy a Subway franchise."

Amy laughed. "Yeah, we suggested it. A nice, normal business where he has very little chance of getting his head blown off. But no. He's not happy unless he's dealing with gun-waving deadbeats." Then her smile faded. "But to tell you the truth, he's not really looking for some*thing* as much as he is some*one*. He just doesn't know that yet."

Darcy felt a little flush of warmth, thinking back to a couple of times in the past few weeks when she'd seen John staring at her with something that looked like confusion, as if he was trying to figure something out but was coming up short. Maybe he was looking ahead to what his life might be like in the future and imagining her in it.

Or maybe he was just picturing her naked.

Darcy took a quick shower, and then she and Amy went shopping at Wal-Mart. After buying a few things for her kitchen, Darcy picked up some car wax on sale, thinking that sometime she ought to try to spiff up old Gertie a little. When Amy said there was no time like the present and offered to help, Darcy figured she couldn't turn that down. They spent the rest of the afternoon washing and waxing the old car. In spite of a first-class effort on their part, though, Gertie didn't look much better than she had to start with, but Darcy was very happy to have killed a few more hours of G-Day.

Amy left about five o'clock. Darcy had just headed to the bathroom to take another shower when she heard a knock. Looking out the peephole, she was surprised to find Bernie standing at her door, her hands tucked behind her back.

Good God. Not again. Darcy did *not* want to deal with this.

She opened the door with a heavy sigh. "What now?"

"Mr. Bridges would like to speak with you."

"Bernie, will you do me a favor and tell Mr. Bridges to take a hike?"

"I fully intend to. The moment he stops signing my paychecks."

"What does he want?"

"I have no idea."

Darcy sighed. She was still a mess from washing and waxing her car, but so what? If Jeremy dropped by unannounced, he was taking a chance on what she might look like. And what did it matter what he thought, anyway?

She grabbed her keys, locked the door behind her, and followed Bernie to the parking lot, where the limo was double-parked. Bernie slid in beside the driver, and Darcy climbed into the back. As always where Jeremy was concerned, she got a surprise.

He was wearing a tuxedo.

"Hello, Darcy."

For a moment she was speechless. What was he up to now?

"Surprised?" he asked.

"Yes. I wouldn't have thought you even owned a tuxedo."

"I didn't until this afternoon." He tugged on his lapels. "You know, I may eventually like the millionaire look. What do you think?"

What did she think? He looked *amazing*.

"You look . . . okay."

"Okay?" He beamed. "Why, Darcy, I do believe that's the nicest thing you've ever said to me." He knocked on the Plexiglas between him and the driver. "Let's go."

To Darcy's surprise, the driver started the car, and

before she knew it, they'd pulled out of the apartment complex.

"What are you doing?" she said. "Bernie said you just wanted to talk."

"Isn't it amazing what a good liar she is? She blows me away sometimes."

She knocked on the Plexiglas. "Hey! Stop! Take me back home!"

The driver acted as if he hadn't even heard.

"I thought we could spend the evening together," Jeremy said.

"Well, you thought wrong."

"Have a nice dinner."

"Dinner? I don't want to have dinner with you!"

"In San Antonio."

Darcy froze. "What?"

"My private plane is waiting at the airport to fly us there."

Darcy just stared at him, dumbfounded. "You want to take me to San Antonio just for dinner?"

He grinned. "Nothing's too good for the birthday girl."

Birthday. That god-awful word she didn't want to think about, much less hear somebody say. She started to ask him how he knew it was her birthday, but why? By now the man probably knew everything from the number of fillings she had to the brand of feminine-hygiene products she used.

"Have you bothered to look at what I'm wearing?" she asked.

"Not a problem. We're dropping by my house first. I have a wardrobe consultant there with a nice selection of evening dresses for you to choose from. Size six, isn't it?"

Darcy sighed. Did this guy *ever* let up?

"Hmm," he said. "You don't seem particularly happy about my plans for this evening."

"That's right. Your plans. Not mine."

"Just think of it as a very nice surprise."

"Surprise? Technically this is kidnapping."

"Technically, you're right. Are you going to call me on a technicality?"

"I don't like being manipulated."

"It's just a date, Darcy. What could possibly be wrong with that?"

"I already have a date this evening."

Jeremy frowned. "Then you'll just have to cancel it."

"How many times do I have to tell you? I don't want to have dinner with you!"

"Sorry," he said with a gleam in his eye. "You're stuck. This limousine is on an irreversible course to my house, and then to Love Field. You're just going to have to suffer through a flight on a private jet and a gourmet dinner whether you like it or not."

Jeremy sat back with a smirk of satisfaction, but Darcy had no intention of letting him get away with this.

A few minutes later, the limo turned onto a property surrounded by a massive iron and stone fence. The house was tucked away down a gently sloping road lined with trees, a sprawling French chateau with arches and columns trimmed in carved limestone. The massive oak front doors were flanked by diamond-cut glass that shimmered in the evening light. It was even more spectacular than she imagined.

Out of the corner of her eye, she saw Jeremy watching her, a devilish smile on his face. That was what he was.

The devil. Trying to lure her into selling her soul for the opportunity to enjoy the kind of luxury only the wealthy could consider.

She got out of the limo and followed Jeremy and Bernie into the two-story foyer. A dazzling chandelier lit the space, which was complete with a marble tile floor and a hand-carved Palladian arch leading to the great room beyond.

"So, what do you think?" Jeremy asked. "*Architectural Digest* wanted to do a spread of it last year, but all those people running around my house would have irritated the hell out of me."

As much as she wanted to, there was no way to lie about this. "It's beautiful."

"Give a decorator a blank check, and this is what you get."

Yes, it was amazing. And normally at the sight of this kind of elegance, she'd be salivating like Pavlov's dog. But for some reason, she wasn't thinking about the beauty of this house, or the cachet of a private jet, or about a dining opportunity that didn't involve two-for-one coupons. She was thinking about the man she'd be with.

Or, rather, the man she wouldn't.

Jeremy's cell phone rang. He took it out of his pocket, looked at the caller ID, and frowned.

"I have to take this," he said. "Just go up the stairs to the first bedroom on the right. The wardrobe consultant is waiting for you. Then we'll head to the airport."

"And just when do you intend to take me home?"

He stopped at the doorway, a sly smile playing over his lips. "Actually, Darcy, I was hoping you'd want to stay tonight."

With that, he disappeared into the other room.

Darcy couldn't believe it. What exactly was he offering her? She wondered if it was possible that he was actually getting serious, or whether he was simply spending more money to play the same game.

But then she realized it didn't matter. She wanted out of there. She wanted to go home to her crappy apartment and get ready to go to John's house. Instead of a gourmet dinner complete with fine wine, he'd probably shove a bag of popcorn into the microwave and they'd chase it with a couple of beers. For reasons Darcy still was a little fuzzy on in light of the elegance Jeremy was offering her, the thought of that put a smile on her face.

She went to the kitchen. Bernie sat at the breakfast room table, reading the newspaper. Darcy headed for the telephone to call John, knowing he'd drop whatever he was doing if it meant getting her away from Jeremy Bridges. Then she realized his phone number was programmed into her cell phone, but she didn't know it off the top of her head. And as a former cop, the last thing he'd have is a listed number.

"What are you doing?" Bernie asked.

"Calling a cab."

"Yeah? Got money for cab fare?"

Darcy froze. No, damn it, she didn't. Not only had she gotten away without her cell phone, she'd gotten away without her purse.

"I don't suppose Jeremy has a cookie jar full of money around here somewhere, does he?"

"Nope."

"Bernie, can I borrow—"

"Nope."

"If he won't take me home, you do it."

"Sorry. No can do."

"This really is kidnapping."

"So call the cops."

Darcy put her fists on her hips. "Hey, whatever happened to sisterhood? Women are supposed to stick together."

Bernie made a face. "You saw that *Ya-Ya* movie, didn't you?"

God. This woman was even more infuriating than her boss.

But then Bernie's gaze slowly swept across the kitchen to the back door. Through the big window next to it, Darcy could see Jeremy's umpteen-car garage. Next to the back door was a board where half a dozen sets of car keys hung. Bernie focused on it for a few long, deliberate moments, then looked back down at her newspaper.

"The code for the garage doors is two-eight-one-nine," she said.

Darcy looked over her shoulder to the door Jeremy had disappeared through, then walked quickly over to the board that held the keys. Hummer . . . Cadillac SUV . . . Maserati . . . *oooh.* A Porsche 911. She'd always wanted to drive one of those.

"Door number three," Bernie said quietly.

"Just how mad is he going to be?" Darcy said.

Bernie looked up, and a sly smile inched its way across her lips. Then she looked back down at her newspaper again.

Now, *that* was sisterhood.

With a whispered thanks, Darcy slipped out the door and headed to the garage, hoping Jeremy couldn't hear her starting the engine. As she motored down the road toward the front gate, she glanced in the rearview mirror and didn't see him standing in the driveway shaking his fist, so she figured she'd made a clean getaway.

Fifteen minutes later, she swung the Porsche into her apartment complex and pulled it into a parking space next to Gertie. It was a nice car. *Really* nice. But Gertie had her advantages, too. Her paint was shot a long time ago, so she didn't need a garage, and because nobody would ever think to steal her, all those expensive antitheft devices weren't necessary.

And she did have four really nice tires.

Darcy had just stepped inside her apartment when she heard her cell phone ring. She hurried to the kitchen counter where she'd left it, smiling when she saw the caller ID.

She hit the TALK button. "Hello, Jeremy."

"You do realize you just committed car theft."

"Tell you what. If you won't have me arrested for car theft, I won't have you arrested for kidnapping. Deal?"

"I don't get you, Darcy. I arrange a really nice evening, and this is the thanks I get?"

"Your car will be at my apartment anytime you'd like to pick it up. And if I were you, I'd make it snappy. I saw a couple of sleazy-looking guys scoping it out, and they weren't just admiring the paint job."

Over his protests, she hung up the phone and went to take a shower. That beer and popcorn was sounding better all the time.

And what was going to come after it was sounding pretty good, too.

Chapter 19

Jeremy hung up the phone, astonished at this turn of events. He turned an irritated expression toward Bernie.

"Bernie? Did you not see her going for the key?"

"Must have been looking the other way."

"Uh-huh. And how did she know the security code for the garage door?"

"Lucky guess?"

He threw up his hands. "Do you even know the *meaning* of the word *insubordination*? My enemies treat me better than you do!"

"That's because they don't know you like I do."

"Have you thought about maybe *helping* me once in a while?"

"Sure. Do you want me to go to her apartment? Maybe wrestle her to the ground, tie her up, and throw her in the trunk?"

Jeremy sighed with resignation. "No. She'd probably just gnaw through the trunk lid."

"Shouldn't that tell you something?"

He sat down at the table. "It tells me she plays this game better than I thought she would."

"Maybe it's not a game with her."

"Oh, yes, it is. I know her kind. I saw the look on her face when she saw this house for the first time."

"I know it offends you to your very soul that you're actually going to lose at something, but there it is."

"I'm not going to lose."

"Hard work has never been your thing. Why don't you just find yourself an easier target?"

"Because I haven't finished with this one yet."

"Leave her alone. She's too good for you."

Jeremy bristled at that. "Oh, yeah? She spent fourteen years as a trophy wife, and *she's* too good for *me*?"

"Yeah. Because she's trying to get over that, and you won't let her."

Jeremy ripped the bow tie from around his neck, then unfastened the top button of his shirt so he could take a breath for the first time in an hour. Bernie just didn't get it. No matter how it looked right now, women like Darcy couldn't stay away from this lifestyle for long. It was just a matter of time. He wasn't sure what it was going to take for this one, though. Every time he thought he had her, she slipped right through his fingers.

Bernie said it wasn't a game to Darcy, but that was exactly what it was. She was toying with him, turning down the small stuff to get him to step up to the plate with something really substantial. What irritated him was that the more she pulled back, the more he wanted her, and he couldn't remember ever being in that position before.

Another opportunity would present itself. And when it did, he'd be waiting.

At seven o'clock that night, Darcy knocked on John's door. As soon as he opened it, she came inside and gave him a kiss. Then she turned around, and her heart sank.

Flowers. Candles. Presents. And—*oh, God*—a birthday cake.

John smiled. "Happy birthday, Darcy."

She sighed. First Amy, then Jeremy, and now John. How did one go about banning the word *birthday* from the English language?

"I didn't want anyone doing anything for my birthday," she said.

"Sorry. Too late. How about a beer?"

"Drown my sorrows? Sounds good to me."

John grabbed two beers from the fridge, nudged the door shut with his heel, and popped the tops. He handed one to Darcy. She took a long swig. *Ah*. There. Three or four more of these and she might forget she was one year closer to that AARP membership.

"Presents first," John said, setting his beer down. "Then cake."

He grabbed three packages from the dining room and brought them to the coffee table. He sat down beside her, handing her a small cylindrical one.

"This one first."

Darcy pulled the ribbon, then unwrapped the package. She laughed out loud. "A can of Raid?"

"Yep. I've always thought you could win the battle with conventional warfare, but it never hurts to have the nuclear option."

She smiled. "Thank you. I'll cherish it always."

Next he handed her a wide, flat box. She tugged open the wrapping, lifted the lid, and laughed all over again.

A gift certificate from Taco Hut?

She smiled. "Hope you really love that cellulite, be-cause you're going to be seeing a lot more of it."

"That's my plan. I like curvy women."

"Right. Pretty soon I won't be able to get through the door."

"One more," he said.

He grabbed the biggest box and set it on her lap, and she wondered what other gag gift he'd managed to think of. Whatever it was, it was bigger and heavier than the first two. She unwrapped it, preparing to laugh, but when she saw what the box contained, all the silliness faded away.

Ice skates?

For a moment she sat transfixed, unable to believe what she was looking at. Beautiful skates with blinding white boots and shiny silver blades, a nine-year-old girl's dream come true. Tears came to her eyes, and for a mo-ment, she couldn't find her voice. She just stared down at them, all kinds of emotions swirling through her.

John remembered.

No gift of Warren's had ever meant anything. He al-ways just gave her one more bauble to add to her jew-elry cabinet, or maybe the occasional car if she needed one. And Jeremy. He figured the more money he threw at her, the more impressed she would be. But none of that had ever made her feel the way she did right now. And it wasn't just the skates. The other gifts were inside jokes that had meaning only for them, gifts that made them laugh and cultivated a kind of intimacy between them she'd never expected.

"Is something wrong?" he asked.

But words still wouldn't come. Finally she just set the skates aside and wound her arms around his neck, managing to murmur a "thank you" in his ear. She kissed his cheek, then pulled away again, sniffing a little and wiping a tear from beneath her eye.

"Does this mean you'll take me skating?" she asked.

John froze, his smile evaporating. "Uh . . . I didn't get any for me."

"That's okay. You can rent some. Tomorrow's Sunday. We can go to the ice rink at the Galleria."

"But I don't know how to skate."

"Neither do I. We can fall on our asses together."

She tilted her head and looked at him plaintively. A calculating expression came over his face.

"We'll do your recreational activity tomorrow," he said, "as long as we can do mine tonight."

That was a win-win situation if Darcy had ever heard one.

After cake and ice cream and a glass of champagne, Darcy was feeling marginally better about turning forty, and when they retired to the bedroom to enjoy John's choice of recreational activity, her age slipped her mind completely. Afterward, she went to the bathroom, and when she came back, John lay on his stomach on the bed, the sheet pulled to his waist, sound asleep.

Drowsy with satisfaction herself, she sat down on the bed next to him, and for a long time she just leaned quietly against the headboard, watching him sleep.

It was almost unfathomable to her that he was the same man who'd shown up to take her car the day her world fell apart. She couldn't have imagined him giving her a job and a deadbolt and ice skates and sexual satisfaction beyond her wildest dreams, or holding her in his arms and looking at her as if she were the only woman on earth. But acquiring wealth didn't make even the top ten on his list of things to do. So how could she have fallen for a man like him when she still missed her old life so desperately?

Or did she?

Her heart did a little flip-flop. She swallowed hard, and her cheeks grew hot.

Maybe not.

He lifted his head groggily. "Darcy?"

"Yeah?"

"What's the matter?"

"Nothing."

"You look like you're going to throw up."

"Uh . . . probably not."

"Good. I can do without that right now. Come to bed."

She crawled in next to him. He rolled over and took her in his arms, closing his eyes again.

"Jeremy Bridges wanted to take me to dinner in San Antonio tonight."

John's eyes sprang open. "He what?"

"New evening gown, private jet, the whole nine yards."

"That son of a bitch. You know what he's doing, don't you, Darcy? You know when he gives you expensive gifts like that—"

"I know. He's going to want something in return."

There was a long silence. Darcy heard nothing but crickets chirping outside, mingling with the low-pitched rattle of the air-conditioning unit outside the bedroom window.

"Did you consider going?" John asked.

For maybe the first time since she'd met him, his words sounded hushed and uncertain.

"Not for one moment," she said.

He kissed the top of her head and tightened his arms around her. Darcy couldn't imagine being on that plane right now, or anywhere else that wasn't in John's arms.

After an hour of fumbling his way around the railing of the ice rink, John concluded that ice skating was, without a doubt, the dumbest sport ever invented. How in the hell was anyone expected to balance on blades a quarter-inch wide while standing on *ice*? He wanted to blame his ineptitude on his bum knee, but it wasn't a ligament problem. It was a balance problem. As in, he had none.

A child maybe three years old sped past, followed by one not much older going backward. And more were in the middle of the rink, jumping and spinning and otherwise defying gravity in ways he couldn't fathom. He was lucky to stand up, and these kids were swirling around like dust devils.

"This is insane," he muttered as he picked himself up off the ice for the umpteenth time.

"Just hold on to the railing," Darcy said.

"I was holding on."

"And you still fell?"

He came to his feet, breathing hard. "I want you to know that I don't make an idiot out of myself for just everyone."

She smiled up at him. "Why don't you sit out a few

rounds? Rest up a little? Then you can give it another try."

"That," he said, "is a *really* good idea."

He dragged himself around the rink, hand over hand, until he reached the exit. He plopped down in a chair with a huge sigh of relief. As much as he griped about the skating, though, it was worth every bump and bruise to see the look of pure joy on Darcy's face. It was probably the only time in her life that she'd been at the Galleria and shopping was the last thing on her mind.

"You're right, Amy. This was *so* worth the trip."

John spun around, surprised to see Tony and Amy standing behind him. What the hell were they doing here?

Amy plopped down in the seat to John's right. "Darcy called me this morning and told me you were taking her ice skating."

"And Amy told me," Tony said, taking the seat on John's left. "John Stark on ice skates." He grinned. "There was no way on *earth* I was going to miss this."

John glared at Amy. "You have a big mouth."

"Uh-huh."

"How long have you two been here?" John asked.

"Long enough to see you fall on your ass about a dozen times," Tony said.

John yanked the laces loose on his skates. "Stupidest sport on earth."

"Is Darcy still out there?" Amy asked.

"Yeah. She's a glutton for punishment."

"I don't know," Amy said, pointing. "Looks to me like she's getting around pretty well."

John looked up. The moment he saw Darcy, he froze,

watching as she scooted around the rink, her dark hair a brilliant contrast to the white ice, looking so beautiful it took his breath away. He had the most uncanny feeling that if she were standing in a crowd of ten thousand, she would still be the only person he saw.

"Ice skates," Tony muttered, shaking his head. "Are you nuts? Didn't you know what you were in for the moment you gave her those?"

"Don't listen to him," Amy said. "It was a very nice thing to do. Darcy was thrilled."

John just shrugged, even though the world would come to an end before he'd forget the look on her face when she opened them.

"So, John," Tony said. "You gonna get one of those stretchy leotard things with tiger stripes? They're all the rage among male figure skaters."

John glared at Tony and yanked off one of his skates, wincing in pain. Blisters. *Damn.*

"You'll have to wear one if you expect to try out for the Ice Capades," Tony said.

John held up the skate. "This blade is sharper than you think. Don't make me use it as a weapon."

Tony just laughed, then turned his attention to a pair of twentysomething women in criminally short skating skirts. He waved a little and gave them a glowing smile, which they returned with equal enthusiasm.

"Oops," Amy said. "Darcy's down again."

John turned to see Darcy getting up off the ice for the umpteenth time. This time, though, a pair of little girls, maybe nine or ten years old, grabbed her hands and led her around the rink, showing her how to move her feet. When they finally let her go, her movements had smoothed out a bit, and she made it a few more times around without falling once. John fought the goofy smile that insisted on pushing its way across his face. The fact that she could look wildly clumsy and strikingly beautiful all at the same time just boggled his mind.

"She's the one, isn't she?" Amy said quietly.

John opened his mouth to respond, only to realize that the knee-jerk remark he was about to make, the one about it just being casual between them, was so far from the truth he couldn't even speak the words, and he closed his mouth again.

But how could that be? He hadn't known her long. Only a matter of weeks. But still . . .

Usually, after he'd been with a woman even a few weeks, he got itchy to get out of the relationship before it actually became one. But with Darcy, every day he only wanted to see her more. She was vain and irritating and argumentative and occasionally so exasperating he wanted to pull out every hair on his head, but *God*, he'd never felt about another woman the way he felt about her. She was tough and resilient, far more than she realized, and he admired the hell out of that. And beautiful, no matter how much she protested about her advanced age and imaginary physical flaws.

He'd told her it was more than just sex between them, even though at the time he hadn't known exactly what that meant. He still didn't know. But the more time he spent with her, the more he saw her being part of his life for a long time to come.

Finally Darcy stepped off the rink and trundled over to where the three of them sat, flashing a bright smile. "Amy! Tony! What are you guys doing here?"

"We just happened to be at the mall," Tony said. "Imagine seeing you two here."

"Yeah, right," John muttered, then turned to Darcy. "Tony thought it would be funny as hell to see me on ice skates. I think it's time we put a pair on him and watch what happens."

"You know, that's not a bad idea," Tony said. "If I fell enough, I'm betting those two lovely ladies over there would take pity on me."

John stared at him dumbly. "Is there anything you won't do to pick up women?"

Tony thought about that, then shook his head. "Nope."

Amy rolled her eyes. "Come on, Lover Boy. The fun's over. We're out of here."

Tony turned to John, shaking his head. "Man, she's got you *ice skating*. What's next? Crocheting doilies?" He leaned in and spoke in a loud stage whisper. "Take my advice. Get out while you still can."

He turned and gave Darcy a wink. Amy grabbed Tony by the arm with a roll of her eyes and pulled him away from the rink.

"Okay," Darcy said, circling the railing to sit down next to John. "I've had enough for one day. I think I've got bruises on top of bruises."

She took off her skates and packed them up, and John returned his to the rental counter. A few minutes later, they emerged from the mall, and even at eight o'clock at night, the strong night wind felt like a blast furnace compared to the cool air inside.

"You know what would taste good right about now?" Darcy said.

"What's that?"

"Iced coffee. There's a Starbucks down the street. Let's stop."

"Caffeine at eight o'clock at night?"

"We'll get decaf."

"I hate Starbucks."

"You have to have been there before you can hate it."

He scowled.

She got the gift card out of her wallet and held it up. "Jeremy Bridges is buying."

"Well, then. By all means, let's have some coffee."

A few minutes later they walked into Starbucks. Only a few people were there—a granola-head in scruffy clothes sat on a sofa reading the newspaper, and a guy in the corner was glued to a laptop and a cell phone at the same time.

Darcy went to the counter. "Two Mocha Frappuccinos. Grande."

"Grande?" John said.

"That's a medium," Darcy said.

"Sounds like a large."

"A large is venti."

"Venti? Why don't they just say *medium* and *large*?"

"Because I guess then they'd have to say the next size down was a small, and that sounds, well . . . small. Like you're not getting much."

"Then what do they call a small?"

"A tall."

"A tall is a small?"

Darcy smiled. "Exactly."

John shook his head. "I knew there was a reason I stayed away from this place."

A few minutes later they grabbed their drinks and sat down by the window.

"Why do you like this place so much?" John asked.

"It's the atmosphere. The music. The people. The scents. Oh, and the pastries." She sighed. "I swear if I could, I'd have sex right up next to that dessert case."

"I always had a feeling you were a pervert. Is it the discovery fantasy about doing it in a public place?"

"No. It's the dessert fantasy of intensifying the brownie-eating experience by having an orgasm."

John eased closer. "Tell you what, sweetheart. You eat the brownie"—he slid his hand over her thigh under the table—"and I'll take care of the rest."

Never in her life had a man looked at her the way John did, as if he wanted to gobble her up in a single bite. She thought about being alone with him later, and her stomach swooped with anticipation.

She smiled to herself. *Why wait?*

She pulled out her gift card, went to the counter, bought half a dozen brownies, then came back and grabbed her drink off the table. John looked up at her questioningly.

"I have the brownies," she said. "What are you waiting for?"

Chapter 20

John figured if he went ten miles over the speed limit all the way back to Darcy's house, he had maybe a one in twenty chance of getting caught, but he also had maybe a one in two chance of being stopped by a cop he knew who would let him slide on a ticket. Those were odds he could live with, particularly when Darcy spent the entire trip running her hand up and down his thigh and speaking only one word.

Hurry.

Fifteen minutes later, they were at her front door. The wind was up, and she was having a hard time getting the key in the lock with her hair flipping into her face. Finally John took over, unlocked the door, and pulled her inside, dragging her up next to him for a kiss. She reached over to close the door, but the wind blew it back open. John gave it a push with one hand at the same time he tugged up her skirt with the other, wrapping his hand around the back of her thigh and pulling her up against him. He heard the soft thud of the sack of brownies as they hit the floor. A second later, when she reached between them for his zipper, the world seemed to slip out of focus, and he stopped thinking about anything except getting naked.

After leaving a trail of clothes all the way to the bedroom, they fell into bed. Darcy curled her hand around his neck and pulled his mouth to hers. When he slid his hand between her legs to find her hot and slick already, the urgency he felt took a quantum leap.

No. You can't hurry. Take it easy. Take your time. Make it good for her.

He stroked her incessantly, then delved inside her, then pulled back to tease her again. He did it over and over, kissing her lips, her breasts, then coming back up to whisper dirty little nothings in her ear. She squirmed beneath him, and then all at once she shimmied and shook him away.

"Darcy?"

"Now."

"No," he said. "Too soon."

"I said *now!*" She grabbed him by the arm, but he shook loose and reached for her again.

"No," he said. "It can't be. Just let me—"

"Oh, for God's sake!" She pushed him away, shoved him over on his back, and straddled him. She pointed down at him.

"Don't move!"

She reached into the nightstand drawer, found a condom, rolled it down over him, guided him to her, and plunged down hard.

John squeezed his eyes closed, gritting his teeth against the sudden indescribable feeling of being inside her all the way to the hilt. She picked up his hands, shoved them over his head, and before he knew what was happening, she laced her fingers through his and pinned him to the mattress. And then she was moving against him, her warm breath spilling across his neck, her nipples dragging along his chest with every stroke.

Holy shit.

"You're such a know-it-all," she said breathlessly, finding a hot, even rhythm. "A hardheaded know-it-all who never listens to anyone. Did I ever tell you that?"

He arched up to meet every stroke, astonished how quickly the feeling was building. "Repeatedly."

"Well, I'm telling you again." Her fingers flexed against his, her face tight with passion. "From now on, John, when I say *now,* I don't mean next week."

"Yes, ma'am."

She kissed his neck, then whispered in his ear. "So I have your attention?"

"Oh, sweetheart," he said through gritted teeth. "I'm hanging on every word."

But then she moved faster, with hard, grinding strokes, and her words fell by the wayside. He rose to meet her, wanting everything she had to give him any way she chose to do it.

She moaned softly. Then let out a tiny gasp. She threw her head back, and seconds after she cried out, he was coming, too. He clasped her hands so tightly he was in fear of breaking bones, groaning at the flood of heat that spilled through him.

She fell against him. He shook his hands loose from hers and wrapped his arms around her, stroking his hands up and down her back. He felt as if he'd been hit with a sledgehammer. No pain, though. Just pleasure so complete it was almost unbearable.

Darcy finally rolled away, falling to her back with all the muscle control of a marionette. She took a deep, cleansing breath, then rose on one elbow, fumbled in her nightstand drawer and pulled out her vibrator. With a sharp underhanded toss, she threw it toward the corner of the room. It bounced against the wall, then fell into the trash can with a satisfying clatter. She rolled back against John, resting her head against his shoulder and twining her leg with his.

John smiled to himself. What man wouldn't love the ego boost of beating out your average battery-powered device?

Darcy put her hand against his. He turned it over and laced his fingers with hers. She looked at him, her eyes sparkling in the dim light.

"You know what?"

"What?"

"Everybody has best days of their lives."

"Yeah. I guess they do."

"This was one of mine."

Her words flowed over John like warm honey. As crazy as it seemed, he couldn't imagine a time in the future when she wouldn't be part of his life.

They lay there a moment more, and then he rose and went to the bathroom. When he came out, he decided he'd go back to the front door, get those brownies, and feed every last one of them to her while he did unspeakably carnal things to every inch of her body.

He rounded the doorway into the entry, surprised to find the front door standing open. He thought he'd shut it, but evidently he hadn't done it hard enough, and the wind had blown it open again.

Then it dawned on him. Pepé was nowhere to be seen.

Darcy's heart pounded with apprehension as she and John hurried along the sidewalks of the apartment complex, calling Pepé's name.

"I can't believe the door was just standing open," she said. "I swore we shut it."

"So did I."

"He's probably scared to death."

"He has tags," John said. "If somebody finds him, they'll call you."

"As long as he doesn't get scared and do something stupid first, like run right out in front of a car."

"Take it easy. We'll find him."

"How long were we in the bedroom? How far could he have gotten by now?"

"I don't know. Surely he'll stay around the complex, won't he?"

"John, I love my dog to pieces, but I'm afraid he's not terribly smart. I'm just so afraid he's going to—"

"Wait! There he is!"

"Where?"

She looked where John pointed and spotted Pepé huddled against a wall behind a shrub. She hurried over and scooped him up.

"Oh, he's so scared! See how he's trembling?" She kissed his furry little head. "We have to be more careful about the door from now on."

"We will." John reached up to stroke his head. "Wow. He really is shaking, isn't he?"

"Poor baby," Darcy said, hugging him closer. "It's a

big bad world out here, isn't it? You have to watch out
for all kinds of—"

"Is that a dog?"

Darcy spun around, and she couldn't believe who was
standing behind her. *Damn*. Was it too late to try to stuff
Pepé into her pocket?

She sighed. "No, Charmin. This isn't a dog. It's an
elephant."

"I know a dog when I see one. You haven't paid a pet
deposit."

"I was going to, but I was a little short, and—"

"You owe me three hundred bucks."

"Come on, Charmin! Most hamsters are bigger than
he is!"

"Doesn't matter. You got a dog, you pay the deposit."

"Oh, all right! I'll pay it! But you have to give me a
little time."

"You've got twenty-four hours."

Darcy recoiled. "Twenty-four hours? I can't get that
kind of money together in twenty-four hours!"

"Pay the money, or the dog goes."

Charmin gave Darcy one last snotty look, then shot
one at John for good measure. Most people wouldn't take
the chance of irritating a man like him, but Charmin was
too mean to be intimidated.

"What am I going to do?" Darcy asked as Charmin
disappeared around the corner of the building. "I don't
have three hundred dollars! I barely have enough money
to survive until payday! Can she really make me give up
my dog?"

"Technically she could get a court order."

"And she will, too. I know her. God, three hundred

dollars? It might as well be three thousand." She put her hand to her forehead, her mind reeling. "Do you know Warren and I used to have dinners at our country club that cost almost three hundred dollars?"

"I don't doubt it. What a waste of money."

"Okay. Maybe it was stupid. But a lousy three hundred dollars shouldn't matter this much to anyone."

In the distance, she heard the door to the apartment next to hers open, and one of its many scroungy residents came out. He locked the door behind him and headed for the parking lot, the hot evening wind blowing his scraggly hair in a swirl around his head.

"Will you look at that guy?" Darcy muttered. "I swear everyone who lives here looks like a drug-addicted serial killer. Those who aren't transvestite hookers, anyway. Not exactly Mr. Rogers's Neighborhood, is it?"

John was silent, which meant she'd spoken the truth so he didn't know what to say. Darcy hated this. She hated that she lived in this crappy place. Hated that she drove a crappy car. Hated that she had to watch every dime she spent. She *hated* it.

"John?" she said. "I know this is a lot to ask, but I can't give Pepé up. I can't. Do you think . . ." She exhaled. "Do you think you could loan me three hundred dollars?"

He sighed. "I don't think that's a good idea."

"But I'll pay you back."

"I know you will. It's just that . . ."

"What?"

"You need to do this on your own."

"On my own?" she said incredulously. "How am I supposed to come up with three hundred dollars in twenty-four hours?"

"Tell you what," John said. "Why don't you let Killer here come stay with me until you can get the deposit together? He's used to me by now. And it'll be like a vacation for him. He'll love running around in my backyard."

She shook her head. "No. It would feel like I'm giving him away."

"It's only temporary."

"Temporary could turn into a long time."

"Do you trust me to take care of him?"

"Of course, but—"

"Then I'll keep him as long as you need me to."

"Okay. That's fine for this time. But what about next time?"

"What do you mean?"

"What do you think I mean? I'm just one paycheck away from being on the street!"

She spoke louder than she intended, and Pepé squirmed in her arms. She hugged him closer and lowered her voice, but her frustration seeped through just the same.

"Gertie could break down any minute," she told John. "The IRS could hit me with back taxes. My electric bill could be even bigger next month. As long as I'm living paycheck to paycheck, it's *always* going to be something."

"And there's always a way out. You'll find it this time, and next time, too."

"None of this would be an issue if you'd teach me to be a repo agent."

John closed his eyes with a hard sigh. "You know how I feel about that."

"You won't loan me money, yet you won't let me make more?"

"You make enough money. You just need to learn how to manage it."

"Will you *stop* patronizing me?"

"You're making too much out of this."

"Don't you get it? If a lousy three-hundred-dollar pet deposit sends my finances into a tailspin, how am I ever going to—"

All at once, a loud *boom* shattered the night, sounding like lightning striking the ground only yards from where they stood. John grabbed Darcy and spun her around, shielding her body with his as pieces of debris fell to earth.

With her ears ringing, Darcy looked around John's shoulder, trying to see what had happened. And when she did, the most horrible feeling of dread slammed into her.

The door of the apartment next door to hers was blown off its hinges. Windows were shattered.

And the building was on fire.

Minutes later, the apartment complex was a whirlwind of activity. Tenants poured outside to see where the explosion had come from. Red and blue lights of emergency vehicles swirled around the scene as firefighters hit the ground running to try to put out the blaze. The sun had slipped below the horizon, and the red-orange sky behind the burning building made it look as if the entire landscape had descended into hell.

Fortunately there hadn't been anyone in the apartment where the explosion occurred, and everyone else in the building had gotten out without injury. When the police arrived, they directed all the tenants who were standing around to the front of the complex to clear the way for more emergency vehicles and personnel. Vans from local news stations that had been tuned into the police band were already parked at the front of the complex, and reporters and cameramen were covering the story live. As they milled around, Darcy heard one of them tell another one that they should just let the whole crappy complex burn to the ground. They were probably right, but still it made her feel awful. This horrible place was the best she could do, and now she didn't even have that. She could only stand there beside John, watching as the fire consumed everything she owned in the world but a beat-up car, a terrified dog, and the clothes on her back.

"Well, it looks like there really was a meth lab next door to you, huh?"

Darcy turned to see Charmin walk up beside her, and she almost groaned out loud. She did *not* need this woman right now.

"Yeah," Darcy said. "I guess it wasn't just a rumor."

John's eyes widened. "Did you say meth lab?"

"Don't know what else would cause an explosion like that." Charmin huffed with disgust. "Damn. Dealing with this is going to be a pain in the ass. The owner's gonna go nuts."

"I don't really care what *you're* going to have to deal with," Darcy said. "Not when I don't even have a place to live!"

"Cheer up, Darcy," Charmin said. "You know that pet deposit you owe me?" She chuckled. "Looks like you're not going to have to pay it after all." She looked back at the burning building. "And while you're at it, looks like you can forget about the rent, too."

As she walked away, Darcy gritted her teeth. "Did I tell you I *hate* that woman?"

"You knew there was a meth lab next door to you and you didn't tell me?" John said.

"Nobody knew for sure."

"But you should have told me, anyway! I could have had the cops all over this place!"

"John—"

"Damn it, I should have known. I saw all kinds of people coming in and out, night and day. I should have *known*. I should have—"

"John! It's done! The damned thing blew up! So why are we still talking about it? And it doesn't really matter, anyway. If it hadn't been this, it would have been something else."

"What do you mean?"

"Crazy Bob would have left a cigarette burning, or an electrical short would have popped up somewhere, or the owner would have burned the place to the ground himself to collect the insurance money. At a place like this, it's always going to be something!"

"Take it easy, Darcy," John said. "Everything's going to be okay. You have renter's insurance, right?"

"Renter's insurance? You must be joking."

"Are you telling me you don't have—"

"No, I don't! What was I supposed to buy it with? My extra disposable income?"

"Forget it. It doesn't matter. You can start over again."

She looked at him incredulously. "Half an hour ago, I

couldn't even come up with a lousy pet deposit, and now I'm supposed to start *over* again?"

John took her by the shoulders. "Things aren't as bad as you think. We'll evaluate where you are financially and put together a plan to get you back on your feet. Then we'll go from there. Everything's going to be okay."

"Will you *stop* saying that?" Darcy said, shuddering away from him. "Everything's *not* going to be okay! How many more times am I going to lose everything before I just can't take it anymore?"

When John turned away with a sigh of resignation, she knew the truth. He didn't really believe the things he was telling her. For all the times she thought she'd been at rock bottom, she hadn't even come close. *This* was rock bottom, and she didn't see any way out.

Suddenly John came to attention. He lifted his chin, focusing on something over Darcy's shoulder.

"That son of a bitch," he muttered.

Darcy turned to see a sleek black limousine pull to the side of the road in front of the apartment complex and come to a halt. The back door opened, and Jeremy Bridges stepped out.

Chapter 21

John's hand tensed against Darcy's arm. "What the hell is he doing here?"

Jeremy walked over to where they stood, zeroing in on Darcy and completely disregarding John. "I heard a news report on the radio. Did the fire get your apartment?"

"Yes."

"Everything?"

She nodded.

"Get out of here, Bridges," John said. "Nobody needs you here."

"Shut up, Stark. I'm talking to Darcy." He turned to her. "What you've lost tonight wasn't worth having. It's meaningless. Of no consequence at all. Do you understand?"

"Darcy," John said. "Let's go."

Jeremy turned on John. "Where? To that pitiful hovel you call home? Is that where you're taking her?"

"You don't know a damned thing about where I live."

"Forty-four seventeen Caldwell Street. You think I haven't been keeping tabs on her?" He turned back to Darcy. "It's time to stop this. Time to get out of this low-class life and back to the one you know. Look around you. If you stay with him, you'll never have anything more than this. Is that what you want?"

Her eyes filled with tears. No. God, no, it wasn't. She wanted things the way they used to be. She wanted to wake up in the morning and worry about where she was going to have lunch with her friends, or what to wear to the club that night, not about whether she'd be able to make it to her next paycheck.

"We'll go to my house tonight," Jeremy said, his voice low and mesmerizing. "Tomorrow I'll take you shopping. Then we can get out of town. Where would you like to go? New York? London? Paris? By this time tomorrow, we can be in a five-star hotel in any city in the world."

John inched forward. "Darcy, don't listen to him."

"I can take you away from all this," Jeremy said. "In no time, this life will be nothing but a bad memory."

"Bridges—"

"You know it's what you want. What you've wanted ever since Warren took your life away from you. Come with me, and you'll have it."

"Back off, Bridges."

"All you have to do is say the word."

"I said *back off!*"

Jeremy met John's angry gaze with a coldly indifferent one, and for several seconds, neither man moved. Finally Jeremy backed away.

"I'll be in the car. But you'd better make a decision quickly. I won't sit there all night."

He walked back to the limo and got inside, disappearing behind the darkly tinted glass.

"Listen to me, Darcy," John said. "He's an opportunistic son of a bitch. Do you see what he's doing? He knows how you must be feeling right now, and he's trying to take advantage of you."

"Take advantage? A man offers me a mansion to live in, clothes on my back, money in my pocket, a private jet at my disposal, and he's taking *advantage* of me?"

"Yes, and you'll know exactly when it kicks in. When you get the bill. And it won't be in the form of dollars and cents. You'll pay, Darcy. One way or the other."

"I don't care!"

John drew back. "What do you mean, you don't care?"

"He's right. I haven't lost anything here, because I had nothing to lose. I want *more* than this!"

"You can have more. You can have anything you want. You just have to be willing to work for it. You've been doing a good job at the office. Better than I ever thought you would. You deserve a raise, and I'll give you one."

"Great. Now instead of making minimum wage, I'll be making barely above minimum wage."

"It's the best I can do for now. Maybe in a few months—"

"Don't you see, John? It doesn't matter. No amount of work I'm capable of could *ever* get me the kind of life I want!"

John's gaze grew hard. "It isn't as if you were born with a silver spoon in your mouth. It wouldn't kill you to spend a few years struggling."

"I wasn't cut *out* to struggle!"

She was shocked to hear Jeremy's words coming out of her mouth, but suddenly they rang so true that she shook with the frustration of it. Hot tears streaked down her cheeks, and she swiped them away with her fingertips.

"I just can't do this anymore, John. I can't be the person you think I should be. One who hits rock bottom and claws her way back up again. I just *can't*."

"You're stronger than you think."

"No. I'm not strong at all."

"Will you stop selling yourself short?"

"Will you stop trying to make me into something I'm not?"

John started to respond, only to look away with a sigh of frustration. Darcy glanced at the fire and smoke in the distance, imagining her meager possessions as nothing but piles of ashes. She scanned the clusters of people around her, half of whom were criminals or deadbeats. Then she looked over her shoulder at the shiny black limousine. There was only one thing she had to do to shut out all this ugliness.

Climb inside.

When her gaze lingered on the limousine, John took her by the arm and forced her to face him. "Darcy, tell me you're not seriously considering leaving here with that man."

When she didn't respond, his gaze narrowed fiercely. "I never meant anything to you, did I? You were just biding your time with me until you got a solid hook into Bridges."

"No. That's not the way it was."

"It sure as hell looks that way to me now."

Maybe John was right. Maybe she'd just been deluding herself into thinking she could be happy with nothing. Maybe he really had been just a stopgap, someone she could bide her time with until she could find another man with money, because without it, nothing in her life would ever be right again. What had ever made her think she could support herself? No job she was capable of doing would ever give her the kind of security she needed.

She thought about John's house. It was old and small and cramped, with twenty-year-old furniture and a dishwasher on the blink. His business was up and down, with no certainty of how healthy it would be a year from now. She'd seen him paying his bills once with a worried frown that said he was probably juggling money from one month to the next. Even if he let her become a repossession agent, she would never have more than he had.

And suddenly that just wasn't enough.

"I want to have nice things again," she said. "I want to sleep in a place where I don't keep pepper spray under my pillow. I want to stop worrying every second of every day about where my next meal is coming from. I want to feel *secure* again!"

"He can't make you feel secure. Not in the way you really need."

"Yeah? You should see his house. Tell me I won't feel secure in a place like that."

"So that's what you intend to do? Go through life with no dignity at all?"

"Would you mind telling me what's so dignified about starving? About driving a car that's a piece of crap? About living in a slum? What's so dignified about that?"

"So it's more dignified to be tossed expensive toys by a guy like him? You're worse than Pepé begging for a dog biscuit."

Anger swelled inside her. "You're so damned self-righteous. You think there's only one way to live life, and that's *your* way."

"At least I have some self-respect. You're losing more of yours every time you open your mouth."

Furious, Darcy turned around and started toward the limousine, but John grabbed her arm and pulled her back. "I'm warning you, Darcy. If you go with him tonight, don't think you're *ever* coming back to me!"

Looking at John now, he seemed like a stranger. A tall, handsome, furious stranger who didn't have a clue who she really was.

"With all he has to offer," she said, "why would I?"

She pulled her arm from John's grip, tucked Pepé against her chest, and headed for the limousine.

John called after her, his voice thick with rage. "Fine, then! Go! Get the hell out of here! You and that bastard *deserve* each other!"

His words pounded her with every step she took, but there was no going back, because it was just as she'd suspected in the beginning. She and John were oil and water. Fire and ice. Night and day. Immovable object and irresistible force. Two vastly different people who would only end up making each other miserable. Now she knew for sure the life she was destined to live, and it wasn't this one. She'd been a fool to think, even for a moment, that it was.

Jeremy got out of the limo, held open the door, and she stepped inside. When he got back in and closed the door behind them, the silence was overwhelming. Bernie sat in the front seat, staring dead ahead. She never once acknowledged that Darcy had even gotten in the car, and Darcy sensed disapproval radiating from her like heat off a summer sidewalk.

Jeremy tapped the Plexiglas. "Home."

As the limousine pulled away, Darcy hugged her shivering dog, refusing to look back at John. She'd never expected Jeremy to finally offer her luxury beyond her wildest dreams, and now that he had, it was an opportunity she wasn't going to pass up.

~

Jeremy didn't say a word to Darcy all the way back to his house. Once they were inside, Bernie went into the kitchen, and Jeremy told Darcy he'd send someone out to get dog food for Pepé. Then he handed her off to his housekeeper, who he said would show her to a guest room upstairs where she could take a shower and relax. Then he disappeared into the back of the house.

She didn't know how she'd expected Jeremy to behave, but that hadn't been it. She was thankful for it, though. She just wanted to go to bed and pretend this day had never happened, then wake up tomorrow morning without a care in the world.

A sense of calm settled over her. Relief that she wouldn't have to fight anymore. There were worse things in this world than being pampered by an extraordinarily wealthy man, and Darcy refused to feel as if she was doing anything wrong. Jeremy was unconventional but not unattractive, and she could learn to like him enough to make life worthwhile.

She followed the housekeeper up the curved staircase and into a stunning guest suite complete with floor-to-ceiling windows, a beautiful walnut sleigh bed, and a fireplace. Pepé wandered around nervously before landing on the rug in front of the fireplace and collapsing with a little doggy sigh, looking even more tired than Darcy felt.

Darcy went into the adjoining bathroom to find it as dazzling as the bedroom, with walnut cabinetry, recessed lighting, a double whirlpool tub, and bath towels so thick and fluffy she could lose herself in one. Then the housekeeper showed her a closet that contained a dozen nightgowns, a few pairs of slippers, and a drawer full of lingerie.

Jeremy had clearly entertained overnight guests before.

Darcy took a long, luxurious bath, and when she came out, her clothes were gone, clearly snapped up by the housekeeper to be cleaned and returned to her closet by morning. As much domestic help as she'd had when she was with Warren, it hadn't included a luxury like that.

Darcy slipped into an elegant emerald-green gown. She had a fleeting thought about an ugly-as-sin hot-pink nightie with a feathered hem, but she squeezed her eyes closed and systematically put it out of her mind.

Sleep. That was all she wanted. Just to sleep.

Just as she was pulling back the covers on the bed, though, she heard a knock. She cracked the door and peered into the hall to find the housekeeper standing there.

"Yes?"

"Mr. Bridges would like to see you."

Her heart skipped. "Now? What does he want?"

"You'll have to speak to him."

She thought about the gown she was wearing. It was beautiful. Elegant. And it left nothing to the imagination.

"You don't happen to have a spare robe lying around somewhere, do you?" Darcy asked.

"No, ma'am."

Darcy's heart started to pound. Maybe he just wanted to make sure she was settled and comfortable.

That was what she told herself, anyway.

She followed the housekeeper out of the room. The woman nodded to the tall double doors at the end of the hall, then turned and disappeared down the stairs. Darcy stared at the doors, knowing what lay beyond them.

Jeremy's master bedroom suite.

John sat on a barstool at McMillan's, a beer in his hand, hoping to lull himself into oblivion. It was pointless, of course. No matter how much he drank, he wasn't going to get rid of the god-awful feeling that he'd been played for a fool. That the woman he cared about cared so little for him. That the crazy plans he'd started to make inside his head, the ones that involved him and Darcy together forever, had just blown up in his face.

He finished off that beer and ordered another one, oblivious to the people around him. It was Sunday night, so the crowd was light. In fact, the place would be closing down soon, which meant he'd have to go home alone to a house that was too quiet, with four walls feeling as if they were closing in on him. With as much solitude as he'd had over the past several years, he'd never realized just how wonderful it could be to share his house with somebody else.

Obviously Darcy would never be coming back to the office. Why work for a pittance when a man like Bridges handed her a fistful of credit cards with no limit? She'd just stay at that ostentatious, overpriced mausoleum of his, taking whatever crumbs she could seduce him into throwing her for as long as she could get him to do it. How could she not know how little regard that man had for her? And if she knew, why didn't it matter?

Relationships for her were about all the crap in life that didn't mean anything, all the things she thought she'd die if she didn't have. Even so, for a single crazy moment tonight, John had wanted to grab her and tell her that no matter what she wanted, he'd find a way to get it. That he'd lie, cheat, steal—whatever it took. How deluded had that been?

He remembered the day she'd locked herself in his bathroom and cried her eyes out, right before they spent the rest of the day in bed. For hours on end, she had treated his body like a playground God had created especially for her. He could still feel her hands all over him, her warm lips hovering over his and the gentle sighs and moans that told him what she felt with him was real. It was just as Darcy had said. Everybody had best days of their lives.

That had been one of his.

A blond woman three stools down from him caught his eye. She toyed with her cocktail straw for a moment, then gave him a provocative smile, clearly hoping for one in return. He simply turned away and took another swig of beer. He couldn't even fathom being with another woman when memories of Darcy still loomed so large in his mind.

But she's with Bridges now. And you know what they're doing.

John rubbed his eyes, then let out a heavy sigh, trying his damndest to put that thought from his mind. Darcy had made her choice, loud and clear, so it was time for him to stop wishing things had turned out differently and say good riddance.

Chapter 22

Darcy stood in front of the double doors, her pulse throbbing in her temples and her palms damp. She raised her hand. Paused. Finally she gave the door two soft raps.

She heard Jeremy tell her to come in. She closed her eyes and took a deep breath, then opened the door.

The room was as opulent as the rest of the house, but nothing in particular about the décor registered in her mind. All she saw was Jeremy sitting on a sofa in front of the fireplace, a glass of wine in his hand. On the wall behind the sofa was a king-sized four-poster bed.

The covers were turned down.

"You look beautiful," Jeremy said, his voice low and seductive. "But, then, you know that, don't you? You've always known just how beautiful you are." He nodded toward the door. "Close it."

"I'm really tired, Jeremy. After everything that's happened, I think I'd just like to get some sleep."

"Negotiating already," he said. "I expected that." He set down his drink, closed the door himself, then faced her again. "But tonight is nonnegotiable."

Darcy couldn't believe it. This man wasted no time at all.

"Drink?" Jeremy said, pulling another wineglass from the bar and reaching for an open bottle.

"You're having wine? I thought beer was more your style."

"This is a Chilean Merlot. Outrageously expensive. I bought six cases as an investment, but in light of everything that's happened tonight, well . . . what the hell."

Just the mention of expensive wine used to send Darcy into paroxysms of delight, but now the words seemed to float right past her as if she hadn't even heard them. It was as if the receptors in her brain for the finer things in life had evaporated.

Or maybe her definition of "finer things" had changed.

"No, thank you," she said.

Surprise flickered across Jeremy's face. He set the glass back down on the bar, and as he approached her again, his voice became soft and seductive.

"So what's it going to be tomorrow morning? Paris? London? It's your choice."

Darcy's heart was pounding so hard she was sure he could hear it, but not because she was imagining how wonderful a stay in a luxury hotel was going to be. It was because of the look on his face right now. She had a feeling it was the same expression his opponents saw when he looked at them across a boardroom table as he evaluated their strengths and zeroed in on their weaknesses.

He moved in closer, touching his palm to the back of her hand. She jumped a little, and when his hand glided up her arm, she closed her eyes, stiffening beneath his touch.

"Relax, Darcy," he murmured. "I have all kinds of wonderful things in store for you. Tonight is just the beginning."

Just go with it. Give him what he wants, and you'll have everything you want.

He moved his hand up her arm to her shoulder, where he hooked his finger around the narrow strap of her nightgown. He teased his finger along it for a moment, then slowly edged it off her shoulder.

Darcy told herself not to move, but she couldn't help it. The moment the strap fell against her upper arm, she grabbed it, nonchalantly sliding it back up to her shoulder again.

Jeremy frowned. "It's time to stop playing hard to get. We both know why you're here."

"No. I don't want—"

"You don't want what? Beautiful clothes? A wallet full of credit cards? A trip to Europe? Which one of those things don't you want?"

"Jeremy—"

"You gave Warren what he wanted for fourteen years in exchange for what I consider to be a mediocre lifestyle. I'm offering you far more than mediocrity."

Darcy itched with discomfort, hating the way his voice sounded. He moved toward her again, resting his hand against her shoulder, his thumb stroking her collarbone as his gaze roamed over her body with the utmost appreciation. There had been a time not so long ago when this kind of attention from a man would have made Darcy feel powerful, as if she had him wrapped right around her little finger. But now she realized the truth.

She had no power at all.

This man held all the cards, and right now he was demanding advance payment against everything she could persuade him to give her in the future. All at once, John's words thundered inside her head.

You'll pay, Darcy. One way or the other.

He was right. The moment she gave this man anything and expected something in return, she would be confirming that she was exactly the kind of woman he thought she was. The kind she used to be. Suddenly, all the things she'd thought were so important seemed as insignificant as house dust.

Jeremy moved closer, his hand creeping across her shoulder to rest against her cheek, and every nerve in her body screamed for him to stop.

He can't make you feel secure, Darcy. Not in the way you really need.

John was right. This wasn't security. She was selling herself, piece by piece, for luxury to be doled out to her like candy to a child. She didn't need it, didn't want it, and as of right then, she never wanted to see it again unless she'd bought and paid for it herself.

"Jeremy . . . don't."

He came closer.

"Jeremy—"

He leaned in to kiss her. The instant before his lips touched hers, she put her palms against his shoulders and shoved him away. "I said *no!*"

He stumbled backward with a look of total astonishment. "What the hell are you doing?"

"What part of that didn't you understand? The 'no,' or the shove?"

"Neither one!"

"Good-bye, Jeremy."

She spun around and started for the door. He hurried after her.

"Hey!" he said. "You can't just walk away!"

"Yeah? Why not?"

He caught her arm and pulled her back around. "I thought we had an understanding."

"Actually, I didn't understand anything until I came here tonight. I thought the worst thing in the world was to lose everything I had. It's not. The worst thing in the world is to be treated like a high-paid hooker by a man who thinks there's nobody he can't buy."

Jeremy looked genuinely surprised, but she knew it wasn't because of what she'd said. It was because she'd had the audacity to say it.

"That's a pretty harsh characterization," he told her.

"It's a pretty *accurate* characterization. And I don't want any part of it."

"Do you have any idea how many women would kill to be in your position?"

"No, but I imagine there has been quite a parade of them in the past. I saw the selection of nightgowns in the closet."

His jaw tightened with irritation. "You have no idea what you're turning down."

"Yes, I do. I don't want your money, Jeremy. And I don't want this."

"If you think you'll ever get an offer like this from me again—"

"Actually, I think I will, because you hate like hell to lose."

"Eventually you'll give in."

"Eventually I'll get a restraining order."

His eyes widened at that, and she could practically feel his brain working, trying to figure out a way to come out of this situation on top. After a moment, though, his gaze shifted away, and he sighed with defeat.

"Restraining order," he said with disgust. "Really, Darcy. Do you have to be so dramatic?"

"Do you have to be so relentless?"

"I thought I knew you."

"Believe me. No one is more surprised about this than I am."

"I assume you're going back to Stark?"

Darcy started to answer, but before she could get the words out, her voice cracked and tears stung the backs of her eyes. When she thought about the possibility that she'd never see John again, the longing she felt was almost incapacitating.

How could she have been so blind?

"Actually," she said, "after everything that's happened, I sincerely doubt he'll want me back."

Jeremy shrugged offhandedly. "It's for the best, you know. He's not the one. You'll be shopping at Wal-Mart forever. A woman like you always wants more."

Yes. He was right. She wanted more. She wanted more of John. But because of what she'd done tonight, she knew he would never want to see her again. Still, if nothing else, he had taught her one important thing: an extravagant lifestyle handed to her by somebody else paled in comparison to a meager one she managed to earn on her own.

"You're right, Jeremy. I do want more. And I'm going to get it. After all, I still have a car with four good tires, a neurotic dog, and a twenty-dollar bill in my purse for cab fare to my parents' house." She shrugged. "I can work with that."

"So you think you're going to make it on your own, do you?"

"Yes. I do."

He smiled indulgently, as if she were a five-year-old who'd announced she was running away from home. But Darcy didn't care. She didn't know how she was going to make it. She didn't know how she was going to pay her bills or what she was going to do for a job. She only knew that somehow, some way, she was going to survive, and she was going to do it in a way that made her feel good about herself. And no matter how many times her life got jerked out from under her, she was going to get up and start over again. She'd probably fall on her face a time or two more before she finally got it right, but she was going to make it happen.

Maybe then she'd be the kind of woman who deserved a man like John.

She started toward the bedroom door.

"I think you might be wrong about Stark not wanting you back," Jeremy said.

Darcy turned around, feeling a surge of hope, but she refused even to think it might be true. "No. He told me if I went with you, I could never come back to him. He means what he says."

"Men say all kinds of things in the heat of anger."

Maybe some men, but not John. Darcy had never known anyone so utterly in control of himself, who knew exactly what he was saying and doing every moment of his life. And he wasn't one to tolerate the slap in the face she'd given him by walking away the way she had tonight.

"He has too much pride," Darcy said. "Trust me. He'll never want to see me again."

"Don't bank on that."

But Darcy knew the truth. The very idea that she'd ruined the best thing that had ever happened to her made Darcy sick to her soul. If she saw John again, he'd only tell her how spoiled and willful and clueless she was, and then remind her that when she'd had the opportunity to do the right thing, she'd blown it.

Or maybe he'd say nothing, and that would be the worst blow of all.

"I need my clothes back," Darcy said.

"I'll let my housekeeper know."

She nodded.

"That twenty-dollar bill," Jeremy said. "Don't spend it on cab fare. It might come in handy later."

"Shall I steal one of your cars instead?"

"Car theft won't be necessary this time. After you get your clothes, just go downstairs and wait in the foyer. I'll have somebody there shortly who'll take you wherever you want to go."

"You don't have to do that."

"I know." He turned to face the window, looking out into the night. "Just consider it my contribution to the Struggling Single Women of America."

His words were lighthearted, but as she looked at his reflection in the window, they weren't matched by a lighthearted expression. She sensed an aura surrounding him that was completely at odds with the bravado he usually exuded with every breath. Suddenly she wasn't looking at a successful multimillionaire with deals to make and money to burn.

She was looking at a lost and lonely man.

She still didn't know what to make of him, except it was possible he was missing the same thing in his life she'd been missing in hers, that thing she'd thrown away as if it meant nothing to her when it meant everything in the world.

"Good-bye, Jeremy," she said.

"Good-bye, Darcy," he said. "And good luck."

~

John didn't even bother finishing the second beer he'd ordered some time ago. What would be the point? He could drink a gallon of the stuff and all he'd get would be a hell of a hangover. Then he'd wake up in the morning, take a few aspirin, and Darcy would still be gone.

He signaled the bartender to bring his check. He was just reaching for his wallet when his phone rang. He pulled it out of his pocket and looked at the caller ID. Jeremy Bridges?

Anger rose up inside John, razor sharp. What was the guy doing? Calling to gloat?

Bastard.

He flipped his phone open. "Bridges? What do you want?"

"Listen closely, because I never repeat myself. Two things."

John came to attention.

"Number one. Darcy McDaniel is a seriously misguided woman. I offered her just about anything her little heart desires and asked so little in return. But—funny thing—it turns out she doesn't want to be a kept woman after all. She wants more out of life, but evidently I'm not the man who can give it to her." He paused. "She seems to think you are."

John pressed the phone closer to his ear. Damned music in the bar. Had he heard this guy right?

"Number two," Jeremy said. "Right now that seriously misguided woman is standing in my foyer waiting for the ride I promised her. She's convinced you'll want nothing to do with her anymore, and maybe that's true. But it's your choice. You can stick to your guns and tell her again that after coming with me tonight she can never go back to you. Or you can put aside your considerable ego, drive over here, and take her home with you where she belongs. Now, which is it going to be?"

John just sat there, so dumbfounded he couldn't speak. Go to Bridges's house? Pick up Darcy? Had this man completely lost it?

Actually, Bridges wasn't the problem. Darcy was. John felt as if she'd crawled inside his head and messed with his mind until he couldn't put two consecutive thoughts together.

He had to think rationally about this. He couldn't give in. He couldn't let her yank him around like this. After all, he had a little pride, didn't he? And all kinds of self-control? No way was he going to let her do this to him. No way. After what she'd done tonight . . .

As that thought trailed off, he closed his eyes with a heavy sigh. Oh, hell. Who was he kidding?

"I'll be there in fifteen minutes."

Chapter 23

Darcy sat on a bench in the foyer of Jeremy's house, feeling tired right down to her bones. Pepé sat nearby at the foot of a potted plant, his buggy little eyes shifting back and forth nervously. Poor little thing. First he'd gotten lost. Then came the explosion. Then she'd dragged him to an unfamiliar house. And now they were going back to her parents' house, where peeing on the rug was a capital offense.

She called to him. He slinked over and jumped onto her lap. She hugged him close, taking comfort in his warm, hairy little body, hoping he'd stay reasonably sane until she could finally afford that doggy shrink he was desperately going to need.

A few more minutes went by, and Darcy wondered how much time had passed. How long did it take for Jeremy's driver to bring the car around?

Just as she was starting to think about using that twenty to call a cab after all, she glanced out the window and saw headlights flashing through the darkness. A car was coming through the front gate.

She stood up and went to the window, thinking at first that Jeremy must have called a cab, even though that made no sense. But as it drew closer, she realized it wasn't a cab after all.

It was John's SUV.

As she opened the door and walked onto the porch, John brought the car to a jolting halt. He killed the engine and stepped out.

Darcy blinked dumbly. It was as if she were looking at an apparition. A figment of her imagination. A manifestation of her own wishful thinking. It was as if she'd fantasized about wanting him so much that he'd actually shown up. Only in that particular fantasy, John was smiling.

He wasn't smiling now.

"John?" she said. "What are you doing here?"

He never responded. He just closed the door, went around the car, and started up the walk. His face was impassive. She couldn't read his mood. With every stride he took, she grew a little more nervous.

"I did the dumbest thing on earth tonight," she said as he drew closer.

"Yes," John said. "You did."

"No, I mean the *dumbest*. Really."

"I'm not arguing with that."

"I don't want to be here. I told Jeremy—"

"I know," he said, still walking.

"You know? But how—"

"No man in his right mind would have anything to do with you. You know that, don't you?"

She took a step backward, bumping against the front door. "Look, John, I know you're angry, but I want you to listen to me. I have to tell you—"

Before she could say anything else, he grabbed her

by the wrist, wheeled around, and stalked back down the sidewalk toward his car, pulling her along in his wake. Pepé trotted over, and John scooped him up without missing a beat. When they reached the car, he pulled the passenger door open, deposited Darcy inside, plopped Pepé into her lap, and shut the door behind her. He went around and slid into the driver's seat, moving so quickly that Pepé got spooked and scrambled into the backseat.

"I don't understand," Darcy said. "You said no man in his right mind—"

"Exactly. I haven't been in my right mind since the moment I met you."

"So why did you come here?"

"I heard you needed a ride."

"You heard? How did you hear . . . ?"

"Bridges."

Darcy's eyes widened. "He called you?"

"Yeah. He called me."

She looked at him disbelievingly. "And you came?"

"Hell, yes, I came! I said I was out of my mind, didn't I?" He jammed the key into the ignition.

"I'm sorry, John," she said. "I'm sorry for what I did. I don't want Jeremy. I don't want this house. I don't want his money. I don't want *any* of this."

"I'm not sure I believe that."

He started to twist the car key, but Darcy grabbed his hand. "But you must believe it. You came here, didn't you?"

He didn't respond.

"That must mean something."

He said nothing.

"You came here as soon as Jeremy called. A man you *hate*, by the way. Why did you do that?"

John closed his eyes, his hand tensing beneath hers.

"I mean, you're not exactly the type of guy to forgive and forget, so I don't know why—"

"Because I *love* you!"

For the count of ten, there was silence in the car, John's words filling the space so completely that not a single molecule could move. So this was why he was charging around and grumbling and yelling and doing all those other things John did when he didn't feel as if he was in control?

Because he *loved* her?

Darcy was stunned. She'd always believed that love was something that happened only to a select few karma-blessed people and had no bearing on her reality. But as she looked at John now, she realized it was more real than she'd ever imagined.

She leaned across the console, ran her hand along his cheek, and turned his face toward hers. She kissed him gently on the lips. "I love you, too."

John blinked. Swallowed hard. When he spoke this time, his words were little more than a whisper in the dark.

"Then why did you leave me tonight?"

All his anger had slipped away, revealing the hurt beneath it, and it just about broke her heart. How could she have done that to him?

"I don't know," she said. "I guess when you've had your priorities screwed up for as long as I have, it's a hard thing to get over."

"Just tell me again that you don't want Bridges."

"I don't want Bridges."

"Tell me you're never going back to him again."

"Never," she said, tears welling up in her eyes again. "You're the one I need, John. I don't like the person I was without you. And no matter how tough things get, I'm never going to be that person again."

"Are you sure about that?"

"Yes, John. I mean it. *Never*."

"No matter what happens?"

"No matter what happens."

"It won't be easy."

"I know. But it will be worth it, won't it?"

He smiled softly. "Oh, sweetheart. You have no idea."

He slid his hand against her cheek and stroked it gently with his thumb, then lowered his lips to hers in a long, deep, *loving* kiss. When he finally eased away, he was looking at her so adoringly that her heart melted.

"I didn't think you'd want me back," Darcy said. "I was so afraid—"

John swept her hair away from her face and gave her one more kiss, an almost imperceptible brush of his lips against hers. "Don't look for it to make sense. Nothing between us ever has. I only know that when Bridges called me tonight, and there was the slightest chance things weren't over between us . . ."

"What?"

"I broke every traffic law in the book to get here."

Tears filled Darcy's eyes for the umpteenth time that night. "Oh, John. I was so wrong, and I'm *so* sorry."

"It's over now. Let's just go home, okay?"

She thought about his tiny house on that tree-shaded street, the one with the cracked sidewalks, the honeysuckle growing wild over the fence, and the gutters John had never found the time to clean, and she couldn't imagine anything more beautiful. But it was because she could finally see through the surface to the heart of his house, to the man who was offering her everything. She'd just been so blinded by all her preconceived notions that she hadn't been able to see it.

She wanted to spend every moment with him she could. She wanted to cuss him out for being stubborn and overbearing, then have him pull her back and convince her that he and sensitivity weren't mutually exclusive. She wanted him to tell her what a low tolerance he had for high-maintenance women, then spend the next hour treating her like a pampered princess. She wanted to feel that rush of excitement as they made love, then the slow, gentle descent into the kind of togetherness that made her glow from the inside out.

All at once her throat tightened and her eyes started to burn, and all the tears she'd kept bottled up for the past few minutes spilled out like flood waters over a broken dam.

"Oh, God," John said, his eyes wide with panic. "What's the matter?"

"N-nothing," she said, wiping her eyes.

"Then why are you crying?"

She shrugged helplessly. "I don't know."

"Everything's fine."

"I know."

"Is this one of those crying-in-the-bathroom things, where things are good, but you cry anyway?"

"Yeah. I think so."

With a heavy sigh, John just took her in his arms and

held her tightly. Darcy dropped her cheek to his shoulder, and he turned his head to whisper in her ear, "Do you know what it feels like to be in love for the first time in your life?"

"Yeah," Darcy said through her tears. "I know. Believe me, I know."

He held her until her tears wound down, and through it all she could feel the steady beating of his heart, like a clock ticking away the seconds, the minutes, and soon the hours and days of their lives they were going to spend together.

Before they went to the office the next morning, John drove Darcy back to her apartment complex so she could pick up Gertie. After all, a girl had to have wheels, even when the wheels and the tires attached to them were the most valuable part of the car.

Even several blocks away, the sharp odor of the burned-out building permeated the air. As they drove through the complex, Darcy was astonished at how awful it looked in the light of day. Just the brick shell of the building remained intact, blackened by the flames. Two men were picking through the rubble.

"Who are they?" Darcy asked.

John brought his car to a halt behind Gertie. "Fire inspectors. Trying to determine the cause of the fire. Or at least trying to make the cause of it official."

Yesterday the thought of everything she had going up in smoke had sickened Darcy, but all she could think now was *good riddance*.

"I'll see you back at the office," she told John as she leaned over the console to give him a kiss. She started to get out of the car, only to glance to the far side of the parking lot in front of building four. "John. Look over there."

"What?"

"I think that's Larry Howard's car."

John looked at the car. "Might be. It's a red Corvette."

Then Darcy noticed whose apartment it was parked in front of, and any doubt about whether this particular Corvette belonged to Larry disappeared.

Apparently he was here to see Georgette.

Given Larry's history with hookers, it was pretty clear what kind of massage he was paying for. And how funny was it that he had no clue Darcy lived in this apartment complex, so he'd left his car right out in plain sight?

"It's his," Darcy said. "I'm sure of it."

She turned off John's car and grabbed the keys out of the ignition.

"Hey!" he said. "What are you doing?"

She stepped out of the car. Walking around to the back of it, she opened it up, dug through John's toolbox, and grabbed a screwdriver. When he circled around to the back of the car to see what she was doing, she tossed his keys back to him.

"We'll get Gertie later," she said.

"Where are you going?"

"Stay here."

"Darcy! No! You stay away from that Corvette!"

She turned around and put her palm to his chest. "John. Stay here."

"Darcy—"

"Please! And keep your voice down!"

Darcy strode to the Corvette. She opened the driver's door and slid into the seat, glancing occasionally to Georgette's apartment to insure the coast was clear.

Using the screwdriver, she quickly popped a plastic piece off the steering column, revealing the ignition wires. They looked like multicolored spaghetti.

Oh, God. Now what? Think. Think!

When her father had shown her how to do this, he'd crossed two red wires. But there weren't two red ones here.

She glanced back at Georgette's apartment. *Please, Larry, keep your pants off for a little while longer.*

Wait a minute. Now she remembered. Her father hadn't said it had to be two red ones, just two matching ones, and there were two blue wires.

She looked quickly at John, who stood impatiently by his car with an expression that said he wholeheartedly disapproved even though he was staying put.

She had to pull this off.

She grabbed the two blue wires and twisted them together, her hands shaking like crazy, remembering her father's admonition: *If you get it right, the car will start. Get it wrong, and you'll probably blow the whole electrical system.* She held her breath and sparked a third wire against them.

The engine roared to life.

She wanted to throw her arms up in the air and shout with joy, but that wouldn't have been professional, and her boss *was* watching.

She put the car in reverse, eased off the brake and touched the gas, backing out of the parking space like a pro. Nothing was going to stop her this time. Not a locked garage. Not a stick shift. *Nothing*.

"What the *hell* are you doing?"

Darcy whipped around to see Larry standing in Georgette's open apartment door. At first she felt a glimmer of panic, but when he streaked into the parking lot wearing nothing but baby-blue boxers and a pair of black socks, it was hard to see him as much of a threat.

He ran up to the driver's door. "Get out of my car!"

"Sorry, Larry. Not this time."

"Are you *nuts?*"

She looked at Larry's boxers, a deflating erection still tenting their crotch. "Yeah, Larry. *I'm* nuts."

"You're not taking my car! You don't know how to drive it! You'll just tear up the transmission!"

"This transmission is going to be just fine." She reached for the gearshift.

"Wait!" Larry said. "Just get out of my car, and I swear I'll go straight to the bank to take care of things. I swear I will."

"Sorry. I'm afraid it doesn't work that way. You don't get the car until you make up the back payments." She put the car in first gear, her foot hovering over the gas pedal.

"You can't do this to me!" Larry shouted.

"Sure I can. And Larry?"

"What?" he snapped.

"Your lady friend?"

"Yeah?"

Darcy leaned toward him and dropped her voice. "Georgette used to be *George*."

Larry whipped around to look at Georgette standing

at the open apartment door. She ran her hand up the door frame, her purple peignoir fluttering in the breeze.

"Come on back in here, honey," she said, flashing him a sizzling smile. "We haven't finished our business yet."

Larry's expression went from astonished to horrified. He spun around to Darcy again, shouting as she began to drive away.

"You can't leave me here like this! Take me with you!"

"Sorry, Larry. I'm a repossession agent, not a taxi driver."

Darcy hit the gas, and Larry was still shouting as she circled around the parking lot and pulled up next to John. She'd done it. By herself. And if she did it once, she could do it again.

"I believe you owe me the fee for this one," she said.

John shook his head with disbelief. "Where'd you learn to hot-wire a car?"

"My father."

"Most fathers don't teach their daughters how to steal cars."

"Most fathers don't have daughters who want to be repo agents. He's actually proud of me."

"How does your mother feel about it?"

"She doesn't know yet. But she's going to hate it, of course. Maybe I can tell her it's my talent for the Mrs. America competition."

John just shook his head, then leaned into the car and gave Darcy a kiss. "You're really something, you know that?"

"So it was okay for me to grab this car?"

He sighed with resignation. "Looks as if I couldn't stop you if I tried."

She smiled. "So you'll show me the ropes?"

"Yeah, I'll show you the ropes. In a few weeks, you'll be stealing all the cars you want to. The ones I'm pretty sure aren't in dangerous situations, anyway." He closed his eyes. "God, I hate this."

"I know," she said with a smile. "But I promise I'll be careful."

"Just try to keep all the wing-nut stuff to a minimum, will you? I can't afford to bail you out of jail."

"Whatever you say, John."

He rolled his eyes. "Yeah, right."

Darcy looked over her shoulder. "Oops. Here comes Larry."

As Larry circled around the back of the car, John slowly stood up again, folding his arms across his chest and glaring down at him. Larry stopped in his tracks, his startled gaze traveling up. And up. And up some more.

"Darcy?" John said.

"Yes?"

"Hit the gas."

Darcy flashed him a brilliant smile, then stomped the clutch, shifted into first, and peeled out of the parking lot.

⁓

"You sure this is a good idea?" John said a week later as he and Darcy climbed the steps to her parents' front door. "Maybe I could just talk with her on the phone or something."

"Nope. Meeting my mother is kind of like swimming in ice-cold water. If you just stick your big toe in first, you'll see how bad it is and you'll never get in. It's best just to leap right off the dock."

"I think I'd rather jump in that ice-cold water."

Darcy smiled. "You're actually nervous, aren't you?"

"Nervous?"

"John. You have a death grip on my hand."

John let go of her hand and wiped his sweaty palm on his pants, and Darcy felt a tingle of pure delight. If he didn't love her, this wouldn't matter so much. But it was just a formality. It didn't matter in the least what her mother thought. She was going to love him right back.

A few days ago when Darcy told her mother that Jeremy Bridges was out of the picture for good, she thought the woman was going to collapse with despair. And when Darcy told her she just happened to be in love with another man who didn't exactly reach that same pinnacle of financial success, Lyla tried every way under the sun to get Darcy to see the error of her ways. She cajoled. She whined. She even shrieked a little when she didn't think Darcy was taking her seriously, which she wasn't. In a half hour, she went through every argument in the book, half a pack of Virginia Slims, and three shots of Wild Turkey.

Finally her father had spoken from his La-Z-Boy in the living room. "Lyla. Invite the man to dinner."

"I will not. There's no sense encouraging something like this."

"Darcy," her father said, "we'll see you and John at seven o'clock on Saturday."

Now Saturday had come, and John looked as if he was going to his own execution.

Her father greeted them at the door. He shook hands with John and escorted them into the kitchen, where her mother was bent over the oven. She closed the door and stood up, wiping her hands on a tea towel. Judging from Lyla's frigidly restrained expression, Darcy's father had clearly had a word with her about her behavior tonight.

"Mr. Stark," she said with an icy smile. "How very nice to meet you."

She shook his hand with all the warmth of a cadaver.

"Dinner sure smells good," John said.

"It'll be ready in a moment. I hope you like quiche."

John's smile faltered. "It's my favorite."

Uh-huh. This from a man who could finish off a side of beef and then wonder when dinner was going to be served.

"Vegetable quiche," Lyla went on. "With a side salad of iceberg lettuce and cherry tomatoes. You do like low-fat dressing, don't you?"

"Uh . . . sounds great."

Darcy rolled her eyes. Passive-aggressiveness was *so* unattractive, but since it seemed her father had warned her mother against *active*-aggressiveness, she had no other weapon left.

"I'd be delighted to get both of you a drink. Mr. Stark? What will you have?"

"It's John. And, uh . . . a beer would be fine."

"Of course, Mr. Stark."

John's hand tightened on Darcy's. *Is she going to be this way all night?*

"Darcy? What would you like? Shall I open this lovely bottle of wine you left here when you moved?"

She nodded toward the bottle of Penfolds Grange Shiraz sitting on the kitchen counter. Darcy had forgotten all about it.

"Nah. I can drink beer right out of the bottle. That way I won't dirty a glass."

Lyla's nose crinkled with disgust, but she was still smiling. It was one of the funniest combinations Darcy had ever seen. John, though, didn't appear to see the humor in it, eyeing her mother as if he expected her to bite his head right off his shoulders.

As Lyla went to the refrigerator, Darcy whispered to John, "Don't let her attitude fool you. Her drink is Wild Turkey and diet Coke."

Lyla opened the refrigerator door and pulled out two beers. She started to put them on the counter and froze.

"No," she said.

"What?" Darcy said.

She shoved the beers back into the fridge and slammed it. "No! I just can't do this!"

Clayton raised an eyebrow. "Lyla . . ."

"Our daughter has lost her mind. She could have had a millionaire, and she settles for a repo man?"

A look of thinly veiled horror spread across John's face. He'd spent eighteen years as a cop looking danger in the eye and never blinking, but three minutes with Lyla Dumphries had put the fear of God into him.

Darcy smiled up at him. "Money isn't everything, Mom."

"The only people who say that are people who have plenty of it, which you don't."

"It's love," Darcy said. "*Love*. Never forget that."

"Love. Please. Try eating love instead of food and see how long you survive."

Clayton sighed. "Lyla. Not now."

"Yes, *now*. I'm making a point here."

"So is Darcy."

"Darcy doesn't know what's good for her."

"She knows very well what's good for her."

"Try paying the mortgage with love," Lyla said. "That'll go over big."

"Lyla . . ."

"Or the electric bill."

"Lyla!"

"Sooner or later you'll be freezing in the—"

All at once, Clayton grabbed her, hauled her right up next to him, and bent her backward over his arm. *Oh, God,* Darcy thought. *This is it. After forty years of bottled-up frustration, he's going to gnaw right through her jugular.*

Instead, he kissed her.

Darcy's eyes widened with astonishment because it wasn't just any old kiss. It was a kiss so hot she was surprised the sparks didn't catch the mobile home on fire. Clayton finally brought Lyla to her feet again, and she stared up at him with a dumbfounded expression.

"Now, what were you saying?" Clayton asked her.

Lyla just stood there, her eyes glassy, gaping at her husband. "Uh . . . nothing."

"Good answer." Clayton reached into his wallet, pulled out a pair of twenties, and handed them to John. "John, I want you and Darcy to go to dinner on me. Lyla and I need to be alone tonight."

"W-we do?"

"Do you have a problem with that?"

She swallowed hard. "No. No problem."

"Uh . . . okay," John said, looking so disoriented that Darcy almost laughed out loud. "Well, then. I guess we'll be taking off. It was nice to meet both of you."

"Yeah," Lyla said, still staring up at Clayton. "Nice."

John and Darcy stepped out to the front porch and closed the door behind them. John still looked a little woozy, and for a moment she was afraid he was going to trip right down the steps.

"What the hell just happened in there?" he asked.

"Something that should have happened about thirty years ago." She smiled up at him. "Welcome to the family."

⁓

Darcy wanted to go to Taco Hut for dinner, where they could spend ten bucks and pocket the other thirty, but John put his foot down and told her to stop being a tight-wad. After a nice dinner at an eclectic little restaurant in east Plano, they came home and curled up on the sofa to watch the end of the Rangers game. Darcy couldn't see ever liking baseball to any large degree, but since she'd taken over three-quarters of John's bedroom closet, most of his dresser drawers, and virtually all of the counter in the bathroom, she had no doubt he'd chop off her hand if she so much as reached for the remote.

When the Rangers finally won the game, Darcy excused herself, went to the bedroom, and put on something she'd bought earlier that day. She slinked back down the hall, the feathers at the hem tickling her thighs. When she reached the living room, she ran her hand up the doorway, striking a provocative pose.

John turned, and his mouth fell open.

"It's pink," she said. "My favorite color. And it was on sale. Seven-ninety-nine. Hell of a bargain."

He stared at her for a good ten seconds, his mouth slowly closing again.

"Beautiful," he murmured.

"You said before you thought it was ugly."

"I'm not talking about the nightgown. Come here."

Feeling a shiver of delight, Darcy walked across the living room, and John pulled her onto his lap. He slid his hand beneath the feathers and stroked her thigh, leaning in to kiss her neck. Then he stopped suddenly, his hand tightening against her leg.

"Wait a minute. There's something I've been meaning to ask you."

"What's that?"

He winced a little, as if he was afraid to say the words. "Who was the first man to walk on the moon?"

Darcy drew back. "You don't know?"

"Of course I know. Do you?"

"Sure. Neil Armstrong."

He let out a long sigh. "Thank God."

"What has that got to do with—"

"Never mind."

But as he pulled her down for another kiss, Pepé jumped up on the sofa and stuck his nose under John's arm.

"What's the matter, Killer? Is your mom getting all the attention?"

John scooped him up and plopped him into Darcy's

lap. Darcy lay her head on John's shoulder, stroking
Pepé's ears and sighing with contentment.

"I read a romance novel once where the heroine fell in
love with a man with no money," she said.

"Oh, yeah?"

"Yeah. She threw away her inheritance to marry him,
only to find out he was a prince in disguise who had millions of dollars."

"Hmm. Lucky woman."

"Uh . . . I don't suppose . . ."

"Nope."

Darcy sighed dramatically. "Well, I guess this means I
have to settle for love instead of money."

She smiled furtively and snuggled closer to John, unable to believe she'd gotten halfway through life before
she finally figured out that *this* was what life was all
about.

ABOUT THE AUTHOR

Jane Graves began writing stories at the age of five, and she hasn't stopped since. She's a graduate of the University of Oklahoma, where she earned a B.A. in Journalism in the Professional Writing program. The author of fifteen novels, Jane is a six-time finalist for Romance Writers of America's Rita Award, the industry's highest honor, and is the recipient of two National Readers' Choice Awards, the Booksellers' Best Award, and the Golden Quill. She lives in Texas with her daughter and her husband of twenty-five years.

You can visit Jane's website at www.janegraves.com, or write to her at jane@janegraves.com. She'd love to hear from you!

More sassy, funny,
and sexy romance
from Jane Graves!

• • •

Please turn this page
for a preview of

*Tall Tales
and
Wedding Veils*

Available now.

Chapter 1

They were the ugliest bridesmaid dresses Heather Montgomery had ever seen, and she'd seen her share of them. When you had a family that could fill Texas Stadium, somebody was always getting married, and it was family law that cousins asked cousins to be bridesmaids, even if it meant blood relatives had to stand in line behind five of the bride's sorority sisters.

This time around it was Heather's cousin Regina tying the knot, and she'd chosen these dresses for one reason only: her high-priced wedding planner had convinced her they were the height of fashion. To Heather they simply looked ridiculous.

"Regina!" squealed Bridesmaid Number One, as she fanned out one of the six petticoated, pouffy-sleeved, waist-hugging creations. "They're *fabulous*!"

Two and Three voiced similar opinions, while Four and Five stroked the satin reverently, making breathy little noises of approval. Heather had given up trying to remember five names all ending in "i"—Cami, Taci, Tami, whatever—and which blond woman belonged to each one. In the end, she'd simply assigned them numbers according to hair length.

In the wake of all the *oohs* and *ahhs*, Heather traded furtive eye-rolls with her mother. Barbara Montgomery had come along on this dress-fitting excursion, even though she didn't particularly like her sister *or* her niece. She was there because family weddings always stirred things up, and if she stayed in the thick of things she was sure to be around when the pandemonium began. The whole family thrived on chaos in a way that boggled Heather's mind. Given her own preference for a calm, tidy, organized life, sometimes she wondered if the stork had taken a wrong turn twenty-nine years ago and dumped her down the wrong chimney.

"Oh, yes," Barbara said. "The dresses are simply adorable. Don't you think they're adorable, Heather?"

Was Heather the only one who heard the sarcasm oozing through her mother's voice?

"Yes," she said, sounding almost as Stepford-like as her mother. "Adorable."

"Of course they're adorable," Aunt Bev said, as she fluffed the skirt on Three's dress. "They're by *Jorge*."

"Well, pink must be Jorge's signature color," Heather said. "I mean, look at how much of it he used here."

"They're not *pink*," Regina said, with a toss of her head that sent a shudder through the mountain of lace attached to it. "They're *salmon*. It's all the rage this season." She fluttered her hands. "Go ahead, girls. Try them on."

Heather grabbed her dress, went to a dressing room, and stuffed herself into it. The sleeves drooped to her elbows, at least six inches of hem dragged the ground, and it fit so snugly around her waist that breathing was a chore.

She pulled back the curtain. One through Five had

morphed into gushy, grinning quintuplets with perfectly toned abs that didn't make the slightest bulges in the waistlines of their perfectly hideous dresses. It was like watching models on a Parisian runway wearing ridiculous clothes, yet for some reason, nobody laughed.

The seamstress smiled as she surveyed the perfect members of the wedding party. Then she zeroed in on Heather.

"Hmm," she said, running her hand over the waist of Heather's dress and shaking her head. "It's a little tight."

Heather sighed. "I told Regina to get a fourteen, just in case. I knew it would have to be taken in, but—"

"A fourteen?" Regina said, blinking innocently. "I'm sorry, Heather. I swore you said size twelve."

There wasn't a damned thing wrong with Regina's hearing. It was just Regina's way of coercing her cousin into a smaller size so she wouldn't have five women walking down the aisle who were pencil-thin followed by one who looked like a gum eraser. So what if Heather wouldn't be able to breathe? As long as enough oxygen went to her brain that she stayed upright during the ceremony, that was all that mattered to Regina.

"I can let it out a little," the seamstress said. "But only a little. There's not much seam allowance."

"Can't you order the fourteen?" Heather asked.

"Too short notice."

"The wedding's not for a month," Regina said. "I'm sure you can drop a size by then."

Drop a size in a month? When she hadn't been able to drop a size in the past ten years?

"Try the Hollywood Watermelon Diet," Four said with

a vacuous smile. "I once lost six pounds in a weekend on that one."

Great. Not only did Heather have to be in a wedding she was going to hate, she was going to have to starve herself for the privilege. As the seamstress knelt down to mark the hem of her dress, Heather wondered how many celery sticks she'd have to eat in the next month so she wouldn't look like ten pounds of potatoes in a five-pound sack.

"So, Heather," Aunt Bev said. "Are you seeing anyone right now?"

The eternal question. One whose answer never seemed to change. "No, Aunt Bev. Nobody right now."

"What a shame. But don't worry. I'm sure you'll meet Mr. Right very soon."

The subtext was so thick Heather could barely wade through it, and all of it was directed squarely at her mother. *My Regina's getting married and your Heather isn't even dating anyone.*

"Actually, Heather is concentrating on her career right now," Barbara said. "A lot of young women are waiting until their thirties to marry."

"Is that what all the women's magazines are saying?" Aunt Bev said, looking befuddled. "If so, I'm afraid I wouldn't know about it. It's all I can do to get through every issue of *Modern Bride*."

"What they're *saying*," Barbara said, "is that some women choose to be successful in their own right before settling down and getting married."

"And I think Heather is very smart to do that," Aunt Bev said with an indulgent little smile. "That way if the worst happens and she doesn't find a man, at least she won't be struggling for the rest of her life to put food on the table."

Heather had long since learned to let Aunt Bev's comments roll right past her. Her mother hadn't. Heather could almost feel her mother's brain working, trying to manufacture a comeback, but when it came to sheer bitchiness, she couldn't hold a candle to Aunt Bev.

Heather took off her dress and put on her clothes again. As the seamstress marked the other bridesmaids' hems for alteration, Heather sat down on the bench next to her mother.

"Don't listen to Aunt Bev," Barbara muttered under her breath. "She's just jealous that you have a fabulous career while Regina barely made it out of college."

Truthfully, there was a limit to the fabulousness of a career as a CPA, if it even counted for anything in the first place where her family was concerned. Career women weren't put on the same pedestal as those who chose matrimony and the mommy track. What was valued the most was the ability to wed, procreate, raise progeny to adulthood, maintain a clean house, and sustain enough of a relationship with your husband that he didn't leave you for his secretary.

"Why don't I just tell Regina I don't want to be in the wedding?" Heather whispered. "She doesn't want me there in the first place. If I backed out, it would make both of us happy."

"No. If Regina asked, you have to do it."

"Angela told her no. Why can't I?"

"Angela is with the Peace Corps in Uganda."

"So that's all I have to do to get out of this? Live in squalor in a foreign country?"

"You're being unreasonable."

"What about Carol? She said no, too."

"You know Carol is having trouble getting her meds straightened out. God only knows how she'd behave the day of the wedding."

"So if I pop a few Prozac, I'll become ineligible, too?"

"As if anybody would actually think *you're* unbalanced?"

True. Everybody in her family had a reputation for something. Heather's was being sane.

"If you come up with some story now," her mother went on, "everybody will think you're jealous of Regina because she's getting married and you're not."

Heather started to say she didn't care what her family thought, but she knew her mother did. In front of Aunt Bev, she portrayed her daughter as a high-flying career woman who couldn't be bothered with something as mundane as marriage. But Heather knew the truth. Her mother didn't want to say, meet my daughter, the CPA. She wanted to say, *"Meet my daughter, her handsome husband, and her four lovely children,"* preferably within earshot of Aunt Bev.

Fifteen minutes later, after the fittings were over and they'd suffered through a lecture from Regina on the jewelry they were expected to wear for the wedding, Heather and her mother left the bridal shop. As soon as the door closed behind them, her mother rolled her eyes.

"Could you *believe* those dresses?" she said. "My sister may have money, but she has no taste. None whatsoever. But it doesn't matter. You still looked beautiful in that dress, no matter how horrible it was."

Beautiful? No. Heather was nothing if not a realist. She wasn't beautiful. But that didn't stop her mother from continually professing it, as if repetition would make it come true. As Heather was growing up, she could only imagine how her mother must have watched and waited for her ugly duckling to blossom into a swan. Instead, Heather had ended up somewhere between a chicken and a cockatiel. She had a headful of corkscrew curls the color of a paper sack that were impossible to tame, a bump on the bridge of her nose she kept swearing she was going to have fixed, and a body polite people called "curvy." In the past ten years, she'd lost approximately fifty pounds. If only it hadn't been the same five pounds ten times, she might actually have gained a foothold on being thin.

On the positive side, she had clear skin, blue eyes everyone commented on, and nice white teeth that had never needed braces or fillings. But she'd always felt as if the bad outweighed the good, and if attention from men was any indication, she wasn't the only one who thought so.

They stopped beside Heather's car. "You *are* going on the bridesmaids' trip tomorrow, aren't you?" her mother asked.

Heather groaned inwardly. A weekend jaunt to Las Vegas with Regina and her five picture-perfect friends? She couldn't wait.

"Yeah, Mom. I'm going."

"Good. Aunt Bev and Uncle Gene are footing the bill. Take advantage of it." She gave Heather a quick hug. "Do you want to have dinner with your father and me tonight?"

"No, I'm meeting Alison for a quick drink at McMillan's

and then heading home. I need to get ready to go tomorrow. I'll see you when I get back from Vegas."

"You have a good time, now," her mother said, then shrugged nonchalantly. "And who knows? Maybe you'll meet a nice man."

There it was again. Heather could say she was going to a gay pride parade, and her mother would still say, *maybe you'll meet a nice man*.

Heather hated to burst her mother's bubble, but for her this trip was going to consist of going to a few nice restaurants, sitting by the pool, catching up on her reading, and watching a lot of men watching five blond bridesmaids instead of watching her.

⌒

There was nothing like sitting on a barstool at McMillan's to put Tony McCaffrey in a good mood. He loved everything about the place—the antique bar with the inset mirrors, the big screen TVs, the polished oak tables, the clacking of pool balls, the beat of the music, the hum of the crowd. When he went to heaven, he imagined God would welcome him inside the Pearly Gates and then escort him to a bar and grill just like this one. Somebody would hand him a beer and a pool cue and surround him with a host of tall, leggy women with halos of blond hair whose only desire was to keep him company in paradise.

As soon as he bought this place, he wouldn't have to die to go to heaven.

Jodie slid his usual Sam Adams in front of him, then folded her arms on the bar and tossed him a sexy smile. She'd started working there about a month ago, and she was just his kind of woman—quick with a beer, out for a good time, and *very* nice to look at. Someday soon he intended to do more than just look.

"You're sure seem to be in a good mood today," she said. "What's up?"

He smiled and took a sip of his beer, which tasted even better than usual. "Can't say just yet. But trust me, sweetheart. This is going to be a red-letter day."

She grinned. "Can't wait to hear all about it."

Tony wished he could spill the news, but he wasn't going to open his mouth until the deal was final. The only person he'd told about his plans was his boss, John Stark. John ran Lone Star Repossessions, where Tony had worked as an auto repossession agent for the past few years. It was a good fit for his skills and personality. He kept his own hours, the money was good, and when dangerous deadbeats tried to cause trouble, he generally managed to talk his way out of the situation with a smile and a little bit of Texas good-ol'-boy charm. But when this bar came up for sale, he realized he was destined for bigger things. For once he'd be running his own show rather than being part of someone else's.

John told him he was sorry to see his best employee leave, but he admired the fact that Tony wanted to go into business for himself. Then he'd pulled a bottle of Scotch out of his desk drawer, poured each of them a drink, and toasted Tony's future success.

God, that had felt good.

"Got some champagne in the back," Jodie said. "Is it going to be one of those evenings?"

Tony grinned. "How about you toss a couple of bottles

in the fridge? I'll let you know when it's time to pop the corks."

"You got it."

As Jodie headed for the kitchen, Tony turned on his barstool and looked out over the room. Even though the crowd was a little light at five o'clock, he knew it would pick up considerably in the next hour. Right now, two guys were drinking beer and playing pool. A young couple was deep in conversation at a table near the door. And Tracy had just sashayed over to set a couple of martinis in front of two women who sat in a booth against the wall.

The women weren't exactly his type—a little too ordinary looking—but any people who came through the door with money in their pockets looking for a good time were going to be his new favorite customers. He intended to become Mr. Hospitality, courting every one of them with great food, drink specials, and a big, welcoming smile. A neighborhood bar was all about making people feel right at home, and that was exactly what he intended to do.

"Hey, Tony. Let's talk."

At the sound of the gravelly voice behind him, Tony turned to see Frank slide into a booth near the bar, his belly bumping the table as he maneuvered his way in. Over the years, he'd consumed mass quantities of the food and alcohol his establishment sold, leaving him with a physique that made him a cardiologist's dream patient. He grabbed a Marlboro from his front shirt pocket and lit it with a flick of his Bic. If heart disease didn't eventually get him, lung cancer would, which was probably why he was selling the place. Best to head for retirement now while he was still alive to enjoy it.

A short, balding man slid into the booth beside Frank.

He wore a suit, carried a briefcase, and his pinched expression said that antacids were one of his four major food groups.

Yep. Frank was ready to get down to business.

Tony grabbed his beer, gave Jodie a wink, and slid off the barstool. This was it. A deal in the making. In just a few minutes, he'd be one step closer to making his dream come true.

~

"Bridesmaid dresses are supposed to be ugly," Alison said, as she twirled the spear of olives in her martini glass. "It's the law."

Heather took a healthy sip of her own martini, hoping by the time she got to the bottom of the glass, the memory of those dresses would be obliterated.

Oh, hell. Who was she kidding? She could chug an entire bottle of gin and she still wouldn't be able to forget.

"It wasn't just that the style was weird," she said. "It was the color, too. They were *pink*."

Alison's forehead crinkled. "Pink's not really your color."

"That pink wasn't anybody's color. Take a blender. Throw in a chunk of watermelon. Toss in a dozen flamingo feathers. Top it off with a bottle of Pepto-Bismol. Hit the button, and there you go."

"How about we make a pact?" Alison said. "When we get married, we have veto power over each other's bridesmaid dresses. That'll lessen the chances of either one of us making a tragic mistake."

"Sounds like a plan to me," Heather said.

They locked pinky fingers, entering into the umpteenth pact they'd made since junior high. The first one had been a pinky swear that unless both of them got dates to the Christmas dance neither one of them would go, which turned out to be a non-issue since nobody asked either one of them.

"Do you remember when we were in high school," Alison said, "and we made lists of the qualities we wanted in the men we married?"

Heather remembered. Her list had included *intelligent*, *well-dressed*, and *good sense of humor*. Alison's list had consisted of *nice body*, *good kisser*, and *well-hung*. Even though they'd both been virgins at the time, Alison's intuition told her that size really did matter.

"Yeah," Heather said. "I wanted a professional man. You wanted a porn star."

"Hey! Stamina is a very worthwhile quality in a man. I mean, if it's over in five minutes, then what's the point of—" She stopped short, her eyes following something across the room. "Oh, my," she said. "Speaking of men we'd like to marry . . ."

Heather turned to see one of McMillan's regulars slide into a booth across the room. Her heart always skipped a little whenever she saw him, but only because there were certain basic reactions a woman couldn't fight. Looking at Tony McCaffrey led to heart rhythm disruptions every time, in spite of his reputation with women. Or maybe because of it.

"Please," Heather said. "Marriage? A man like him?"

"You're right. Forget marriage. I'd settle for a nice, steamy affair."

Which was about all a man like Tony would be able

to deliver, since guys like him were all about playing the field. With those captivating green eyes and dazzling smile, he could have a woman stark naked before she knew what hit her.

"Yeah, he's gorgeous, all right," Heather said. "But would you really want a man like him?"

"Please. Would *you* kick him out of bed?"

"I'd never go to bed with him in the first place."

Alison rolled her eyes. "You are such a liar."

"No, I'm not. I like men with brains. Guys like him are so good-looking they've never had to rely on anything else."

"I don't know about you," Alison said, "but I'd be having sex with the man, not asking him to derive a new law of physics."

"Fine. Why don't you hop over there and see if he's free tonight?"

"Right," Alison said. "And the entire time we were talking, he'd be looking over my shoulder at one of the waitresses' butts."

"Exactly. What's the future with a guy like him?"

"Forget the future. I'd be perfectly willing to take him one night at a time." Alison sighed wistfully. "Why is it women like us never get men like him?"

"Because we're B-cups with three-digit IQs."

"Seriously. Look what we have to offer. We're college graduates. We have good jobs with 401(k)s. We own real estate. We're not in therapy. Maybe we're not Miss America material, but we don't scare small children, do we?"

Heather frowned. "Next you're going to say we have good personalities and childbearing hips."

"Trouble is, we have boring professions. You're an accountant, and I'm a loan officer. What man wants to date either one of those?"

"So what should we do? Become flight attendants? Exotic dancers? Dallas Cowboy cheerleaders?"

"I was thinking Hooters girls. Just once I'd like a man to love me for my body instead of my mind."

And that was exactly what it took to get the attention of a man like Tony: a hot body in low-slung jeans and a tight T-shirt that showed off perky breasts, a belly-button ring, and a small-of-the-back tattoo. A woman whose intelligence was inversely proportional to her bra size.

"Hmm," Alison said, glancing over at the booth where Tony sat. "Looks like they're having a serious discussion over there."

"If it's men, and they're serious, it's probably about football. One of the Cowboys must have blown out his knee in the preseason."

Tracy swung by and asked if they wanted another martini. Heather just asked for the check.

"Leaving so soon?" Alison asked.

"Soon as I finish this one. I have to get up early in the morning so I won't have to fight traffic on the way to the airport."

"So you're actually going on the bridesmaids' trip? You said you'd rather sit through a time share presentation in Death Valley."

"Well, it is a free trip, and I've never been to Vegas." Then she sighed. "And my mother really wants me to go. It reminds me of when she wanted me try out for the high school drill team."

"So you could be around all the popular girls?"

"I think she's hoping if I hang out with Regina and the other bridesmaids, there'll be men all over the place. That way at least I'll have a shot at getting one of their castoffs."

"Actually," Alison said, "that's not a bad plan."

"Wrong. It's the sign of a desperate woman. And my mother is more desperate than most. It drives me crazy."

But if Heather were honest with herself, the reason it drove her crazy was because she was beginning to feel a little desperate herself. The closer she got to thirty, the more she felt a million years of evolution bearing down on her. No, she'd didn't want Og smacking her over the head with his club and dragging her back to his cave to make little Oggies, but she wasn't immune to the forces of nature. A forward-moving relationship with a man that eventually led to marriage would be nice, but so far it hadn't happened.

She glanced back at Tony. Yeah, he was hot, all right, but men like him had never been part of her dreams, just as she'd never been part of theirs. She'd always figured that the man she married probably wouldn't be all that handsome, but he would be reasonably attractive. He might not be wickedly charming, but he'd certainly be a good conversationalist. They'd settle down, have a couple of kids, take summer vacations, and plan for retirement.

Heather had always prided herself on being a realist, and *that* was reality.

～

As Frank's attorney pulled the contract from his briefcase and slid it across the table, Tony's heart beat like crazy. Just getting his hands on this document made him feel as if it was already a done deal.

He'd never been like other single guys who squandered their money. He had a nice amount in savings, and the small investments he'd made had turned out well. Still, giving him a loan to run an establishment like this when he'd never been in business for himself was a risk most bankers didn't want to take. So when Frank offered to owner-finance the deal, he couldn't believe his good luck.

Tony flipped through a few more pages of the contract, itching to pick up a pen and sign it, dying to make this place his.

Then he saw something that jolted him out of his euphoria.

"Wait a minute," he said, pointing at one of the figures. "This isn't the down payment we agreed on. This is twenty thousand more than that."

"We were just talking last week," Frank said. "I was estimating."

Tony held up his palm. "Hold on. Are you expecting me to come up with another twenty grand on top of what we already talked about?"

"Sorry, man. Turns out the wife's got her eye on a beachfront condo on Galveston Island. I gotta have more cash."

Tony's stomach sank all the way to the floor. "But you know I'm pushing it as it is. Where am I supposed to come up with another twenty thousand?"

"I'm just telling you what I gotta have. That's all."

"Would you take a second mortgage instead? Short term?"

Frank shook his head. "I need the money up front."

Tony sat back in the booth, trying to get his bearings, his mind spinning like crazy trying to imagine where he could come up with an additional twenty thousand. Nothing was coming to him.

"Can you give me a little more time?" he asked. "A few weeks? Maybe a month? I'll find a way to get the money."

Frank sighed. "I can give you until Monday."

"Monday? *This* Monday? But it's already Thursday."

Frank took one last drag on his cigarette, then stabbed it out. "Here's the truth, Tony. Another buyer contacted me yesterday. He offered to give me the up-front money I need."

Tony felt sick. Another buyer?

"But I still want to give you first shot at it," Frank said. "If you can get the money together by Monday, the place is yours. If not, I'm going to have to take the other offer."

"Come on, Frank! I've spent more money in this place in the past three years than all of your other customers put together! Shouldn't that count for something?"

"Course it does. But I gotta think of myself. And the wife. Believe me, buddy. If she ain't happy, nobody's happy."

The lawyer reached for the contract. "So the deal's off the table?"

"No!" Tony said. "Not yet." He turned to Frank. "Promise me you won't do anything until Monday."

"Sure, man. Like I said, I'll hold the deal. If you can find the money, the place is all yours."

Tony nodded. Frank and his attorney slid out of the

booth, leaving Tony alone with his beer, his frustration, and a dream that was falling apart at the seams.

He sat there a long time, trying to formulate a plan, but nothing came to him. He was completely tapped out himself, and he knew of no one he could borrow that kind of money from, particularly on short notice. No friends, and certainly no family members.

He didn't own a house, so a home equity loan was out.

He glanced over at the pool tables. He had no doubt he could bet on a few games and come out a winner, but betting on pool in a neighborhood bar wouldn't net him twenty grand until the beginning of the next millennium, much less by Monday.

He dropped his head to his hands for a moment, letting out a breath of disappointment. By the time this place came up for sale again, he'd probably be collecting Social Security.

Then slowly he raised his head again as a thought occurred to him. There *was* a way he could conceivably put twenty thousand dollars in his pocket before Monday. Betting on pool might be out, but there were other kinds of gambling . . .

No. He was crazy even to consider it.

But as the minutes passed and his desperation grew, even a crazy plan seemed better than no plan. It was a long shot—such a ridiculous long shot that no reasonable man would even consider doing it—but it was his *only* shot at keeping this opportunity from passing him by.

He took out his cell phone, dialed American Airlines, and booked a flight to Las Vegas, praying that Lady Luck would follow him all the way there.

THE DISH

Where authors give you the inside scoop!

♥ ♥ ♥ ♥ ♥ ♥ ♥ ♥ ♥ ♥ ♥ ♥ ♥ ♥ ♥

From the desk of Michelle Rowen

Dear Reader,

I have a confession to make.

Sarah Dearly, the main character from my novels BITTEN & SMITTEN and FANGED & FABULOUS (on sale now), thinks she's in control, and she is!

When I first conceived of my book about an "everygal" who becomes a vampire after a blind date from hell, Sarah was just a bookworm introvert who longed for a more exciting life. But as soon as I started writing, she let me know that she was no bookworm. More of a DVD aficionado with a love of fashion who uses sarcasm as her greatest weapon. And, she liked her life just fine the way it was.

She had two guys to choose from in the first book, BITTEN & SMITTEN. I said, "Hey, Sarah, you're going to end up with Cute Guy #1." And she said, "No, I want Cute Guy #2." I told her I was planning to kill him at the end. She then kicked up a huge fuss claiming that "she loved him," so I let him live because he was just too hot to die.

Then I got the chance to continue her story in

FANGED & FABULOUS. Sarah still wants to do things differently than I had planned. And she still has a very specific idea of whom she wants to end up with. She thinks that since I put her through so much stress and in life-threatening situations and that as a vampire she has to drink blood (which is a totally gross concept) that I "owe her."

Stubborn characters. Sheesh.

Now if you'll excuse me, the men in white coats have arrived to take me away.

Happy Reading!

Michelle Rowen

www.michellerowen.com

♥ ♥ ♥ ♥ ♥ ♥ ♥ ♥ ♥ ♥ ♥ ♥ ♥

From the desk of Wendy Markham

It's just an hour from New York, but for newly transplanted Manhattanite Meg Addams from LOVE, SUBURBAN STYLE (on sale now), suburban Glenhaven Park feels as challenging—and remote—as the northern Adirondacks. So our heroine adapted the following handy resource:

~~Wilderness~~ <u>Suburban</u> Survival Guide

Even the most savvy ~~hiker~~ single mom can wind up stranded in the middle of nowhere. Be prepared to combat any of these commonly found ~~wilderness~~ suburban threats:

Predators

You never know what creatures might lurk in ~~the forest~~ Starbucks or ~~stream~~ in the soccer field bleachers: venomous ~~snakes~~ snobs, cunning ~~coyote~~ yoga moms, or maybe even a ferocious ~~bear~~ PMS victim. Just remember, if you don't bother it, it won't bother you. But if all else fails, ~~run!~~ offer chocolate, preferably Godiva.

Hunger and Thirst

Foraging may yield ~~mushrooms~~ decent pizza or ~~berries~~ a diner that serves cheeseburgers (just make sure they're not ~~poisonous~~ made of soy). Remember, ~~insects~~ tofu burgers and even ~~grubs~~ low-fat veggie-sprout sandwich wraps may be unappetizing, but they are edible. With luck, you'll find a ~~stream~~ friendly local pub nearby, where you can indulge in plenty of life-sustaining ~~water~~ frozen margaritas.

Loneliness and Isolation

Being alone in ~~the wilderness~~ a rundown fixer-upper with only ~~wildlife~~ a moody teenager for company can drive anyone crazy. It's crucial to ~~keep your mind and body active~~ turn to your nearest neighbor for adult companionship, even if he is your unrequited high school crush.

Cold

Perhaps ~~exposure~~ a broken heart is the most dangerous threat of all. Before embarking on a ~~wilderness adventure~~ new romance, always learn how to create a spark, and gradually, without smothering the flames, build a fire that will burn indefinitely.

If you follow this guide, not only will you survive ~~the wilderness~~ suburbia; you might even ~~thrive~~ fall in love with the dad next door!

Happy Reading!

www.wendycorsistaub.com

♥ ♥ ♥ ♥ ♥ ♥ ♥ ♥ ♥ ♥ ♥ ♥ ♥ ♥ ♥

From the desk of Jane Graves

Dear Reader,

Maybe I shouldn't admit this, but I love torturing my characters. That sounds sadistic, but let's face it. Watching polite people in ordinary situations be sweetie-nice to each other is a bore. Watching strong people face challenges and overcome them— now, *that's* entertaining. After all, would we watch all that reality TV if everybody got along?

Here's another truth: My characters don't think what's happening to them is funny, but trust me, it is. Did Lucy Ricardo think it was funny when she was trying to make candy, but the conveyor belt went so fast she couldn't keep up? No! Did Bill Murray's character in *Groundhog Day* think it was funny when every day was *not* a new day? No! But, we laughed, didn't we?

Darcy McDaniel, the heroine of HOT WHEELS AND HIGH HEELS (on sale now), is facing the biggest challenge of her life. Her wealthy husband sends her on a vacation with a friend and, in her absence, cleans out their bank accounts, sells their house, and disappears.

Darcy is terrified of being destitute, but tough times call for tough measures. When ex-cop turned repo man John Stark repossesses her beloved Mercedes, she starts working for her sexy adversary with the goal of moving from receptionist to repo agent so she can make some decent money. However, John refuses to turn a spoiled ex–trophy wife loose to legally steal cars, and soon, their battle of wits and sexual one-upsmanship burn hotter than a bonfire out of control.

I require all my characters to have one quality: No matter how hard they're hit, they get back up again. And the results will leave you laughing. Pick up a copy of HOT WHEELS AND HIGH HEELS, and ride along with John and Darcy on their rocky road to happily ever after!

Enjoy!

Jane Graves

www.janegraves.com